THE VAST MEMORY OF LOVE

ALSO BY MALCOLM BOSSE

Mister Touch

Stranger at the Gate

Captives of Time

Fire in Heaven

The Warlord

Incident at Naha

The Man Who Loved Zoos

The Journey of Tao Kim Nam

THE VAST MEMORY OF LOVE

MALCOLM BOSSE

Ticknor & Fields

NEW YORK

1992

For information about permission to reproduce selections
from this book, write to Permissions, Ticknor & Fields,
215 Park Avenue South, New York, New York 10003

Library of Congress Cataloging-in-Publication Data
Bosse, Malcolm J. (Malcolm Joseph)
The vast memory of love / Malcolm Bosse.
p.   cm.
ISBN 0-395-62943-8
I. Title.
PS3552.O77V37   1992   92-7590
813'.54 — dc20   CIP

Printed in the United States of America

Book design by Robert Overholtzer

AGM 10 9 8 7 6 5 4 3 2 1

All illustrations by William Hogarth. Reproduced by
courtesy of the Trustees of the British Museum.

CONTENTS

But still this world (so fitted for the knave)
Contents us not. A better shall we have?
A kingdom of the Just then let it be:
But first consider how those Just agree.

— ALEXANDER POPE, "Essay on Man"

I desire of the philosophers to grant, that there is in some (I believe in many) human breasts a kind and benevolent disposition, which is gratified by contributing to the happiness of others. That though the pleasures arising from such pure love may be heightened and sweetened by the assistance of amorous desires, yet the former can subsist alone, nor are they destroyed by the intervention of the latter.

— HENRY FIELDING, *Tom Jones*

PROLOGUE

He arrived in London on the same day that *Amelia* appeared in the bookstalls. Grim and realistic, this last of Henry Fielding's novels was to prove both a critical and commercial failure, although Nathaniel Carleton wouldn't know it had even been written.

He came by stage from Nottingham, carrying his few belongings in a pouch once used for holding the game he trapped. His long hair was plaited into a queue in the style of shepherds. Patently he was a country boy with a battered felt hat pulled low over his brow. He wore turned-back cuffs, yarn stockings, and wool breeches below which appeared large rough clouted shoes.

No sooner had he stepped off the coach at the staging inn than a tall fellow called to him in a haughty voice of command. The man asked Ned did he understand horses.

"I do, sir."

The tall man was house steward for a nobleman and sometimes met incoming coaches on the lookout for country youths, who were regarded as more trustworthy than Londoners. After looking Ned up and down like a buyer of rams, the steward said curtly, "Maybe you'll do."

So in a moment of remarkable luck the country lad had found employment in a great household. After a week of training (and his hair cut short, then rolled upward at the sides under a silk cockade), Ned Carleton could open a landau door with a flourish and stand on the rear roost with his white-gloved hands clasped firmly at the small of his back. He felt like a prince in his new leather boots, silk garters worth two shillings, gilt buttons, with a velvet stand-up collar to his coat, and a riding crop thrust under his armpit.

Grooming a horse was something he'd learned to do before he could spell his name. Once the head coachman and the stable keep were satisfied that he didn't drink too much porter, the "bumpkin," as they called him, was secure in a job that half of London might envy.

Every fortnight he was given a free afternoon. In his old sheep coat and breeches unfastened at the knee, the twenty-year-old newcomer tramped through the city, agog at its bustle. From London Bridge he stared at a dizzy procession of sails heading for the sea. He visited the Tower and in the Armoury gawked at the sword which had severed the pretty head of Anne Boleyn. In the Tower Zoo he regarded lions and tigers, unlike anything he had trapped in the thickets of Sherwood Forest.

He crossed the Thames in a boat oared by a uniformed waterman and for a shilling ambled through the pleasure garden of Vauxhall, gazing at Turkish minarets, columned ways from Arabia, at waterfalls and shell grottoes and pillars hung with lamps. He saw the rouged fops dicing up chickens in booths near the orchestra and young women strolling under long-stemmed parasols, their lampblacked eyes meeting with arrogant stares the glances of gallants in flowered waistcoats and bag wigs.

On the Artillery Ground he watched men play at long bowling and cricket, amusements more complicated than the greased pig contests at country fairs and the wheelbarrow races he used to enter. He paid his half crown at Bedlam and strolled with other curious visitors among the insane. The hooting and screaming unnerved him, yet he emerged with only a fleeting recollection of the misery there, having before him again the giddy prospect of London.

To come to the great city he had mustered up the coach fare by selling his most prized possession, the watch left him by his father. The first year of his manhood he had remained at home because of his mother's declining health, and after her death, another year because of his love for a farmer's girl who abruptly married a well-to-do innkeeper. Thereafter, nothing else held him in the village, so Ned succumbed, as many country youths did, to the blandishments of the city.

Now almost every day in the great household he saw things that amazed him. There were masquerades, drums, routs, great squeezes to which the beaux came with their orange water and musk and Jamiee canes topped by amber heads, disdainfully munching on Seville oranges and lemons. From his postilion roost on the chariot, he overheard milord's family discussing where to buy things: cricket equipment from that famous turner of Kentish bats and balls, Wilks on the Strand; lavender water at the Sign of the Civet Cat; pistachio nuts from the confectioner Richard Robinson; and shops for crimson Genoa velvet, embroideries from the Levant, silks from Japan.

Like his father, who'd been a sailor, Ned meant to see the world, and the world was here in London. To his innocent ears the tinny blast of hawker trumpets was exotic music. He'd halt in his tracks to hear the carefree song of piemen, "Colly Molly Puff." His lips studiously formed the names on painted shop signs, as colorful and plentiful as stiffened battle flags: FUNERALS FURNISHED HERE. FOREIGN SPIRITOUS LIQUORS SOLD HERE. CHILDREN EDUCATED HERE.

The variety of life overwhelmed him, especially away from the fine neighborhoods, when he made for the deepest heart of London town: workmen carrying twelve-foot ladders, draymen in traffic slashing out with whips; a drover's bull running amok near the Haymarket; bales, kegs, scurrying bootblacks, ballad singers and Punch-and-Judy, brewery men rolling barrels into vintners' cellars, ladies carried in snug chairs on poles, ladies stepping daintily from sedans, revealing a flash of silken leg beneath swaths of petticoat.

It was a world of wood and cotton and flesh moving like an immense tide, a river more incessant and powerful than the Medden on which he'd fished as a boy. Ned Carleton would stand on a Cheapside corner and let the human flood eddy around him as if he were a rock in a stream, and in these ecstatic moments of new wonder he'd wish for his father to whom he would declare, "I never lived till I saw London."

Part One

THE HAND

[1]

ACROSS THE ENGLISH CHANNEL on this bright wintry morning Jean-Baptiste Chardin was adding a dab of black to the muzzle of a scruffy dog he was painting on a canvas to be named *The Blind Beggar,* a work that critics would praise in the Paris Salon Show of 1753 for its startling truth to nature.

Goya was a small boy in Fuendetodos.

Reynolds and Gainsborough were in early career, but it was Hogarth who was enjoying the pinnacle of fame in England for his satires of a London the artist both hated and loved. In York the painter George Stubbs had temporarily set aside his portraits of race horses to do engravings for a book on midwifery to pay his passage to Rome.

On this brisk morning three years before the birth of Mozart and three after the death of Bach, aging, half-blind Handel was practising scales on a harpsichord. He was scheduled for an evening musicale at the home of the fourth earl of Sandwich.

In preparation for the maestro's appearance the Sandwich household was already at work this morning. Footmen polished the grates with oil and scouring paper. Rough hands of housemaids scrubbed clean the princesses being wooed by elegant herdsmen on porcelain jars. In the salon the festooned curtains had been taken down for cleaning, and on a tall ladder the underbutler, who trusted such important matters to none but himself, dusted the gilt branches of a chandelier. The kitchen clerk disputed with French and English chefs, while the confectioner looked on gravely. At issue was the nationality of the third course.

In his study John Montagu, earl of Sandwich, sat with his left leg resting on a gout stool and both elbows propped on a writing desk. Logs crackled behind a plushwork fire screen. A huge mastiff snored on the Turkish carpet. His lordship wore small round spectacles on wire frames; a velvet coat lined with satin and faced with ermine was taut across his fleshy back. His unwigged brown hair was tied behind with a black ribbon like a common tradesman's, but his thighs were sheathed in white silk breeches — it was vogue to affect a combination of the vulgar and the elegant. A snuffbox and toothpick case were in reach.

He had a wretched hangover from too much claret last night, which made it difficult for him to concentrate on domestic matters. He was writing an irate letter to the New River Company. After paying those villains ten pounds sixteen a year for his water supply, he was rewarded yesterday when one of their elmwood pipes burst under the pavement and left a gaping hole that twisted the axle of his carriage.

"Gentlemen, observing the pipes belonging to you are continually breaking, I give you this notice in order to . . ."

A wretched hangover. Ever since the duke of Newcastle had conspired to oust him from the Admiralty, he'd filled the long empty hours with more pleasures than even he, admittedly a man of appetites, could reasonably manage. He glanced around at the sleek marbles, a loo table, the paintings in this room. He disliked this stuffy chamber and the whole cluttered town house, preferring the airy rooms of his Henchenbroke estate where there was fox, quail, sunlight, no politics, and no crime.

Crime was what they'd talked about at length last night, he and Bedford. He pointed out that politics and intrigue had cost him the Admiralty, though none in the post had ever curbed crime as successfully. As First Lord of the Admiralty, he'd managed to halt all smuggling on the Thames. That's why his subordinates had respected him. Indeed, they had named his austere lunch of bread and meat, which he'd eaten while working at his desk, a "sandwich." And he said, "I have spoken of this before, I know, but it's a measure of their appreciation of my effort." His friend Bedford had readily agreed.

And Sandwich had said next, "Fools in Parliament are talking of a halt to impressment. Any sane man knows you must use impressment to keep the navy afloat. How else can you manage ships unless the press gangs round up people to sail them? It's a time-honoured practice. But Newcastle goes round complaining of poor lads being forced at sword point to serve at sea. What are we, a nation of fops like Newcastle? The silly bastard. He fears to cross the ocean himself, but tells the English navy it can't use the press."

Bedford had then shifted the conversation to the magistrate from Westminster, Henry Fielding, who had recently disapproved of public executions because they glorified the condemned. Fielding, so reported Bedford, had declared that an execution should be swift while people remained indignant, and solemn since it emphasized punishment, and secret because it would terrify wrongdoers with the prospect of dying unnoticed.

Sandwich had scoffed, even though Fielding's proposition made sense. After all, the magistrate was in truth no more than a writer, to say nothing of being a follower of Newcastle and therefore a scoundrel. And so another bumper of righteous claret last night and so the hangover today.

He pictured Newcastle simpering through the halls of Parliament, a lace kerchief dangling from his fingers while that whining voice called out, "Oh, the sorry fate of innocent men! Took by press gangs!" It was a disgrace for such fops to have the king's ear. Newcastle was a harebrain without understanding of the English seadog who to say true was a foul beast ashore, but glory in the rigging. A sailor was like a child, for he lacked judgement, and needed his betters to point him in the right direction.

This reverie was broken by a footman who asked milord's permission to bring in a jeweler. Silversmith Williams had fashioned two collars inscribed with the Montagu coat of arms. His lordship took the bigger collar from the jeweler, leaned over, and clamped it around the neck of the mastiff. He instructed the footman to have the matching collar placed round the neck of his little African page. It would go prettily with turban and pantaloons.

Finishing his letter to the water company, Sandwich turned to the pile of bills. Most of them had been incurred by his wife. This, for example:

Hoop Maker, R. Whitely
Hoop Petticoats

The Right Honourable the Lady Judith Montagu's Bill.
10 January 1753

For eleven yards of lutestring at 6s per yard
For pinking the flounce
For flouncing the hoop
For a box hoop

More than seven pounds for such frippery. It put his lordship out of patience. Then the waiting woman burst into the chamber without a trace of formality and exclaimed breathlessly that her ladyship awaited with urgent business.

Sandwich got up immediately. He knew his wife. Whatever melodrama was in progress might assume outlandish proportions within moments. Hurrying upstairs, he recalled a foolish hysterical woman in one of Fielding's books who reminded him of Judith. Fielding should have stayed with such amusements instead of undertaking the law and serving that unstable sonofabitch Newcastle. In courting the arrogant Austrians and promising good English coin to a number of shaky duchies in exchange for alliances that would fade into thin air at the first hint of French aggression — Sandwich huffed as he mounted the staircase — Newcastle, the loathsome little prick, had thrown out of the Admiralty a Montagu of substance who had so conducted himself in office that his accomplishments would go down in history. John Montagu, fourth earl of Sandwich, had compelled the Navy Board to render accurate accounts. He had drawn up precise regulations for promotion to Flag Rank. He had overhauled the system for inspecting dockyards —

And suddenly there he was, standing in the doorway of the Red Damask Room, staring at his family. His son was a fat child with knock-knees, a grim reminder of Sandwich's own physical awkwardness. The boy was lavishly dressed in a bob wig, gold-laced waistcoat, and pink breeches. He held a cane on which he was leaning as slit-eyed and listless as an old man.

Little Julia was seated at a desk, pouting over a stack of books.

She was dressed exactly like his wife in a hooped skirt and flowing robe, hiding the thin figure which in womanhood would be no fuller or more desirable than her mother's.

The new governess was also there: a bony, unattractive female who stood next to his wife at ramrod attention.

"Julia won't do her lessons," his wife complained. Glaring at her daughter, she said, "Milord, this girl will not do her lessons! She won't! Nanny and I despair of her learning her numbers. She is such a *friponne!*" Judith bit her thumbnail in mounting panic. "Isn't she, Nanny? Tell how this saucy piece defied her mama all morning!"

Tight-lipped, the governess nodded.

Little Julia was bending lower at the desk. "I'll learn my numbers," she muttered, "but not from a book. I hate a book."

"Hear that?" her mother cried triumphantly. "She hates a book!"

Sandwich hesitated a moment, an odd thought flashing into his mind: Fielding might have written this scene. Then he shuffled toward the desk, but was brought up short by his daughter's sudden malevolent glare.

"Dear child," he began soothingly, "a book can't hurt you."

The girl shook her head. "I hate a book."

"Will you incur your papa's displeasure?"

Grimly, she stared at the pile of unopened books.

"Ah well, you see!" Judith waved her arms dramatically. "I wash my hands of this child!" But then, after fluttering her hands in anguish, she rushed to the girl and fondly stroked the long brown hair. "It shan't have a book then," Judith cooed. "Mama will throw the naughty books into the fire if the pretty thing can't abide them. It shan't have anything it doesn't like, if only it will learn. Will it learn its numbers? For mama?"

Sandwich glumly appraised his wife, a tall plain woman with no breasts to speak of. Worse, she had a thin unmusical voice that grated on his nerves. Of all things in a woman, he most admired a musical way of speaking.

Thank heaven his Judith carried a fan near her mouth most of the time. Sweetmeats had rotted her teeth until not even breath tinctures could hide the stink. Mercury water and lead salves had pitted her skin until she looked like a poxed whore. Once an ointment of carmine dye — a cosmetic newly in vogue — had brought on a terrible gastric fit, causing much of Judith's hair, which was her only good feature, to fall out. For its restoration she'd consulted a quack, who sold her a poisonous concoction that filled the house with the stench of fermented pigeons so virulently that every window had to be flung open during the coldest days of winter. Whenever his lordship marshaled up the courage to make an appearance in her bedroom to complain of her wild extravagances, he had to confront a night mask and straps of leather wrapped around her forehead to prevent wrinkles that multiplied anyway.

Alas, his fretful daughter would grow into a bleak copy of her.

Suddenly the little girl shrieked and with a wild sweep of her arm sent the books flying. Her brother then let out a cry, lunged forward, and began whacking her across the shoulders with his cane. A fierce hubbub ensued, a blur of velvet and silk in the Red Damask Room.

Spinning on his heel, Sandwich hurried out, hearing behind him his wife screaming at Nanny to remove the horrid books at once.

No sooner had he returned to his study than new problems awaited his lordship. The head valet came in to charge a footman with exacting outrageous tips from visitors. Only yesterday he'd stood impudently in the path of the duke of Bedford and demanded a handsome vail for helping his grace into his coat.

Next to the head valet stood the house steward to whom the earl said, "Dismiss the man without pay."

"Milord, the man is not here to dismiss. Last night he absconded with plate worth at least ten guineas."

Before Lord Sandwich could react, yet another member of the household entered the study — the clerk of the kitchen, a small obese fellow with tiny eyes inflamed by wine. He had come to accuse a young postilion of pilfering the larder. His account of the alleged crime was rambling and vague, but included these facts: last week a brace of partridge had been missing and this week a shank of lamb, and yesterday the pigeon soup had tasted as if someone had removed the fat to sell to a vendor and had replaced it with tallow — a bisque so evil it had to be thrown out — and this morning the postilion had dragged mud into the kitchen.

Lord Sandwich turned to the house steward. "What do you say of the postilion?"

The house steward reported that in nearly two years the lad had done his work without incident.

Lord Sandwich glanced at the furious clerk. The man kept peace in the kitchen, even managing to control the French chef, who was perpetually in temper but served up the finest fish sauce — chopped anchovies, shallots, lemon, spices, horseradish, white wine — in all London. Next to the house steward, a man of uncommon good sense, the kitchen clerk was the value of the household.

"Have the postilion in here," his lordship ordered the house steward.

[2]

A TALL FELLOW in horse livery soon appeared. His square peasant face was matched by broad shoulders, a powerful chest. Lord Sandwich recalled how in recent months he'd noticed the lad whose brawn atop his coach had made him feel especially secure. Studying the postilion's open expression, he liked what he saw, for the manliness of it reminded him of weathered salts cheering him from the rigging.

"Your name, lad."

"Nathaniel Carleton."

"Your lordship," the house steward corrected in a low voice. With a slight bow of apology to the earl, he added in explanation, "The lad knows better, milord. It's his nerves. This be the first time in two years he has spoke openly in the household."

"Nathaniel Carleton, your lordship."

Sandwich smiled to reassure him. "You don't have a London look."

"I'm from Nottinghamshire, your lordship."

That wasn't far from Sandwich's beloved Henchenbroke with its meandering streams and shady hollows. He felt a little tug of kinship with the lad. "Were you a shepherd there?"

"I was, your lordship."

"The finest sheep in England come from there."

"They do." The postilion smiled faintly.

"Your lordship," the house steward whispered loudly.

Sandwich dismissed the correction with a sweep of his hand. "Why did you ever leave such good country, lad?"

"To seek my fortune, your lordship."

Sandwich guffawed at this simpleminded optimism, which reminded him of British tars, the terror of the seas. Give them bread full of weevils, they called it hearty fare and went to meet superior forces convinced they'd just dined like kings. He was inclined to treat the boy with good-humoured tolerance. "Very well, Nathaniel, did you steal from the larder? The truth will put a very good countenance on my judgement of you."

"I stole nothing."

"I stole nothing, *your lordship!*" snapped the house steward.

"But you took maybe a partridge?" Sandwich asked with a wink.

"Nothing, your lordship."

"Come, no snuffling answer," said the earl. "Be a man and own up. It's not the end of the world."

"Nothing, your lordship."

"A scrap of lamb, then? A soup bone?" He glanced at the kitchen clerk, who was fidgeting in a rage.

"I eat in the stable, your lordship. I eat hearty. I have no wants. I never steal."

A believable air, Sandwich thought. These stout peasants were too dim-witted for sharp practice. "Clerk," he said, "be you absolutely certain it was this lad who nicked the larder?"

"I'm certain, milord. Today I found him at high ease with a scullery wench."

"Maybe that was the delicacy he'd come to the kitchen for and not partridge." Sandwich cocked his head in amusement. "What say you to it, lad?"

"Say, your lordship?"

"Have you had her?"

"I stole nothing. I never steal."

"Come now, can you answer a question?" It was the sort of question that Sandwich expected any man to answer: Did you have her? Was she good?

"I never steal," the boy persisted.

This time the postilion's failure to add a formal address of respect annoyed his lordship. Even so, the boy was surely innocent, if downright foolish in his assumption of a defiant air. Sandwich decided to give him one more chance, though it anger the kitchen clerk.

"What says the head coachman of him?" Sandwich asked the house steward.

"Vigilant, milord. Industrious."

"Well, what do you say?" Sandwich turned to the kitchen clerk, whose lips were trembling.

"He took the victuals, milord. As I am honest, he did."

As the man was honest, Sandwich thought, he was jealous of the lad having taken the scullery wench. It was no deeper than that.

"If you say it is so, clerk, it must be so." The earl couldn't fully suppress an ironic smile. "I propose the following." Turning to the postilion, he said, "You beg forgiveness for your error." Then to the kitchen clerk, "And you accept the apology."

"I beg forgiveness for nothing, your lordship," Ned Carleton declared.

"Have you heard me?"

"I didn't steal. I never steal!" His voice, rising in frustration, roused the mastiff from a dream, and the huge animal raised its wedge-shaped head.

"Control yourself," the house steward muttered close to the boy's ear.

"I swear it! I never steal!" Hands fisted at his sides, Ned stared at the bulky man behind the desk.

Lord Sandwich had the unnerving sensation of being, for an instant, on equal footing with a servant. He couldn't have been more shocked had they faced each other with dueling pistols. "You are insolent," he told the boy in a cold voice.

"I took nothing. I won't say I did."

"If you can't say it, you are dismissed." Waiting a few moments for a response and receiving none, he turned to the house steward. "This surly boy is dismissed." He added, after further consideration, "Pay him not one farthing. Cast him out today. I won't endure impudence. Not in my house. I won't have insubordination. Clerk," he said to the fat little man, who for the first time was smiling, "your vigilance gratifies me. Now all of you be so kind as to withdraw."

The clerk and house steward turned to leave, but the postilion remained at the desk, hands fisted at his sides.

Again Lord Sandwich met the dark intense gaze of the lad. They might have been arguing like old friends over a wench in a bawdy house. It was an insufferable situation. "I will have a constable here if you fail to go this instant," he warned.

At this threat the postilion went to the door, but before departing cried out, "I'm no thief! I won't say so!"

Alone once more, the earl noticed that his hands were trembling as he picked up another bill, this one for white candles. Thirty-five pounds worth. Scarcely a month's supply. But of course Judith would have a dozen burning at midday in a room drenched by sunlight. Clumsily he got to his feet and poured a glass of claret. His consolation for such a terrible morning was the anticipated trip to Medmenham next week, where he'd enjoy the company of merry friends and pretty doxies and leave behind the interminable bills, the unmanageable family, the bickering servants.

A footman knocked and entered to announce that Mister Scarrat awaited his lordship's pleasure.

"Desire him to walk in."

A couple of years ago Scarrat had been a footman too, but the earl had found better use for him outside the household. Scarrat had a knowledge of vice that made him exceedingly valuable. In his days at the Admiralty, Sandwich had found much need of spying and for this purpose had bought an ale house frequented by watermen. Scarrat was put in charge of it. The idea was for him to sound out customers and keep an ear cocked for trouble on the waterfront. Sandwich held the mortgage but allowed Scarrat to pocket the tavern proceeds. The investment paid off handsomely. Through his spy, the First Lord of the Admiralty got wind of dockyard pilfering at Spithead. The scheme was soon in ruins, the thieves in irons. Then he brought to justice a gang of river pirates who cut lighters adrift and plundered them ashore. Because of Scarrat's ability to ferret out information, Lord Sandwich had taken control of the Thames, which had puzzled and distressed the duke of Newcastle. Sandwich claimed that success in such matters had led Newcastle to dismiss him from the Admiralty. Perhaps Scarrat would help him regain the post — a good spy was worth more than a seat in Parliament.

Scarrat had another talent besides the ability to listen while drunken watermen blabbed their guts. The rascal was a keen judge of women and knew where to find them. For some time he had procured for John Montagu.

Scarrat now bowed his way into the study, a tall lean fellow in a long coat and dark wool breeches. His face was narrow, his black hair unruly. A boyhood of chimney sweeping had left him with a permanent hacking cough and skin a cadaverous grey. His brown eyes were dully cold within their heavy lids. Lord Sandwich wouldn't want such a fellow athwart his own path at night.

"I have need of eight nuns for next week," he explained to Scarrat, who stood in front of the desk. "It be my turn to supply them."

"Only eight?" Scarrat was circling the edge of a frayed cocked hat in his hands.

"The others are provided for by the monks."

"So you'll be needing eight." Scarrat put the back of a gnarled hand to his mouth and coughed. "Milord, two days ago I was passing through Aldermanbury and heard a girl singing so cheery and I told myself this was for his lordship. So I spoke with her and found her compliant."

"Is she on the town?"

"Not Betty. Eighteen with skin of roses and she knows her betters. This is something clean."

"Then she'll be for me." Sitting back, sipping his claret, for a few moments he thought of his Judith's strident voice in the Red Damask Room. "You say the girl's a songbird?"

"Milord, trust me in this."

"And you reckon her handsome?"

"Skin of milk, voice from heaven."

He always discounted Scarrat's glowing reports. Even so, the man did well by him for the most part. "As for the others, don't choose them so common they might be poxed. See to it they all bring armour with them."

"I understand, milord."

"My brothers must not be clapped or otherwise diseased. To say true, sometimes they forget to bring armour, especially in their cups."

"I well understand, milord. Who comes will bring armour and they will see to it it's used."

"Eight of the finest, hear."

"Have I ever failed milord in anything?" Scarrat smiled broadly enough to show teeth that reminded Sandwich of his own wife's mouth.

That dismal comparison encouraged him to reply petulantly. "Don't challenge me, Scarrat. I remember, sir, the chit some months ago with a lilting soprano but no gift for frolic."

"I warrant I failed then, milord."

Having asserted himself, Sandwich gestured the failure away. A man of substance did well to gather round him a few fellows such as Scarrat who were capable of providing access to a world otherwise denied him because of circumstance.

After Scarrat had bowed himself out of the study, Lord Sandwich idly picked his teeth — from habit, since he'd not eaten a thing after breakfast — and poured himself another claret. He reached down to pet the mastiff, whose silver collar gleamed in sunlight flooding the long window. Then he stood at the window, seeing in his mind's eye a vast stretch of ocean, a fleet of ships bearing down on the enemy. Batteries unmasked. Sails rippling. A veer, a tack into glory. Far above such stuffy rooms in imagination he breathed the pure air of combat like a seadog.

It was good to think so, but aboard ship these days he'd cut a sorry figure. Since leaving the Admiralty he'd gained considerable weight from a sedentary life. He used to be a cricketer and when the Thames froze over went skating and on rainy days swung dumb-bells for exercise.

Now all the exercise he got was with nymphs he paid for in flash houses or when he went for a black mass at Medmenham. He longed for the days to pass quickly until the friars assembled again at the old twelfth-century Cistercian abbey near Marlow and put on their cowled robes and prepared with bumpers of Hollands for a weekend of riot.

The Hell Fire Club, so named by Francis Dashwod, used to meet at taverns like the George and the Vulture and ale houses near Pope's villa in Twickenham. The public rooms had kept them in restraint; Sandwich, for one, had felt reined in like a lapdog — so did he declare to the others. But then they'd acquired freedom when they rented the abandoned monastery safely out of London. In refurbishing it, they were careful to bring in artisans from beyond the neighbourhood to do the work. Secrecy, of course, was paramount. Many of the Medmenham Friars (members of the Inner Circle and their "novice" guests) held high posts in government or were prominent in other walks of life: Dodington, Whitehead, Churchill, Potter, Lloyd, and Selwyn, among others, though fine rakebellies all, answered to one sort of constituency or another.

Now the Amorous Knights had their own place, and their own "superior" in Francis Dashwood, whose first name fit properly into the humour of their "religious" enterprise. So they were Franciscans, and the earl of Sandwich was himself a "sub-prior" of the Order of Saint Francis.

Sipping claret at the window, looking down at the gaping hole where that damnable River Company's elmwood pipe had burst yesterday, Lord Sandwich felt an overpowering desire to get away from here. This was a great mansion but not a home, and it lay in a city that had rejected him by allowing the sniffling cur from Newcastle, that waspish and jealous complainer who feared ocean voyages and damp beds, that mole of a man, to dismiss the First Lord of the Admiralty with a curt note ending "You shall always find me yr affectionate and humble servant." It was unbearable for John Montagu to remain in this city, let alone in this house, for too long a period.

He anticipated his first sight of the Medmenham abbey: the Thames, the towerless building among trees, the entrance way with its carved exhortation from Rabelais: FAY CE QUE VOULDRAS. And it was true! The company of merry monks, weary of London, in this sylvan hideaway did exactly what they damned well pleased: slept in outsize cradles, celebrated the mass of Satan, cracked untold bottles together, and entertained a bevy of masked nuns, either purchased from reputable madams or brought secretly at their own request and for their own amusement from reputable families in London.

Long ago he disliked Dashwood, who'd been elected archmaster of the antiquarian Dilettante Society only months after the earl had been suspended for "misbehaviour to and contempt for the Society" — a matter of biased interpretation, in his opinion, since the charge had been made by fatuous clergymen. Now he and Dashwood were fast friends, bound by a sense of defiant daring. Of course, he still despised Wilkes, who was an improvident upstart, and he considered Bubb Dodington no more than a lout whose only consistent act in life was to fall asleep in his cups. But all in all he loved his brother monks and the frolic they stood for.

Pouring another of claret, Lord Sandwich shuffled back to the writing desk for a look at more of Judith's bills. Dipping a pen into the inkwell, he paused before signing yet another check drawn for signature by his agent-in-chief. His head no longer throbbing from hangover, he allowed himself a moment of leisurely memory. It was at cards. Horace Walpole, having lost a hand, was in the mood for bitter observations about government. What he said then in his pompously elegant way still resonated in Sandwich's ear: "This world we agree to live in is quite silly. But who wouldn't laugh at a world where so ridiculous a creature as the duke of Newcastle can overturn ministries?"

[3]

Past the three balls outside a pawnbroker's shop lay an ale house that Scarrat sometimes visited when in this part of town. Good Victuals and Spirits was its name, its sign a man's head on a plate. He came in coughing, for it was cold today and his task had wearied him. Scarrat ordered a small beer, the strongest spirit he would touch.

Workmen and artisans were coming in for their afternoon drams. He studied them for tell-tale signs of the infirmities of their trade. A man like Scarrat, who felt his own chimney sweep's body ever threatened by disease, could tick off the fault of every occupation. Tailors became humpbacked, potters splenetic, chandlers developed vomitous stomachs, gold refiners had the asthma, sawyers got hernias, anchorsmiths wore out, gilders suffered paralysis, and hatters went mad. As for himself, Scarrat had managed to escape the chief hazard of a grog-house keeper — that of drunkenness. Not once in all his days at the Sign of the Frigate, listening to the boasting and blabber of watermen, had he ever tasted a strong liquor, not once, not ever.

He knew about sickness, having it seep through his lungs since he could remember. And he knew remedies. He knew that Keyser's Pills were good for claps. He knew there was Mrs. Stephens' Remedy for bladder stones, and if you suffered a broken bone you could have it set by that grizzly bitch Sara Mapp of Epson. He had sundry pills at home for curing looseness, worms, the jaundice, ague, itch, boils, vertigo, and sore eyes. He was a sober, careful man who looked out for himself.

Scarrat had brought a daily with him; he sat back to read and rest awhile. In the service of his lordship he'd spent half the day arranging for nuns to travel out to Medmenham the following week. Years ago, when Scarrat had first procured, he'd consulted *The New Atlantis,* a brothel guide, which was sold under the piazza of Covent Garden; it listed whores and singled out for special mention those establishments where flagellation was practised. But after a while he'd no longer needed help from pamphlets, having a map of pleasure in his mind that ran from fancy houses in Little Russell Street to the stews of Field Lane where it was a shilling a fuck.

This morning he'd stopped first in Hoop Alley, the abode of sign painters whose stocks of wood, carved to resemble teapots and sugar loaves, leaned shining against their shop walls. He was here to find a girl in a grocer's stall. As was his custom, he'd marked her one day while passing by — spoke to her politely of good fortune that might come her way, which she'd understood with a bold nod, and so he had writ down her name and place in a notebook kept for such purpose. She was a thin, dirty girl but when washed she'd show a lovely face, for though Scarrat rarely touched a woman himself he recognized beauty when he saw it. And this girl made it exceedingly clear that she would go to it for six shillings, no less, if the grocer decided she must, he taking half.

Then Scarrat moved on to a modish house of accommodation in the West End, run by Charlotte Haynes, where he negotiated for three more fillies. Then his duty took Scarrat to the Pink Swan near Clare Market, where Jews slaughtered oxen according to their heathenish custom. The Pink Swan had fine ladies of pleasure — he got one here — although next door was a notorious house for buggery, where clients pretended to the names of women and dressed in finery at tables laden with the pomatums and carmines worn by true ladies on Sunday promenades. Scarrat's own brother, before dying of lung sickness, used to frequent the place.

Scarrat went next to the Magpie and Stump in Skinner Street, a boisterous stew where naked women postured obscenely in candle-lit windows, beckoning the passersby in. Sometimes, however, there were new girls, none of your nightbags, your fireships with the clap, but rosy-cheeked maidens from the country. Today was his lucky day, because Scarrat found just such a one. The girl was going to cost milord Sandwich and his brother monks a pretty penny, the procuress at the Magpie and Stump being experienced, crusty, and as full of greed as the devil himself. She well knew a main chance when it came along.

He found a seventh girl in the purlieu of Drury Lane. She was known already by one of the monks and liked by him for having pissed on his naked chest. Nevertheless, Scarrat wouldn't hire the wench till satisfied she was neither poxed nor clapped, which he believed only after taking her into an alley and behind some barrels slipping two fingers into her and then inspecting her thighs and armpits for buboes.

He sipped his small beer while reading the paper. In a high wind yesterday a tradesman's sign in Bishopsgate tore loose and crushed a man's shoulder. On Monday last there were four malefactors executed at Tyburn. As one was a woman, they weren't all of them MALE-factors. Scarrat grinned at the levity. He carefully perused an advertisement for a kind of pill that cured many distempers such as scurvy, chilblains, cramp, colt-evil, twisting of the guts, sour belching. He doubted that all these claims could be true, though he never doubted there was always prey for every quackery.

Then there was an advertisement for Magistrate Fielding's *Covent Garden Journal,* along with the following notice: "All persons who suffer by criminals are desired immediately to bring the best description they can of such robbers etc., with the time, place, and circumstances of the fact, to Henry Fielding, Esq., at his house in Bow Street." So the judge meant for all the crime in London to be reported to him there — the Fielding house would serve as a central clearing station.

Scarrat pooh-poohed the idea. Let Mister Fielding and his Bow

Street Runners just try to stem the tide of crime. Godspeed to the arrogant fools! And yet Scarrat had a certain grudging respect for them. He had often seen Saunders Welch, chief of the Bow Street thief takers. Welch was a handsome, robust fellow who liked to attend executions at Tyburn in a powdered George-the-Second wig and a tall three-cornered hat, holding a crop tipped with silver and riding a white horse. Despite the show and finery, this was a man to reckon with; surely Scarrat had no wish to cross him. Unlike most constables and watchmen, who stood aside when trouble began, Welch and his boys worked hard and even recklessly to bring offenders in. Scarrat had once seen Fielding himself on one of those quick violent raids — a hulking man with a protruding jaw and nostrils that curled like the horns of a ram. Despite gout, Judge Fielding had climbed off his horse and followed Welch into a slum house in Ludgate Hill from which, after some minutes of yelling, they emerged with a cuffed miscreant whom they then shoved into a carriage for the trip to Bow Street and thence to Newgate Prison.

Even so, a long experience of London convinced Scarrat that no man could succeed in bringing under control the black hearts of this town. Fielding and his lot would end up laughing-stocks.

Finished with beer and paper, Scarrat left the tavern. Clutching his coat lapels against a keen gust of wind, he plowed through a mire glazed like cake. With no more than formal viciousness he kicked at a dog shivering across his path. He paused in a narrow lane until a wagon waddled by, then opened his breeches and pissed in the gutter. A well-dressed woman gave him a disapproving frown to which Scarrat responded with a grin. A show of modesty in women, be they cloaked in the finest fur, was nothing more than monkey nonsense. Under linsey-woolsey or bombazine, be they stinking or scented, they was every one of them brazen tarts. He knew them well. Before joining the Sandwich household, he'd served as a twang for countless whores. In his day he'd found girls of nine or ten for certain patrons. He'd located one-legged women, women with boobies as big as pumpkins, milkmaids who liked being whipped. But such specialties had been easier to find than milord's songbirds. In Scarrat's opinion most women made the noise of hens running from the ax.

So he'd been fortunate passing through Aldermanbury that Thursday last and hearing a sweet voice from an open window. It was true what he'd told milord Sandwich. Without even seeing the wench, he knew from such song that she had to be for his lordship. He'd tied his horse and walked about town, learning soon enough that Betty Canning was maidservant to a carpenter. Smoking a pipe in the dram shop across the street, he'd waited for her to appear. And in a while she'd come from the carpenter's house, a girl of pleasing enough figure with a wealth of brown hair and a regular if simple-looking face. He had overpraised her to his lordship, but so lovely was the voice she possessed — and knowing his lordship's love of song in a woman — Scarrat believed her lack of beauty would soon be forgotten when she sang for him in bed.

Betty Canning, though obviously inexperienced, had not shrunk away from the prospect of going to a nobleman. With hardly a moment of hesitation she had swallowed her virtue and murmured, "Yes, I would think kindly of a great gentleman taking me some-wheres for a lark." He had merely warned her to keep mum and be patient and he'd come for her. So he would come for her sooner than he'd expected. Tomorrow he'd ride out and give her the news and plan where to meet her, for it wouldn't do to make public in a small place such as Aldermanbury that a young girl was leaving town with a strange man.

So he had his songbird, the eighth of the nuns bound the week next for Medmenham.

Icicles were melting and dripping from eaves onto his great-coat as he leaned into the wind. Faggot fires were smoking in alleyways to keep the beggars warm, though they danced round and smacked their gloveless hands together to keep the blood flowing.

This morning, coming from his own waterfront tavern, he'd watched the smoke of fires rising along the riverbank. The Thames had glowed brown and murky beneath the winter light, as water-men plied their wherries near London Bridge with its timbered arches and haberdasher stores. All bridges, including that great one, were hated by watermen for taking revenue from them that they'd get on a crossing. If a bridge was burned down, you knew how to seek who did it. Look for a smiling waterman.

Scarrat was thinking how much he knew. It seemed to him sometimes that London ran in his veins like blood, that there was nothing separating his beating heart from the pulse of this terrible city. Few could know it as he did. He knew, for example, where thieves at night cooked in open ovens the lapdogs and cats they'd stolen during the day. Scarrat was thinking of the stink of burning dog just as he approached Ludgate Street. What he actually smelled was smoke and what he heard was a crackling sound. When he turned the corner, a street fire confronted him.

It surged through adjacent buildings, one of which had already been consumed by flames, another blazing, and a third engulfed in eddies of black smoke blown around by a rising wind. A crowd had gathered at the site like filings around a magnet. Already a fire wagon had arrived with its score of men in blue and orange livery, iron helmets, and silver badges pinned to their sleeves. They had rolled out a small-bore leather hose and plugged it into a streetside watercock; the oil which kept it from cracking made the hose glisten like coils of a snake. Two men held the nozzle and sent a feeble jet of water at the inferno. Standing on top of the wagon's cistern, another fireman directed a copper waterpipe at the house not yet afire. Other brigade members stood on ladders and with long preventing hooks pulled at the house already half burned, trying to isolate the fire. Still others hauled water in leather buckets from neighbouring buildings. Other firemen, holding hand squirts, leaned from nearby windows to shoot a few gallons of spray at the burning walls.

Children, whipped by the excitement into a gay frenzy, skipped beneath the quaking façades and dared one another to go closer. A fellow on stilts comically directed the firefighting above a crowd that rewarded him with bursts of laughter.

Joining the onlookers, Scarrat stood next to a fellow whose coffee-coloured hands were those of a tanner. The tanner was explaining to anyone who'd listen just how the fire started. An overheated glue pot in a cabinet-making shop had exploded. Blazing sawdust had then rushed up the stairway like a river. This explanation was peppered with such gross obscenities that a few ladies among the spectators edged away. The leather-stained man kept laughing and cursing and providing commentary on the fire's progress.

Scarrat regarded the scene with both indifference and fascination. In his day he'd seen dozens of such fires, yet they never failed to hold his attention. This one, for example. Inside the house the fire was swelling like something alive, like a thing growing, like an enormous monster bracing its shoulder against mortar and brick, its broad crimson back snapping the timber. For a few awful moments Scarrat remembered milord Sandwich calling up devils in the stone chapel at Medmenham. The fellow monks had been laughing all the while, but outside, eavesdropping against the cold wall of the abbey, Scarrat had felt a chill along his spine, just as he did now, and he was frightened near witless when at the next moment he heard voices raised in a chorus of "Jesus Christ Our Saviour!"

Turning in panic, he saw a black knot of bystanders singing the hymn. They had come upon the scene and were raising their voices in supplication to God. Damn Methodists! Onlookers were already taunting them, but faces ruddy in the glow, the Methodists continued their singing, this time a triumphant rendition of "Onward, Christian Soldiers."

The crowd had pushed dangerously close to the buildings so that coals shot into their midst. This merely caused squeals of merriment as a flurry of hands beat out the sparks falling on shoes and hats. Freed from the memory of Medmenham devils, Scarrat started to grin, secure in his rightful element here: the fury and blare and wild alarm of London town. Through the seething flames he glimpsed suddenly a woman leaning from a top window of the third building that had finally caught fire too. Half her body was out the window, her mouth a black O of fright as she kept screaming for help.

"They can't get her out," observed the tanner with bland certainty. "She's dead as a fish." He pointed to three men, none in brigade livery, who were running at a low crouch toward the building. As they charged inside, burning timber crashed behind them. "Fart heads!" yelled the tanner. Grinning, he turned to the crowd. "Those whoreson assholes can't get her out. The stairway must be fallen. They have turds for brains, they." But others cheered the rescue attempt. The man on stilts, asway from all the jostling beneath him, began a chorus that drowned out the Methodist hymn-singing: "Go to it, bullies! Go to it! Go to it, bullies. GO TO IT! GO TO IT! GO TO IT!"

"I wager a shilling the stairway's out and they can't get her," shouted the tanner.

A bystander took the bet. While they were shaking on it, the first house collapsed. Its floors fell through one another, sliding onto the street like the smoking bowels of a butchered animal. A rampant coil of flame enfolded a spectator so quickly that he fell writhing and dying before hands could snatch him to safety.

Firemen on top of the cistern yelled for more water, but the pressure was too low and the stream they played on the third building, where the woman still called for help, hardly reached the ground floor. The house was quaking and sizzling, aglow like the brassy light of a furnace.

Abruptly from its entrance staggered the three defeated rescuers, the last one out a tall brawny lad onto whose hat a burning brand had fallen.

For a terrifying moment Scarrat saw him as an apparition, the flame licking up from the hat brim like the horn of Satan. And another image flashed through his mind — that of his drunken master in a cowled robe praying to the Powers of Darkness. And in this heightened moment Scarrat mixed the scenes, so that the stumbling lad in the blazing hat seemed to be a demon conjured up at Medmenham.

The crowd roared in dismay as the woman plunged forward from the window into thick clouds of smoke, her body turning in descent like a flung doll.

A few miles eastward on London Bridge the Italian painter Canaletto was at work on a sketch. He paused to study the vermilion glare above the spire of St. Paul's. The fire might add a touch of melodrama to his composition, but he decided against it. His intent was to sketch a London as serene as a Swiss landscape, and so did he continue.

The man who'd lost the wager to the tanner was slipping away, but the tanner cried out and onlookers wrestled the loser to his knees. "Pay up, damn you!" screamed the tanner, standing over him. "She croaked. You lost. Pay up!"

"Pay up," threatened others until sullenly the loser produced a shilling and thrust it at the tanner.

Scarrat shoved past them to stare at the husky lad who for a bad moment had given him such a fright. The young man had flung away the burning hat and was now sitting cross-legged near the dead woman spreadeagled just beyond the dwindling fire. He held out his left hand stiffly; it was blackened, severely burned. The lad's eyelashes had been singed off, a huge welt was rising on his cheek.

Kneeling, Scarrat studied that face. It was familiar in some way, and in a few moments he placed it: this was a postilion in his lordship's household. During one of Scarrat's visits, he had noticed the lad in the stable and another time had sent him for snuff. Scarrat had liked his obedience and calm nature.

Now, however, he said coldly to the lad, "You played the idiot."

Reeking of smoke, holding the wrist of his burned hand, the boy grimaced.

"Do you know me? Do you know who calls you idiot?"

Ned Carleton stared from bloodshot eyes, then nodded.

"It was simple-minded what you did. Who told you to go in there? Had you saved the bitch, you'd get nothing for it, not a farthing. She'd tip you a curtsy and go her ways. What a cock sparrow you are," he added with a grin.

Turning slightly, Ned glanced at the dead woman, whose bare arms, rosy in the firelight, were jutting out at odd angles.

"As I know his lordship," Scarrat continued, "he'd not want a simpleton atop his chariot."

"It's of no account. He has cast me out."

"What for?" Getting no answer, Scarrat said, "Did you tumble a kitchen wench?" He guffawed, reached out and good-naturedly patted the lad's shoulder. The hectic scene had filled Scarrat with a sense of well-being, as if crowd and flame had transmitted energy to his own body. In this expansive mood he might even do the country oaf a good turn. "Speak up, boy. What was the dodge that got you cast out?"

"Kitchen clerk said I stole, but I stole nothing."

"Come. Did you nick a slice of mutton?"

"It's what milord asked, but I stole nothing." Staggering to his feet, Ned looked around and sucked his breath in with a startled groan.

"What now?" Scarrat asked with a smile.

"I had a sack with belongings." Turning around, Ned scanned the debris-strewn street. "I dropped it when I saw the woman up there."

"*Dropped* it?" Scarrat cocked his head in disbelief. "Dropped your goods in the midst of these fine Londoners? You put belongings in trust of this crowd of honest Englishmen?" Scarrat did a rare thing for him: he threw his head back and laughed.

Ned regarded the burning embers, the torn clothes, the bits of furniture and chinaware that had been blown out of the buildings. "That sack was all I had."

"I warrant no more than rags in it," crowed Scarrat, his chuckle turning into a fit of coughing. "God in heaven, these fucking bumpkins!" He coughed harder, feeling his lungs heave and tighten and a dry rale begin pumping up from deep within his body. He looked at the boy. That rosy young face had never been smeared with coal dust. That robust frame had never been doubled up in a soot-filled chimney. That lad had eaten good victuals his life long. Scarrat was abruptly weary of him. "Go to," he mumbled, as a few bystanders came closer and began poking through the debris for something of value.

Having breath again, Scarrat shoved his face forward at the boy and grinned spitefully. "You can't last long at a simpleton's game here. This be London, boy. How do you like it?" Taking a step closer, he glared at the former postilion. "Tell me, dimwit, how do you like it? Hey? How do you like it! Tell me — ah, a fucking pox on you!" Wheeling around, Scarrat went a few paces, then halted at a loud crashing sound. Preventing hooks were pulling down molten streams of brick. The crowd roared and edged back. At his feet Scarrat noticed a vellum-bound volume, half of it charred, the other half wet from the fire hose but still smoking.

He saw himself for a moment looking up the narrow sooty passage of a chimney into the sky. He was already coughing then, at nine years of age. He was staring at blue sky, wanting nothing more in the world but for God to reach down and grasp him and pull him out of there and carry him to heaven.

Bending down, he picked up the book and turned back to Ned Carleton, who stood holding his blackened hand out. "Here," Scarrat said, thrusting the book forward. "Can you read?"

"Some."

"Take it. Find a place on the riverbank and sit like a fine gentleman and calm yourself reading." Scarrat couldn't remember the last time he had given anyone anything, and here he was offering a book, a half-burned one, to a foolish boy who had lost his goods while trying to save a doomed bitch and had then lied about something as common as theft from a larder. Scarrat amazed himself. But he persisted, "Here, take it. It's a book. Go sit and calm yourself. Turn pages with the good hand. Go read awhile like a gentleman." He heard the strange note of gentleness in his voice.

The boy took the book in his good hand.

Scarrat turned again and at a brisk pace quickly left behind him the noise, the smoke, the fire wagon, two corpses among the rubble, and a simple country lad who stood by himself in the midst of all that confusion, hurt and robbed and dumbfounded by the world.

[4]

NED CARLETON HAD PAID scant attention to crippled beggars until now. In his village there had been only one of them, and everyone fed the twisted fellow till his hunched figure grew stout, his lopsided face sleek. Now, however, Ned stared in dismay at the begging poor: women rendered sightless from the pox huddled in doorways and whined for a penny; legless men in flat carts scooted at great speed through the crowds, thrusting the wood blocks in their fists over the cobblestones in a spleenful forward rush; their limps both real and fake, small children wheedled coins from customers as they left shops. Sleeves fluttered emptily. Suppurating cankers loomed out of shadows. Legs dragged. Crutches punched holes in the mud. It seemed to Ned that London was a charnel house inhabited by the half dead.

And now he was one of them.

Yet without reckoning the reason why. His whole life long he'd believed in reward and punishment for deeds committed. What had he done to be cast from the household? He hadn't even tupped the kitchen wench. They had merely talked about their villages far north of London, he being from Nottinghamshire and she from Yorkshire. All they shared was the common memory of countryside and forest. They talked of tambour lace and coal mining and felt homesick together. No more than that. Not even a touch of hands.

Yet his lordship, winking and laughing, had accused him of having taken both her and a partridge and to compound the insult had disbelieved the truth when he spoke it. Things had happened then so quickly that he found himself in a crowd at a fire, watching a woman call for help from a window, and on impulse to save her he was somehow inside the building, choking on smoke and with flaming brands falling on his coat and in his hat and his hand gripping a banister that was suddenly ablaze. And then he'd lost everything the head coachman had allowed him to take away in a sack. There was nothing left now but two guineas in his pocket.

His first task was to find lodgings, which he did in a Smithfield boarding house. It was boxy quarters, smaller than his room back home in Warsop, but he shared it with four other men, one of them a virulent drunkard, though the others were decent enough. There were two beds, two to a bed, and as the newcomer Ned had a blanket and the floor. His first night there he pulled out the book given him by Mister Scarrat and studied its look in candlelight. With but slight handling, a good third of it had already crumbled into ash, and many other pages were too ruined for deciphering. The gist could never be read through, but then his skill with words had never got him much further than reading signs and quips in a gazette. But he meant to keep this book. After all, it had been given him by Mister Scarrat, a known tavernkeeper and a mysterious confidant to his lordship (stablemen hinted of dark secrets between them, maybe even an unnatural relationship, as milord Sandwich had always carried about him an unsavory repute). Ned would keep the crumbling book because a man of substance had given it to him, and because it was all he still had.

He tried parsing some of the writing at random, skipping burned portions and words so smudged by ash and dirt as to be unintelligible:

> . . . to say the truth, this gentleman (who was no ——r than the celebrated Mr. Peter Pounce, and who preceded the Lady Booby, only ——— miles, by setting out earlier in the morning) was a very gallant person, and loved a pretty girl better than any thing, besides his own money or the money of other people.

One of the boarders, sitting idly at the window and smoking a pipe, asked Ned what that was. So Ned showed the book, wondering if the man knew two of the words, and the man did, explaining "celebrated" and "preceded."
And there was this:

Adams had soon put on all his clothes but his breeches, which in the hurry he forgot.

Ned studied this sentence a long time before accepting the humour of it, as at first he couldn't understand how a man might dress himself entire without thinking of his breeches. Then flipping pages, he came to this:

. . . imprinted numberless kisses on her lips without considering —— —— present. If prudes are offended at the lusciousness of this picture, they may take their eyes off from it and survey parson —— —— —— the room in a rapture of joy.

More smudges. Again he consulted his roommate, who kindly offered interpretations until he knew every word that was visible and could judge the author of them to be humorous and bold.
But the next day he had no time for reading. There was work to get. As for his hand, because it had given him little pain after the first hours, he'd not worried over much about it. Buying some white salve at a barber shop, he rubbed it on the charred fingers from which a colourless fluid was seeping. He wrapped the hand in a kerchief and simply washed the cloth in water when it got dirty. Thanks to his youthful vigour, the infection failed to spread far. Within a fortnight new skin began to appear at the edge of the wound. Nevertheless, the shock left him cold and sweaty, too weak for seeking long after work. And when nerve endings started to renew themselves under the blighted tissue, he felt a throbbing ache radiate up his arm from each finger. It was more pain than he had felt initially. But worse than pain were the ridges of scar that webbed his fingers together like a duck's foot. When he tried to move his fingers, they seemed to be encased in plaster, remaining in a half-clenched attitude that made of them a single unyielding mass as if someone had attached to him the rigid hand of a corpse. He

kept hoping for improvement, but none came, and there wasn't time to wait for it. He must find work soon. Down to his last shillings, he could not much longer afford the luxury of lodgings.

Each day he walked the icy streets of town, the truth grew deeper in his mind: at twenty he was too old for an apprentice and too unskilled for a journeyman. Master craftsmen turned him away from guild doors — even before seeing the hand. Combmakers and cobblers and silkmen needed to ask but a single question about their trade and his confusion sank him.

One night he found a half-used torch in an alley. With this he hoped to set up as a linkboy, hiring himself out as a guide through the dark streets. But no sooner had he walked the length of a lane than a dozen men surrounded him. They carried lit brands and thrust them at his face, demanding to know his name and was he the trusted acquaintance of Sam Cutter or Will Billings or other linkboys of the district, because if not, damn his balls, he had no business hereabouts and he'd finish tonight with the torch he'd stolen jammed down his fucking throat. Perhaps what saved him was his appalled and puzzled look, because after handing over the torch, he was motioned to go his ways and stay clear of here forever.

Once near St. Mary Magdalene he came upon fishmongers squatting on the ground and quarreling over their sprat, their whitings. Ned told them he had a strong back for work. They grinned from bearded faces at the leather leggings and riding coat that marked him as a country shepherd without knowledge of fish.

"You look to have a strong back," said one of the fishmongers. "And so have we — strong enough to cool your courage, chum. We could throw you down in your own shit and not worry about it."

Another said, "He's got but one good hand anyway."

"Get clear of us," another added, "or we'll pound a bung up your filthy ass."

Each day he walked the streets, telling people in desperation that he was out of a place, that he could earn his victuals, that he had a strong back for work. It seemed to him that he'd collared every man in London: drovers, coal heavers, fellmongers, soap boilers. "I'm out of a place," he told snuff makers, stock weavers, sawyers. He stood humbly in the doorway of tripe shops and breweries, hiding his bandaged hand and with his good one plucking the sleeves of delivery men as they rolled huge barrels into cellars. "Do you need another strong back, sirs?" He pleaded with woolmen to let him help haul their bales and with wine merchants to lift their heavy casks out of storage. At rare times he nearly got a morning's employment, being husky as he was, but when the ruined hand came into view the hiring men no longer wanted him.

With the last of his money he went to a register office. The gloomy waiting room was filled with mousy chambermaids and haughty footmen looking for employment. Officious clerks were seated within the inner office at high desks. After a long time he was summoned by a crooked finger to await a clerk in a disheveled tie wig. Ned sat on the chair's edge, knees together, his back straight in the rumpled riding coat that after all these many months still smelled faintly of sheep. He answered questions that were put sharply to him.

"Name?"

"Nathaniel."

"Nathaniel *what?*"

"Nathaniel Carleton."

"Age?"

"Twenty year by the parish register."

"Where born?"

"At Warsop in Nottinghamshire."

"Your last place?"

"Postilion to His Lordship the Earl of Sandwich, sir."

The clerk put down the quill and glared. "Why, man, did you leave a thing like that?"

Ned paused to consider a dissembling answer, but only the truth came to mind. He explained being cast out for thefts he never committed. "I touched nothing."

"Spoke like a man," the clerk commented with a sarcastic grin. "What came you away with?"

"Sir?"

"What did you bring away from the house with you, man?"

"Head coachman let me keep a pair of white stockings, stout boots, silk garters worth two shilling each, a bob wig, livery breeches — for he was a good man unwilling to let me go empty-handed — and five gold buttons and a tricorn, but I lost it all."

The clerk nodded with a fierce smile. "Of course, you lost it all. You country fellows be all alike," he said. "What cole is left you?"

"Sir?"

"Cole, man. Money. Have you got as much as a guinea?"

"Less now."

"Well, how much?"

With his good hand Ned placed the coins on the desk to count them, but the clerk, also counting, declared, "Six shillings."

Finishing his own count, Ned agreed.

"So you're in luck, man," said the clerk. "I have a place for you."

After a moment's hesitation, Ned raised his bandaged hand timidly. "I have this, sir."

"Never mind. For five shillings I have a place for you."

For this fee Ned was given the Hatton Garden address of a family of substance who needed a groom, but when he went there, no such family existed. Indeed, no such address existed.

Returning to the register office, he demanded in the waiting room to see the clerk and get his money back, but three husky fellows came out and ordered him to leave. Ned was prepared to fight, but then thought better of it, for he might reinjure the hand and find himself more helpless. What had Mister Scarrat, surely a man of the world, warned him of? None lasted long by playing a fool's game in this town.

Without more words, Ned crept from the office and allowed the men to grin at his back. Retreating from a fight was a queer sensation for him. In his village he'd never refused a challenge, not even when it was blacksmith Jimmy Hawkins, the strongest man around. Long after he was beaten, Ned had met those sledgehammer fists, rising even after he felt a rib give way, after his own blood blinded him, but he kept staggering into the huge blacksmith until the fellow's great hands dropped from exhaustion like weights of lead, and they both of them sprawled side by side, neither a winner in the dust, though Ned was laid up for a week and Hawkins returned to the forge that afternoon.

Taken altogether, those three men at the register office wouldn't make up among them one Jimmy Hawkins. Yet Ned had walked away from them, leaving both his money and his honour behind. Mister Scarrat had said in a jolly if scary way, "This be London.

How do you like it?" In faith this was surely London, and he in it without money, not enough to leave with even if he wanted to, which to his amazement he was not sure he did. He had but a shilling, a cold night ahead, and nowhere to stay.

At sunset he drifted toward the docks, coming to a boardwalk from which he could see the Thames. Bobbing on the violet water were six- and eight-oared wherries, many of them with awnings and lanterns in the bows. Fashionable passengers lolled on cushions. Tilt boats passed, running toward Gravesend with sailors jammed together like fish in baskets. He gazed long at the shadowy timbered arches along London Bridge and heard the swirling noise of mill blades clacking beneath its span.

Suddenly from the far end of the boardwalk a commotion started up. People scattered like sheep as a phalanx of men approached, brandishing clubs and swords.

"Press! The press!" yelled someone stumbling past Ned in the gloom.

Waiting for the press gang to come closer, Ned stayed his ground. The gang was swearing and laughing and pushing three captured men forward in wrist irons. Two members of the gang shot out from the pack and grabbed a fellow sneaking along a warehouse wall. When he struggled, a cudgel came down and opened a gash in his head.

"You scurvy sonofabitch," grumbled a press sailor. Leaning over the fallen man, he clamped on a pair of irons.

Calmly Ned waited for two men to approach him, one with a sword raised threateningly.

"Yo ho, brother!" called the man with the drawn hanger. "Come along!"

"Gladly," said Ned.

"I said come along!"

"I will."

The two men eyed him suspiciously. The one without a sword crouched in readiness to prevent Ned from escaping.

"Gladly," repeated Ned. "I will go gladly."

"It's to sea with you then," the swordsman told him. "In His Majesty's service."

"Gladly."

"Devil take me if you run and I don't skewer you."

"No need of irons. I will go gladly." Proving it, Ned walked over to join the impressed men, one of whom was weeping.

"I don't want to go," the man sobbed, as the gang continued down the boardwalk.

Another captured man said, "It's a frigate for us. Three-year voyage, I heard one of them say."

"Meaning four-year," another said, "or five. Last time I was pressed it was five."

"What of my wife? Who can tell her where I'm taken? What's to do?"

"By God, shut up!" A sailor dug his cudgel into the man's stomach, doubling him.

The gang trudged slowly down the wharfside, drawing into their net, as they went along, a drunken waterman and a boy eating gingerbread who had unluckily turned the corner. At the dock's end lay a boat and beyond it in midstream a pressing tender with lanterns defining its long low shape. Some of the gang jumped into the boat, ordering the captured men to do the same.

Pulling his bandaged hand from his coat, Ned prepared to jump, but a sailor shoved a torch forward to have a better look at him and called out, "Wait, you! What's the rag for?"

"Hurt my hand some." Ned shoved it into his coat pocket.

"Let's see that."

Hesitantly he withdrew his hand.

The sailor yanked the dirty cloth off with a few furious motions. "Ho, look at that. Bosun!"

A burly fellow came up and held his torch toward Ned. One look at the ugly hand and he exclaimed, "Why, the lad's bad hurt!"

"Will he do, Bosun?" asked the sailor.

"I will do," Ned urged.

Studying Ned a moment, the bosun turned and guffawed at his mates. "He wants to go. Let's see you move the hand."

Ned tried, but the clawlike fingers remained rigid.

"He can't," the sailor observed, "but he's stout. Will he do?"

"Will he do?" repeated the bosun sarcastically. "You piss-ass, what do you think? Lieutenant would have my gizzard for pressing such a rotten one." With a disgusted glance at Ned, he added, "Crippled as a three-legged dog."

Pushing Ned back, the sailor let another prisoner jump into the boat.

"I can work," Ned insisted.

"Get your ass away, you piss-ass," the sailor yelled at him.

Ned stood to the side and watched the loading. The prisoner with a wife was still weeping. Another argued with a sailor and for his pains got rapped with a cudgel. There was a rhythmic splash splash splash as the boat left the pier and headed for the tender. Torches and lanterns, bobbing above the black river, cast flickering light against a forest of masts and furled sails, like fireflies along a tree-bordered road at dusk. Ned watched until the boat reached the tender, then looked around the boardwalk for his kerchief, but couldn't find it. The sailor who ripped it from his hand must have tossed it into the river. So Ned removed his linen neckcloth and wound it around the proud flesh. He tried again to move his fingers, but with the same result: they felt thick, woolly, something like the backs of sheep. Sheep. Home. Where he'd stood up to men better than any in the press gang.

Father used to counsel him, "If a man speak to you in a threatening way, don't think on it or palaver or threaten back. Just lend him a douse and be done with it."

Father would have bit his lip in shame — who had spent a lifetime at sea, returning home but long enough to make another baby, seven in all, none surviving childhood save Ned and a girl now married. Father would come roaring home with a sea bag on his shoulder, his weathered face breaking into a smile of pleasure at the sight of children still alive. Five years ago he'd died of a wasting disease on a barque carrying rum and sugar from the Indies. At least he'd lived to see his only son grow tall. On his last visit home he'd coughed frequently while they strolled in the cottage yard, scattering chickens into the phlox. Father had coughed with the same cold seriousness as Mister Scarrat coughed. He stopped to pick a flower with a shaking hand. Holding it like a child, he gazed beyond the woodpile toward a rippling stand of trees on the distant hillside.

"Sonny, you be tall as me now," he said. "Taller to get, I wager." Looking at the phlox lost in his massive hand, he said, "We must all die. That's certain. Best make no fuss about it. As the saying goes, Death's like a good bower anchor. It will bring us all up."

Then he and Ned had returned to the cottage. Along with Mother (hardly a year of life left to herself) and Ned's sister Sarah, they'd sat down to rye bread soaked in buttermilk. Never again did Father speak of solemn matters, but teased Sarah about her young men and winked at Mother and jabbed Ned in the ribs while making a sailor's jest.

Father would die of shame, Ned told himself grimly, to see me treated so. Bending forward into an icy wind and with nowhere to go, Ned reentered the dark streets of London.

[5]

THAT EVENING in his study Magistrate Henry Fielding was putting the finishing touches on a treatise entitled *A Proposal for Making an Effectual Provision for the Poor, for Amending their Morals, and for Rendering them useful Members of the Society*.

He reread the introduction which harshly denounced the present handling of this matter:

> That the poor are a very great burden, and even a nuisance, to this kingdom; that the laws for relieving their distresses, and restraining their vices, have not answered those purposes; and that they are at present very ill provided for, and much worse governed, are truths which every man, I believe, will acknowledge.

Once done with this pamphlet, he would take up a charge by the duke of Newcastle to develop a plan for curbing the worst crime wave in history. Fielding felt — and so communicated to his grace — that he could bring to this worthy task the same forthright optimism that had suffused *Tom Jones*. If his proposal was accepted, a magistrate would remain on duty for twenty-four hours at Bow Street. The small band of thief takers already through him assembled would gradually be augmented by other men of unblemished character who were willing to risk their lives in hazardous enterprise. Three horses would be kept saddled in the Bow Street stable for instant pursuit of malefactors. All reported crimes would be duly noted in a register. By governmental order it would be incumbent on newspapers to give full details of felonies and thereby alert pawnbrokers against accepting stolen goods and stablekeepers against hiring out horses to escaping felons. A grand scheme. And he meant to put it in proper form within a few months, but at the moment he had stomach cramps of such fierceness that he couldn't hold a pen.

Henry Fielding was ill. For many years he had suffered periodically from gout, but in recent months he was never free of a crushing pain in his left foot, which allowed him to walk only with the aid of a crutch. When bandages were changed, he stared gloomily at the hot shiny skin, as purple as boiled ham. He slept only with the aid of too much brandy, and then, likely as not, his asthma flared up. No longer did he consult a mirror to verify the destruction of his youth. The rugged six-foot frame had shrunk into that of a chronic invalid. Loss of teeth had caved his lips in, further aging his face. The long distinguished Roman nose had become ruddy and bulbous and testified better than gossip to his drinking habits. Continually he sought improvement in his health, but nothing worked. He doused himself with powders and at Glastonbury took the spring waters, which did not prevent his asthmatic attacks, nor did the drinking of tar water relieve his gout. Yet another remedy was abroad that he might try. It was said to cure, according to the advertisement, "Worms, Obstructions of the Veins and Passage of the Chyle, the Jaundice, Hypochondriac Melancholy, Surfeits by Hard Drinking, and was good in any Clime." Any clime? Was it good in English clime, he thought, it would do for the whole world.

He tossed aside the advertisement, knowing full well that he shouldn't put faith in such a wonder. And yet this very day he might douse himself with the potion and hope to heaven it didn't kill him. Friends warned him against quack medicine, but a man must put his faith somewhere when sick. Samuel Richardson did that while writing *Pamela*. Being too fat and short of breath, he had taken a diet prescribed by Doctor Cheyne of vegetables, milk, bread, and light beer. Fielding sighed. Not the specter of death itself could persuade him to get such sops down his own gullet. But prim Richardson had followed the regimen, allowing him to finish his silly book on schedule, and for that result Fielding should feel grateful, as *Pamela* had provided a satiric source for his own *Joseph Andrews*.

A knock on the study door, and an elderly manservant entered with a tray and the announcement that Madam Fielding wished to remind his worship it was time for medicine. Fielding drank off the bitter brew offered him thrice daily. It was Doctor Ward's Drop, a mixture of antimony and arsenic, made nearly palatable by a following glass of port.

"Joseph, another of port."

"Madam begs to remind your worship, two glasses of port will not have a salubrious effect."

Fielding waved him away. A man had fallen on bad times when he was denied a second glass of port. Gone were the days when he could drink champagne and chew tobacco and write ten hours at a stretch. Gone too were the days of promise and hope when debts blithefully incurred were as blithefully paid. Upstairs depending on him were a pretty daughter by his deceased first wife, two girls and a son by Mary, and soon Mary would present him with yet another mouth to feed.

Sitting back he awaited the effects of the drop. On his tongue was a familiar metallic taste, on his breath a strong garlicky stench. In minutes his stomach would burn, his skin grow clammy, his head throb as if he'd swilled bumpers all night.

To employ the time until he might attend again to important tasks — for though wracked by cramps he refused to sit by and do nothing — Fielding drew out from his desk a personal journal which he had recently begun in secret. He meant to keep an honest record of his thoughts in it, the impulse coinciding with his new sense of mortality.

Picking up a quill, grimacing from a new spasm, he nonetheless continued an account of events last evening:

❡ Be it known, Reader, that when I returned from supping with Lyttelton and my elderly manservant opened the door, I threw a guilty glance at his threadbare livery which, to say the truth, he had been wearing nigh on ten years, ever since in one of my reckless moods I had purchased new livery for all the servants and, as a consequence, had spent almost the entire earnings (however

modest) of *Joseph Andrews* on such frippery. The faithful man —
I say faithful because most other servants, seeing the way the wind
was blowing, had long since quit our household — went by the
name of Joseph in honour of *Joseph Andrews'* success with critics
(but a failure with booksellers), although his true Christian name
was Peter. Joseph still wore with consummate grace the brilliant
orange frock-coat, albeit it was patched, torn, and faded, in all too
perfect harmony with the state of my literary reputation.

Fatigued by the day, yet unwilling to relinquish it — for in my
state of health I begrudged the dying of each hour — I went to my
study for a perusal of the latest journals. The presses had lately
been pouring out a veritable flood of printed matter: memoirs writ
by traveled ladies and listless moral essays filled with Latin tags
and pompous articles describing the waterproofing of boots, the
manufacture of curl papers, the breeding of monkeys.

In the midst of all this indifferent paper I found in *Old England*
still another unfavourable estimate of my last work, *Amelia,* which,
for two years, had occasioned scurrilous abuse and ridicule. Never
hath a book been more severely handled, as one after another of my
habitual detractors (among them Richardson, whom I have often
tried to befriend as a fellow writer — and one of a wonderful
talent, I might add, if a bit stuffy in aspect and still smarting from
the farcical use I made of hypocritical Pamela), all hailed the
unlucky book as poor stuff, wretched stuff, bad stuff, sad stuff, low
stuff, and paltry stuff, to which could now be added the final
judgement of judgements: "The corpse of this poor wretched
Amelia."

This of a fiction that hath been the favorite child of all my
literary endeavours!

We must everyone of us bear up, Reader, under adversity in his
own way, as wise Horace observed. So I called for a bracing glass
of port, which Joseph brought along with Doctor Ward's Drop,
which I swallowed down and followed with the port. Wanting
another and with a hopeful smile that was meant to ingratiate
myself with Joseph, I asked for port, to which he replied in his
elegant manner that Madam Fielding would surely beg to remind
his worship that two of port together could not have a salubrious
effect. And with his grandiloquent refusal, the old devil, bowing
deeply, retired in triumph. You will doubtless agree, Reader, that
a man hath fallen on evil times when he cannot have a second of
port.

Debts plagued my mind while upstairs were four children and a wife soon to present me with another mouth to feed, all of these dear charges depending on talent and vigour no longer at my command.

But you may be pleased to hear that I was not left long in such a brooding way, for the door opened and in trooped young William and little Sophia, aged six and three, along with their mother, my good Mary. I greeted them warmly with all my heart and set each child on a knee, wincing from the pain occasioned by William's weight on the gouty left leg. But I would have borne any pain for the sake of this sweet-natured boy, whose bodily proportions were large for his age albeit well knit like those of his parents, Mary and I possessing the solid frames of country folk. Most likely our William will grow into a sturdy size. He had come into this world less auspiciously than I hope he will leave it. William had arrived no more than two months after I had wedded his mother in St. Benet's, Paul's Wharf, the which arithmetical calculation my enemies have never ceased to make whenever other methods of securing merriment at my expense have failed. Poor Mary hath suffered from the shame beyond my comprehension, and to no avail have I tried to keep from her eyes those vicious broadsheets which have called her "his late wife's personal maid" and "his plain speaking but even more plain looking housekeeper" and finally "his nurse to whom he applied in his mental and physical distress for more than medicinal solace."

Then into the room came my eldest, Harriet, a girl in first bloom, whose handsome looks have often recalled to me Dryden's line "All paradise is opened in a face." I kissed her briskly on the cheek, struggling not to show partiality to this issue of my first marriage, for I knew that Mary could not help observing closely my treatment of the girl. Mary hath not a mean bone in her body, yet methinks that a wife aware of being forever second in her husband's affections cannot without dismay witness his tender regard for a child whose mother is forever first in his heart.

I was therefore careful to show equal regard for the children of both women and, indeed, so I did feel, Reader, at least in my conscious mind. But in my heart of hearts still dwells my Charlotte for whom I will ever grieve and whose delicate features seem to shine forth again in the fifteen-year-old face of Harriet.

I asked my wife how did our Louisa, an infant but six months old, who had been sickly of late. I was pleased to learn that she had shown improvement. While having thus around me my family before I must retire for the night and hoard up what strength there

could be for tomorrow's work, I thought of something I had
read — or perhaps myself had written: Domestic happiness is the
end of almost all our pursuits and the common reward for all our
pains. My poor friend Lyttelton. Like myself, he had lost his
beloved first wife, but unlike myself, he had not found a kind-
hearted woman to give him a second chance at happiness.

But last night as I prepared for bed (Joseph having removed the
bandage on my gouty foot, the hot shiny skin of which looked as
purple as boiled ham), the domestic calm of my spirit was shaken
again by the last attack on *Amelia*. Once I heard drop from the late
Mister Pope that nature hath never produced a more venomous
animal than a bad author; and I would amend his remark to
include a bad critic. Even after a lifetime of literary turmoil, I
cannot stomach a malicious thrust at my work; it is in faith like
someone pushing my own child into the mud. This holds
especially true of *Amelia* which hath been decried for lack of wit
and quite neglected for its portrait of a naturally noble woman.
Reader, you may smile at the vanity here revealed, and I must
confess that I am wounded in part by such criticism because I do
inwardly acknowledge the loss of a comic spirit with which I once
attempted to laugh mankind out of its favourite follies.

Perhaps there is little hope of an overworked man in fear of his
health and deeply in debt to proceed merrily like a seaworthy
vessel through a storm and not look up at the rigging and down at
the bilges. I grant myself a new caution. Nor hath being a Justice
of the Peace produced a genial effect on my humour. Confronting
men whose deeds in villainy go far beyond mere folly hath given
me a new and sobering view of the human heart. If *Amelia* is
somber, then so is the life it describes. I believe I might aver that I
have writ little more than I have seen.

Calling out to Joseph, I demanded another of port, but the old
rascal pretended not to hear me and shut a window which I had
opened minutes before and with a very low bow, the meaning of
which you may interpret as you will, he left the room.

I reopened the window and looked out upon a black London,
put in motion here and there by streaming little lights from link
torches. I have believed in reason throughout my life, yet perhaps
approaching the end of it, I am no longer certain of reason. Indeed,
I would go further and suggest that men are ruled by their
expectations of pleasure.

It is in the nature of a confession, Reader, that I offer myself as
an example of this thesis; for though I have long resolved to build

an estate and leave my family provided for in the event my various
illnesses prove fatal, I have put aside the resolve whenever some
merry friends happen along, so that I have spent my bounty on
feasting and have made loans without security and have bought
gifts at a dear price merely to light up a companion's eye with
momentary joy; the which prodigality hath each time drained
off household funds and left my family once more at the edge of
insolvency.

Prodigal of prodigals! From early youth on I have put too much
trust in my powers. A sly voice always whispered in my ear that
today I might spend and tomorrow restore. Along with Terence I
accepted the view that nothing human can be foreign to me —
nihil humani a me alienum puto — and by extension of that
deceptive view, that nothing human can be beyond my capacity to
perform. This is an arrogant philosophy indeed, for often it pushed
me to the brink of endurance, so that my continual labor as writer
and magistrate now leaves me old in mid-years, without leisure to
recoup the lost strength; but on the contrary, with time snapping
at my heels like a mad dog and forcing me to scribble pamphlets
for little reward, to hear interminable cases at law for meager
salary, and to sacrifice a worn body at the publishing of a journal
in hope of obtaining the modest estate of a tradesman. Is there
any wonder I have lost the taste for genial comedy?

So did I ask myself last night when Joseph left me in nightshirt
and cap, standing before the bedroom mirror. I did not need a
consultation with that piece of glass to verify the destruction of
Henry Fielding. A loss of teeth had caved the cheeks in. The
Roman nose, of which I admit to some liking, had become swollen
and ruddy and testified better than Grub Street gossip to my
frequent need of a dram to buoy up flagging spirits. This did I see,
along with a yellowish skin and gauntness, whereas below the
mirror's view lay more ruin: the dropsical belly that soon must be
tapped, according to my surgeon; the gouty foot and ankle which
virtually have crippled me; to say naught of the pièce de résistance,
a hacking cough which seems to proceed from somewhat south
of my knees on a long and difficult journey by way of a tortuous
routing into the greying forest of my chest and traveling from
thence issues forth with such violence from the mouth that persons
in a room never fail to turn and dolefully observe the individual
whom they hold responsible for this untoward interruption of their
thoughts and conversation.

As I survey that last sentence, I think of good Parson Adams, who might have spoken it long-windedly to Lady Booby, and for a moment I recall with melancholy the good fun of writing that book.

But if I have no longer a robust constitution, my heart is still strong and it beats with a vigour and a pleasure in life. Last night I looked forward to tomorrow, and here I am, at this very moment enjoying it, as I remember what Pindar tells us: The best of healers is good cheer.

[6]

THOUGH HE HADN'T EATEN since yesterday and then only a half-dozen oysters at a stall, he needed shelter more than food. He could go to a gin shop and for a modest sum have a drink and then sleep in a back room. At the lodging house the man who knew about words had given him this advice. "If you lack money, try a grog shop. I warrant half of London has spent a night in the back of a grog shop."

The chill lanes were crowded with gentlemen going to pleasure and with labourers returning home. Passersby huddled in their coats, pulling their hats low, and Ned was thankful to have a last possession from home — his warm riding coat with a flared skirt that whipped round his trousers. But his feet were freezing in flat shoes; the leather had cracked through.

A shivering girl whistled at Ned from a doorway. "I'm two shillings, pretty lad! But two shillings!"

Sedan-chair bearers cursed him as they staggered across his path. Children weaved in and out, scooting close to prancing hoofs. As Ned entered the lousy district of St. Giles, the crowd grew thicker, more raucous and tumultuous. Carriages didn't dare to enter the narrow lanes, and linkboys stayed close to their customers, as drunken people jostled one another in the darkness, filling the air with laughter and shrill oaths.

Glancing up at the half moon sailing through a clear sky, Ned wished himself home on a feast day, when meat was roasting on a spit and in every hand was a mugful of tepid ale and beyond the circle of evening fire was a moonlit field, tempting the young couples, among them himself and Priscilla — the lass married now to a man of substance but still in Ned's mind, so strong in his mind that he must never go home for fear of seeing her again.

The London moon was a different moon, hanging cold and remote, while around him the tumult grew. Ahead he saw an open door; a beam of lamplight lay across the churned mud at its entrance. A man, lurching out, fell into the mire; giggling, he staggered to his feet again.

The light from the grog shop beckoned Ned, drawing him toward its warmth. Standing in the doorway, he stared at rows of tables at which people were sitting elbow to elbow, each with an earthenware mug. They were laughing and quarreling, though some of them sat in stupor.

Timidly Ned entered and sat down on a bench at one of the tables. A swarthy girl in calico, her breasts bubbling over the top of a dirty chemise, came up with a tray.

"What gets a penny?" Ned asked.

"A pint."

"Does cheese come with it?"

"No cheese." She banged a mug down, pocketed the coin, and went off.

Ned's breath steamed across the surface of the clear liquid. He had never cared much for hard spirits, preferring beer, but now he drank deeply. He felt as though a burning coal had been rammed down his throat. When he gagged, a little old woman across from him cackled at his plight. A tide of heat surged through his chest. When he had breath again, he drank again, and again he gagged, and again the old woman chortled.

"No great lifter, you," she said with a wink. Turning, she poked her neighbour, a little man nodding stuporously. "Wake up, John, in God's name, wake up." Leaning toward Ned and smiling, she revealed an empty mouth save for two snaggle teeth. Most of her wrinkled face was hidden by a floppy hat. "No great lifter, you," she repeated. "Ale's your meat, I wager."

"For a gin, I was told, I might sleep here. Is it true?"

"Not true. Leastwise if you ask. Not in this miserable shithole.

They'll call you blockhead and send your sweet ass to kingdom come."

"But I was told —"

"Sure you was told. We all of us was told of good fortune when we was young. But do we believe it now? Ah —" She gave him a sudden grimace of pity, as if looking into her own past. "Here be the truth. You can sleep here be you so elevated on gin you can't reach the door. They don't want bodies piled outside their shop, bringing constables who have got to be bribed. Do you have my meaning?" Reaching across the table, she meant to tap his hand in assurance; seeing the bandage, she thought better of it. "But stay clear of the coal bin."

"The coal bin? What coal bin? Why?"

His questions sent her into a gale of laughter.

At this moment a fight broke out between boys not more than half grown. They flailed at each other, fumbling at homespun caps, each pummeling the other's slack face with open hands, while the slow-motion spectacle brought a few spiritless calls of encouragement. Finally a big fellow appeared from behind the counter and without a word lifted both boys up, carrying them by their coat collars like a bitch carrying pups. To general hilarity he tossed them into the street and stood formidably in the doorway to watch them stumble out of sight.

Ned drank. Now the gin burned less going down, but generated heat through his limbs; he felt cosily warm for the first time that day.

The old woman, slapping her friend, was unable to rouse him. She squinted fearfully at Ned. "I can't handle him. When his head gets to the table, there's nothing to be done. They'll throw him in the bin."

Sure enough, the watchful big fellow came round the counter, grabbed her companion under the armpits, and started to lift.

"I beg you," she cried, "don't put him back there!"

"We run a proper shop. If ever a baggage knew that, you do." Yanking the drunken man roughly from the bench, he carried the inert body through the back door like a bundle of logs.

"He won't get air," sobbed the old woman. "My bowels ache to think of it. Poor John."

"Where be his place?" asked Ned.

"Cross the way. But I can't handle him," she whined.

Draining off the gin, Ned wiped his mouth and walked to the back door. Opening it, he peered into a coal bin where half a dozen bodies lay. In the light from the doorway he distinguished John. Leaning over the bin gate, he reached in and lifted the old man out and carried him over his shoulder through the crowded shop, then waited at the entrance for the astonished old woman to join them.

She led the way down the street to a dark cellar below a chandler shop. One candle on the wall illuminated a narrow passageway off which were a number of cubicles. From one of them came the sound of ecstatic panting, from another some voices raised in cards.

"In here," said the old woman.

Ned flopped the senseless man on a mattress in a tiny room.

"You're a Christian soul," the woman told Ned as she lit a candle and placed it on the dirt floor. Unhappily she studied her friend, who snored among quick little jabs of breath. "He has room here, do you see. There's no air in the coal bin. Last time in it he near perished. Young gentleman" — she showed Ned her two teeth in a grateful smile — "you was sent from heaven. You could stay the night but for the landlord. God never made a meaner creature. He comes through with his pistol at twelve of the clock sharp, demanding his night's rent. He'd make you pay."

"How much?"

"Got you a shilling?"

"No."

The old woman shook her head. "He brings a tough with him too, both armed. They'd break your head before tossing you out." She turned to the snoring man. "John was prenticed to my husband. No man could purify gold as pure as my husband. Jewelers flocked to him." She sat down wearily on a three-legged stool, her floppy hat at an angle, her breath coming in cold steady plumes. "My husband's was a God-given gift. But he had no head for business, he. His partners bilked him, but John never did. John here never stole a thing from him. Bless John. He never took from me neither, though others got every thing I had, every farthing of it, for, damn me, I had no head for business either. I could wind cotton with any wench alive, but for counting numbers I was no better than these two hands. Men saw the ninny I was and robbed me blind, plucked me clean as a chicken. But not John here. He

never took a thing, not once." She smiled at the snoring man. "It's
the breath they lose," she murmured, bending to rub a swollen
ankle. "Mercury does it to them. Mercury makes the gold pure, but
it took my husband's breath and it's taking John's too." Crossing
her legs and rubbing the other ankle, she sighed. "Leastwise my
dear Dicky didn't live to see what evil I've fallen to. Hear John
rattling?" She cocked her head. "Same way. He'll go from the
mercury. I know the signs in faith. When they got no breath, they're
like a child begging for it. You should see the eyes of a man who
can't get breath. Poor John, he never robbed us once, neither of us,
not Dicky, not me. The mercury, you see, they can't get the gold
pure without it. They know it takes the breath, but they use it all
the same." Her voice trailed into silence, but she remained ramrod
straight on the stool, facing the mattress in her vigil. The little man
snored and at intervals snuffled for breath.

Returning to the gin shop, Ned bought another pint for a penny
and squeezed between two labourers at a bench. Sporadic fights
broke out. Pipe smoke drifted in a roiling haze above the benches.
A girl too young to have breasts leapt on a table and did a drunken
jig to loud applause. The man sitting next to Ned bent over and
quietly vomited on the straw-littered floor.

Starting the second gin Ned felt nauseated himself. He noticed
the big fellow, joined now by an equally rugged companion, lift up
half a dozen stupefied customers and carry them back to the coal
bin. The more Ned drank the more favorably he viewed the coal
bin. It was warm in there and dry. He gulped down the last drops
of gin which smouldered in his blood like faggots in a hearth. So it
would be the coal bin for him tonight. He'd feign senselessness.
The liquor gave him sly pleasure in the idea of deception.

Resting his head on the table, Ned closed his eyes and waited.
Moments later he felt hard fingers grip him under the arms.

"This one must weigh fifteen stone!"

Then he was being dragged along the aisle. Someone poured gin
on his stomach. Opening his eyes, Ned saw a receding face, livid
from drink, smirking down at him and his own feet, splayed out,
trailing through the straw. Closing his eyes again, Ned waited
through the odd journey until he felt himself hurtling through the
air. He landed on something yielding. A moan followed. He smelled

the sweetish fumes of juniper berry and acrid coal dust. Feeling around, he touched either cloth or flesh — they'd flung him into the midst of bodies. Opening his eyes, he found himself staring at a belly. Losing consciousness, he came to when a warm liquid trickled down his face — someone was drooling on him. Wiping it off with his sleeve, Ned pushed out and struck a cheekbone. He was no longer on top of the pile but within it. Shoving on all sides with his arms and legs in sudden fear of suffocation, he struggled to get free, but lifeless bodies rolled back against him, warm and wet, as if he'd been tossed into a mound of giant maggots. Folding his arms and drawing his legs up, he made a ball of himself which moved but slightly when the flesh round him surged like waves. He was a human buoy floating on a sea of flesh. God in heaven. The nausea returned. He felt light-headed. His last waking thought was of the sea rhythmically breaking around him, a relentless tide.

The cottage was on fire. He heard his mother screaming for help, but when he broke the door down, she was gone, and Blacksmith Hawkins sat grinning behind a desk in an ermine robe. Ned tried to escape, but the door was shut behind him, and Hawkins, reaching out, took him by the throat.

He awoke then in a panic, finding himself in the midst of bodies. Managing with a great effort to rise on his elbows, Ned pushed the wedging flesh aside and thrust his mouth free into the muggy air. Once again he fell drunkenly asleep, rushing through dreams till his opening eyes stared at a bearded chin.

There was light enough from the doorway for him to see what had transpired during the night. Not more than six feet square, the coal bin contained at least a dozen people, their limbs tangled like worms in a fishing basket. In his sleep Ned had managed to push upward and stay near the top. The stench of gin, vomit, urine, and excrement was overpowering. Retching, he got free of the pile and slid over the bin gate, which had kept the bodies, like so many chunks of coal, from littering the floor. Others were also stirring. Ned crouched in the dirt, aware of wet clothes, for the body heat of sleeping drunkards had turned the bin into a steam room.

Another man hoisted himself over the gate and lay near the door, groaning, "Christ in heaven." Another squirmed over the gate and fell heavily. A woman came next, her fat thighs exposed to the crotch as she rolled over and lay face up, touching her lower lip feebly.

"He's cold," someone wheezed from inside the bin. "Get off, you hear? The man's cold!"

A few others scrambled clumsily out. Ned staggered to his feet, gripped the gate, and peered down into the bin. A woman sprawling there met his eyes, her own round with horror. "He's . . . cold. He's cold." She lifted the arm of someone who had been near the bottom. Just as Ned reached down to help her from the bin, there was a loud growling noise behind him. He turned to see an enormous man in the doorway, wearing a leather apron.

Clearing his throat — this was the growling noise — he bellowed, "Out, rascals! Out, turds!" Shoving aside someone with his foot, the huge man advanced to the bin.

"This man's dead," Ned told him, pointing inside.

"Out, fuckers!" the man yelled at three people still in the bin. A man and a woman stirred, groping for purchase on the gate, and Ned helped them out.

The huge man in the apron bent lower to study the last body, which lay motionless. "Well." He scratched his large shaggy head. "Leave him be," he told Ned and the others. "He's our charge now." Turning to the door, he wiped his hands on the apron. "Out, rascals. You had your free sleep."

Another stout man appeared in the doorway. His bald head shone in the soft light like a pewter plate.

"One's mutton for worms," the huge man grumbled.

Reaching down, the bald man roughly shook a woman by the hair until she whined. "Out of here, cunt!"

There was a shuffling exodus from the coal bin room, while the two big fellows hauled the corpse onto the floor.

Leaning against a wall, Ned watched them strip the body. In the haggard light the dead man looked like a big white fish. Then the bald man ordered his companion to go get the wagon.

They both noticed Ned. "Get a cudgel first," said the bald man.

Ned lurched from the room, past empty benches and gin-soaked tables, into a cloudy morning.

The street was nearly deserted. Only a few carters led their squeaky wagons through the frosted mire. Somewhere a dog was yapping. Ned held the damp lapels of his coat to his chin, feeling a keen breeze sting his sweaty legs through the cotton breeches. He shambled along, aching in his bones. Within a minute his teeth were chattering. Ahead a grocer was setting out vegetables in a stall. Halting, Ned stared at a peck of weazened potatoes. His mouth watered at the sight, but he couldn't find a penny — perhaps someone had robbed him in the coal bin or he had none left. Nevertheless, he continued toward the stall, and even before he got there the grocer's girl understood his intention. Her little mouth opened in fear, but she made no sound as he leaned forward and grabbed some potatoes.

Coming from the other side of the stall, the grocer nearly collided with him. Stooped and elderly and bearded under a felt hat, the man backed away. "Do no harm," he muttered. "Take them, lad, but leave us be."

Ned trudged away, voraciously chewing a potato. Never had anything tasted so good, and the potato was gone in a moment. He ate another before walking a block, then nausea doubled him. He vomited black bile and the hastily masticated potato. Sitting on the muddy cobblestone, the other potatoes scattered round him, Ned ignored a horse-driven cart that showered his legs with icy water. He was not sure of being awake. He did not know his own body. His eyes stared at mud, horse droppings, thick boots passing. Although shivering, he no longer felt cold. His body was like any old wintry object: a muddy barrel, a splashed coat, a glistening axle. He looked at a wall of the rust color of a fox. It was a brick wall. It was a brick wall in London town. He was in London town.

Able at last to rise, he headed out like an old mule set in listless motion by a slap. Aimlessly he tramped through the lanes, watching shops and warehouses emerge from the dawn mist like debris from the depths of a river. People multiplied at the edge of his eye. Someone had once asked him how he liked London. Mister Scarrat had. Eating another potato, he felt it settle fistlike in his stomach. "This be London, boy. How do you like it?"

Part Two

——————————————•——————————————

THE RETURN

[7]

AT LAST she pried the board loose. It had taken a full week of yanking and pulling whenever she mustered the strength to try, but finally with a sucking sound the nails gave way. She inched the board back from the casement with both hands until she could stick her head into the brisk twilight air and see through distant trees a dull sun going down.

The room had been cold enough, a stale motionless cold, but the wind had a fierce bite to it, so she clenched the ragged jacket to her throat. There was just space enough between board and frame for her to wiggle through and climb down to the shed roof. Pain. Touching her right ear, she came away with fingers soaked in blood. A nail had ripped her earlobe. Crouching on the roof, she judged the distance to the ground. Gusts rippled her dirty petticoat. Under it she had on nothing but a rough cotton shift and over it nothing but a torn jacket that the old bitch hadn't known was in the room. The girl glanced up at the window. She was weak, it was bitter cold, should she go back inside? Never. And anyway, her arms weren't strong enough to hoist herself up to the casement again.

She began to creep down the slanting roof toward its edge, but in the frosty thatch her toe snagged, threw her off balance, and tumbled her fifteen feet to the ground. For a few moments she lost consciousness, then squinted up at the first stars of evening that danced and faded and danced again before steadying into brilliant dots. The girl moved slightly to judge if any bones were broken. She became aware of the frozen earth blazing against her naked thighs. Had the old bitch heard her fall from the roof?

Leaves crackled when she sat up. Her head throbbed and there was a dull ache along the left side of her face, as she struggled to rise and then leaned against the shed wall. She could go back, circle the house and knock at the door. The old bitch would let her in all right. And then drag her upstairs again.

It was run away or go without food and this time, because of her disobedience, the bitch would starve her to death as sure as there were stars overhead.

Betty set out across the open field. This much she knew: a road was nearby, because for weeks she had seen through a crack many wagons and coaches bouncing along in the distance. Crossing the bleak field, she came to a stream with a narrow channel. Kneeling at the bank and scattering the edge of ice with her fist, she drank deeply and long, the cold water seeming to scorch her throat. Shakily the girl got up, crossed a footbridge, then another open field where a covey of partridges whirred out of the brittle heather and startled her. She halted then to wind an old kerchief round her ear, staunching the blood. There was no path to follow and some clouds obscured the moon, but eventually she reached a turnpike. Suddenly a coach with one jiggling lantern loomed from the darkness, nearly running her down. Thundering through a pothole, the wheels drenched her with icy water. Hunching into the wind, Betty fought back tears. Was she going wrong on the road? Somehow she had lost all sense of direction, as if she'd been whirled around in blind-man's-bluff. Ahead was dark, behind a flickering of lights. That could be the village of Enfield where the old woman was. She feared going toward the lights, but feared the darkness as much.

Mister Scarrat had named Enfield that day weeks ago in the coach, when she threatened to loosen her tongue less he gave her more gold. She would never forget his voice then.

"Threaten me? *You* threaten me?" he had asked in a cold fury. "I'll tuck you away till you know your betters. Threaten your betters? A chit like you? Do you know, girl, who you was with?"

"A fine gentleman."

"A fine gentleman," he repeated in a voice so tight from controlled anger that it sent a chill down her spine. "So fine a gentleman you're not clean enough or good enough or pretty enough or singer enough or woman enough to wipe up his shit let alone sleep in a bed with him. You? Threaten him?"

"I beg something more, sir, that be all I meant."

"Threaten your betters like him and me? You? Thomas!" Scarrat had leaned through the coach window and thumped the side with his fist. "Make for Enfield! We'll show this little baggage who can threaten and who can do!"

The long ride in silence. In blackest night they had come to the house of that terrible woman at Enfield.

Now the girl halted on the road and looked toward the flickering lights. Be that Enfield?

Another coach, heavy with luggage, swayed by. To avoid a splashing, she jumped into a ditch and scratched her leg on a bramble bush.

Coming along the road was a burly figure pulling a cart. Betty could make out a wide-brimmed hat, a big coat on broad shoulders. From the ditch she called out plaintively, "Which way, sir, to London?"

He halted and leaned forward to see better. For a wild moment she feared he might come at her, but then he stretched his hand back at the flickering lights. "That way."

"Be that Enfield?"

"It is."

"No other way to London?" she asked. Enfield would take her close to the terrible woman.

"None other way, less you take across the fields." He grunted irritably. "Then you fall in a pond somewheres and drown." The man trudged off, pulling his cartload of faggots.

So the way must be through Enfield, near the old bitch's house. Heaven help me, Betty thought. Minutes later she was hurrying past the cottages of Enfield, alongside the inns aglow with yellow light. Not far from the road that terrible old woman must be sitting over a bowl of strong ale. If she knew the prisoner was on the road to London, old Tabby Howard would howl like a mad dog.

And then Betty was clear of Enfield. It was behind her, and so was the terrible creature. Betty needed a rest, but who knows, at any moment old Tabby Howard might clomp up the stairway and find her gone and go out looking in a murderous rage for her charge.

Betty feared to slacken her pace, but gritted her teeth and went forward. Clouds scattered, as though blown away by a giant breath. There followed a long stretch of open road under bright moonlight, and more little villages like Enfield, and more rumbling coaches that splashed her with freezing mud. At last she saw a huge boulder, the number 10 chiseled on it: the ten-mile stone. She had ten miles to go, and then one more. Could she go that far? Had she strength enough for so many miles?

Any moment old Tabby Howard might push aside the bowl and tramp upstairs to find her prisoner gone.

The fearful thought of it gave Betty strength. She kept up her pace by counting each step. One foot forward through the icy mire, and she lifted a thumb to mark that progress. Then the first finger, the next, the next, the next, beginning with her thumb again. Fear kept her counting through the windswept chilly night. Fear, the bloodshot eyes of Tabby Howard.

Hours later, her stiff fingers still counting, Betty shuffled under the high wall of Bedlam Hospital and down the gravel path of Moor-fields. It was late, so only a few people passed her by and none gave her a glance. Then the watch came along, an ancient fellow muffled to his nose, swinging a lantern, and called out the hour of eleven. She had been walking for many hours, driven beyond endurance by the memory of a woman who had given her not so much as a crust in days or a mouthful of water, but had stood cackling outside the door, threatening her with death. "Don't you think I won't do for you, trollop? Scarrat's a titmouse compared to me." Her voice rose drunkenly. "You need breaking! He said teach the insolent slut a lesson, so I say aye to it and more! No victuals till you lay measured for the grave. Spread out for dead. Hey, miss! Not a crust. Then we'll see who crawls to me with a humble nature!" Loud laughter, feet stomping on the stair. The memory of that hoarse croak, that shambling footstep had followed the girl every mile of the way.

Behind her was the bitch, but ahead were other dangers. She'd been gone from home a whole month, and one thing was sure: she must never say what happened. Tell the truth, Scarrat would have hcr dead — or the public would. Did they still flay people alive for the outrage she'd been part of? In the days of witches they did — flayed and burned heretics.

Halting in a moment of terrible fancy, she thought of her skin bloodied by the hard little balls of a cat-o'-nine-tails.

Then stumbling on, she was wracked by remorse, not for what she'd done with the fine gentleman, but for what she'd said to Scarrat. Dreaming of finery, excited by a gentleman who used perfumes and spoke like a prince, she had thought herself grand and in that foolish mood had demanded more gold, which if not forthcoming would result in the world knowing what had happened in the devil's place. Why had she done so? Where had come the weakness? After all, she'd been sworn to secrecy and had gold enough in a money pouch to seal that vow. Alas, she'd been grievously blinded by visions of brocade and Chelsea vases and silver shoes. Whatever had possessed her, pray God, to mouth such words from two-shilling romances to a man like Scarrat, who was Satan's own? Yet without a heavier purse, she'd told him, the world would know of her being handled wickedly in Lucifer's chapel. She had quite simply let herself go, following fancy phrases down a path of dreaming.

This had often been true. She'd imagine herself in a book. While peeling onions at the hearth, she'd become a lovely heroine married to a handsome captain of the guard. Fancy, not greed, had led her to the silly threat. She saw herself as a virgin (which she'd not been in two years) kidnapped and whisked out of London (to which she had heartily assented), who had then been decked out in a nun's habit and a black mask (which in truth had thrilled her) and then had been made to frolic with heathen monks (a fate no worse than that suffered by other heroines) and finally had been forced into the bed of a wicked gentleman (which she had gone to out of curiosity).

But Scarrat, grimly silent through her haughty demand and threat, had taken her at her word. For a bit of daydreaming she'd spent a month in captivity and almost died of it.

Each dragging step homeward, she grew more aware of the need for a convincing tale to explain her absence. When people demanded the truth, she could not describe her willingness to accompany a gentleman somewhere out of London, much less relate what happened when they got there. She must fashion a wondrous tale or suffer punishment. Pillory? Prison? Would they brand her? Betty saw herself in filthy rags, staggering down a street with people reviling her on either side — as in a book she'd once read.

Spin a tale or suffer. Those were her choices. At least she could start with the truth. On New Year evening she'd actually left her aunt and uncle Colley on the corner of Houndsditch.

And there, at the start, the truth must end. Minutes later a grinning Mister Scarrat had helped her into a coach for the long ride to a fine gentleman in a strange place.

New Year evening. It had been cold and dark.

Betty's pace slowed as she thought.

Cold and dark. Instead of going straight home from the Colleys, she had walked . . . strolled idly . . . She had strolled through Moorfields, just as a few moments ago she had done. Dark. Wind shaking the leafless trees, as they were shaken now. The watch coming through inky night like a ghost. In faith, Moorfields was the proper place for something wicked to happen. She had taken a bit of a stroll through Moorfields before heading home. It had been pitch black, dark, without a moon at all, and suddenly . . . out of the shadows . . . out of the shadows two men came! They handled her roughly. Two? Three of them. Aye, they did, as heaven is witness! Three men took her up and dragged her off somewhere.

The idea appealed enormously. It was like a romance in which the young maiden is beset on every side. Bullies took her up, mercy and salvation. And such did happen in truth in London town. Innocent girls suffering bad usage. Rakes got them, hauled them into bawdy houses where they submitted or else died for honour. It was like the romance of a Distress'd Maiden swooning in the arms of a Lascivious Brute. Having been rendered witless during the bestial attack, the maiden could not later recall at which precise moment her precious treasure had been so violently taken from her!

A most appealing idea.

It made Betty shiver to think of it. Her voice lifted in wordless song as a tale unfolded. Bullies knocked her into . . . into a fit . . . from which she did not recover until . . . finding herself away in Enfield —

But not at the house of Tabby Howard.

But in Enfield. Where in Enfield? That must be sorted out later.

The thing was . . . they took her away . . . spirited her in a coach out of London . . . all the way to Enfield.

At long last Betty Canning was going to be a heroine, and in a tale of her own devising. Only Scarrat was an obstacle in her way, because he must agree to the story. Would he? Surely he wished the truth to be hid. He would agree. God in heaven, he must, or she was done for.

[8]

THE YOUNG APPRENTICE SAWYER in Aldermanbury Postern was ready for bed. Tomorrow he must saw a load of thick planks for his mistress, the widow Canning, who was a hard woman to satisfy. She had taken on fancy airs since her husband died. Neighbor women held her in awe because she could read without following the words with a fingertip, for during service as a maid in a good household she'd been taught to read by the waiting woman. Tomorrow the widow would stroll round the lumber yard, clasping a book and scolding James for work that her husband, a kindly man, would have called good work and proper. Sighing, James gulped down the last of his nightly beer. He was rising from the hearth when a loud scraping at the door startled him. The latch was lifting. Before he could call out, a young woman staggered in and slumped down into a chair. He gawked at a bloody rag, a bruised face, at hollow eyes.

"It's her!" he yelled.

A querulous voice warned from an adjoining room, "You'll wake the children. Quiet."

"It's her!"

The bedroom door swung open, a puffy face framed in a soiled bonnet appeared. "Hush, you —"

Wildly the apprentice pointed.

Squinting, her mouth working, the woman finally murmured, "Ah, no — it cannot — a ghost!"

Two girls and a boy in night-shirts appeared in the bedroom doorway, just as the heavyset woman took a step forward and collapsed.

Seeing their mother down and their sister alive in a chair, they began to jump in terror. "Mother! Mother!" they shrieked. "Betty! Mother!"

Rushing to his fallen mistress, James rubbed her hands while the trio of children danced round in panic. Widow Canning began to revive, mumbling, "Ghost . . . it cannot . . ."

"Betty in the flesh," the apprentice claimed, but glanced back at the chair to make sure. After all, she'd been a month gone and looked horribly wasted.

"James," Betty murmured feebly.

So leaving the mother, he rushed to the daughter. In a faint voice she told him to find Mister Scarrat at the Sign of the Frigate and bring him hence.

"A month gone!" James exclaimed, staring at the girl. "How be you, Miss Betty?"

"Fetch Mister Scarrat," she panted. "The Frigate near Temple Bar Gate."

The apprentice seemed rooted there.

"Hear me? Mister Scarrat. Fetch him."

"You mean now?"

"Fetch him!" she demanded in a shaky but forceful voice.

Throwing a coat around his shoulders, the apprentice rushed from the house with the little Canning boy trailing him. James stopped and gripped the boy's arm hard. "Go get some neighbor woman," he ordered the boy and ran into the night.

In his old age James would rock before a roaring winter fire and bore his grandchildren for the hundredth time with the story of Elizabeth Canning's return.

Robert Scarrat was sitting with some watermen when the door of his tavern flung open and a ragged youth burst in with a shout. "She's come back and alive! Miss Betty's come home!"

James stared at the seated men. "If any be Mister Scarrat, come quick, for she wants you!"

"Betty Canning?" Scarrat rose to his feet, astonished.

"Yes, this minute. Come out of the night as bloody as a ghost.

Mistress thought it a ghost, for she fainted away at the sight of all that blood, and I was sent for Mister Scarrat."

Grabbing his coat, Scarrat said, "By whom? The girl sent you?"

"It was her first thought."

"Come along then."

They hurried into the night, with Scarrat thinking the bitch should have come home in a box. He should have let Tabby Howard slit her throat and good riddance. He'd been soft, no more resolute than a fop. Look at the business now facing him: the girl free, home, and likely to live. Instead of instructing Tabby to break the girl and starve a bit of sense into her, he should have handed over a knife to the old horror and told her to use it.

The excited apprentice was babbling away at his side.

"A whole month! We thought her dead and gone. Mistress put a notice in the journal. A woman writ it out for us, for mistress reads like a king but can't write. *Lost,* it said, *a girl of eighteen.* Two notices paid for. And at the Wesley Meeting House they said prayers. And mistress went to a cunning man who told her fortune in cards. Beware of ghosts, she was told. Mistress will live long and prosper. Said never fear. Miss Betty cannot fail to come home and come home she has done!"

Linkboys were weaving down the rutted thoroughfare, lighting the way for gentlemen to clubs and coffee houses. Gentlemen. High-born persons kept good fellows like himself at hard duty, Scarrat thought. They wanted the most troublesome of women. Give him a simple baggage any time when the need was on. He'd rather a wiggish girl, be her crawling with pox, than a greedy songbird like Bet Canning.

Ahead was the ramshackle house in Aldermanbury Postern. Before reaching there, Scarrat had certain facts clear in his mind. The girl had sent for him, which meant he was known to her. How so? And why would she send for him? God was with him here. He meant to draw upon his stint service as a constable of the parish. Forced upon him by law as a tradesman, he had served reluctantly for six months last year, having received no pay for it. In the course of serving, he'd not apprehended one criminal, not even touched one, for like so many other citizens called to serve, he had ignored the irksome duty and had kept clear when trouble was afoot within the district. This troublesome service would at last bear fruit.

Without knocking, Scarrat pushed open the front door to the Canning house and walked in.

Widow Canning was sitting with a neighbor woman beside the bed where Betty lay wrapped to the chin in blankets.

"The girl sent for me," Scarrat said with a long face. "How does she?"

"Ah, poor," said the neighbor woman.

Widow Canning studied him closely. "She sent for you?"

Scarrat approached the bed, trying not to glare at the girl. "Poor little miss," he murmured, but his voice had a cold edge.

"Sir, do I have the pleasure of knowing you?" asked the mother.

"I've been a constable in the parish, so I must be known to her. Is Constable Scarrat known to you, girl?" he asked Betty, who after a long stare at him nodded feebly. To the mother he said, "I have a public house by the waterfront."

That seemed to impress the woman, who gave him a smile before beginning to sob. "My poor saint has come back to me, but broken."

Scarrat had not taken his eyes off the girl. "What has happened, child?"

"Bullies got her," volunteered the neighbor woman. "She walked in from Enfield all the way home."

"Bullies?" He studied the swollen face, the bandaged ear. "This girl is poor indeed," he said, turning to the women. "Get her soup and some mulled sack." He made the motion of hurrying chickens out of a yard. "You women have got her in a fright. Get her food and leave her to me. I'll calm the poor lass."

When they were gone, he bent over the girl and whispered, "Keep your wits. What account have you made?"

"Please, sir, that I was taken up by bullies near Bedlam on New Year." Anxiously her eyes sought his for approval.

"Where was you took?"

"To a bawdy house, I said. A woman there . . ."

When she hesitated, he reached out and pinched her arm sharply. "Be quick."

". . . kept me captive this month. I 'scaped from a window and walked home. That's true, sir, I did."

"Did you name the woman?"

"I could not." Her tongue flicked across chapped lips. "I mean, I would not. I would not cross you, Mister Scarrat, sir."

"What happened there?"

"Tabby Howard near starved me to death. I had to get free or die. She gave me nothing to eat in days."

"Punishment you deserved."

"I own it. I did you a terrible wrong."

"Well, you did right in sending for me," Scarrat told her with less severity. "You said a house in Enfield?"

"It was what came to mind."

He stroked his chin thoughtfully. "Then you was held all that time in Enfield. A house in Enfield." He turned to listen to the women bustling in the kitchen. Leaning closer to the girl, he whispered, "I know a house in Enfield where you was kept. Do you follow? It was not at Tabby Howard's. You was in another house there. You was at . . . the house of Susannah Wells. Held by wicked people. A den of harlots in the Wells house, they had you. Do you mind what I'm saying?"

"I do, sir. At Mother Wells' house this month. I'm on a good footing with you."

"You appear to be now."

The door swung open and in trooped a dozen people, led by Mister Wintlebury, an old brandy vintner who had once employed the girl as a maidservant in his household. Wintlebury commanded everyone to step back, while he bent over the bed. "It's known in the streets," he said.

"Did you hear that, dear?" the widow Canning exclaimed. "It is already known."

"Poor girl," Wintlebury said gently. "Tell me from the start what happened."

A neighbor woman entered with a bowl of soup and held a spoon toward the girl's mouth.

Pushing the spoon away, Wintlebury snapped, "Give her time to make answer."

In a shaky voice the girl explained that leaving her aunt and uncle on the corner of Houndsditch in the evening of New Year's Day, she had become accosted near Bedlam wall out of Moorfields by two, that is, three lusty big fellows who handled her in a rough way, tore her bonnet, and stripped her of her gown and apron. "When I screamed, they cried out to keep shut or they'd kill me."

Women gasped. Betty's eyes took on a sudden luster. "They stuffed a kerchief in my mouth."

"Did they take you then, child?" asked a neighbor woman, crooking her head around Wintlebury's shoulder.

Betty glanced round at the ring of expectant faces. "I cannot say —"

"Say true," said the woman.

"One gave me a rude blow on my head."

"Then did they take you, child?" another woman asked.

"Leave her be!" Wintlebury yelled with a furious scowl at the woman. Bending closer to dominate the girl's attention, he whispered, "What did they do then, poor Bet?"

"I don't know. I . . . went into a fit."

"And then?"

"When I waked, they was dragging me into a house." Her voice was stronger, almost lively.

"Where?"

"They said Enfield." Her eyes sought out Scarrat, who gave her back a calm look.

"Who was in that house?" Wintlebury continued.

"Some women. One said, 'Go our way, miss, you shall have fine clothes.' Then she held my hand."

Widow Canning groaned loudly.

"When I said I would not, the woman took up a knife and cut my laces and pulled off my stays. Then slapping my face, she called me bitch and promised to keep me shut up till I did what she wanted."

A murmur of dismay.

"Then, child?"

"I was pushed upstairs to a room and kept there out of sight this month."

"Who came up to you?"

"None."

"What food had you, child? You look remarkable starved."

"They shoved in some dry bread and a jug of water."

Widow Canning cried out. A woman put a comforting arm round her shoulder.

"Poor creature," Wintlebury murmured. "God was with you. It's a miracle you live." Turning and glaring around the room, the old man said, "We shall carry her to a justice on the morrow. This girl has been monstrously used. I swear to have satisfaction for it."

At this declaration Scarrat moved forward. "Come, sir, I share your sentiment, but the girl's too poorly to see a justice."

"Who are you, sir?"

"Robert Scarrat, sir. Last year a constable of this parish. I have been called in to be of service."

That seemed to mollify the old man. "Then when she's fit." Despite his years, Wintlebury was still vigorous, with a determined ruddy face and a gold watch fob across his paunch. "What treatment this girl received is not endurable under heaven. The guilty must answer."

"As God is my witness, I do agree. I mean to lend my experience as a constable to this poor family." Scarrat had hoped for the nasty business to end here and now, but the old man obviously retained an affection — perhaps more than an affection — for his former maidservant. Wintlebury would never let the matter drop, nor would the mother, who was already enjoying the fame her daughter had brought home. Scarrat was not someone to waste time on lost chances or mistakes. He should have freed the girl sooner or let Tabby deal with her for good, but now those choices were gone and he must look to the future. A public inquiry into her reappearance could no more be stopped than a Billingsgate fire in a high wind. But this too was clear: the wench would not defy him again. She had felt the awful reach of his power. Proof of that was her fear of returning without his knowledge. And he could depend on her native avarice. Drop a purse into her lap, Bet Canning would keep mum in front of King George himself.

Scarrat felt a grudging admiration for the little bitch, all muffled in blankets. Her story had merit, a few improbables notwithstanding. Fear, greed, and the pleasure of spinning a lively tale would keep her safe. He'd seen many Bet Cannings in his day. What amazing creatures — with the fortitude of cats prowling the lanes of London. You could hoist a pair of those mangy beasts on a pole with their tails tied together and let them rip each other's guts out; you could stone them, eat them for want of better; you could run them down with horses, drown them in the Thames, set dogs on

them and litter the streets with their fly-blown carcasses; and in
spite of everything they'd return at daybreak on the rooftops, cater-
wauling, peering from yellow eyes down at the world below. That
was Elizabeth Canning and her ilk. Amazing creatures.

Approaching the bed, he said, "Poor miss. We shall see you don't
want."

The girl smiled in a sly way that meant she understood.

"She needs sleep," observed old Wintlebury and motioned for the
crowd to leave. Everyone shuffled into the parlour and stood there,
as yet unable to break the spell of the evening. Something porten-
tous was happening. For the neighbor women it was the moment of
a lifetime, the stuff of fancy.

Scarrat decided to embark on the next stage of this unavoidable
journey. He called loudly for attention. "Friends," he began, "the
poor child named Enfield. I have some recollection of the place. I
think, in faith, I can judge where she was held."

In the abrupt silence a faggot crackled in the grate.

"Where, sir?" asked Wintlebury.

"In a house there with a reputation for bawds and bad fellows. I'd
wager a guinea to a farthing she has been at Mother Wells'."

[9]

ELIZABETH CANNING WAS UNFIT the next day to appear at the
Guildhall. An apothecary was called in to examine her. More than
a year later Sutherton Bakler would so testify: "I found her in a low
condition so extreme I could scarcely hear her speak. She had cold,
clammy sweats upon her. She complained of being faint with a pain
in her bowels, and small wonder — she had not moved them once
during her confinement. I ordered her a purging medicine."

All day the Canning house was besieged by mobs of the curious
and sympathetic. Well-wishers stood around waiting in vain for the
girl to give an audience. The other Canning children were relegated
to the attic. Apprentice James sawed few planks that day, but ran

errands for everyone. Surrounded by women, Widow Canning wailed without letup, stopping only for a taste of sweetcake washed down with strong ale.

By nightfall the girl's sensational return was being hawked in penny broadsheets throughout London, until the wildly augmented details had reached West End mansions and East End bagnios, until her name was on the lips of lady and whore, member of Parliament and lace peddler, until King George himself turned to a minister and in his thick German accent gruffly inquired, "Vat iss dis voman? Should ve know her?"

It was something like the question Lord Sandwich asked himself when his man Scarrat came with the bad news. His lordship had to think hard a few moments before recalling the wench who had sung for him at Medmenham. A full bosom, a lilting voice, but no real gift for frolic. Her hips, as he remembered, had been as unyielding as the deck of a ship, and her mind, if there had been one, seemed to have gone elsewhere in a dream. He had taken little pleasure of her, yet the mousy distracted creature had it in her power to bring trouble down on him. Damn her. Damn Scarrat too. At the end of the man's account — her blackmail threat, imprisonment for it, escape, and now public notoriety — his lordship shook his head in burning dismay and said to Scarrat, "You chose me a sorry slut."

"I own it. But she's too frighted to give more trouble."

"She has already given enough."

"I swear, milord, I have her in hand."

Sandwich tapped his snuffbox against the desk. "She had heart enough to get free of your confinement. She also had spirit enough to ask for more gold when a good purse already lay in her lap. She had impudence enough to threaten a peer of England. Can I then depend on your control of her?"

"Please you, I've set about correcting that error. The girl's safe or I'm not Bob Scarrat."

Sandwich squinted hard at the grey face. He was comforted by the thought that Scarrat would do anything to keep the ale house. Damn the woman. Had she been a common whore, none would care what she claimed. But this was a girl of decent enough reputation from a tradesman's family, and she'd been imprisoned by the confidant of a nobleman. Such a thing might kick up trouble with the Church, Parliament, even the king. It would be insufferable if the secrets of Medmenham were exposed by a girl who'd been with one of the friars. Rapping the snuffbox hard against the desk, he muttered, "This is damn vexing. I must not have my name abroad or those of my friends. I warrant you mean to buy her silence?"

"I mean to have it how I can."

"How you can," Sandwich repeated, savoring the implications. "Very well. I wish never to know what you mean by that."

"Yes, milord."

"But be assured whatever gold is necessary is at your disposal. Where's the girl now?"

"At home near mortal ill, but she'll recover. Then I'll follow her each step of the way."

"See I am kept out."

"I vouch for it, milord, with my life."

"Am I not kept out — consider the seriousness of what I am saying — we are quits."

"I vouch for her silence."

"You had better." Fearing to lead Scarrat into rashness, he added, "However, I urge you be prudent."

"I would not be reckless and thereby injure your lordship."

"That is good to hear." Sandwich could imagine the duke of Newcastle's response to such a scandal: the foppish bastard whispering through the halls of Parliament, asking behind a silk handkerchief in a voice of mournful concern was it true that milord Sandwich had whisked a decent girl from London to an unholy place and then starved her near dead in a disreputable house. Loading snuff on his thumb, his lordship inhaled, awaited the pleasurable sneeze, and it came. "Stay clear of this house till the matter's resolved," Sandwich told his man.

"Have no worry, please. It *will* go right for us."

"Could I not believe that . . ." He left the threat dangling.

"Milord, I know my duty."

Watching the grey fellow bob his way out of the room, Sandwich took another pinch of snuff and sneezed. Such a mishap occurring at a time of political unrest was simply intolerable. He picked up a quill and ended his domestic effort of the morning. Another bill: fifteen yards of bombazine for a gown that Judith would probably forget to have made. Damn her. Damn all women. Damn Scarrat for lack of judgement. Damn the simpering duke too.

Then he subscribed twenty pounds to the ensuing publication of a treatise by Thomas Chippendale. The Yorkshireman had recently designed a lovely chair for the sitting room. It had been one of the few reasonable purchases Judith had made in years.

In spite of her weak condition, Betty Canning was taken next day before an Alderman Chitty in the Guildhall. Chitty was a small peppery man whose irritable nature was worsened by a head cold. He stared with displeasure at the crowd accompanying the emaciated girl. Ordering a chair for her, he waved back the sympathizers and sent a bailiff to stop the chanting of *"Bet! Bet! Bet!"* now booming through a crowd gathered outside the Guildhall. He gaveled and began the interrogation.

In a feeble but determined voice the girl described her vicious reception at the Enfield house of a woman named Wells.

"Where was the room you was took to?"

"Up a long stairway, your worship."

"Can you describe the room?"

"I laid on a bare floor." She ticked off items briskly on her fingers. "There was a grate with a chimney, a stool, a bit of bread, a jug of water." Her mouth was set in a faint smile.

"Nothing else?"

"No, your worship."

"You say a bit of bread. How much was a bit?"

"Four, five pieces, your worship."

"How long did these bits last?"

"For the whole time."

"Young woman!" cried Chitty. "You lived a month on a few pieces of bread? It cannot be possible."

"I swear," the girl said coolly.

"Once you'd refused her, did the procuress apply again for your cooperation in her designs?"

"No, she did not, your worship."

"You were held a month. Why did you not try sooner to escape?"

"I was frighted the Wells woman might cut my throat." Pausing, she looked grimly at the spectators. "It took beyond a week to get the boards free. I'm no lusty girl."

Chitty glared at the murmuring crowd. "Who here can speak for her character?"

Her present employer stepped forward, a sober-looking man in muscular middle age. "I be William Lyon of Aldermanbury, a carpenter by trade. This girl belongs in my household as maidservant. I give her a good Christian character."

"I give her as good," declared Wintlebury, stepping a pace in front of Lyon. "She worked for me longer."

Scanning the honest red faces of tradesmen who tensely awaited his decision, Alderman Chitty could not otherwise believe but that the girl had told a wild tale, much like the silly romances his wife kept nightly at her pillow. No girl could live on some few crusts of bread for a month. Yet in aspect she was demure enough, not much older than his own daughter. And rogues did set upon girls in Moorfields. But why had the lass chosen to stroll in such a dangerous place and why had the bullies robbed her *before* carrying her off? And why had the procuress failed to opportune her further? Had they meant to murder the girl, there was no need for waiting so long. Chitty studied the decent but restless crowd again. These advocates of hers would set up a nasty roar did he dismiss the accusation for doubtful evidence. Surely there were rogues in Enfield who deserved scrutiny. Let others concern themselves with it.

"Mister White," he said to a young officer of the court. "I charge you with serving a writ for search of the Wells house in Enfield, whose keeper I hold under suspicion of robbery. Girl," he said to Betty, "what was the worth of those stays?"

"Fourteen shillings," she replied without hesitation.

Chitty smiled. None but ladies wore stays of such worth. But he continued with the charge. "— whose keeper I hold under suspicion of robbery of stays worth fourteen shillings and of assault upon the person of one Elizabeth Canning of Aldermanbury Postern. The writ shall be issued now and you will serve it on the morrow." He gaveled.

The satisfied crowd trooped out of the Guildhall, most of them crossing the yard to celebrate in taverns the success of their poor Betty's complaint.

Wintlebury and Mistress Canning assisted the weary girl into a hackney coach. Instantly the mother opened a calf-bound volume in her lap. She read at a theatrically high pitch of a young husband grieving at his wife's grave:

"In this dissolving Rack of Misery he continued, still kissing of her
Lips! wringing his Hands! and lifting up his Eyes and Voice to
Heaven in Prayers to follow her! till working Nature to her utmost
Bent, with a furious Groan he broke the Thread, and let him down a
Companion for the Grave."

Widow Canning paused to exclaim "What sentiment!" before
continuing to read. Betty stared hard at the book, while a rosette of
color appeared in her wan cheeks. Wondrous events unfolded in her
imagination: swordplay, moonlight trysts, shipwrecks, and recon-
ciliations ending in rich marriages.

Mistaking her blush for the embarrassment of a young woman
forced to endure public scrutiny, the old brandy vintner leaned
forward and patted her hand, sadly recollecting the times when he
had touched far more than her hand in the back room behind some
kegs, before the cruel impotence of old age had transformed him
from lover into protector.

"Don't fret, child," Wintlebury said gently. "The world's behind
our cause. We shall have justice done. We shall have satisfaction."

"Three cheers for our Betty!" people shouted in the Guildhall yard,
as the carriage swayed out of sight. The cheers kept going up. Ned
Carleton joined in for the mere joy of clearing his lungs. He felt a
surge of renewed strength, as if the people packed close to him were
warming his heart and marrow. This elation turned to surprise
when he noticed Mister Scarrat pushing through the crowd to a
carriage. It seemed as though they had met at the Ludgate fire a
long time ago, instead of Tuesday last. Ned was glad just to be
alive, although since leaving the coal bin his luck had changed a
little for the better. Only this morning, for helping a lady to cross a
muddy street, her gloved hand on his arm, his hand held threateningly up at oncoming wagons, Ned had received a shilling.

He nearly went after Scarrat, for perhaps such a man might help
him. Ned tapped his coat pocket; the book, what was left of it, was
there. And besides the book Scarrat had given him advice —
warned him to be hard in this town. And yet he remained where he
was in the warm crowd. People were still milling around, unwilling
to let go of the magical moment when a newfound heroine had just

left their midst. In fact, the crowd tightened hip against hip for a last few moments, surged together so that Ned was brought up against the fat buttocks of a gentleman in a velvet coat. A fine cambric kerchief was peeking out of a side pocket. The delicate cloth fascinated Ned as if it were something alive, peeking rakishly from the velvet slit.

Without more thought Ned grabbed the trailing end of the kerchief with his good hand, yanked, and began plowing through the throng that had raised its collective voice a last time in the chant of *Bet! Bet! Bet!* Fighting his way through, Ned awaited a cry of *Thief!* Without glancing back, he kept going, freeing himself from people and bursting into the street. At last he looked over his shoulder; to his surprise and relief no one was following. He stopped and leaned against a cobbling shop wall. A steady procession of coaches and wagons was moving through drizzle. Not a soul gave him a glance. Looking down at the wadded cloth in his fist, he considered what had just happened. He had committed a theft, he, Nathaniel Carleton from Warsop in Nottinghamshire, whose mother had believed in hellfire.

Pocketing the cloth, he walked rapidly in a state of sudden elation. In his coat lay a thing of worth, and a king's ruby couldn't have meant more to him than this piece of cambric. As he headed through the rainy streets, Ned reached many times into his pocket to make sure the kerchief was there. A voice seemed to be whispering from it. "Goods have no master. They belong to him that has them." The world looked different to Ned. It was nothing more than streets and buildings and a cloudy sky above, without a fearsome power staring down at him in severe judgement. "Yours for the taking, lad. Goods be yours for the taking."

Immersed in these odd but thrilling thoughts, Ned found himself once again in St. Giles, only this time with something of value on his person. In the narrow lanes he watched his pocket, for they were crawling with sullen people, lean and watchful as hounds.

He noticed a bearded man in a threadbare cape on a corner, holding a staff, gazing ahead from sightless eyes.

Going up to him, Ned asked boldly where a fine kerchief might be sold.

"Let me feel it," the blind man said, holding out his hand.

Ned gave him the kerchief, which he rolled thoughtfully between thumb and forefinger. "Worth ten shillings," he declared. "You could get four. Go to the shop on the next corner west. Be you from the north?"

Ned told him yes in surprise.

"It needs no cunning man to tell your mouth's from the north. And none from hereabout would risk a kerchief in *my* hand." He snorted merrily. "I've got a sly hand, boy. It could make the cloth vanish before your eyes, and in its place I'd put cotton and you not the wiser." He gave the kerchief back.

Ned inspected it carefully.

"Let no one take it less they pay you first," the blind man warned.

Ned found the pawn shop, a small hovel smelling of leather and smoke. Down the aisle, past a welter of saddles, bed warmers, copper pots, and past tables with swords, wigs, clothing, a wea-zened little man came limping. He wore a torn robe tied at the middle with a piece of rope. He was smiling tightly. He held a cocked blunderbuss at Ned's chest.

Without a word Ned thrust out the kerchief, but when the man touched it, Ned held firmly to one end. Lowering the gun, the man shrugged.

"It's poor cloth. Two shilling."

"It's worth twelve."

"Maybe eight in Cornhill shops, but here two."

They held the kerchief between them, while the man squinted at it in candleglow. "Three." Letting go, he backed away and raised the pistol.

"Three then," Ned agreed.

After the pawnbroker gave him three shillings, Ned was sur-prised to see the gun raised again. "You needn't the pistol. I won't rob you."

"But someone has robbed someone, hey, spark?" The pawn-broker grinned over the barrel. "Next time you mill a good piece of cloth, bring it to me. I deal honestly."

Outside in the drizzle Ned studied the lane, on either side of which stood a clutter of shacks and old tilting houses, many of them still bearing traces of scorched brick from the Great Fire nearly a hundred years ago. Yesterday these hodge-podge lanes had seemed threatening, but today, with ill-gotten coin in his pocket, they were as familiar as friends, their labyrinthine jumble a kind of haven. Passing the blind beggar, Ned halted and thanked him.

"So my lad got his cole. Good."

"Why did you help me?"

"Because you'll be back, and when you do you'll have more to sell and I warrant then you won't forget me." He laughed. "I know my good lads."

"Where do I get a night's lodging and a wash?"

"Black Boy Alley. Home of more rascals than you care to rub elbows with. Mind yourself. Sleep with coin in your fist. But the pie's good and the lodging cheap."

That evening Ned ate a hot pork pie and washed the coal bin dust from his body with soap in a pan and then slept in a cellar with half a dozen beggars, holding one shilling six in his good fist as he curled up under a lousy blanket which the cellar owner had lent him for half a pence. In another nightmare a wigged judge bearing the florid face of Lord Sandwich pronounced the sentence of death, but the next day Ned awoke strangely refreshed. His sentence for committing a crime was to live.

The coins in his pocket jingled a merry tune. Yours for the taking. Yours for the taking. Yours for the taking.

[10]

℘ Shortly after daybreak, Reader, I awoke with words on my lips, a snatch of remembered song from one of my early plays: "The dusky night rides down the sky and ushers in the moon."

The fine word there, I hope you agree, was "dusky," and it gave me some pleasure in the chill air of morning to consider that I had conjured it when hardly more than a boy.

Soon I was up and about, yelling for Joseph from my doorway, and happily grumbling at his slowness in bringing breakfast so I

could get at business. His stern face nearly broke into a smile when
he found me so energetic upon his arrival with the tray. I ate four
slices of bread and butter — Yorkshire butter, and let no man
within my hearing ever argue against Yorkshire butter — along
with three dishes of tea and a good deal of sugar. Then Joseph
bandaged my foot. It proved too swollen even for a slipper, so I
would have to endure a cloth casing and a damnable crutch
throughout this day.

But the inconvenience scarcely altered my humour. I read
Cervantes awhile, as each morning I alternate between him and
Lucian. Today I came upon these lines the good Spaniard wrote
but four days before his death:

> Goodbye, thanks; goodbye, compliments; goodbye, merry
> friends. I am dying, and my wish is that I may see you all soon
> again, happy in the life to come.

Aye, Reader, that was a man. To such a person death can be no
great misfortune, for it is but the beginning of another existence
where his virtues will become the foundation for new happiness, as
he meets old friends in a union everlasting.

I went down to my chambers where Joshua Brogden was
already at work, preparing reports of recent crimes for insertion
in the *Covent Garden Journal*. My half brother John, seated at
another desk, was dictating to a clerk some puffs for our little real
estate and insurance agency, the Universal Register Office. He had
to dictate the squibs, for at nineteen he had been accidentally
blinded at sea — powder burns from a defective cannon charge —
and so wore patches over both eyes.

Joshua Brogden put into my hands a large sheaf of cases we
would be hearing this day; after my perusal of them, Joshua
informed me of the latest news, which included the grisly murder
of a customs officer whose bones had every one been broken before
his captors had deemed it right to dispatch him. Then Joshua
offered me a new guide to brothels. Glancing at names of popular
houses such as Wetherbys and Murphys and Blasted Bet's Place
and a sly reference to the White Swan, well known for unnatural
acts, I threw the guide back at Joshua and rallied him. "Have we
got this guide for the benefit of Bow Street or of you, Joshua?
Perhaps you may have need of it, yet don't know what it contains,
whereas I know what it contains but have no need of it. You're a
rogue."

Chuckling in reply, he placed before me an unfinished article I

had begun yesterday. One of a series on the problem of the Poor, it
dealt with grave defects in the laws which govern the disposal of
the indigent. I firmly believe that all such laws should be repealed
and a single comprehensive statute take their place. I wish to
push for a large city workhouse rather than a multitude of parish
institutions. In a central place the tools can be provided, along
with instructions, for the use of the able-bodied poor, and the
administration of such a dignified establishment should attract
men of dignity and help do away with the corruption of the present
system for allocating poorhouse funds.

In the year we have been publishing the twice weekly *Covent
Garden Journal,* I have written more essays than I can count. So
this morning I had to study a moment before discovering the exact
subject of this piece. I picked up a quill, dipped it into ink, and
began to scratch out the rest of the article. It carried me forward
into anger and frustration which so often becomes, at the end of
my pen, an attack on human folly.

I conclude then that much religion supports the original design
of government, which is to keep the poor from encroaching on
the possessions and privileges of the ruling classes, for if the
poor can be persuaded that the Kingdom of Heaven will be
theirs in the next world, they may be more willing to resign
pretension to a share of good things in this one.

I read this conclusion to my brother John, who declared that
such a sally might raise a pretty hullabaloo in both state and
church. That hardly upset John. He never shrank from trouble,
egads, he never did, not that fellow with his cane, his cape, and eye
patches. He hath a remarkable memory that I have always envied,
as he can identify from a single hearing the voice of anyone.

I was pursuing ads from booksellers when Mary came into the
room complaining mildly of tobacco, for Joshua and John were
puffing on pipes while I was chewing my usual plug. She had
domestic news of a mixed nature. Calculated to please me was
the easing of little Louisa's croup; equally to displease me was
an account of little William's gluttony and its consequences, for
having hid himself in the pantry and consumed a load of raw
bacon, he had promptly disgorged it on the salon carpet.

Then Joseph came in with word that Doctor Ward awaited me
downstairs. We went down, I silent and Mary assuring me that the
doctor's Drop had already shown good effect. We found Doctor
Ward in the foyer with his coat still on. An enormous birthmark

disfigured his face. I had been warned against him by my surgeon who took him for a quack, and indeed, I have always considered men who busy themselves with our bodily ills to be somewhat ill themselves. But to be brief, I liked this fellow Ward with his huge red mark and arrogant manner and wicked tongue with which he had once explained a failure to back out from the king's presence. "His Majesty suffers no harm by my turning to see where I walk, but were I to break my neck from a regard for ceremony, it would be a sad loss for the poor." True indeed, as every day the fellow ministered to them while his more regular colleagues, who abused him for a charlatan, treated only the well-to-do.

This morning, with scarcely a word of greeting, Ward peered into my mouth, thumped my belly, frowned at my unslippered foot, and declared with some warmth, as if I had wronged him personally, that in future I must add the drinking of tar water to the regimen and increase by twofold the amount of his Drop. Having never removed his great-coat, he was gone without more to-do, before Mary could express added concern for "His Worship," which is what she hath persisted in calling me, though I have told her I am her husband, not her magistrate.

I then proceeded by crutch to my legal chambers where Joshua waited with the full wig of my office. Shortly thereafter I entered the crowded room on the first floor of Bow Street house, which serves as a court, and gave a stern look at the people assembled there. I was aware, Reader, as I am sure you are, that a sick man's last support is the courage in his eye.

With a bold stare at men rosy cheeked and vigorous, I took a chair at the desk, propping my bandaged foot on a stool my constable was kind enough to bring forward. So began a long day on the bench. I heard evidence, conducted examinations, admitted persons to bail, ordered commitments, and busied myself with the particulars of fraud, theft, and assault. The gavel rose and fell in my mottled hand, as I signaled up my best judgement of fellow creatures, many of whom had failed most dismally to observe prudence in the conduct of their affairs and as a consequence had tangled themselves in a web of foolish intrigue from which, in an effort to extricate themselves, they had struck out on reckless impulse and were to finish the sorry business here before me.

Two cases stood out today, the first dealing with the most gruesome murder of a small child.

The bailiff brought up a woman whose lank hair lay matted

about a sullen face. She wore a dirty smock, a ragged coat, decrepit boots. A violent tic agitated a long purple scar running from cheek to mouth. She was, you may guess, one of those unfortunates so common in town, oft-times seeming more animal than human, from that primal breed which hath been fostered on evil in dark cellars since birth; and indeed, this sorry creature had come to the worst end possible, for she had strangled her own child in a Bethnal Green ditch, stripped it of clothes, and sold them to purchase gin. She taxed the principle by which I have lived, namely, that few if any natures are wholly corrupt, as some elements of goodness can be found intermingled with the foulest vices. Still elevated on liquor, the woman grew lively before me and bold enough to boast of her capacity for Bung Eye, after which she casually acknowledged, as if it were the simplest thing in the world, that necessity had forced her to sacrifice the child, as it was already sick enough to die. This confession was sufficient for me to bind her over for capital trial, and I had no doubt but that, following the present quarterly session, the creature would hang.

The other case which held my attention had nothing about it of rare interest; indeed, it was common fare, save that I thought the principals more amusing than pathetic, both acting together, as it were, the comic role of the porter in *Macbeth* after the murder of Duncan. The burden of this second case was as follows. A certain Mister Francis, poulterer of Leadenhall, had charged a Miss Allen, milliner, with the theft of three pounds six from his person. I looked the pair over. Mister Francis was of a round figure, had a plump face with a kind smile on it, and seemed to borrow an air of rectitude from the watch fob his left hand never left. As for Miss Allen, she was thin and sallow, with stringy hair all limp under a bonnet, and otherwise dressed in wrinkled finery. Some minutes of questioning revealed the following pertinent facts. The alleged theft had taken place not in the shop wherein Miss Allen was employed or in the poultry shop, but in a private room secured for them as married persons by Mister Francis.

Said Miss Allen: "He called me his mellow little pear and painted in lively colors the happiness I should soon enjoy as his legal wife, but only if I did not refuse him my person. Whereupon divining his true purpose, which was to leave me after my dishonour — that I blush to say had been accomplished — I thought it proper and fitting to punish him by securing for myself

a few of the coins that constitute the only things in this world the
scoundrel loves." In short, she had taken his money. Her air of
injured innocence did not square convincingly with an appearance
and bearing more of faded harlot than shop girl. Indeed, she had,
in my opinion, got her phrases together with difficult practice. I
suspected the language of elegance was no more in her keeping
than French is in his who can sing a bawdy Provençal catch. To
give the best-natured turn I can to her disposition, I would call her
indifferently honest, a mortal of that tribe who shuns the safe road
to fortune but spends a reckless effort on any fanciful scheme that
comes along.

In reply to the accusation of having debauched her, Mister
Francis ungallantly observed, for one thing, that she was no
flincher with the bottle and, for another, that he would never touch
her, not her ever, for the jade was scarcely meat for a fishmonger.
After which Miss Allen let out a screech of fury and called him
(beg pardon, Reader) an old fart bag, which, needless to say, had
the courtroom in a gale of laughter, so that it was worth half my
strength to gavel order into the assembly.

I then gave my ruling. To Miss Allen I quoted the old adage
that it serves no purpose to lock the barn after the horse is gone,
meaning, in this instance, that she ought always to obtain her own
reward before dispensing it. A titter swept through the room,
which I again gaveled into silence.

Then in a most severe tone, you may be sure, I informed Mister
Francis that men of a certain age are commonly prey to romantic
notions, often causing them the loss of either money or sense or
both, and therefore, in his interest, I recommended him to forget
the three pounds six and recall it henceforth only as a warning
should he be tempted again into intrigues with young women,
whose experience of fools has been known to exceed their
innocence of life.

That ended the session, after which I shuffled wearily by aid of
the damnable crutch into my private chambers, where Mr Salt, an
attorney with whom I had done business in the past, was awaiting
me anxiously. He mentioned the affair of Elizabeth Canning, of
which I had heard that morning, and offered me a fee to read the
particulars and give an opinion, which I speedily did, for to tell the
truth, when lawyers come with fees in hand I am ever at their call.
I read the assertions and learned from Mr Salt that on the morrow
a search of the Wells house would be conducted. In my opinion the

warrant was in order and so did I indicate. Clearly the poor girl
had been kidnapped and held in bad circumstances. Her life had
been saved by her own courage and ingenuity. The guilty needed
to be found. Salt thanked me and begged to consult further if
needed.

Going upstairs then to the dining room, I was joined by Mary
for a small repast. She laid by me a broadsheet puff for a new
potion, the salutary effects of which would cure Coma, Lethargy,
Caries, Apoplexy, Convulsions, Falling Sickness, Sour Belching,
Looseness, Worms, Hypochondriac Melancholy, and Gout. It
looked familiar to me, though the order of illnesses might have
been different.

"It be the last cure, Mister Fielding," my wife said, "I was
thinking of."

Leaning forward, I patted her hand in the hope of relieving her
mind somewhat, my poor condition plaguing her even more than
it did me. How often, looking across the table, had I hoped to see
in Mary the woman I loved but alas had seen only the woman I
admired. She wore her brown hair pulled back from a broad
forehead with a severity appropriate to, though rather too much
emphasizing, her straight lips and grave eyes. Her features
remained faithful to a piety which though commendable was
sometimes oppressive, or to be frank, at least that way to someone
who could recall the rippling laughter of Charlotte Cradock, my
dearest Charlotte, in our days of courtship.

To turn away from my state of health, I asked after the little
rogue William, who, I learned, had forsworn raw bacon while
coaxing a slab of kidney pie from the hands of good-hearted Cook.
Sophia, however, may have caught the croup from Louisa, and
had been sent by Mary to bed to a beef broth and plasters.

I lunched on a cold mutton bone and two large glasses of hock,
for it is my unshakable conviction that hock, contrary to port,
allays the gout rather than increases it, a thesis for which Mary
hath shown little enthusiasm.

Joshua Brogden came later with hopeful news concerning the
Covent Garden Journal. A coalition of publishers had shown an
interest in buying it out of our hands. I would gladly be rid of its
responsibility, as we had made no fortune through it this whole
year, principally, I confess, because of my insistence on printing
the early issues on good paper. I told Joshua that in this venture
we had been (as Seneca observed in another context) shipwrecked
before we got under way. We were best shut of the journal and

should count ourselves lucky to be free of it and seek our salvation elsewhere.

Then I lay down for a rest. There were other cases in the afternoon to be heard, but a noise in the distance prevented me from napping. I sent Joseph to inquire; he returned with news that people were chanting the Canning girl's name in the streets. Well, I had made a fee from the kidnapping, and only hoped that the search tomorrow would turn up the miscreants who had treated her so badly.

In drowsiness my mind wandered back many years, almost thirty in fact, to my own attempt at kidnapping. The fifteen-year-old face of Sarah Andrews floated lazily into dreamy view. Such a face had taken powerful hold of my heart then; indeed, I had followed the lovely pied piper through every salon of Salisbury and then on to Lyme Regis, whence she had been spirited by her guardian uncle, and secured against my attentions. I remember the abduction was to take place on a Sunday. And with the charmer's merry consent, for each night we conversed secretly — she from her bedroom window and I from the limbs of a locust tree.

On that Sunday I waited with a friend beside the road, three horses with us, and when her church-bound carriage came along, we rushed out and waved it down. Out sprang pretty Sarah from the carriage, and we might have made off had not her uncle, Mister Andrew Tucker, come galloping down the road with his men. There was a quick little battle — of the pell-mell sort I would later describe in *Joseph Andrews* and *Tom Jones* — and I had the pleasure of leveling Mr Tucker with a single blow before his bullies drew me away. It was no luck for me that Mister Tucker was Mayor of Lyme Regis. For my transgression he had me bound over a few days by the local magistrate before releasing me on the road to London. By the time my ensuing letters of passion reached Sarah, she had other beaux (for I later learned I had been merely her third suitor). She soon married a young Oxonian bound for a career in divinity, and as I recollect she is now Mrs Rhodes of Kingsbridge.

A snatch of bad poetry (to say true, my own) came to my lips, the words said outright into the afternoon:

> "Ask you then, Celia, if there be
> The thing I love? My charmer, thee."

Better lines came to mind then. They were from Mister Pope's "Sappho to Phaon," his translation of one of Ovid's Epistles:

No Time the dear Remembrance can remove,
For oh! how vast a Memory has Love?

Oh vast, indeed.

[11]

NEXT DAY, the fifth of February, 1753, a dozen armed men were mounted and waiting in front of the Canning house for a signal to set out for Enfield. Their aim was to search the Wells house before Elizabeth and her party arrived by coach.

The wintry thoroughfares of London throbbed with the din of hurdy-gurdies, blind fiddlers, church bells, street criers, screeching pulleys, and horses snorting in collision, when old Wintlebury stepped to the door, raised his hand, and added to the noise by leading *Hurrahs!* for Bet Canning.

Scarrat, in the raiding party, joined the outcry, then with the others spurred his horse into a trot. Progress for the dozen men was slow through the morning lanes clogged by commerce. A drove of cattle, being led to butchery in Smithfield, squeezed all traffic to the walls — wagon, sedan chair, pedestrian — leaving in their heavy-footed wake the odour of steaming manure to mix in the brisk air with smells of coffee, fish, charcoal smoke. Scarrat nearly ran down a porter carrying on his back a dozen chamber pots strung together at the handles. Glancing up at Scarrat, the porter swore a formal, indifferent oath, as this was nothing more than a hazard of his work.

Riding alongside Scarrat was Gawin Nash, a thick-set baker, the self-styled leader of the group. Abruptly, from a second-floor window, a stout woman emptied a bucket of slops on the rump of Nash's horse. Nash shook his fist at her. "Ah, a fart for you," the woman yelled contemptuously. Nash was furious. To get on the good side of the baker, Scarrat called her "a loose fish." Nash was worrisome. The supercilious fellow had an eager air, and thus far Scarrat hadn't been able to charm him one whit. Nash was riding out there to uncover the truth.

The dozen reached Bishopsgate, a wider thoroughfare, and broke into a canter. Heading toward them was a small boy, his face coated with soot, a burlap sack bulging with rags across one thin shoulder, the black hole of his mouth piping, "Sweep for hire! Sweep for hire!"

Scarrat pulled out of the group and reined in sharply before the boy. "Stay," he commanded, while scooping a pence from his coat. "Here." He flipped the coin at the filthy boy, who scrambled for it in the mud. Getting it, he looked up then at Scarrat from bleary astonished eyes.

Scarrat glanced around and noticed a burly fellow in a black smock lurking nearby. "You be the sweepmaster?"

"I be." The man showed broken yellow teeth.

Scarrat threw a pence his way too. The man grabbed it up with the same alacrity as the boy. "Now you have yours. Let the boy keep his."

The sweepmaster tipped his battered cap. "Aye, your honour."

Scarrat clucked, moved his horse into a gallop, and soon joined his companions. He well knew that the sweepmaster would yank the coin from the boy's hand as soon as they turned the corner, but it didn't matter, because Scarrat couldn't help himself. When coming upon a sweep that young and beaten, Scarrat always flung a coin his way in the vain hope that his sweepmaster would let him keep at least a farthing of it. In those ageless little faces Scarrat saw his own. In recurrent nightmares, which marred most of his attempts at sleep, he climbed the narrow chimneys again, coughing from the soot, blinking away the falling ashes. In sleep he experienced again the old panic when his small thin body got momentarily stuck in a sharp bend. Once, in truth, he had refused to climb higher after such a fright, and his enraged master, to teach him a lesson, had lit a fire in the grate below. He returned in nightmare, oh he returned to that self-same chimney, his legs roasting, his lungs drowning in the rising smoke, his fleshless bones inching upward through the black tunnel, as his screams reverberated along the bricks: "I go up! I go up, sir! I go up now! I go up, I go up!"

He felt sweat breaking out on his forehead as the raiders emerged from the fetid airs of Shoreditch into the windswept countryside. Cows huddled in the bare fields. In the distance, shorn of foliage, willows and poplars marked the passage of icy little streams. Overhead a flock of swallows dipped in the breezy blue currents. But for Scarrat none of these things mattered. A landscape without cobblestone, without hovels leaning crazily together, without clots of whining beggars around a bonfire was unreal to him. But now beyond Shoreditch not even the young sweep or his own memories held Scarrat's attention. No longer serving a sweepmaster, he had another sort of man to please, and one to fear as much. His mind held to Enfield. His fortune depended on the outcome of events at Enfield.

When the raiders drew up at the Wells house, Officer White from the Guildhall was there to meet them. He was a raw-boned young man with the stiff manners of someone unsure of his role. He held an unsheathed sword and gave a nervous account of his actions. Getting to the house an hour ago, he had herded its inmates into the parlour where a local man stood guard over them with a pitchfork. Officer White led the raiders into a kitchen that smelled of tainted mutton and boiled turnips.

Eager to assume command, Gawin Nash stepped forward and declared, "It's our bounden duty to examine this place before the girl and her party arrive." He added with a grand sweep of his hand, "to piece out the truth."

"Aye, piece it out," said a silversmith named Aldridge, a small fat man who wore a velvet waistcoat and blue breeches, as if rigged out for a Sunday stroll.

At Nash's command they ascended a long staircase in the main hall. The second floor consisted of three sparsely furnished bedrooms. Returning to the kitchen, the raiders opened a side door and climbed six steps into a narrow sun-filled hayloft that ran the length of the house.

"I found a lousy woman here," said White, leaning on his sword guard. "Touched in the head."

Glancing around, Nash declared, "This cannot be the place where Betty was kept. She said a small, darkish place."

"And square," added Aldridge. "This cannot be it."

"All this hay." Nash kicked at it. "Betty said a bare floor."

"That's right," agreed Aldridge. "She laid the month on a bare board."

The raiders milled around thoughtfully. In one corner stood a battered chest of drawers, which Betty had not mentioned. Nash pointed out this discrepancy. On the other hand, there was neither chimney grate nor stool, both of which she had sworn to before Alderman Chitty.

It was painfully obvious to Scarrat that the girl had described, for want of something better, the actual room in which Tabby Howard had detained her. With growing dismay he watched an inspection of the window: unboarded, with a casement wide enough even for the fat silversmith Aldridge to get through.

Nash leaned out of the window. "No shed. She named a shed under the window. This is close enough to the ground for a child to jump without harm. This can't be the room."

"There is this, gentlemen, to think on," said Officer White, still holding the unsheathed sword. "Come with me."

The raiders trooped outside through a flurry of chickens, past a fallow vegetable garden. Curious people of the neighborhood followed them silently.

Scarrat was relieved not to see Tabby Howard's ugly mug in the crowd. She was a vicious old tart, but shrewd enough in her way not to come among men searching for trouble.

Officer White took the party around the house to the hayloft window. "Look." He pointed with his sword at a large mound of dung directly under the window. "Someone shit from it."

"Then it couldn't be boarded up," declared Nash.

"I asked the Natus woman — the one touched in the head — who did the shitting," continued Officer White, proud of his investigation. "Claims she and her husband —"

"Who?" Nash interrupted.

"The Natus woman. I have got her in the house waiting. Claims she and her husband — the man is nowhere around — she claims they have lived in the loft this whole past month. Her husband shits from the room when it's too cold for a walk to the necessary." He pointed the sword at an old privy beyond the house.

"Seems like shit enough for both man and woman and a lot more," said a raider.

"Could be Betty was held elsewhere," Aldridge suggested.

"But where?" Nash asked grimly.

As the party started back to the house, a raider named Adamson volunteered to go look for the Canning coach.

Nash wanted to know why.

"They might have took a wrong turn. It's late. They should be here and then we could ask Betty herself where she was kept."

"Let me go," Scarrat offered, wanting a chance to speak privately with the girl about that hayloft.

But eager for his own glory, Adamson rushed to his mount and had a foot in the stirrup. In a moment he was galloping down the rutted turnpike.

The party re-entered the house, this time squeezing into the gloomy parlour where a local man stood with his pitchfork over the seated prisoners.

Slumped near the hearth was the Wells woman: fat, shabby, peering from nearsighted eyes at the incoming men, a bowl of tea gripped absently in her hand.

Scarrat wondered if she might recognize him, but she glanced from face to face stuporously. And of course she'd seen him only when he'd watered his horse at her trough.

Next to Susannah Wells sat the ugliest woman he had ever seen. The creature was deeply wrinkled, with a mouth twisted at one corner toward a squinting eye, as if that side of her face had been shoved together from chin to brow by an irresistible force. She was thickly mustached; long grey hairs stood out on her nose like thistles, and her fearsome visage was partially hidden under a brimmed straw hat. One of her hands held a clay pipe, while the other lay gnarled against an enormous belly swathed in numerous patched skirts. The raiders stared dumbfounded at her.

"That," said Officer White, "be the gypsy that boards here. Calls herself Mary Squires." He smiled. "It's a plain name for such as that. They be her daughters."

He meant the two girls who huddled at the gypsy's feet. One had large beautiful eyes in a face as coarse as her mother's; the other was altogether coarse. Behind the huge woman stood a brawny lad in rough wool pants and shirt. Although he too had his mother's features, a kind of idiotic smile gave him a softer expression.

"Her son," explained Officer White, leveling the sword point toward the boy. "And that be Virtue Hall." The blade moved beyond the hearth at a thin girl with straw-colored stringy hair. A thick scar ran from her upper lip to her cheek.

Nash chuckled. "Bless me. That be named Virtue?"

The raiders laughed until the yellow-haired girl stuck her tongue out at them — but laughed too, good-naturedly.

"Where be the Natus woman?" Officer White asked suddenly.

The local man swung his pitchfork around and pointed it at a far dark corner where a little woman was squatting behind a stool, nearly out of sight. She wore nothing but a filthy shift and a rag around her bony neck. Long grey hair lay chaotically around a face even more vacuous than that of Susannah Wells. She was holding her naked toes in both hands, as if for comfort.

"This is a sad crew," muttered silversmith Aldridge and drew back toward the door, fearing one of these people might brush against his clean breeches.

Officer White led the raiders back into the kitchen, where Gawin Nash took charge again. He explained that they must confront Betty Canning with the whole gang at once and see could the girl identify Susannah Wells.

It was exactly what Scarrat feared. If the women were brought in singly, he could let Betty know by a nod which was Susannah Wells. "What's the need for so much caution?" he asked Nash. "We have the poor girl's word."

"We must make sure."

"Of what?" Scarrat glanced at the others for support. "We believe our poor abused Betty."

"Damn but we do!" It was Rossiter, the burliest man present.

"And so do I," said Nash stiffly. "But for the magistrate, should it come to that, we must be official in what we do."

"*Should* it come to that?" cried Rossiter. "And do you think we'll let them handle one of our girls in such a way and not have justice?"

There was a flurry of argument between Rossiter and Nash, but it lasted only moments, because Adamson reappeared, flushed and panting from a furious ride. "I met the coach at Ponder's End. We be all right, gentlemen," he announced gaily. "She said there was hay in the room. A chest. It is verified."

"Did you tell her there was hay?" asked Nash.

For a moment Adamson considered the question. "I might have done. I can't remember. But I swear she said there was hay."

"Then damn but there *was* hay," said Rossiter.

The kitchen was silent. It filled with pipe smoke, as the raiders awaited the carriage. At a sudden commotion outside, they all rushed from the kitchen and into the road, where carpenter Lyon and the coachman were lifting the girl from a landau. A crowd of townspeople were staring at the huge bandage that swathed Elizabeth Canning's head.

Scarrat was pleased by her composure. Indeed, as she was carried bodily into the house, the haggard wench assumed the air of a princess. Officer White ordered the onlookers to stay clear of the yard, but a few crept in behind the raiders and entered the house. Everyone squeezed into the kitchen, where Betty was set down in a chair.

[12]

"MULL HER SOME WINE," demanded old Wintlebury, who had held her hand while she was carried in.

Rossiter began rummaging through cabinets for wine and spices.

"Now, Miss Betty," Nash said, after calling loudly for silence in the crowded room, "does this fit the place you was kept in?"

Looking around, the girl said nothing.

"Is it?"

"Be gentle with her," warned her present employer, carpenter Lyon. "She is weak, man."

"Indeed, be gentle," put in Wintlebury, still holding her hand. "No need to hurry a girl so exhausted."

Cowed a little, Nash cleared his throat and said, "Let's to the bedrooms first."

After Betty was picked up, the party gathered in the hall and faced the long staircase. The cradled girl judged the stairs a long time before declaring, "I believe I was held up there." Carried through each second-floor bedroom, at last she shook her head. "None of them is the room."

Her statement relieved Scarrat, for the bedrooms were unlike her description before Alderman Chitty. Had Scarrat not known otherwise, he would have believed the dissembling wench's every word. Not greed nor fear had brought her to such a pitch of certainty, but the two-shilling romances had done it for her. Good for Betty, he thought. The little tart was living one of her romances.

Everyone returning to the kitchen, Rossiter offered her some heated wine with cinnamon. Betty wanted none, but Widow Canning took a steaming mug and drank heartily. "Bless me," she sighed, "I was near a faint."

"Dear Betty," said Scarrat, pressing forward and pointing to the kitchen door which led to the hayloft. "Was this the stair you was pushed up?" He gave her a long look.

"Aye, this one, Constable. I recollect it."

Scarrat knew she couldn't resolve all the errors of her already given description, but the hayloft was better believed than the second-floor bedrooms. As Nash had already suggested, no other room in the house could be the prison save the hayloft, though that was queer enough.

Carried to the loft, Betty studied the hay, the chest, the wide unboarded window, the sunny length of the room. Her face remained calm as she declared in a low voice, "This be where I was confined."

"Aye," said Widow Canning with a sob, "this be where my poor dear angel was confined."

"Good woman," Nash said to the mother, "was you confined here too that you know it so well?" To the girl he said, "You never mentioned hay to the alderman."

"I didn't recollect it then."

"No? So much as is here, you forgot?" He swept his arm out dramatically.

"It seems more now than I remember."

Scarrat pushed forward. "No doubt there's more now," he said. "After you got free of the rascals, they must have piled more hay in and added the chest and disguised the room in every way they could. That's plain." Scarrat held high a gallon jug with a broken handle. Unobserved, he'd brought it up from the kitchen, having found it in a cabinet while the party was climbing to the loft. "Here be the jug our poor Bet slept with a full month!"

"Where did you get that?" Nash asked fiercely.

"Why, near the hay here."

"We never did see it. You, sir" — Nash sought out the face of Officer White — "did you see this jug before now?"

White shook his head glumly. Since the arrival of the girl he'd been ignored, his little authority quite lost.

"We never did see it," Nash said, turning to Scarrat.

Scarrat shrugged. "It was pushed under the hay."

With a scowl Nash walked to the window. "Here, girl. Come here."

"Lift her! Lift her!" urged Wintlebury, and Lyon and Rossiter lifted her from a chair brought upstairs for her to sit in.

"You spoke of a board you pried off," Nash said when they carried her to the window.

Betty nodded. "There was a board here."

"What held it, pray? I see no nails."

Scarrat came up. "Come, it's plain the rogues pulled the nails out. Such people are clever enough."

"Where?" demanded Nash. "Where was the nails?"

Scarrat made as though to pry loose a piece of casement wood, then gave it up. "Too crumbly to tell, but they was pulled out."

"Where be the holes?"

Controlling his frustration, Scarrat gave the tough-minded baker a smile. "Wood's too crumbly to tell."

"Crumbly?" Nash began to pound on the casement in a test of its solidity.

"The girl spoke true!" exclaimed Wintlebury. Others took up his cry. "She spoke true!"

"The nails was pulled out," Scarrat affirmed, raising his hands in a gesture of triumph.

Nash mumbled under his breath; his square red face was puffing out.

"This is the place, gentlemen!" cried Scarrat. "As God is our witness, it's the place they starved our Betty for her innocence!"

A general shout of agreement followed. Nash, his authority broken, drew away from the window.

"Set the child down gently," said Wintlebury. "She's near the end of her strength." When she was seated again, the raiders shuffled around the loft, poking with minimal enthusiasm under the hay, in corners. They had already decided that this was the place.

While the half-hearted search for more evidence continued, Scarrat moved close to the girl and whispered suddenly, "Wells sits near the hearth."

"What did you say?"

Scarrat turned to meet the suspicious gaze of the fat silversmith, Aldridge. "I asked her how she did."

"I will ask something other." Aldridge looked coldly at the girl. "How much bread did you have here when you was held?"

"A quartern."

"What? A quartern?" Aldridge turned in astonishment to the others, who turned from their searching and stared at him. "Hear that, gentlemen? She says four pounds of bread, but to the alderman she declared but four small pieces. Now it's a quartern. Bless me."

Betty never changed expression, but calmly explained that by four pieces she'd meant four large ones — a quartern — when before the alderman.

Wintlebury came up and patted her hand soothingly, with a glare for the silversmith. "Sir, do you expect from this abused child the accuracy of a solicitor?"

At Scarrat's suggestion they returned the girl downstairs, through the kitchen, and into the hall. There her present employer spoke to the girl. "You are going in now to see them," said Lyon. "Don't be daunted, for you have friends about you. Even so, challenge no one less you are positive of them."

"I will do as you command, sir."

"Then you shall see them." Lyon nodded to Officer White, who opened the door.

Scarrat saw trouble. The gypsy had moved closer than Susannah Wells to the hearth. The mountainous woman was lighting her pipe with a coal.

Lyon said, "Now, Betty, discover the one who robbed you."

From the chair where they had seated her, Betty looked steadily around the room and finally pointed a finger at the gypsy near the hearth. "That was the woman."

"That's not Wells then," declared Gawin Nash in triumph. "She named wrong. She named the gypsy."

"She named right," said Lyon. "At the alderman's she said a woman dark in the face. That's the gypsy."

"Aye, the gypsy," put in Rossiter with a glare at Nash.

"She might not know the name, gentlemen, but she knows the face," Scarrat said, thinking nimbly. "It was not Wells who did it but the gypsy."

The girl with beautiful eyes jumped up and ran to the huge woman. "Mother! The gentlewoman says you robbed her!"

Mary Squires struggled to her feet, a tall and muscular figure made gigantic by the voluminous skirts. Pushing back the straw hat, she glowered at Bet Canning. "I meant to wait for you to see me clear, but I will speak now. I robbed you, ma'am? Look at this old mug of mine. You never saw it until today."

"I saw it before," said Betty.

Mary Squires guffawed. "Not on your life. Pray, ma'am, when did I rob you?"

"On the New Year."

Slapping her thigh, the gypsy chortled. "New Year, ma'am? Bless you! You have just named yourself as a liar. On New Year I was a hundred mile from this place!"

"Where was you, dame?" asked Nash.

"At Abbotsbury in Dorset and I can prove it."

"By other gypsies? Betty named right," declared Lyon. "She said a tall woman dark in the face. Wells, look you, gentlemen, be short and whitish. As Constable Scarrat told us, our Bet mixed the names is all. At the Alderman's she meant the gypsy."

Rossiter spoke up gruffly. "None but another gypsy could trust the word of a gypsy."

There was a murmur of assent in the crowd.

Scarrat was amazed by this turn. Betty had made virtue of a bad mistake by picking out the wrong woman. Had she named Wells, someone would have recalled her description of a tall, dark woman. As matters now lay, Betty had done all to perfection. A gypsy was worse liked than a dull baggage of Wells's ilk. In spinning the tale Betty had lit upon a tall woman of a dark complexion. Probably a villainness from one of her romances. Women and fate were queer things.

"Where's that creature," Nash asked suddenly, "who swore to laying up all month in the loft with her husband?"

Officer White stepped through the crowd and from the corner yanked the cowering Judith Natus to her feet.

"When did the gypsy come to board here?" demanded Nash.

The woman blinked.

"Speak up, ninny."

"These last few days."

"Not till then?"

"No, your honour." She curtsied to the baker. "Me and Fortune — "

"Who?"

"My husband, Fortune. Me and Fortune, we slept in the loft and saw nothing of Egyptians till some days ago."

"Fiddlesticks!" cried old Wintlebury, laying a protective hand on Betty's shoulder. "It's a bald lie."

From the far corner Virtue Hall began to giggle. She tossed her yellow hair and laughed uncontrollably until tears ran down her face.

Nash went up close to Susannah Wells, who slumped on a stool, munching her lips in a bovine way. "Have you ever seen this miss," he asked her, pointing to Betty, "until this day?"

"No, milord, your worship."

Virtue Hall, still cackling, stared hard at Betty Canning. Betty glared back. The girls fixed each other like gamecocks.

Now it was Lyon's turn to lead the investigation. Kneeling at Betty's side, he asked did she have more to uncover about this gang.

"I do, sir. That one stood by while the gypsy took my stays."

"Do you mean Susannah Wells, child?"

"I do." Then turning, she regarded the yellow-haired Virtue Hall, who was yet snickering. "That creature too. She stood by and watched. She laughed when I was asked to go their way."

Virtue Hall stopped laughing. "God forgive you, chit. I never saw you in my life till now, say what you will."

Lyon then asked if the gypsy's son had been there too. "Was this fellow one of them who brought you in, child, from Moorfields?"

Betty studied the smiling idiot. She coloured slightly under his innocent gaze. "I can't be sure. Perhaps he did not. No, he did not."

"Come, come, enough," Scarrat said loudly and stepped forward. "We talk too much here. We have a pack of rogues in our hands." He stood in front of the hearth. "Plainly they rigged it to debauch a poor girl. Let's get them to a magistrate!"

A roar of approval, a general movement toward the Wells people.

"Get a wagon to secure them," Scarrat told Rossiter. "Officer," he said to White, "we prevail upon you to do your duty."

[13]

THE YOUNG OFFICER drew his sword, flourished it grandly, and nearly swiped some bystanders in the packed room. Then he and the local man with the pitchfork and raiders with drawn pistols began to herd the prisoners into the road. In a few minutes Rossiter came running up alongside a wagon driven by an Enfield ostler. Grumbling and fearful, the prisoners climbed into the wagon. Virtue Hall, leaning out, grimaced as she screamed, "The chit's a shameless liar! I warrant a slut in the bargain!"

Nash approached the young officer. "What do you make of this affair, White?"

Officer White stared at the man who had usurped his authority all day. "I have done my duty," he said loftily. "I think, sir, I have done my proper duty."

"Indeed." Nash walked over to Aldridge, who had been the only raider save himself to have questioned the girl boldly. They talked in whispers, then crossed the road together to the village inn.

With the wagon loaded, the Canning group seated in the landau, and the remaining raiders mounted ahorseback, Officer White stood in the road and delivered a short oration. "I was ordered by Mister Alderman Chitty, did I find evidence of misdoing by persons in the house of Susannah Wells, to take those persons up and to the magistrate in Edmonton. I have so found. Let's there with haste and God save the king!"

From the inn the two skeptics watched the procession grind into motion.

"I'm heartily sick of the damn thing," Aldridge observed sourly. "Will you take some cold mutton with me, sir, and a half of wine?"

Nash agreed. "I can't like this affair," he declared. "Dear God, the girl didn't know that room."

Aldridge flicked some dirt from his velvet sleeve. His feasting clothes, worn in the spirit of bringing about justice, had been rumpled by the day's work and their state made him fretful. "She didn't know it. She said a bare floor, not a blade of straw on it, till that damn fool Adamson rode out and told her of the hay."

"No board on the window and a latrine below it for half an army," continued Nash. "No shed. No hard jump to the ground either. I peeked at the loft door — no lock. She could not tell the difference betwixt one staircase and another. Hell, man, she was never here before today."

Aldridge pursed his lips judiciously. "Yet we must also consider the gypsy. They're smugglers and thieves, every gypsy you'll meet without exception. This black giant is thief and murderess too if God ever made one."

"But she was nowhere near. She was in Abbotsbury."

"So says the gypsy. Who will countenance word of smugglers and thieves?"

They fell silent over their wine.

"The sum I collect," said Nash after a while, "is against the girl. She has fobbed us."

"I believe it."

Halfway through the mutton, Nash threw down his fork. "I want no part of the affair."

"Nor I." Aldridge glanced slyly at his companion. "Yet called to witness in a court of law, would you speak your mind?"

"I would not go to court less by writ. I would not go by choice."

"Why so?"

Nash leaned forward, knife held vertical next to his plate. "Think of the friends she has. And of them soon to come. They'll go hard on someone set against her." He rapped the table with the knife handle for emphasis. "I won't say a word against that girl."

"Nor I. It's a business to stay clear of."

Merry Tyschemaker was a justice of the peace for the County of Middlesex and for two hours in his Ford's Grove residence heard the Canning accusations and the Enfield denials.

He believed the girl, because accompanying her were clean ruddy-faced tradespeople, whereas the other crew was motley, shifty-eyed, and stupid. He had insufficient cause, however, to hold the yellow-haired whore and the idiot son and the filthy Natus woman and the two gypsy daughters, one of whom had exceedingly beautiful eyes. But the black-visaged giant was plainly a sullen thief and her accomplice, the Wells creature, would not say ten words in her defense, doubtless for fear of uncovering worse crimes.

So he bound over the two, charging Mary Squires with theft and Susannah Wells with running a disorderly house. Squires was to be taken to New Prison and Wells to Bridewell.

The Canning party withdrew in a mood of dissatisfaction. Carpenter Lyon spoke for them all. "This magistrate of little count has set no date for trial, nor did he mention assault of Betty's person. He's here in Edmonton with no concern for our girl. He'll let the culprits stay at ease and I shouldn't doubt but they bribe their way to freedom. We must plead before a known magistrate of consequence."

"As to that," said Wintlebury, "let me speak. I have already hired a solicitor and sent him for opinion to a famed magistrate, Justice Fielding."

"I heard of Justice Fielding," put in Rossiter with an approving nod.

Wintlebury continued. "Fielding has told Salt we are so far proper."

"I heard of Salt too, a good solicitor," added Rossiter.

Startled by old Wintlebury's independent action and taken aback by his own loss of initiative, Lyon said testily, "I too have heard of both men. Fielding is my choice for a good magistrate, though I've yet to have an opinion of Salt. But to plead our case strongly we must raise subscriptions in our Betty's behalf." Fired by his new vision, Lyon went on. "We must get friends loyal to her and to the cause of justice and with them support her cause. We must prepare for a protracted struggle, as the wicked have always their own support."

The band of raiders cheered.

Then they set out for London, all save Robert Scarrat, who slipped away in the growing darkness.

In the coach headed home, old Wintlebury held the weary girl's hand, while Widow Canning opened a volume.

After the tender and now happy Father had raised them both up, and they had embraced one another all around, he proposed them a certain Day to Solemnize their Nuptials.

She lowered the book with a happy sigh.

That night, exhausted beyond further endurance, Elizabeth Canning collapsed and fell into a delirium from which people feared she might never recover. All night long she shouted of devils and raised her voice in song, many of the verses blushingly improper, and called out for mercy until women in the outer rooms, sitting in vigil, wept and prayed for her soul.

After leaving the homeward-bound raiders, Scarrat galloped back to Enfield and reined up at Tabby Howard's house in a blustery darkness.

For a long time he pounded on the door before it finally opened a crack and he could shoulder his way roughly inside. Three steps across the threshold, he struck the woman.

Tabby Howard reeled back against a table, knocking a gin bottle over on its side, where it spun crazily.

She clutched a threadworn jacket to her throat, while slowly wiping blood from her lips. "Bless me, leave off, sir," she muttered drunkenly.

"I told you. Keep her rations short, break the bitch down, but I never told you to starve her dead." Scarrat's voice was low and tight in stifled rage. "I paid for her food, but you chose to starve her and pocket my coin."

Looking up from the blood on her fingers, the woman said, "Wait. Hear me."

"Hear what? Lies? What ails you? I know you for a stinking fucking baggage!" Raising his fist, Scarrat stepped forward.

Tabby held her ground, giving him a grin from her bleeding mouth. She was nearly as tall as Scarrat. "Do what you will, man."

"Ho!" He struck again, this time with greater force, and sent her thudding against the wall. Somehow keeping her feet in spite of the blow and her state of drunkenness, Tabby mumbled something he couldn't understand.

Her strength and balance made him angrier, so he struck again, this time sending her down.

"Go to," she snuffled. "That's enough. Help me."

After a moment Scarrat lowered his fist and pulled the woman to her feet.

"The girl's out causing trouble," Scarrat said, panting from his exertions. "And you to blame."

"I was following you. You said break the jade, so I did."

"Sure I wanted her broke. But not starved, not killed, but killed rather than getting loose that way and going home. None was done right." He had raised his fist again in fury, then dropped it. The creature was no good to him beaten senseless. For that matter, she was hardly good to him as she was — sodden with gin, capable of knifing him if he turned his back. "Well, what's done is done," he said more calmly. "We must go from here. Did you hear what happened in this village today?"

"She came with armed men, took some people up. I stayed clear."

"You did right for once."

"Took Susannah and a gypsy."

"Do you know them?"

Tabby shrugged. "Not the gypsy. Susannah's a rip, an old stinkard with half a brain. She rents out her rooms to sweatboxes for bringing men there."

"No formidable person," Scarrat said with a touch of levity.

"Ah, Susannah's but a nightbag. If she's in court, the judge has only to take one blink at her, he'll pronounce her for hanging."

"Maybe so. But to make sure, I want good witnesses. Is there a safe man hereabout?"

"Not many."

"I asked *one*."

Dabbing a rag at her mouth, Tabby stared at the gin bottle lying on its side, fortunately corked. "Could you want some Bung Eye?" She made for the table.

"Touch that, I'll brain you!"

She halted in her tracks.

"Be there?" Scarrat said.

"What?"

"A safe man hereabout!" he bellowed in exasperation.

"Ah." She eyed the bottle. "Well, there's one I know of."

"Go on," Scarrat said when she paused.

"Sells fish at Waltham Cross. He'd slit his mother's throat for a shilling."

"I don't want a murderous kind of rascal."

"It was a way of speaking."

"All right, then. Will the man perjure?"

"John Iniser?" The woman snorted. "John Iniser would sell the Christ child for a sum." She held the rag against her mouth, against her split cheek. "I have done business with him. Believe me, I know John Iniser."

"That's the man, then. And he'll keep mum?"

"In his own interest."

"Tell him he had seen the gypsy woman this whole last month in and around the village."

"In and around the village. What be she like, so John will know?"

"Even uglier than you. A giant dark woman. Sells linen at doors and tells fortunes, I suppose, like gypsies do. Likely a smuggler and a thief as well."

"Of course."

"Ugly." Scarrat pulled one corner of his eye down and twisted his mouth up."

Tabby smiled. "Uncommon beast, hey?"

"Tell your man he had seen this thing a whole month hereabout." Scarrat tossed a guinea on the table. "Half for him, half for you. You keep your wits."

Her eyes roamed from money to gin.

Scarrat watched her ogling the bottle. "Do you follow? I said keep your wits! Say nothing of the gypsy yourself. I don't want you in it."

"I don't want in it."

In three strides he was at her side, taking her jaw with one hand and jerking her head back. He squeezed until her mouth opened from the pressure into a figure eight. "Correct your error, you miserable cunt." He squeezed harder. "Or you'll know me for sure." He squeezed harder. "I don't care a whit for your disgusting life. Is that clear?"

She tried to nod.

"Make a clumsy hand again, I'll turn you off. Like nothing. Like a dog in the street." Abruptly he let her go.

Tabby's head jerked forward, with crimson stripes on both cheeks.

Scarrat walked briskly to the door. "I'll be back to check on your man. If you need more money for him, you'll have it. That's no difficulty. The difficulty is everyone keeping their wits and doing right. Mind yourself."

"I will."

"I know you will. Mark your man closely. Make sure of him or I'll make sure of you. You know my meaning in that." Flinging the door wide and letting the cold air whistle in, Scarrat strode into the darkness.

Tabby shut the door. Spitting blood, she sat at the table, righted the bottle, and pulled out the cork.

Part Three

THE CANNING
CASE

[14]

NED'S FORTUNES had improved after the cambric kerchief had told him that goods were his for the taking. He had managed to keep himself in food and modest lodgings by snatching kerchiefs and scarves in crowds. Sometimes he was chased, sometimes not, but he learned soon enough that citizens would not pursue less the crime was great — and usually not even then. As for constables, he quickly developed a petty thief's contempt for them, as they showed up only when a neighorhood, usually a group of tradespeople, had cornered a law-breaker — had done the work, so to speak. It was then common practice for a constable to haul the malefactor off to his own home and keep him cuffed there until a session judge charged the felon and sent him off to prison. For his minimal service the constable often asked an outrageous fee of the parish.

Back home Ned Carleton had believed in English law and God's law, both equally powerful in restraining evil. But now it wasn't the wrathful voice of God or that of a London constable he listened to. At his ear these days was the silken voice of a kerchief, telling him the world was his for the taking. His heart beat powerfully. He would live, and he would live right here in London town.

Strolling through the grimy lanes near Houndsditch, he came to the weekly rag fair. Rabble buffeted him along the stalls where tainted meat and spotty potatoes were haggled over. Baskets of fish, roots, and herbs lay next to stolen goods displayed on the muddy ground. Buying a penny loaf of bread, Ned leaned against a tripe shop wall to eat it and became aware of a man watching him.

This man was short, portly, in a rumpled coat and baggy trousers, but he carried a brass-headed cane and a ring sparkled on his hand. His face, stubbled with grey whiskers, broke into a grin when Ned returned his stare.

"Ah, sir —" Approaching, the man tapped the brim of his tattered hat in greeting. "I see your bewilderment. You are none of these London rogues either." He turned to grimace disapprovingly at the crowd. "A guinea to a farthing, sir, you come from other parts."

"Yes, from Warsop."

"And Warsop is . . . ?"

"In Nottinghamshire."

The man nodded in satisfaction. "I knew it. You're the salt of the earth. I never fail in my reckoning of quality. Your trade, sir?"

"Sheep," Ned replied. As naturally as night follows day, a new cunning had come in the wake of thievery. He had already decided, if asked about himself, not to mention his last two years of household service in London. He'd have no past here. Pretending to ignorance of London, he'd allay any suspicion of his honesty, for though he'd done no more than grab a few kerchiefs, Ned viewed himself as a hardened criminal already.

Poking the muddy ground with his cane, the man studied Ned for a few moments. "Have you sold a flock here, sir?"

"I have."

"God prosper you. A young man with sheep is in luck. There's fortune in sheep. I saw you in your great-coat, a strapping fellow, and I told myself, he's come to the drawing room of the devil to sell his sheep and then leave this nasty place. Will you do me the honour of your company over a glass?"

They crossed the marketplace to a grog shop. Hesitating in the doorway, the man pointed imperiously with his cane at a distant table, as if choosing a suitable box at the opera. Taking Ned's arm familiarly, he led the way and with a soiled kerchief wiped some spilled beer from the designated tabletop.

"This place, sir, is beneath us, quite beneath us," he muttered sadly, "but any port in a storm, as they say. Sheep, there's good fortune in sheep, sir. How long since you parted with your flock?"

It was over two years. For an instant Ned recalled their knock-kneed legs carrying them down a hillside, rolling like boats in choppy waves. "Just the other day."

The man sighed as if he too understood that for a shepherd such animals were living friends and not just mutton on a plate. "Was it a big flock?"

"Middling." Ned had herded them for Robert Syton, a kindly man who usually drank up the profits and failed to pay full wages.

The fat little man winked. "Even in a middling flock there's fortune." He called loudly for mugs of ale. When they came, he raised his and licked his lips. "This will do," he said, taking a couple of deep swallows. Foam settled below his flattened nose like a white mustache. "It's the very thing to fortify the heart and preserve the liver, sir." He drank again. "Ah, the very thing." Wiping his mouth with a dirty sleeve, he eyed Ned with a frown. "Come, sir, what are you thinking?"

"Thinking?"

"I read your thoughts, sir. I warrant you take me for the sort who hunt for flats."

"Flats?"

The man called for more ale. "It's but the flash language of criminal London, sir. Not that I know much of it, albeit the nature of my business has taught me a thing or two about the practitioners of infamy." He sighed at the memory. "A flat is a poor victim. I warrant you took me for a sly rogue who seeks to do mischief against a gentleman from the country."

"I did not, sir."

"Then my compliments, sir. Let me explain my business as a measure of respect for your trust and good will. I am an inventor of remedies." Pushing his coat aside, he took from a soiled waistcoat a thumb-worn card. With a majestic flick of his wrist, he gave it to Ned. "You read, sir?"

Ned patted his pocket, wherein lay the book. "I do, sir." With difficulty and the man's help, he read the card:

Samuel Bostock, Dispenser of Bostock's Balsam of Life to cure Scurvy, Dropsie, Colt-Evil, Toothache, Scorbutick Gums, Black or Yellow Foul Teeth, Worms, Itch, Kibes, Chilblains. Stumps of Teeth drawn with Ease and Safety. Let Blood. For One Shilling each and

Welcome. By the Doctor who puts forth this Announcement you may be taught Writing, Arithmetick, Latin, and Greek at Reasonable Rates.

When Ned returned the card without comment, Doctor Bostock grunted in disappointment. "I detect you have no need of my balsam. Sir, I despise quackery as much as you do and never take medicine but what performs its operation in a rational manner and whose effect I can account for." He replaced the card in his waistcoat. "I mean, sir, as either braces up the relaxed fibers of the stomach or such as divides the viscid humours and prepares them to be thrown off by insensible perspiration or such as strengthens the nerves, comforts the brain, and revives the spirit." He sat back proudly and hooked his thumbs in his waistcoat pockets. "I could tell you many things, sir. How the cramp is caused by wind in the blood. I can foretell the course of illness by looking at a man's water. I told a woman whose husband she brought me for examination, I told her, I find by his water your husband has drank too much cold beer when he was hot and by this error so mixed his grease with his blood that there's no longer remedy. I told her, woman, you'll be a widow in a fortnight, and as I am a Christian, in a fortnight she was. Sir, may I inquire what happened here?" Doctor Bostock was staring at the bandaged hand that Ned had just removed from his pocket.

"I was burnt."

The doctor leaned forward. "What? Glimmed by sentence?"

"Glimmed?"

"Was you branded?"

"I was burnt in a fire."

"A fire." The doctor touched his lower lip thoughtfully. "Did you set it?"

"God in heaven, no. I never did." It was a strange question, and although Ned was impressed by the doctor's card and professional manner, he felt offended by such an accusation. It reminded him of Lord Sandwich. "I went into a burning house and tried to get a woman out."

"Ah, a Christian act," observed the doctor with a smile. "Good work."

"But I failed."

"In any event, good work. Done like a man." The doctor drained off his ale.

"Done like a fool."

The doctor raised his eyebrows. "A matter of viewpoint, sir. There's some to call you fool. There's some to call you Christian. I myself call you Christian and take pride in your company. My compliments."

Such gentlemanly treatment pleased Ned. "And mine to you, sir."

"Would you be so good as to dine with me?" asked the doctor. "Not here, though. Nothing here but boiled mutton and poisoned bread."

"Poisoned bread?"

"Oh, don't doubt it, sir. They mix the flour with bone-ash from charnel houses. The stuff whitens the bread, you see, but sows the blood with minute seeds of infection. The pernicious threads of disease draw under the skin and" — he turned his palm over emphatically — "tumble you into the grave. You must know your eating houses in London. I am privileged to say I know one with a fish sauce fit for a king. Good Canary too." He kissed his fingers. "None of your Sherry and Malagas mixed together that some rogues call Canary. I know my Canary." He fumbled in his waistcoat. "Now the reckoning."

Ned hauled out a shilling.

"No, no, good sir. I won't hear of it. I'll discharge this reckoning." He tossed a coin cavalierly on the table. "My pleasure, sir." Rising, he twirled his cane. "So you be in sheep. There's a fortune in sheep. A lucky man, indeed. No frills in your life, no foppery, but hard work and just rewards. Sheep is an honest fortune. I can't deny that and I can't deny my own be honest too, for I have made it in the service of mankind."

Last daylight undulated along the rooftops like water. Smoke curled into the darkening sky from numberless chimneys, as the two men strolled along the twisting lanes, proceeding farther into the maze of Smithfield.

Ned felt his heart knocking, his legs grow weak, as he imagined a terrible deed. They were entering an area of town where anything might happen, where he, a boy of Warsop, a God-fearing shepherd once, might do more than think of robbing this man with a brass-headed cane and a ring on his finger — might actually do it.

The doctor was chatting about this and that, unaware that his invitation to dinner might lead to the loss of ring, gold, and cane. Ned wondered if he could do it. It was one thing to snatch an askew scarf or kerchief from a nameless person in a crowd, but quite another to meet and know a man and then, face to face, threaten him or actually handle him with roughness. Ned had the strange sensation of listening to the money pouch that dangled from the doctor's belt. Yours for the taking, yours for the taking. But can I do it? Can I? Ned asked himself, sweating in the chill air.

As they moved deeper into the shadowy depths of Smithfield, a young woman stuck her head from a window, leered down, and called out gaily while jiggling her breasts.

The doctor shook his cane angrily at her. "Have a care, harlot, or we'll have you branded next sessions that all the world may see your trade in your bosom!" To Ned he declared with a deep frown, "As I am Christian, it's the only way to deal with trollops or they'll tear at your clothes next. Follow me, sir, I am at your disposal. I know my way through these vicious lanes." With these reassuring words he turned into an alley strewn with garbage and broken barrels. Daylight was wholly gone, in its stead a hovering mist that ballooned around their legs and obscured the tiny footpaths leading away like spider webbing.

Ned felt a sudden chill and was about to ask Doctor Bostock were they nearing the chop house when a blow across his back knocked him to his knees. Glancing round in time to avoid another blow from a raised stave, he scrambled up and charged, hearing the doctor yell, "At him! At him, Lemuel!"

Ned clutched the stave and wrenched it free, then delivered a tremendous blow that leveled his attacker. From the corner of his eye he saw Doctor Bostock hurrying away, the fog billowing like surf around his fat legs and flying coattails. Within an instant Ned was in pursuit. Before the doctor reached the end of the alley, Ned had him by the collar and spun him back in the direction of his fallen confederate.

"Oh, sir! Do no harm, I beg you!" pleaded the doctor, as Ned pushed him roughly along until they reached the assailant, who had risen to a sitting position and held his head in both hands. Ned threw the doctor down beside him and stood over them.

"Do no harm, sir, I beg you!" The doctor drew his knees to his chin, shielding his face with his arm. "We thought we could mill you without a wink."

Ned felt exceedingly foolish. He'd been led into ambush by someone he was working up courage to rob. He dropped his fists to his sides.

"What goes on there?" someone yelled from a ground floor window.

"Our companion fell," the doctor called out quickly. "No harm done." He grinned shyly at Ned. "Can I rise, sir?"

"Stay."

The confederate was moaning, wiping his bloody cheek with a rag. By shoplight falling into the street, Ned could see that the fellow was long and skinny, with a mop of curly hair, a haggard face. He was young, perhaps fifteen.

"No harm done, sir," said the doctor with a hopeful smile. "This fucking blockhead" — he jerked a thumb at his companion — "got what he deserved. I confess our error, sir. I do, I confess it. But we've lost all our movables. In desperation, in utter desperation" — he lowered his knees and defensive arm — "we thought to take a mere shilling and go our way. Forgive us as you are Christian." Cocking his head, he smiled tightly. "Recall the woman you almost saved. A Christian act, sir, you have a Christian soul. We meant no harm. I told him, Lemuel, damn you, I said use no violence, but this redheaded stupid asinine ninny did it anyway."

"A shilling's all you'd have of me," Ned told him coolly.

The doctor raised his eyebrows. "You jest, sir. You have just sold your flock."

"All told I have four shillings five pence."

"A dealer in sheep? Was you already milled of the proceeds by someone?"

"I had no sheep."

"But, sir, you vowed you was in sheep."

"Long ago I herded them."

The doctor shook his head. "A shepherd. A fine manly fellow like you, you had the air of an owner. No big flock, but a middling would do. Well, a shepherd. Odd's fucking heart."

Ned motioned for him to rise and the fat little man did, cautiously, with profuse thanks. Ned turned to the injured lad. "Can you get up?"

"May I beg to ask your scheme with me?" said the doctor, while retrieving his cane — he'd thrown it down in his haste to flee. "Was I to be your flat?"

"I was thinking of it," Ned told him honestly.

The doctor chortled and twirled the cane. "Hear that, Lemuel? This shepherd thought us worth the setting."

Lemuel struggled to his feet.

"I say, sir, you can tip a man off with a single blow," the doctor told Ned admiringly.

"Oh, he can, he can," agreed Lemuel. "I have knowledge of it."

"Shut your mouth, you simpleton. You've undone me." Then the doctor turned back to Ned. "You have no movables?"

"None but a book."

A group of ragged children whistled by, staring with mild curiosity at the trio, one of whom had blood streaming down his face.

Pursing his lips judiciously, the doctor said, "Then come along with us, sir. Our lodging's nearby. We've got a dram there."

"So you can brain me at leisure?"

"None can brain *you*, sir, with impunity. Least of all this carrot-topped long-legged skinny shit of a Lemuel," he said, glaring at the boy. "And why for would we brain you? There's little profit in braining someone as out of luck as ourselves. Look at your hand. It's hurt again."

There was blood seeping through the bandage.

"Come along. I'll minister to the wound. For the truth is I do know something of remedies." Taking a hopeful step toward the lane, Doctor Bostock looked back and gestured at Ned. "Come along. We have business together."

"What business?"

"Isn't it true we three need movables — extra trousers, boots, maybe a snuffbox? You have got a book, I a cane, and this moron here has nothing. As the French say, there's good in something bad. Though this night went bad, it may prove lucky for us all. So to my lodging." With his cane he jabbed Lemuel in the ribs. "Come, you turdish blockhead." With a bright smile he turned to Ned. "Come, sir, there's fortune in our meeting."

[15]

So NED ACCOMPANIED THEM to a shanty in Bishopsgate and before finishing a second bumper of gin had agreed, as the doctor grandly put it, "to join his destiny with theirs." That night and succeeding nights he slept on the bare floor alongside Lemuel, while the doctor lay on a filthy cot above them. In a short time Ned developed a vast admiration for the doctor. For one thing, the doctor took a single look at the damaged book and pronounced it without hesitation to be *Joseph Andrews,* authored by a man named Fielding, whose tampering with the law had already sent a number of jolly fellows to Newgate Prison. The good doctor had been by his own account an army surgeon against France in the Netherlands; he could spout words of French and Dutch. He knew wine, he knew strong spirits. He knew the worth of linen at a glance. He was a philosopher by his own confession. Had fate given him the chance, he could have stood for Parliament. He might have been a poetaster the likes of Mister Alexander Pope (a gentleman unknown to Ned) with whom for many years by his own admission he had corresponded on technical matters of poesy. His knowledge of the London underworld was so great that Ned wondered how the man had ever found time for all those other things.

Doused with gin each night, Doctor Bostock sat cross-legged on his cot and regaled his two companions with tales of the past when criminals had been popular heroes. He claimed to have known the fabulous Jonathan Wild, who once organized hundreds of thieves into a veritable army and rented Southwark warehouses for storing their stolen goods. Wild's teams of craftsmen had altered jewelry before smuggling it from the country in his own ships. Doctor Bostock had been a surgeon on one of those ships. Once he'd saved

Wild from dying of fever. "Jonathan was as brave a fellow as ever cracked biscuit. His health!" And drank to the memory.

One night when Bostock had fallen into a drunken slumber, Lemuel confided, "He's an old lappy with the bottle, but his heart's of gold." Covering him with a blanket, Lemuel beamed down like a doting son. Lemuel had been apprenticed at six years of age to a Spitalfields silk weaver. He threw the shuttle seven days a week for a bowl of gruel and a bed of straw in the attic. Never taught the finer points of weaving, Lemuel was kept at menial shuttling fourteen hours a day. Out of spite his master didn't feed him on days the prices dropped. Lemuel had the physique to show for years of poor food and foul air: narrow chest, bowed legs, rounded back. He worshiped the doctor for having taken him out of Spitalfields and for apprenticing him to crime. No matter how cruelly the old man treated him, Lemuel seemed happy. Each morning Bostock would scream at him, "Fucking radish! Get me water to cool my cheeks! Out! Go! Or I'll make you smart!" To which Lemuel would grin and go do the doctor's bidding.

Most days Bostock sat on the cot and filled the room with clouds of pipe smoke. It was then he started to teach Ned "the ways of the world," as he put it, which meant the ways of the underworld.

"You'll not be a prig till you learn the flash words of the trade," he told Ned. "Fail to know them in these streets, you're fair game, as fellows will set on you for a country oaf."

So Ned listened keenly.

"To be hobbled" was to be arrested. "To mill a kin" was to break into a house with a crowbar — something the doctor maintained they themselves would never do. "Starring the glaze" meant to cut through a shop window with a glazier's diamond. When describing thievery on the road, Doctor Bostock waxed eloquent, because to his way of thinking this was the glory of the trade. "The drag lay" was theft of bales and trunks from wagons, the which accomplished by giving the waggoner some laudanum in a tankard of ale at a wayside inn and then slipping his goods into a cart when he fell asleep some miles down the road. "Touching the rattler" proved a most daring enterprise, for the thief must run from a hiding place into the road and with his knife on a long pole cut loose a portmanteau from the rear of a moving chaise.

"I knew a rogue," the doctor reminisced, "could touch the rattler as well as any scamp alive. Handled the pole like a surgeon's needle. I cured the bugger thrice of claps, but he was took off last year with a musket ball in his throat."

Lemuel hoped some day to become adept at picking pockets, but his mentor scoffed contemptuously. "You could never do it, simpleton. But you," the doctor told Ned, "might have done had you started young and kept the use of both hands." There was a training school in Smart's Key where boys learned to remove coins from a pocket without ringing a hawk's bell tied to the coat. After three hard years of training, a boy might become a true foist. Did he specialize in cutting pouches loose with a knife, he'd be a nip. An agile lad could hoard up gold enough in four, five years to buy a chandling shop, maybe an inn. "For the kingly art of foist, none of us three are prepared," the doctor noted sadly. "Had I put in my time learning such matters rather than serving mankind for farthings, we should have a gang of foists and nips such as would shake the world. But I'm glad," he said, patting Ned's knee, "you made one with us. I warrant the world shall take notice before we're done. So it's time for a lay," he announced and explained to Ned that a lay was what they'd tried on him.

"I won't carry knife or sword," Ned declared. He had thought this through already.

"Odd's fucking heart, I want no killing. Not me. That's for cutthroats." Bostock drew himself up. "I'm no bully, I'm none of your egregious coxcombs. I'm a surgeon of distinction thrown on evil times. To be short, we can do business more cunningly than that. With you, dear Ned, we missed at the lay. I frankly confess it, though it was the first time we ever did miss." He glared at Lemuel to forestall a contradiction. "Tomorrow, Ned, we do our first work together. One caution. Never run at the first blush of trouble. Stand your ground. Cheats are a good sort with their own chums. They're brave together."

"I won't run," Ned promised, though he knew that the good doctor was capable of it. And yet an image of the little fat man scampering away through the fog, coattails flying, did not diminish the Warsop shepherd's admiration for such cunning and accomplishment.

*

At twilight the doctor selected a man whose appearance marked him for a country flat, most likely in London on business.

"I fancy a merchant worth setting on," Bostock whispered to his companions. Then, flourishing his cane, he approached the man boldly, just as a fortnight ago he had done with Ned. Off went the man with the good doctor for a drink together, then for a stroll into Bishopsgate, bound for a chop house which didn't exist, and in an alley much like the one in which Ned had been ambushed, the two confederates leapt from the shadows.

While Ned tied the man's wrists with hemp and Lemuel stuffed a kerchief in his mouth, Bostock rifled through his pockets. It took but a minute, yet afterwards the doctor, in reviewing their performance, was displeased. There had been too much activity, too much busy holding and tying, all of which might have attracted attention and resulted in the dread cry of "Thief!" Constables might have come running, though that was unlikely, but quite possibly the commotion might have roused the neighborhood — tradesmen with knives — or even worse, the local footpads who guarded their own territory jealously.

When they sat down to count their shares of the loot, however, the doctor's gloom vanished. "He was a gager, a sly fucker, that merchant!" he exclaimed. "He'd let me, a generous stranger, buy him a kingly meal when he had on him fifteen guineas! The miserly bitch!" He gave Lemuel two guineas, Ned three, and kept the rest himself, for "I be the wit here, the brain of it."

Quaffing off a dram, he hissed theatrically between his teeth. "The world shall know of us. Now listen. I've a good stomach for another kind of lay." He studied his companions before continuing. "Ned, can you swim?"

"I can."

The doctor frowned at Lemuel. "I warrant you can't."

The boy nodded sheepishly.

"No matter. It's in truth better if you can't." He paused thoughtfully. "More tragical. Be easy on it, boy. Ned here will save you."

"What's this lay to be?" asked Ned.

"The queer plunge."

*

Next morning Doctor Bostock shaved with cold water and a dull knife, wincing at each stroke, his skin reddening as though rouged. Unfolding a white neckcloth saved for special occasions, he studied the neat linen before putting it on. This bit of finery was followed by black silk stockings, buckled shoes, buff-colored knee breeches, and a silk waistcoat ornamented with brass. Then with the fastidious care of a French hairdresser, he drew a brown wig over his head; it was parted in the center, full at the sides, ending at collar level in back; as he himself observed, "a wig in full fashion."

Ned was so impressed by this transformation of Doctor Bostock into a portly gentleman of consequence that he didn't wonder out loud at the earlier claim of the man having no movables anymore. In fact, the doctor filled an old portmanteau with what else he had. "An old habit," he explained. "When I put on good lurries, I pack the old lurries and take them along, for who can know what fate has in store out there? I'll have my things along. You have your book?"

"I have," said Ned.

"Of course, the skinny moron has nothing to his name but what you see him in."

The trio crossed the Thames to Vauxhall and strolled along a pier where boats were debarking passengers for the pleasure garden. Near the end of the jetty, without warning, the doctor bumped Lemuel into the river, although the lad had been promised a decent warning to prepare his nerves for it. The abruptness of his drop and the immediate danger of his situation had Lemuel instantly in a real panic. He flailed and gasped, his red head bobbing in the icy water, his pale face rigid in fear.

Ned removed his coat and was preparing to leap in after the boy when Bostock growled, "Not yet, you fool!" He turned to regard passengers farther along the jetty, nearer the shore. "Help! Help!" the doctor yelled. When a group of people turned and started for them, he ordered Ned to jump.

Ned did, and succeeded in hauling half-drowned Lemuel to a piling, where some boatmen helped them out. They sat shivering on the wharf with bystanders gathered curiously around them.

The good doctor, glancing around, began to harangue the crowd. "Look at this brave fellow. One sound hand. Yet he risked his life to save another." With a sweeping gesture he pressed a guinea into Ned's hand. "Well done. Brave fellow." Looking around he added, "The least we can do. As I am a Christian I have never seen braver." He glared at the onlookers, singling out a half-dozen fashionable couples who were obviously bound for the pleasures at Vauxhall.

Blushing under his accusatory look, a woman whispered to her escort, who, with a shrug, took a guinea from his coat and tossed it at Ned's feet. Other money followed.

Solicitously the doctor bent down to Lemuel. "How was it, boy, you fell into the water?"

"I didn't fall, sir, I jumped."

A murmur swept the crowd.

"Jumped!" cried the doctor.

Lemuel glanced around sadly. "My mother has the fever, my sister too, and I lost my place at the mill and I can't pay for medicines. I can't go on."

"Odd's heart," murmured the doctor, "he wanted to die."

Lemuel began sniveling and blubbering. His brick-red hair was plastered to a wet and ghostly face.

"Poor fellow, poor, poor fellow." The doctor placed a coin in the boy's hand. "The least I can do as a Christian." He glowered at the bystanders. "His family has come on such evil times that the boy can no longer endure it. He'd take his life to the everlasting damnation of his soul!" Women came forward, opening their beaded purses shyly, and after some coaxing, so did their male companions. Coins piled up in front of the sobbing lad. Removing his own coat in the chill wind, Doctor Bostock placed it gently over Lemuel's shoulders. To show equal concern for the shivering hero, he asked a bearded waterman nearby for a boat blanket.

The crowd began dispersing, and when they had all returned to shore, Bostock took his coat back from Lemuel. "The waterman is peery," he warned his shivering companions.

Sure enough, when the waterman returned with an oilskin and tossed it at Ned, he smirked and said, "You fucking scamps."

"This is an oilskin you brought, not a blanket. It's not wanted," said the doctor loftily.

"I saw you push the lad in. Give me a guinea or I'll set up a cry and have you took."

"Very well, it's done," muttered Bostock. "Will you row us back to London?"

"For six shilling more."

"Done."

Halfway across the Thames the good doctor began to count the haul. He cackled triumphantly. "Now that, lads, was how to work the queer plunge. I'm heartily pleased with you both. Even with you, Lemuel. If there is one thing you can do it is weep."

Sharing the oilskin, his confederates shook in the brisk river wind. The doctor pointed at Ned's bandage. "We'll have you a proper famstring for the hand. In this kid it received due sympathy, but you can't be known by it. A bad hand, a gimp leg, a milky eye can distinguish you and lead straight to Newgate. We'll see to it."

On their return to London they went directly to a Holborn haberdasher. Bostock removed the cloth and studied Ned's hand. Scar tissue had so disfigured each finger that the hand looked, in the doctor's words, "like the webbed foot of a beast." When the haberdasher hissed in disgust, the doctor rapped his cane on the counter and explained with righteous annoyance that his brave companion had burned this hand while rescuing a lady of fashion from a Cornmarket millinery fire and for his selfless heroism had received one hundred pounds from her grateful ladyship, a tiny portion of which would now be used to cover these heroic fingers.

The doctor selected a calfskin glove of normal size for Ned's good hand and another large enough to encompass the thick misshapen fingers of the other. After Ned had managed to draw the glove on, Bostock nodded approvingly. "That famstring has made a gentleman of you. So let's to pleasure."

He commandeered a hackney for hire and they set out for Covent Garden. Leaning forward, he touched Ned's arm. "You're one of us now. A true prig. And you'll share in our pleasures."

"I'm cold," muttered Lemuel, huddled against the corner of the coach.

"Hold your tongue. Never a day goes by but I regret the taking of you from the weaver. You're good for nothing but crying."

"But you said, sir, I wept good today."

The doctor patted the boy's knee. "And so you did. As for being cold, you'll soon be warm, believe me."

Ned was surprised by the familiarity with which the bawdy-house mother greeted the doctor. Pushing the mob cap back on her squarish head, she roared with good cheer as they trooped into the parlour. "I have got such pleasing new goods! All roses and lilies. None of the rotten regiment you get elsewhere."

Bostock pinched her flabby cheek. "I'd rather frisk with you could I trust you not to have distemper. Bring wine and wenches quick. Fetch and squire them hither, good woman, at a rush!" Sitting down at a table, he motioned for his companions to do likewise.

In the lambent candlelight Ned could see men seated with girls in homespun gowns and muslin caps. The young women looked demure but for the low-cut bodices that exposed their nipples. One couple was playing a drinking game.

"Do you like the fair sex, Ned?" asked the doctor.

"I do."

"You country fellows start young, don't you?"

"We do."

In came a half-dozen girls led by the mother.

"Here come the flirts!" cried the doctor.

"Here they are, you old rogue." The mother pushed girls forward, one after another, like chess pieces. "Every one uncommon fair."

Winking at Ned, the doctor said, "You first, lad. Go to it."

All six girls smiled, but one caught Ned's eye: a young brunette with the ample figure and rosy cheeks of a country lass.

"La, child," brayed the doctor, "my spark here has blessed you with such a liquorish look I'd hate to be you in the morning! Come, come here." He motioned for the girl to sit beside Ned. "What? Is it you, beauty? Don't I know you?" He was squinting at a short, plump girl. "Come here, you comely piece."

She stepped up, hands on hips.

Reaching out, he patted her breasts lightly. "Pit-a-pat boobies! Sweety-sweet boobies! Must be touched by none but old dad." Bending down, he stroked one of her shoes. "And these peep-a-peep footies be my goods and chattels. Bless me, I like a girl's foot.

Ho! And what's here?" He thrust his hand roughly up her petti-coats, making the girl squeal. "Give old dad a cuddle," he muttered and drew her down on his lap.

Lemuel chose a girl as skinny as himself, long-jawed and pale. A black boy came along with a trayful of glasses and a jug of wine.

After a sip of wine, Ned turned to his girl and tried to slip his hand into her bodice, but she grabbed his wrist.

"You get none of me," she declared coolly, "till you pay up and we go to my room. I care not for public mauling."

Hearing this, the doctor slapped the table gleefully. "She has country notions of bashfulness. To her, Ned. Roger her! Make her blush!"

Instead, it was Ned who blushed and, in deference to the girl, poured her another glass of wine.

"Good lad," she murmured. "I'm glad it's you of the three."

New patrons and girls were coming into the parlour, causing a general hubbub. The mother of the house admonished a client for tripping the black boy and breaking glasses. Soon drunk, the good doctor became so quarrelsome and boisterous that his wench slapped him and huffed off.

"A surly bitch," he grumbled. "Old mattress-back, old night-bag." He watched her climbing the stairway. "I'm no gull to scoun-drels. My cock's as good as any man's alive."

Beaming, the mother approached. "You're too much for that sorry jade," she told the doctor, mollifying him. "What you need is a lusty, surly, big-assed bitch."

"Like you," cried the doctor, reaching out.

She backed skillfully away, wagging her finger.

Ned's girl took his gloved hand suddenly and draped it over her shoulder. "Do you wear famstrings in bed?"

"He does," the doctor answered for him.

"You scamps," the girl said, laughing. "You all belong in Bed-lam."

"Bedlam, is it? Well, *there's* one who belongs in Newgate with the hangman in sight!" The doctor spoke while rising to stare at a man who had just arrived. Turning to Ned and scowling, he said, "Is there no end to human perfidy? What's just come in is a shitty sneaking dog!"

The man who had taken a far table was beetle-browed and mas-

sive. He had a droopy mouth. A white plume stuck gallantly from a
tricorn on his shaggy head — the hat of a former generation.

The doctor gripped Ned's arm. "That's a damnable cheat, lad.
He can shift a card with such address there's no chance of discovering it." Hardly had the doctor noted this with a mixture of admiration and hatred in his voice than the man rose from the table and
started over.

"Old pussy face! Old muttonhead!" the man whooped, smiling.

Bostock squinted at him coldly. "Do you treat for friendship, we
are pleased. Or answer to my chums."

With an elegant gesture the man swept off his plumed tricorn and
sat down.

A girl arrived for him and a bouncing new miss for Doctor
Bostock. The black boy came with more wine. In a short time
Bostock had one arm around the girl and the other around the
"damnable cheat."

He bellowed at Lemuel and Ned. "This be William Summers,
the staunchest fellow in the kingdom!" He squeezed the big man
affectionately. "Deny it and deal with me!"

"So our differences be forgot?" asked Summers.

"Forgot now, chum."

"Be you still a three-bottle man?"

"Four in my old age. How's Kate?"

"Last time I saw Kate her belly was up to her chin."

"What, Kate? Not careful Kate!"

"She's been taking Tinkly Mirth and a mort of doctor stuff for
the dropsy because that's what she calls it. Dropsy," Summers
guffawed. "The midwife must tap her is all. But she won't think of
it. She can't believe it at her age. Old as a camel and with her guts
out to here!"

"The midwife for Kate," said the doctor, shaking his head at the
wonder of it.

They laughed uproariously and called for more wine.

Looking around, Ned realized that Lemuel had gone with the
pale skinny girl.

"Let's to your room," Ned whispered to his own girl.

Minutes later, having settled his account with the mother, Ned
followed the strapping country lass up a flight of stairs to a tiny
room stinking of onions, and by the dim light of a nubbin candle

undressed himself and lay down to watch her do the same. The girl seemed to flow out of the petticoats. They were soon together, a quick flailing, a rhythmic slapping of belly to belly, that left them exhausted. He lay there thinking of Priscilla, who must be lying tonight beside the dull man of consequence she had chosen over him. She had not chosen a husband for love, that was sure, as the shepherd of Warsop remembered their loving, the long slow building of passion between them, no harsh flailing like tonight, but her breath coming soft and then quickening against his ear and their mutual soaring into the great moments.

Ned watched sleepily as the country lass left the room to douche herself, with a petticoat wrapped around her naked waist. The last thing he saw until morning was the heavy sway of her moonlit hips.

When he awoke, she was gone, the sun high and the heaped coverlet awash in light. When he swung his legs off the bed, his head throbbed. Going downstairs he called for the mother and asked if his chums were still asleep.

"Asleep, child?" She thumped her hands against her hips. "Why, they left long ago in the company of William Summers."

"Did they leave word where I should meet them?"

"I heard them speak of Bath."

"Bath? No. They wouldn't go out of London without telling me."

"Did the doctor owe you cole?"

Ned recalled that they hadn't yet divided the loot from the queer plunge. His expression of dismay must have so informed the woman, because she made to shoo him out of the house, as if he were a wayward chick. "Go to, boy, you're best rid of that crew. About ship and good riddance," she told him, cackling. "You've been fobbed."

[16]

℘ Yesterday Ralph Allen came up from Prior Park and supped
with me and Lyttelton at a chop house I know. I know it so well,
in truth, that a serving man there raised his voice in a rousing song
from my *Grub Street Opera*, censored out of public existence these
many years because of sport I made of Minister Walpole.

> "Oh, the roast beef of England,
> And old England's roast beef!"

Over a tasty ragoo, we were put in a good mood by his lusty
chorus.

We talked then at length of crime, using as text my *Enquiring
into the Causes of the late Increase of Robbers,* published as a tract
two years ago. I still argue as I did then, that the principal cause of
crime was general luxury and the improper regulation of the poor.
Luxury encourages people to seek what they have not. The
nobleman wants what the prince has, the gentleman wants what
the nobleman has, and so on until the very lowest of people wish to
ape anyone above them and in order to get funds enough for such
disguise they often go to crime. I strongly insist now, as I did then,
on the importance of prevention of crime by means of investigation
and a study of its main causes.

Ralph Allen, of a gentle but cunning heart, was still not pleased
with my idea of restricting through licenses the amusements of the
vulgar — among them drink, gambling, routs, and drums — as a
way of suppressing crime. He argued that human nature being
what it is, there's always a way of circumventing law. I could not
in all honesty disagree. Yet I was proud of the new Gin Act, which
my *Enquiry* had influenced. It more than doubled the tax on gin
houses and gave judges extended power in dealing with certain
grog-shop owners, who poisoned their spirits knowingly.

After more conversation on less troublesome subjects, I said to
my companions, flourishing the last of a sweet wine, "As Horace

tells us, 'You have played enough, you have eaten and drunk enough, it is time for you to quit the feast.' "

So ended a good evening with friends.

Reader, you may be pleased to know that this morning I received word from his grace the duke of Newcastle: funds have been released for my Bow Street Police — enough to keep three horses saddled in the stable and to provide a modest emolument for my picked men. They are thus salaried, and as such achieve the recognition of justices and members of Parliament, for they will now be paid by their country for what they contribute to the general good. There is money enough to disburse small sums to persons bringing information, carrying messages, watching suspects, and otherwise rendering service to the pursuit of justice. I shall hire a clerk whose duty will be to maintain a precise record of crimes committed throughout London, with the nature of the offense, the time, location, and other details supplied locally. There is not money to maintain a judge both day and night at Bow Street, but in spite of my infirmities I shall increase my own time on duty as a grateful acknowledgement of the government's aid.

But my moment of victory was not long to be savored, for there was work to be done. A law clerk entered my study to announce that two companies of people were downstairs awaiting my pleasure: one group led by Counselor Salt and the other consisting of a bailiff and two women.

Having already accepted Salt's fee for giving an opinion on the Canning case, I was somewhat reluctant to act also in the capacity of magistrate. It was indeed irregular to act as both consulting attorney and examining judge on the same case. Yet not even in matters of law must I forgo my deepest intuitions, as what is law save the judgement of men exercising good will? And Salt, who had seen me yesterday, argued convincingly for a London-based judge to hear the girl swear an information before him and to examine others suspected of involvement in the crime. Otherwise, so Salt warned, a proper trial might not be forthcoming and justice remain unserved.

So I had agreed. Getting my crutch, I went down.

When Salt produced the girl for Magistrate Fielding's perusal, her manner and appearance seemed to support her claims. Fielding was

impressed by her calm explanations. But what spoke most eloquently in her behalf was the girl's humble demeanor. His own
Salisbury childhood had been filled by plain wholesome young
women much like Elizabeth Canning. It was not in him to believe
that such an artless little creature, not more than eighteen, could lay
a heavy charge on the innocent. What possible motive could she
have for condemning a woman who had never harmed her? That a
young girl of decent family would deliberately commit such an
atrocious crime went counter to his long experience of felons.

And when Betty sat before him to give her sworn statement,
there were a few breathless moments when she reminded him of
his Charlotte. The girl had the same pale almost translucent skin,
bespeaking a frail constitution, a delicate inner life. And the large
eyes, if lacking Charlotte's warmth, were the same limpid shade of
brown and they met his own without guile. Indeed, the girl possessed the vulnerability of a beleaguered heroine. At the end of this
interview Fielding patted her hand, just as he used to do when
Charlotte came to him in tears with a domestic worry.

He decided forthwith that the girl's charge against the gypsy
woman was valid.

Setting upon his head the full-bottomed wig of his office, he
ordered the other party to be brought in, but before this could be
done, Counselor Salt requested that others of the Canning party be
permitted to be present. With Fielding's consent the rugged tradesman Lyon and the paunchy old gentleman Wintlebury came in. So
too came in a tall man with a dark face. Fielding was startled — the
dust of a lifetime seemed to have stained every pore of the fellow's
skin.

Counselor Salt introduced Robert Scarrat as a former constable
and a loyal advocate of the poor girl.

Fielding studied the grey face a moment longer, before turning
his attention back to Salt. "Has Elizabeth Canning had any communication with Virtue Hall since the gypsy was taken into custody?"

"She has not, your worship."

"I ask," said Fielding, "to dispel any suspicion of the girls having
laid up a story together."

"You doubt our Betty?" cried Wintlebury.

"It's in her behalf," Fielding explained, "that I ask. Mister Salt,

did the girls overhear each other's account before Justice Tyschemaker?"

"They did not. They was brought before him separately."

"Then that is good."

A bailiff entered with Virtue Hall, who came in warily, her lips
trembling and agitating the long scar from cheek to mouth. She
stroked her yellow hair while the clerk swore her to her oath.
Mumbling "I swear," she dropped her listless hand and the clerk
sat her directly in front of Justice Fielding.

"Child," Fielding began gently, "you need not be under fear and
apprehension. If you but tell the truth, I give my word as far as it is
in my power to protect you, you shall not come to harm for what
others did." He watched her pluck at the strings of her dirty bodice.
"Do you know Elizabeth Canning?"

"By sight I know her."

"Had you seen her prior to the day she came with men to take the
gypsy up?"

She plucked at the strings, looking down.

"Be a good girl. Tell me plainly."

"I —" Virtue tossed her head. "I can't remember when I saw the
chit."

"Is my question unclear?" He watched her continue to pluck
sullenly at the strings, but increasingly she glanced to the side in
the direction of the former constable, the dark man named Scarrat.
"Come, had you seen her before the gypsy was taken up?"

"I —" She struggled for words, like a child reluctant to recite. "I
saw her before then."

"Tell me when and under what circumstances."

"I can't say when, for I don't know what the month was." The
scar twitched. "I can't keep dates."

"Well, at least tell me under what circumstances."

"Her stays was took." Now she turned and looked directly at the
dark-faced man, so that once again Fielding studied him.

"Who took them?" Fielding asked.

"Women of the house." She added quickly, "But not me. I took
nothing of the chit."

"By women of the house, whom do you mean?"

"Squires, the gypsy."

"So you mean Squires took the stays from Elizabeth Canning?"

"I warrant I might. Perhaps I do." The scar moved violently.

"Perhaps?" Fielding clamped a large hand against his prominent chin. "What is perhaps in this instance?"

Scarrat moved forward and bowed deeply. "Your worship, the girl is frighted."

"Have I asked for your opinion?"

"Forgive me, your worship."

Fielding dropped his hand and glowered at the assembly. "If the girl cannot or will not answer truthfully, I'll examine her no longer." He turned to Counselor Salt. "I advise you to prosecute this woman as a felon, for she's guilty of prevarication before this court in a matter of deepest importance. This Virtue Hall says that *perhaps* she was witness to the stays being taken. Either she does or doesn't know the women of the house and does or doesn't know if she watched one of them take the stays."

Virtue began sobbing and rocking. "I be sorely frighted, your excellence."

"Of what? Of whom?"

"I warrant of the gypsy," Scarrat volunteered.

"Sir, if you speak again I will hold you in contempt," warned Justice Fielding and turned to the girl, whom he addressed gently. "Child, calm yourself. I have given you my word. No harm will come to you if you say calmly and plainly what happened. Let me ask once again. What did the gypsy do?"

"She did it, your excellence."

"With force?"

"Ripped them off, she did."

"Are you claiming you saw Mary Squires forcibly remove the stays of Elizabeth Canning on the evening of New Year?"

"I was, I did, I swear."

"Take this witness to the next-door chambers," Justice Fielding told the counselor. "Put her information in writing." He instructed the others to accompany Salt as witnesses. Everyone trooped from the room, leaving him alone with stomach cramp and headache. Rapping his crutch against the desk, he ordered a clerk to get him a glass of port. When it came, Fielding drank it down. Enheartened by the port, he leaned back and for some idle moments dreamed of leading raids against the wicked of London, bursting into their bolt-holes, rousting them out in the company of Saunders Welch and the other Bow Street Runners.

Then he saw other cases, among them an action of trover between two tradesmen which featured the possession of a bundle of Spanish fans, some tortoise shell combs, and Sheffield-plated buttons. It so transpired that none of these goods belonged to either man but by contract to a tall, smartly dressed woman who had bilked them quite legally. Their lust for her had brought them both down in secret, which she laughingly revealed to them only this day.

Then the Canning group returned. Virtue Hall seemed less fearful, and Counselor Salt fairly glowed in triumph.

Fielding read the statement obtained from her. She identified the two women and added a vital bit of information about the Natus couple, who she claimed had moved into the loft *after* the escape of Elizabeth Canning, and not the month prior to these events, as Judith Natus had stated before Justice Tyschemaker in Edmonton. In addition, the Wells woman had repaired the window, "so that the said window-place might not appear to have been broke open." The statement of Virtue Hall concluded:

> This informant saith, that she, this informant, hath lived with the said Susannah Wells about a quarter of a year last past, and well knows that the said Susannah Wells, during that time, hath kept a very notorious house; and that the said Susannah Wells was privy to the confinement of the said Elizabeth Canning.

Fielding had the girl make her mark, then affixed his own signature to the statement. He turned to Salt. "This last information will have the Wells woman as an accessory after the fact of capitol felony. As for the rest, it accords properly with Elizabeth's tale. I can't pretend to infallibility, but this testament seems irrefutable. This is your case, sir. Now child" — he turned to Virtue Hall — "have no fear of either Wells or the gypsy Squires. I give my word on that account. Do you see how truth is served? It does no harm to say true. Indeed, it has done you good. Now bring in the Natus person."

In came Judith Natus in a filthy smock and decrepit boots. Her vacuous face was wreathed by lank grey hair. When she was sworn — the clerk had to lift her hand — Fielding said calmly, "Woman, are you drunk?"

"No, milord. Not since yesterday."

"Sit down, then. Are you a friend of Mary Squires?"

The woman stared as if unable to comprehend the question. Then finally she spoke. "Me and Fortune, we slept in the loft this month and saw nothing of Egyptians till some days ago."

"When did you see Elizabeth Canning?"

"Milord?"

"The young woman who came with the men," he explained carefully, "who took the gypsy up."

"I never did see such a miss."

"You did not see her when she came with men who took the gypsy up?"

"I saw her then."

"And you spent the month of January in the hayloft where she claims she was held prisoner?"

"Me and Fortune slept there this month and saw nothing of Egyptians till some days ago."

"May I, your worship?" Salt stepped up.

"Proceed, counselor."

"Virtue Hall has affirmed this woman and her husband were introduced into the loft after Elizabeth had escaped from it. It was to give colour to the Wells defense."

Fielding turned to the woman. "What say you to that, Judith Natus?"

"Me and Fortune, we slept —"

Salt interrupted angrily. "Your worship!"

"Counselor?"

"I'm desirous of having this person committed for prejury, as we know she was introduced into the loft to lie there after my client had escaped."

The dry little man reminded Fielding of a sparrow hawk ready to pounce on a chicken. "That would be contrary to law," Fielding observed coolly. "For I might as well commit Virtue Hall or Elizabeth Canning, for that matter, upon the evidence of Judith Natus. Listen to me, Judith Natus," he said to the woman. "I confess I think you guilty of perjury, though unaware of its consequences, so

I give you caution, if you intend to speak thus at Old Bailey during trial. Be sure of what you vow."

"Fortune and me slept this month in the loft."

"You must mean last month, I assume. This is now February. You have the times mixed."

"We saw nothing of Egyptians till some days ago."

"Understand me, woman. If you testify, be sure of yourself." Her stubborn calm unnerved Fielding. "You are discharged," he said in weary frustration and ordered the bailiff to remove her.

"Your worship, may I request to speak?"

It was the dark-faced man. Fielding gave him permission.

"It's well known in Enfield and thereabout, your worship, that the woman be a foul whore and was whipped through Cheshunt for theft. Her husband left one of their children exposed on a tombstone in Ware churchyard and it died, and once he tried to hang himself when drunk and his whereabouts is now unknown."

"I beg your pardon, sir. Your name again?"

"Scarrat, your worship."

Courts of law, thought Fielding, harboured many such faces: the hound jaw, the bloodless lips, the unearthly eyes. Unhampered by crippling vanity, they lived without illusions. For a moment Fielding let his mind wander toward the edge of a new fiction, with this fellow a personage in it, quite unlike any story or character he'd yet imagined. All his life he had poked fun at the vain and the hypocritical: those who took pride in their virtues but without an understanding of their vices, and those who practised vices while pretending to virtues. But he'd not really seen into the dark corners of human life. This man Scarrat had. Fielding felt a kind of grudging admiration for him.

The urge to create nearly hypnotized Judge Fielding till he shook it off fiercely. "Mister Scarrat," he said, "I'll be plain with you. You've related this village gossip about the woman for a purpose, I warrant. Do you fear I might believe the sorry woman instead of the injured girl?"

"Your worship, I spoke only what I know."

"Be assured I need no hearsay to make up my mind. Facts here are plain." He turned to Counselor Salt. "Virtue Hall corroborated the story told by Elizabeth Canning. As far as I can judge at this juncture, it's the sum and substance of the case." He picked up his gavel and rapped. "I confirm the detention of Squires and Wells and shall make sure to have them bound over in Newgate Prison for trial in the immediate session — Squires for capital felony and Wells as accessory after the fact. Please clear the court."

Later that day Justice Fielding jotted down words concerning the Canning affair that would in future be expanded into an essay: "I am firmly persuaded that Elizabeth Canning is a poor, honest, innocent, simple girl, and the most unhappy and most injured of all human beings."

At that instant he beheld his hapless Charlotte gasping for breath in the final hour of agony. He dropped the quill. He was still in the grip of the terrible vision when Madam Fielding came into the chamber. He tried to smile.

Mary's broad face was framed in a bonnet too lacy for features which seemed to emerge rough hewn from a block of wood. Bending down, she kissed his forehead tenderly but admonished him for forgetting to take his new drop. A Doctor Simpson had come yesterday with the theory that his chief problem was dropsy, which could be remedied with Simpson's Drop for Dropsy. Good-naturedly Fielding obeyed Mary, though in his mind were lines from *Tom Jones,* "There is, perhaps, no surer mark of folly than the attempt to correct the natural infirmities of those we love," which led him to other lines from that selfsame book: "Every physician hath his favourite disease, to which he ascribes all the victories obtained over human nature."

He inquired after baby Louisa.

"Still with crouping cough, but she'll mend." Mary stooped to pick up his crutch. "Now to porridge."

"What you call porridge is not porridge," he grumbled. "It's a cawdle fit for invalids and women in childbed, a paltry gruel I won't eat."

"First the porridge," Mary told him quietly, placing the crutch under his armpit. "Then you must see the children."

With a sigh, as he hobbled from the room, Fielding muttered, "Yes, the children. With all my heart."

[17]

THE TRIAL OF MARY SQUIRES and Susannah Wells, widows, for assault and felony, took place at the Sessions House in the Old Bailey before the Right Honourable Sir Crisp Gascoyne, lord mayor of the City of London, on February 21 and continued until February 26, 1753, in the twenty-sixth year of the reign of King George II.

The first witness, Elizabeth Canning, was examined and cross-examined at length.

Spectators in the gallery, among them gentlemen of the press, were struck favourably by her lucid account of the kidnapping, assault, and imprisonment. Wearing a blue bonnet, she gave evidence in a low but unfaltering voice.

After the girl left the bar, Mary Squires rose to ask a question of the court. "Tell me again what day was it the young woman was robbed?"

The recorder replied, "Elizabeth Canning says on the morning of second January."

Squires: "I return thanks. I be innocent as the child unborn, and you all of you shall know it."

The lord mayor silenced her.

Virtue Hall was then sworn and behaved with striking composure, claiming the gypsy Squires had torn off the stays and imprisoned the girl and the landlady Wells had cooperated in the latter action.

The prosecution: "What was you in that house?"

Virtue Hall: "I went as a lodger, but was forced to do as people there would have me."

The prosecution: "How long had the gypsies resided at the Wells house?"

Virtue Hall: "Six or seven weeks in all. Came about a fortnight before the young miss was brought in and robbed."

There was a murmur in the gallery and someone yelled, "The gypsy done it!" causing an uproar which Sir Crisp Gascoyne had to gavel into submission. Minutes passed before the trial could proceed.

The Canning girl's uncle came next to the bar and testified that Betty had spent New Year's Day at his home in Salt Petre Bank. Thereafter, he and his wife had accompanied their niece to the corner of Houndsditch, almost to the Blue Ball, where they left her to go her way home.

John Wintlebury and Edward Lyon gave detailed accounts of the girl's return and of the raid on Enfield. Their testimony corroborated Canning's story throughout and they both gave her a splendid character.

Gawin Nash and Robert Aldridge, resolute in caution, though called to testify, were nowhere in sight.

The prosecuting officer then called Robert Scarrat. "Have you heard the evidence given by other witnesses?"

Scarrat: "I have and what they said be true enough. I also heard Elizabeth Canning examined before the sitting alderman and before Justice Tyschemaker and she gave the same accounts as here."

Edward Rossiter testified that the girl had given the same accounts there as here.

Sutherton Backler, apothecary, swore to the girl's feeble condition upon her return. There had been no indication of venereal salivation and no pregnancy. Her claim that she hadn't passed a stool in nearly a month was justified, in his opinion, by her low state of health. On the other hand, she could have survived on a quartern of bread and a full jug of water.

The prosecution rested.

The court-appointed attorney for Mary Squires — a young fellow eager to prove himself — had in a pretrial fortnight hustled throughout the Enfield district and beyond, gathering his case. In the gypsy's behalf he called the following witnesses.

John Gibbons, an innkeeper from Abbotsbury, nearly a hundred miles southwest of Enfield, claimed that the gypsy band had come into his house on the New Year, peddling kerchiefs and muslins. On that day his wife had purchased two checked aprons from Mary Squires.

William Clarke, also of Abbotsbury, testified that on the New Year he had seen the gypsies in John Gibbons's inn, when he went there for a pot of liquor. Upon cross-examination he declared, "Was I to die for the sorry woman, I speak the truth!"

At his defiant words in her defense the gallery became unruly again. Hats aimed at the witness careened through the air, and angry curses resulted in yet another warning from the lord mayor.

The final witness for the defense was another innkeeper, Thomas Greville, of the Dorset village of Coombe. He swore that the gypsies remained overnight in his public house on the fourteenth of January.

These three witnesses showed their subpoenas, issued in behalf of Mary Squires, as the cause of their coming to give evidence.

Then a fishmonger from Theobalds, near Enfield, was sworn to testify in the Crown's name. Swarthy and disheveled, John Iniser limped to the bar, casting nervous glances at the assembled court officers, the justices ranged above him, the solemn jurors. He had volunteered his testimony freely. He said, "I know the prisoner Squires by sight. Last time I saw her was several times every day up and down Enfield, ere she was took up."

Court: "Are you certain of that?"

Iniser: "I am. I saw her a month ere she was took up. She walked into houses pretending to tell fortunes. I come forward to swear it in God's name."

Susannah Wells used no legal counsel in her defense, but stood in the dock and stated, "As to my character, I confess it's indifferent. I once had a poor husband who was hanged. But I never saw the little miss." She pointed a trembling finger at Elizabeth Canning. "Never, not once, till they took me up. As for the Egyptian, I never saw that one at my house till maybe three, four days before I was took up."

The jury filed out. Within minutes they returned with the verdict, finding both women guilty as charged.

When the lord mayor asked Mary Squires what she had to say before sentencing, the huge gypsy struggled to her feet and declared in a ringing voice, "On New Year and following days I lay at Coombe at the widow Greville's house!"

There was abrupt silence, while the audience considered her statement, after which another roar went up from the gallery, for the gypsy had just contradicted the testimony of her own witnesses, who claimed she had lodged in Abbotsbury on the New Year and at a public house in Coombe on the fourteenth. She could not, therefore, have been at the widow Greville's on the New Year or in mid-January.

"Proof of guilt! Proof of guilt! Proof of guilt!"

During the clamour, which threatened to grow worse, the justices leaned together at their curved bench to whisper tensely until Sir Crisp Gascoyne returned to the chair of the chief justice and gaveled once again for silence.

"We're prepared to pass sentence without delay," he announced.

Only after repeated cries from court bailiffs of "Quiet, the sentence! The sentence!" did the gallery come to order.

A small, wiry man made imposing by the flowing black robe and leonine grey wig, Sir Crisp Gascoyne glared haughtily at the rabble. "Death," he said, "for Mary Squires. Branding for Susannah Wells."

Hats and biscuits sailed through the air. Three cheers for Betty resounded through the Sessions House, followed by three cheers for the jury and three cheers for the lord mayor, who swept out of the courtroom scowling, the other judges at his heels.

The Canning party exited in triumph, as people strained to have a touch of the girl's cloak.

In leg manacles and wrist irons the gypsy was led back to Newgate Prison to await a time of execution, while Susannah Wells remained in the Old Bailey, awaiting her own punishment, which would be carried out forthwith, as soon as the coals were hot enough to heat a branding iron.

On his way from the Sessions House, Scarrat paused at the iron door and whispered to the bailiff there, "Did she come?"

"Yes, the Natus woman came with her subpoena and with her man. I told her, Get your fucking old face out of here, but she was all for staying until her man yanked the subpoena from her hand and tore it up and forced her off."

"Here's this to go with that before." Scarrat pressed a coin on the bailiff.

A good day's work, Scarrat thought. He whistled breathily between his teeth and pushed through the crowd waiting in the yard for the branding to take place. He'd stay for the treat, but his lordship expected news of the outcome.

Now that the excitement was over, Scarrat felt a bit let down. He'd been on his toes this whole past month, ever since the apprentice sawyer had appeared in the Frigate doorway, screaming poor Betty had come home. A whole month at very hard duty. So much might have gone wrong, especially because so much had depended on the behaviour of women.

Look at Virtue Hall.

He'd been thunderstruck by her faltering performance in front of Justice Fielding. She'd nearly failed to support the Canning story, in spite of the consequences if she failed, because at Enfield in her sleazy room he'd given her a goodly taste of his fist and a warning of worse, along with a pouch containing five guineas, which was more than she'd had at one time in her life, more than her lousy body could have earned in weeks with drunken ostlers on one of Susannah Wells's stinking beds. Virtue had nearly ruined everything for no better reason than her hatred and envy of a girl whom she considered as much of a whore as herself. Women.

Look at the Canning widow.

She had nearly offered a different brand of trouble. When Salt had originally come with news that they'd be taken before Justice Fielding, the woman had caused a wonderful stir. "Is Fielding a name I'm acquainted with? A gentleman who writ a book? I read one such of his to my Betty. Though I could not read his Latin and skipped many pages of no consequence, of which to be frank there was many, I did read much of it. It was — not three year ago. It was called . . . I can't remember, but will come back to me. A poor foundling is discovered the heir of great wealth, he is wed to a pretty miss, the villain is cast out. It ends on this fine moral, though Mister Fielding took precious long getting to it and the Latin and all the fine fiddle-faddle made me weary." The silly woman, drawing a quick breath, had refused to let Counselor Salt move on to other matters. "Betty too. I mean, she was weary of it too. Had the book not cost so dear and been so much in vogue — we purchased the volumes second-hand from my cousin who, with a moneyed brewer for husband, buys everything with uncut pages but never loans out since she is miserly — we'd have left off the uncommon long tale altogether." Fortunately the shrewd Mister Salt had connived to keep the woman home. He explained that by the mother being absent from court there was added sympathy for the daughter, as the world would look upon the maternal absence as a measure of her grieving concern for her child. The idiot liked that and remained home, thank God. She'd have been harmful in front of Justice Fielding, whose known humorous nature might well have been distracted by her antics — or worse, her fawning over him might have been annoying — and by her very presence put the entire issue at doubt. Or worst of all, she might have interrupted the proceedings to scold him on the length of his fictions. Women. They never behaved the way a man could count on. They veered off, rushed after fancy.

Look at the Egyptian.

Just now in court she had contradicted her own witnesses, probably because she couldn't keep steady the difference between the first and the middle of a month. Women.

And then Bet Canning had amazed him by learning to believe her lies so thoroughly that she related them with unshakable conviction, with a fetching sincerity that any warm-hearted fellow would find irresistible, be he ever so experienced in cunning. Women. Women.

How much easier to deal with a nasty oaf like John Iniser, who knew to pocket a bribe and without a murmur to do what was necessary — a limping vicious rascal who for a farthing would deny his own mother and lose not a moment's sleep on it. Treating with someone steady like Iniser was a comfort. And even Nash and Aldridge behaved predictably, like true men, by avoiding the trial altogether. They were reasonable, knowing well that giving evidence against the girl might lead to broken windows and broken heads. Such men, though enemies, could at least be counted on. Even the Natus fellow had shown manly sense by appearing today and dragging his asinine subpoenaed wife away from the sessions. In the face of Justice Fielding's warning to tell the truth, the crazy old slut might have gone in there and babbled it. Women, oh these women. They even had the power to make his lordship cringe and grow confused. Such creatures as they were called the delicate sex?

Ahead was the rising spire of St. Sepulchre's Church, which always gave him a shiver, as on execution days its bell tolled from midnight till hanging time at Tyburn. The tolling had been the last sound heard by a half-dozen acquaintances, and the uneasy notion filled him, whenever he saw the grey walls and high steeple, that the bell of St. Sepulchre's might be the last thing he himself might hear on earth.

Waiting in front of the church at this moment was a handsome coach-and-six, with an embossed dragon crest on its door, the emblem of John Montagu, the fourth earl of Sandwich.

The coachman doffed his tricorn when Scarrat approached. They grinned at each other in the affectionate way of conspirators, for they'd served their master on many an escapade. Opening the carriage door, Scarrat climbed into the leather-lined interior. He never did so without feeling a measure of awe. Here inside the coach was the ageless world of nobility and kings. Seated on the crinkly leather, Robert Scarrat felt at one with those generations of men who'd served their betters loyally and well. It gave him assurance. God save the king, he muttered under his breath. It was like a prayer.

The coach began to rumble away from the steps of St. Sepulchre's, but the wheels hadn't revolved three times before its door was shaken by a tremendous blow.

Scarrat saw a blur of dirty cloth, a raised fist. And in the instant before the trotting horses carried him beyond view, Scarrat saw the square youthful features of someone familiar, though the eyes were bloodshot like those of a horse gone mad and a huge gloved hand was raised to strike again. It was an unsettling apparition, and as the carriage moved rapidly down the lane, Scarrat wasn't sure if he had actually seen the young postilion, that handsome fool who'd nearly perished in a fire. Instead of a fresh country face, what had been angrily thrust at the window was the low, mean, brutish countenance of a Londoner bent on violence.

So the boy has learned, Scarrat thought with satisfaction. Everything was orderly, in its proper place: the richly appointed coach, the restless crowds, the inevitable come-down of a country boy. Scarrat leaned from the window, but the coach was already around the corner. Too bad, in faith. He'd have shouted back at the young gull, "This be London! So how do you like it now!"

Scarrat sat back against the leather and let the world go by. He heard a ticking in his head, the comforting sound of time ratcheting by. He found comfort in a secret world of his own — so secret that when he got himself a doxy he never brought her to his place, where she might wonder at the world he'd created there.

[18]

THE DAY AFTER his friends had abandoned him, Ned found himself idling by a dry goods shop near the Temple. When the sun lowered behind the rooftops, leaving the street awash in undersea light, he chose his first cove, a beefy man emerging from a draper's shop with a package of rolled fabric.

At first Ned despaired of finding a chance to attack. Just when he was preparing to break off the hunt, his man turned into a tiny deserted lane. In three strides Ned was on him, dropping the fellow with a single blow of the crippled hand and with the other grabbing the package.

What amazed Ned was the ease of attacking a man. One blow, it was over. Hurrying away, he felt the package was whispering to him, "Yours for the taking." And he felt detached from what had happened. A tall burly fellow had struck someone down with a gloved hand. Only after selling the roll of cloth in Black Boy Alley did he feel united again, in mind and body.

Each time thereafter that Ned felled someone, he underwent the same sense of detachment, mind from body. Remorse came later, once the coins jingled in his pocket, and it never lasted long, because then his attention was on how to spend the gold. Mind and body assumed the rough but steady rhythm of life in St. Giles. During the day he usually lounged in his tiny case, sprawled on a quiltless bed, staring at a window clotted with rags or at the grate, behind which a few pieces of charcoal gave off a brassy glow. He counted folds in the window rags. He fancied all kinds of shapes in the lazy flames.

Sometimes he talked with neighboorhood beggars, with the Abraham-men, who counterfeited insanity; with the dummerers, who feigned muteness; with the limbless souls who huddled in doorways. He took meandering walks through the warrens of Whitechapel and drank bumpers with the outcasts of Old Kent

Road. When the flesh moved him, he visited bawdy houses in Field
Lane and Bishopsgate, getting on familiar terms not only with the
madams and their bunters, but with the thief takers as well, those
denizens of the tough world who lived in the gap between crime
and law. They lurked around bagnios frequented by criminals,
waiting for a chance to peach upon footpads who'd committed
offenses of merit. Such crimes were rare enough, because few citizens dared to carry large sums abroad anymore — a new public
campaign fostered by the *Covent Garden Journal* was seeing to that.
But let a rogue swagger into a bawdy house with a bagful of
significant loot and a thief taker would soon be sniffing around,
encouraging the boastful fool to drink, waiting for helplessness, and
then sending for a constable and later collecting a reward when the
footpad came to justice. Thief takers regarded someone like Ned as
a petty rogue, good only for a snuffbox or a bit of linen. Thus, they
treated him with indifference or good humour, sometimes even
buying him a dram of Hollands.

Evenings when not on the hunt, Ned fell into the habit of drinking and wenching till his coin was gone. After one drunken night,
he contracted a venereal distemper for which he doused himself
with Doctor Kennedy's Powder, bought for half a guinea at a
perfumer's on Orange Street. The powder had been recommended
to him by an old trollop who lived in the Alley, a fat, swarthy, good-
humoured woman whose face was deeply pitted with smallpox
scars.

"Mark this verse," she told Ned with a grin.

> "Happy the Man who in his Pocket keeps sound
> A well-made Armour with Scarlet ribbon bound."

Some days later, having taken the drop, he emerged from his
room weak and haggard, a metallic taste of mercury in his mouth
that persisted a week. He resolved always to use armour. From the
old trull he bought a half dozen of fine linen, with scarlet silk
drawstrings.

Ned sallied forth only when the need for drink and food required
a robbery. He spent but a pittance to repair his threadbare clothes,
so that his appearance was almost indistinguishable from that of
sorry beggars. When his pockets were full of coin, he emptied them

quickly in the grog shops of Barbican, in the flash houses of Houndsditch. Each day he woke to a world of ruins, tilted hovel and crumbling shanty, an undersea graveyard of shipwrecks rising from the mists like the hulks of yesteryear. His pulse seemed to lag, his arms hung loosely, his step lost its youthful resilience, as mind and body grew accustomed to the rhythm of nightmare in which time was marked merely by bolts of violence. All that roused him was a flagon of wine, the naked breast of a Blackfriars whore.

No longer was the underworld filled with the carefree heroes of Doctor Bostock's description. Ned saw his fellows for what they were, desperate and brutal. In a recurrent dream he was aboard a battered frigate on storm-tossed seas. It carried its human cargo toward a whirlpool and always upended, always rolled over, scattering women and children across the water. As the swirling funnel sucked him toward its center he heard their screams, which awoke him violently, but before he'd reached the whirlpool's fatal edge.

A deepening sense of doom began to detach him from the world around him. He turned indifferent eyes on the unwanted babies who lay frozen on doorsteps, their wrinkled old faces set like plaster in the morning light, unnoticed save by those furtive scarecrows who stored corpses in a Tottenham shed and sold them to anatomy students. Without emotion he watched an angry mob plunge a frail pickpocket into a cesspool, keeping him in black water interlarded with garbage and dead rats for upward of an hour. He stared coldly at a young woman dying of convulsions in a street of Blackfriars. Someone said she'd strangled her child and sold its clothes to buy the gin now killing her. As if told the weather was turning round, Ned walked away with a shrug. Each day he looked straight through misery to his next victim, his next meal, his next drink, his next wench. His sense of the world dwindled while his body developed the instincts of a animal. The air around him sent out faint signals of alarm to which his legs responded while his mind remained in a dream. Sometimes he scampered out of danger without ever seeing it, without even knowing why he had run from the next alley, the next shadow.

One thing he'd learned: his chief enemy was not the law or outraged citizens but the lawless like himself, the rovers who fed on their own kind. A thief was fair game for other thieves; and acting on this bitter knowledge Ned Carleton never stalked a cove if he sensed his own ilk nearby. A brotherhood, as Bostock called such people? What a brotherhood! Morning lanes yielded up dead foot-pads who'd become prey, robbed of their swag and slit up their bellies. And before the watch could have the corpses hauled away, countless hands searched everywhere. When carters arrived, likely as not the dead were often naked, picked clean like carrion.

So much for the brotherhood. It had never been more than the idle notion of Doctor Bostock, whose tales of heroic criminals, Ned saw now, was the stuff of shilling romances.

A rippling swell of *Huzzah!* filled the Old Bailey yard when the verdicts against Squires and Wells had reached the waiting crowd.

Often these days Ned Carleton joined such mobs. Within them, safe as a lamb in the midst of a flock, he could study people around him and pick out a likely cove. He shouldered his way to a vantage point from which he had a glimpse of the departing saint, her loyal train, the manacled gypsy bound for Newgate, and the tall lord mayor in a double cockade of scarlet silk.

Then he saw a grey-faced man, lean as a hound's tooth, stooped, coughing, make his way through the crowd. Without a thought Ned followed, as if Mister Scarrat, who had given him a smoking book, might also give him new hope, even a new life. He walked rapidly to keep Scarrat in sight along the thick walls of Newgate and then the open vista in front of St. Sepulchre's. The street widened, the spire reached into the damp air. Beneath the church's damp façade a coach waited, and he saw Scarrat climb inside. For a moment Ned failed to recognize the coach, so intent was he on Scarrat, but then it registered: the crimson and gilt, the sleekly crafted curves, the gleaming axles, the heavily spoked wheels, the powerful team of sorrel horses, the embossed dragon crest on the door, and on the front bench the head coachman who'd been good to him.

Only later would Ned marvel at the profound effect this coach had on him. At the moment he simply rushed at it, growling in his throat, his gloved hand uplifted like a club. Forgetting that it was Scarrat who'd climbed inside, he imagined instead another pres-ence — someone ponderous in ermine, someone who'd dismissed him with the disdainful flick of a ringed finger. The hateful image prodded Ned into a wild sprint that brought him alongside the coach as it was moving away. He pounded the shiny side hard — twice, three times, missing on the fourth attempt as the carriage rolled beyond his reach.

Panting, he watched while the horses sent plumes of vapour into the rainy air and swayed out of sight, their churning hoofs lifting sizy gouts of mud from the street as if parting foam. Ned stared at his hand, feeling the pain shoot from fingers to shoulder. He experienced the odd conviction that if those twisted immobile fingers could reach his lordship's throat, they'd find life again and grip with the old power. He'd taken nothing from the larder, but had combed and groomed the horses to perfection. He'd waxed the side panels, oiled the axles, and on the rear roost had stood proudly erect and protective of the carriage's occupants. All he'd done was seek his fortune in London. He'd done nothing wrong. Often he recalled the smile on his lordship's face, the amusement, the disdain, for it was clear to Ned now that the nobleman had known the truth but had chosen to disregard it.

The man ruined my life, Ned thought, staring in dismay at his aching hand. With lagging step he returned to the Old Bailey yard, having no other place in mind, and stood on the outer fringe of the crowd whose black tricorns looked like crows nesting in the rain.

A man grumbled, "What a fiery set of people here. It's made of nothing but combustibles. I'm for safer pastures." He freed himself from the restless mob and walked away.

A shout went up as bailiffs appeared with Susannah Wells in tow. They pulled her roughly into a space cleared by soldiers wielding pikes and waited until other bailiffs bore a smoking kettle on a rod from the prison. Coals inside of it sputtered from raindrops when the kettle was placed in front of the prisoner. The long rod of a branding iron stuck out from the kettle.

Susannah Wells began to whimper.

The assistant sheriff of Newgate, wearing a black jerkin, came forward, withdrew the iron, and held it high for spectators to see. Above the massed tricorns Ned saw something like the snubbed crimson head of a snake.

The mob swayed and rippled like a huge animal stretching after sleep. A low expectant murmur filled the yard. The sheriff plunged the glowing iron back into the kettle. Raindrops sizzling on the coals could be heard everywhere in the yard. The prisoner's wet hair lay flat against her sallow face and in streaks across her trembling mouth.

One of the bailiffs produced a wooden box on which they ordered the prisoner to stand, so as to be visible throughout the yard. The glowing iron, raised again, swung through the air. Little black dots pocked its red surface when the rain hit. In vain the prisoner struggled against the securing grip of three bailiffs, while a fourth yanked her arm forward and held it firmly at the wrist.

"Open your hand, woman, for the execution of the sentence," the sheriff demanded.

Though whimpering, Susannah Wells obeyed, letting the mottled pudgy fingers unclasp until the dirty palm lay exposed like a plate.

Once again the sheriff lifted the iron high, swung it down, and laid it red and smoking on the woman's hand.

She howled.

Ned saw through the forest of hats a thrashing figure, a clenched fist, a round hole in a white face from which a scream spiraled into the drizzle like flame from a roaring fire.

The mob went wild. Dancing and cheering, they howled "*Huzzah!*"

Grizzled, unwashed, Ned slogged through the crowd, so filled with a vision of the great coach and the ermine-robed nobleman inside of it that he couldn't select a cove from the separating mob.

Only moments later he would see the dog. Only moments later his life would skitter away on a new tack.

John Montagu, the fourth earl of Sandwich, was winning at the game of Hazard in White's Club when a footman whispered at his shoulder that his lordship's coachman waited outside. He turned a deaf ear to the gibes of other players who warned that his luck would turn sour if he left the table.

John Montagu shambled past diners, whist players, and hard drinkers snoring peacefully on crossed arms. His carriage stood at the entrance, and two doormen assisted him up.

Scarrat sat there hatless, black hair limp against his ears, head dipping rhythmically in submission. Proudly he announced the verdict against the two women and emphasized his own considerable part in the affair.

"It's what I expected," Sandwich observed coolly, handing his man a leather pouch. "Fifty guineas for the Canning wench."

"So much, milord? Not half so much. The mother should waste it on frippery within a week."

"I don't care one whit what the dam and the bitch dog do, so long as I'm shut of them." He climbed down from the carriage and ordered Thomas to take Mister Scarrat wherever he wished.

Lord Sandwich had a final glimpse of a dark face bobbing in respect at the chariot window as Thomas whipped the horses into motion. Returning to the club's mirrors and candlelight, to its crimson-garbed waiters and tippling patrons, his lordship looked forward to a good run of cards, then dining at the Golden Fleece. Perhaps he'd end the evening at a certain Covent Garden bagnio and sample there a tender young songbird, a new creature recommended by Scarrat for his pleasure.

[19]

WHILE THE GYPSY Mary Squires languished in Newgate Prison, awaiting the rope at Tyburn, across the ocean Ben Franklin was trying to prove that lightning and electricity were identical. In the British Isles the Scottish doctor James Lind had just taken to the press *A Treatise of the Scurvy*, which described the first controlled medical experiment in history; it proved that the lack of citrus fruit caused scurvy. Percivall Pott was finishing his *Fractures and Dislocations*, an argument issuing from extensive evidence that fractures should be set rather than treated with ointments. Thomas Guy, founder of Guy's Hospital, was also completing an article for Lloyd's *Evening Post* which would include his cure for cancer, a mixture of sulphur, white oxide of arsenic, and herbs.

While the gypsy had been either in Enfield or in Coombe at the widow Greville's if not at a public house, George Berkeley had died, aided in the process by imbibing gallons of tar water, the physic of his choice. The philosopher had believed that the corporeal world exists only as a system of ideas, a doctrine not shared by the physician Sir Hans Sloane, who had died two days earlier, not far from Newgate where the gypsy awaited a different sort of end. Sloane's collection of books, coins, medals, cameos, butterflies, crystals, and plant albums would be left to the British Museum, an auspicious gift as the museum had just been granted a foundation charter and within six years would open to the general public in Great Russell Street.

The lord mayor of London, Sir Crisp Gascoyne, was thinking of neither philosophy nor medicine this morning but of his own dissatisfaction, occasioned in part by the gypsy languishing in Newgate. Gascoyne was unaccustomed to dissatisfaction, having risen by dint of hard work and determination from a Gravel Lane brewer to alderman of Vintry Ward to sheriff of Middlesex and now to lord mayor — the first to occupy the new Mansion House, which people called a kind of "Hallelujah Chorus in Stone," featuring a dining room that accommodated four hundred guests. He was accustomed to getting his way.

Spindly-legged but barrel-chested, the disciplined little man rose each· day at sunrise, doused his face in icy water, and placed his pocket watch alongside his egg dish, thus reminding himself that the frivolous act of eating breakfast was a waste of valuable time. To Sir Crisp the world moved like a geared machine on a plan clearly discernible by reasonable persons. The ultimate goal of this plan was to establish England above all countries of the world, for her system of justice was unmatched by any other. English law was his meat, drink, and religion; he would defend it to the death.

Yet here he was, dissatisfied and even ashamed of the very thing he worshiped.

Presiding over the gypsy's trial, he'd been assailed by the awful possibility that a jury of true Englishmen had been gulled. Or had they been honestly mistaken? Was their performance a travesty of justice? Such questions left him prey to uneasiness, uneasiness led to doubt, doubt led to dissatisfaction, and dissatisfaction was something he could not abide.

The sensational trial, its contradictory evidence, its bullying mob, and its improper handling of witnesses threw him into a funk.

There was no way such a perfectonist could rest until each of the problems was dealt with, starting with the handling of witnesses.

He laid this last impropriety at the feet of Justice Fielding.

Anyone with knowledge of this renowned magistrate would acknowledge, of course, that he would not willfully commit a dishonest act. Yet he *was* a romancer who'd given much of his life to writing fictions — some quite racy — and he *was* a convivial fellow, not overly cautious when a bottle was within reach. Fielding had taken a counseling fee from a prosecuting solicitor — a prosecuting solicitor, mind — then turned round and assumed the rule of committing judge. Outrageous. Moreover, Gascoyne had been flabbergasted to learn that Fielding had allowed a witness, Virtue Hall, to be closeted with that self-same prosecuting solicitor and had then sworn her to the information thus procured.

In his *Address to the Liverymen of London,* composed later in defense of his own actions in the Canning affair, Sir Crisp expressed his opinion of Fielding:

> If Virtue Hall's examination had been taken as she would have *freely* given it; if no threats had been used to frighten her; if Mr. Fielding himself had prepared her information, or perhaps had only been present when it was prepared, the troubles which ensued could not have happened.

But in the lord mayor's view, that wasn't the end of it. Fielding had also threatened the Natus creature, who'd been brought before him on his own warrant, and by this interference most likely had encouraged her to avoid giving evidence at the trial.

At best Fielding's performance had been naïve and careless, at worst an arrogant display of personal bias overriding public justice.

Gascoyne was also dissatisfied with the people who supported the Canning girl. It came to his ears that defense witnesses had been threatened by Canningites at the Old Bailey door — promised bodily harm if they testified. As yet it was only an unsubstantiated report, but he meant to look into it. Later he would write, "The outrages of the mob prevented that solemn and sacred freedom which should attend all trials."

In addition he was dissatisfied with the jury's failure to consider the gypsy's alibi. Three witnesses put her in Dorsetshire when she was supposed to be robbing a girl in Enfield. A "hanging mood" must have prevailed among the jurors for them to ignore such contradictory evidence.

Acting in his official capacity of lord mayor and chief justice, Gascoyne implemented his suspicions by sending out agents to learn if the defense witnesses were of good character — men whose word had substance. The result: a Dorset sheriff pronounced the characters of John Gibbons and William Clarke beyond reproach, and a certificate obtained from parish authorities vouched for Thomas Greville. Moreover, the agents interviewed a number of villagers throughout the West Country and pieced together a credible itinerary for the roving band of gypsies: at the beginning of January they traveled from South Parrot to Abbotsbury, thence to Dorchester, Coombe, Bisset, Chettle, Basingstoke, Bagshot, Brentford, and thence by the Kensington Road to Seven Sisters, Tottenham, and finally to Enfield, which they reached no earlier than the *twenty-fourth*. Innkeepers, drapers, farmers, a whole assortment of rustics including a staymaker, a miller, a footguard, a maltster, and a blacksmith could recall having seen the gypsies here and there or having shared with them some boiled chicken, a bowl of cider, in a wayside tavern.

A number of points now seemed clear to Gascoyne: the gypsies were not *boni et legales homines*, but doubtless a band of peddlers who sold smuggled goods, probably from cargoes run secretly into Dorset coves; yet, just as surely, they'd been one hundred and fifty miles southwest of London on New Year's Day. A certain Mister Ford of Aldenmanbury, a citizen cast in the same civic mould as the lord mayor, had busied himself with obtaining still more affidavits from the people who could testify to the gypsies' travels through Dorsetshire. It was further noted by the lord mayor that the gypsy's claim of staying with the widow Greville in Coombe on the fourteenth — a claim inconsistent with the testimony of witnesses in her behalf, which sealed her fate with the Old Bailey audience, who took it for dissimulation — was a measure of her confusion during the long, wearisome, complicated travel, for in truth on the fifteenth she stayed the night at the widow Giffard's in Bisset. She had named Greville — where she'd stayed the night before — instead of Giffard.

The accumulation of so much evidence in support of the gypsy's alibi encouraged the lord mayor to investigate still further. Again he considered the reliability of Virtue Hall. Taken up after the trial as an accessory to felony, the girl was now being held in the Gate House. On the lord mayor's instruction she was confronted there and confessed to signing a perjured statement. Tearfully she blamed Fielding and Salt for her grievous mistake and begged mercy of the king. She now testified that the gypsy hadn't come to the Wells house until *three weeks after* the alleged imprisonment of Elizabeth Canning. Armed with the full recantation of this principal witness — and vindicated by it for having criticized Fielding — the lord mayor made a formal representation before the Crown. He obtained forthwith a respite of six more weeks for Mary Squires.

The attorney general instructed his officers to look further into the case and report thereon to the cabinet council.

Feeling less dissatisfied, Gascoyne learned from an interview with Officer White that Gawin Nash and Robert Aldridge, though openly voicing their suspicion of the Enfield raid, had not appeared in court for fear of provoking the girl's followers. Gascoyne had them brought before him. Chastened by the stern lord mayor, they readily pointed out discrepancies in the girl's story during the raid.

Gawin Nash, a feisty man and therefore a man after Gascoyne's heart, was impressive in his recall of details. He lit especially upon Canning's inability to recognize the stairway leading to the loft. The girl had let herself be carried through other rooms first, as if uncertain of her whereabouts.

Aldridge remarked on the four pieces of bread that had become four pounds, when it became obvious that no one could have lived so long on so little; and only later had she mentioned a mince pie. Then there was a water jug. He insisted that the initial inspection of the loft had uncovered none; only later did a raider produce a jug out of thin air, as it were.

At last Gascoyne was satisfied. Their suspicions confirmed his own, and wholly convinced him that Elizabeth Canning, possibly in league with others, had cheated justice in a most treacherous way, conniving to bring an old woman, albeit a gypsy and a smuggler, to a most untimely punishment. And that said nothing of Wells, the accessory, who would carry on her hand a terrible mark to the end of her days. Of course, Canningites would argue that the girl's erratic behavior at Enfield was the result of weakness and distraction.

To meet that objection the lord mayor sent out an agent for still more evidence. This time he learned that a village publican, one Ezra Whiffen, had climbed to the loft *in early January* in the company of Mother Wells. The purpose had been to find and purchase a piece of board from there to hang as a sign above his tavern. They had found a good board all right — under the straw on which Judith Natus lay sprawled, incoherently drunk. Sarah Howell, daughter to Wells, deposed that the Natus couple remained the entire month in the loft; moreover, that she herself and Virtue Hall had exchanged pleasantries one January afternoon through the hayloft window with three men lopping tree branches nearby. The pruners all swore that indeed there had been talk of a lively nature between them and the two young women in mid-January, with the girls leaning so far from the sill that two pair of white bosoms nearly touched them in the face.

The following facts now seemed unassailable to Sir Crisp. Canning had failed to describe the loft in which other people had lived throughout January; and more than thirty people had seen the gypsy far from Enfield at the time of the alleged assault and robbery.

When the lord mayor presented these arguments to the Crown lawyers, they listened favourably but hesitated to pardon the gypsy because by such action they must bring an indictment of perjury against Elizabeth Canning, the acknowledged darling of London. The lord mayor's address was put under advisement.

When this turn of affairs reached the public, a spate of pamphlets were soon printed and hawked on the corners of Cornwall and the Strand — some championing the girl, some the gypsy. A surgeon questioned the possibility of a frail girl surviving on short rations for a month, then walking ten miles through a wintry night. A Doctor Cox, at her friends' urging, examined the girl, especially her mouth for mercury scars, and maintained that she'd never been treated for venereal distemper nor had she ever carried a child, though the lack of a hymen put her virginity in question. A response to his opinion was made in the anonymous *The Imposter Detected; or, The Mystery and Iniquity of Elizabeth Canning's Story Displayed,* which advocated the abortion theory.

Of all the anti-Canning essays the most widely praised was written by the Scottish painter Allan Ramsay, who argued that the story was initially a falsehood told by the girl "at a time when her conduct stood greatly in need of an excuse," and then, supplied with hints from well-wishers, she'd woven the fabric of a single lie into a deception of perjurious magnitude, and by this blatant error in judgement had brought grievous harm to women of little means and less sense.

Ramsay's theory was answered by "a Wild Indian suddenly landed in England from America," who wrote in a bitter broadside:

> It is intolerable to all decency that the girl was mewed up in a house for a month without victuals. We cannot accept this cruel, barbarous, unhuman treatment of a virginal maiden who stands for all the martyred of history. She must have justice done. The gypsy must hang.

So the war of pamphlets continued. Nearly two score of them delighted and inflamed the citizens of London, often turning friend against friend, as the populace split into partisan camps of Canningite and Egyptian.

In the midst of this rapidly escalating public turmoil and resentment, the solicitor general reported to the Crown that indeed the weight of evidence lay in the convicted woman's favour.

Upon this legal judgement the king granted Mary Squires a free pardon and released her forthwith into the company of armed sympathizers at the entrance of Newgate.

So the dissatisfaction of Sir Crisp Gascoyne vanished altogether. Receiving this news in the Mansion House, he leaned back and breathed the pure air of matchless England, his mind regaining its belief in the Grand Design.

He was therefore unprepared for what would occur later that day. Leaving the Mansion House, no sooner had he climbed into his carriage than a howling band of Canningites, wielding swords and cudgels, rushed down the rainy street and blocked the way.

Dumbfounded, the little lord mayor stared from the carriage window at menacing arms and mouths stretched wide in fury and blood-dimmed eyes. A stone crashed through the window, spraying glass across his velvet coat. A chant of *Hang the gypsy! Hang the lord mayor! Hang the gypsy! Hang the lord mayor!* echoed through the interior of his coach like the throb of a drum.

Drawing his sword, Gascoyne held its edge out at his chest, while the coachman tried desperately to bring the rearing horses under control. The mob began rocking the carriage until it creaked on its springs, leaning dangerously to one side. An arm plunged through the broken glass, swiping wildly at the resolute lord mayor, whose sharp features betrayed no other emotion than disbelief, as his small fist gripped the sword hilt.

Pulling the reins in with powerful hands, the driver at last subdued the frantic horses. Waywardly they broke into a trot and the coach began careening past the mob that flailed and thundered *Hang the gypsy! Hang the lord mayor! Hang the gypsy! Hang the lord mayor!* at the retreating gilt carriage.

[20]

THE PICK AND FLOWER of London society was at Ranelagh on an early spring evening just hours after a mob of Canningites had attacked the lord mayor in his coach.

Fashionable people considered the older Vauxhall a crashing bore with its rogues begging wine from ladies supping in booths and its vulgar folk gaping for a shilling at the *beau monde* promenading through the gingerwork Music Room.

Ranelagh, the new pleasure resort in Chelsea, was now the rage. Carriages lined up for half a mile, waiting to discharge passengers for a stroll down the broad lanes at twilight. From Chinese bridges they could watch a gondola festooned with flags go gliding down an artificial canal. The real triumph of Ranelagh, however, lay in its magnificent Rotunda, a vaulted room which was said by loyal Englishmen to rival the Pantheon. Painted to resemble a rainbow, its vast honeycombed ceiling overlooked a central fireplace and a double row of gilded boxes where the *haut ton* lounged at ease over chocolate and tea, their rouged, whitened faces illuminated by the brassy light of pendant fire lusters. A crowd of frolics and bloods and all manner of rakes, with their flowered waistcoats, silk knee breeches, and musk-soaked kerchiefs strutted about the circular promenade. The latest in bag wigs were all in view: the intricate blue or white shapes fancifully called the Solitaire, the Comet, the Royal Bird — creations of French hairdressers.

Their female counterparts paraded in hoop skirts, displaying layered swags and flounces edged with fringe, interspersed with tassels or ropes of beads or valances of lace, all of which foamed and rustled about their pretty figures (created to lesser or greater degree by the skillful hands of Parisian *modistes*).

Beneath scores of candelabra hanging from long ropes, there was a rattle of vellum fans, a dazzle of hair dusted with powder — recalling frosted confections — and a wooden swish of thick silk, as the arena buzzed with amorous intrigue, the thrust and parry of flirtation.

"Madam, you have the finesse of your sex. But when, pray, may I wait upon you in earnest?"

"Do be quiet, sir. I don't like your meaning of earnest."

"Permit me to interpret the meaning of earnest my own way, madam. By it I mean a private interview where we can earnestly pursue the meaning of our most earnest feelings."

"I'll hear no more of your earnestness."

"Perhaps if I call, say, tomorrow at noon, you might be in a more receptive mood?"

"I think you mean earnest mood. No, sir, I'm at cards tomorrow at noon."

"Then?"

"Perhaps I'll send word."

"Perhaps?"

"Very well, I'll send word."

"That settled, if not to my deepest satisfaction, madam, will you have a dish of tea? There's no reason for objecting. Your husband's still at cards in the Red Room."

Accompanied by a rattle of the fan: "Sir, you're indeed an encroaching creature." Taking his extended arm: "But as you persist, I believe I will."

For those not engaged in the ballets of dalliance, there were, that evening, three topics abroad. One was the Clandestine Marriage

Act, which prevented runaway couples of good family from making hasty marriages in Fleet Prison chapels — to say nothing of drunken sailors with opportunistic whores and sly fortune hunters with naïve heiresses. The Act would prevent corrupt touts from bullying young people into cheap weddings of dubious legality. So argued many ladies. But many gentlemen countered that the Act encroached on English freedom, and unhappy alliances meant nothing compared to English freedom.

Debate was hotter on the Jewish issue. Passage of the Naturalization Act would allow Jews to become citizens by taking the oath of allegiance without swearing "on the true faith of a Christian." The galleries of Ranelagh echoed with angry voices. The Act would tempt wealthy foreign Jews to immigrate and lend their considerable talents to the country, so why should it not be passed? It should never be passed, reasoned the opponents of the bill, for it was an attempt to profane the Communion.

Of keenest interest, however, was the Canning affair, offering as it did free rein to the fancy. Had the girl run off to rid herself of an unwanted child? Had her paramour abandoned her? Had the gypsies desired to sell her into slavery?

Additional excitement had been whipped up by today's assault on the lord mayor. A romantic account of it drifted above the vellum fans. With drawn sword the lord mayor had withstood a raving pack of rogues bent upon murdering him for championing the poor woman — was it the girl or the gypsy? The courageous lord mayor had run a half dozen of his assailants through. Without a murmur he'd endured a terrible gash in his thigh. Such prating filled the halls.

Snatches of the nonsense reached the ear of Lord Sandwich, whose temper was not improved by this maddening reminder of the Canning slut. It was like pouring salt into a wound already opened today through a damnable foolish action by his old ally Bedford. The fool had played into Newcastle's hand by resigning the post of secretary of state in part as a protest for Newcastle forcing Sandwich from the Admiralty. Without consulting anyone, not even that fat wife of his on whom he so curiously doted, Bedford in a pique had simply resigned. At one stroke Newcastle had rid himself of two troublesome foes. Had Bedford remained firm, others might well have joined the fight against the fatuous, despicable prime minister, the master of trafficking in political jobbery. Only yesterday Sandwich had heard the latest of this booby. Someone mentioned to him Cape Breton, and Newcastle had burbled, "Cape Breton is an island? Wonderful! Show it me on the map. So it is, to be sure, an island. Sir, you always bring us good news. I must go and tell the king that Cape Breton is an island."

There was little chance now, Sandwich thought gloomily, of recapturing the Admiralty. Harassed by Newcastle, Bedford had fallen like a fly into a spider web and thereby cut his closest friend off from regaining a career in government.

Damn Bedford. Only yesterday the fool had been complaining not of Newcastle but of waggoners! Over cards at White's he'd deplored the insolent habits of waggoners who no longer took their path through St. Giles, but turned up less traveled Southampton Street, then across Bloomsbury Square to his beloved Great Russell Street, damaging the pavement in front of his house. He could hardly sleep at night for fear of discovering more unseemly ruts on the morrow. Bedford had been turned out of high office, yet what deeply concerned him was the route of waggoners! How could this country prosper with Bedfords and Newcastles at the reins?

And if that weren't enough — for more salt in an open wound — Newcastle had just appointed Admiral Anson to the post of First Lord of the Admiralty. Very well, Anson was a line officer of merit, but hardly suitable for high posting. He was a commoner who'd worked up through the ranks. He had no breeding, cut an awkward figure in society, possessed a laughable accent, chewed with his mouth open. Anson deserved a ship of the line, but never the Admiralty.

By this mean act of vengeance the duke of Newcastle had undermined an entire department of government and slapped in the face every honoured peer of the land. Newcastle, Bedford, Anson — damn them all.

And damn the lord mayor for keeping the Canning thing fresh and at the forefront of public interest by his infernal meddling.

Half drunk and miserable, impatient for the orchestra to begin the evening's Handel, Lord Sandwich ambled heavily through the arena. In every scented lady he saw his own frivolous wife, who at this very moment was doubtlessly losing at whist among a regiment of women no less bored or foolish.

But was he himself better? He'd come to Ranelagh out of boredom too. In recent days he'd attended a number of great squeezers such as this, each featuring the same aimless strolling, the same chocolate, the same witless talk. During the day he spent vast amounts of time buying gloves in Holborn, lavender water at the Civet Cat. He'd gained so much weight from the idle munching of sweetmeats that his thighs in the silk breeches shook like jelly, notwithstanding his play at cricket and tennis. His nights were spent at the opera or at cock fighting or other diversion. Last night he'd driven out to Spa Fields near Islington for no other reason than to see a female pugilist, "Bruising Peg of Clerkenwell," beat her opponent half to death for a purse of two guineas. He went anywhere for amusement. He'd allowed himself to be dragged to an owl-diving spectacle on the Thames. Sitting in a wherry he'd watched a couple of sports from Boodles tie an owl to a duck's back; the duck dove to shake off the owl, the half-drowned owl hooted wildly upon emerging, thus frightening the duck into another dive, and so on and so on and so on until by this grotesque procedure they both died of exhaustion. He'd nearly died of boredom.

Most of his time, however, was divided between gambling and women. He played at various games — faro, hazard, loo, piquet, macco. He bet fifty pounds on a maggot race at Brookes. After a long night of whist, played at a hundred pounds the rubber, he'd burned his wig, as had his drunken companions, for want of better to do. Lately he was sick of the sight of the iron balcony at number 37, St. James's Street, knowing that within White's smoky interior he'd see the same ruddy faces, stupefied by hours at cards and too much claret, hear the same dull gossip, eat the same overcooked mutton.

But of course he was a man out of office. What could there be for a man of his station save idleness and dissipation unless a high post occupied his time? He prided himself on his energy and English determination. Now he wasted his powers on the flesh of women who could sing. Or who thought they could sing. Or whom Scarrat, who had a tin ear, thought could sing. His lordship's nights were filled with bleating voices in rank rooms.

He wished heartily for the renewal of rites at Medmenham. Paul Whitehead had directed repairs to the old abbey this winter, causing a suspension of the friars' meetings. Last week Sandwich had seen Bubb Dodington at a rout and they'd expressed their nostalgia for the abbey. Bubb had just come from Prussia where his friend Voltaire was sniveling about Frederick's treatment of him. Bubb loved to drop names. But he was a fine old soul, one of the merriest of the monks despite his age and bulk. They had both agreed that the order was being corrupted by newcomers such as John Wilkes, that squinting upstart with the jaw of a mule. But not even a corruption of the membership could dissuade Lord Sandwich from thinking of Medmenham as the most wonderful jest in the world. He longed for the casting off of public care, the first warm greeting of Potter and Hopkins and Stapleton and Selwyn and Earl Temple. He longed for the cowls and masks and the thick smell of incense drifting across the luscious body of the Altar. He longed too for the sudden chill along his spine during the black service when, nearly always, he felt the awesome presence of something terrible, something threatening, eternal, damned.

Impatiently he waited for the music to begin. Musicians had not even appeared on the dais with their violas, hautboys, and horns. Nor did the crowd show any inclination to disperse, but continued to engender heat in the hall until rouged cheeks were rivuleted by sweat and the lamp black on eyelashes dripped down on lips.

Milord Sandwich was ready to leave in disgust when a commotion took place at the entrance to the Rotunda. A breathless whisper flew through the assembly — the gallant lord mayor had arrived.

Sandwich shoved forward to have a better view of the worrisome hero who'd added to his own troubles today. Then he saw the little man, decked out in white silk, bowing low to Elizabeth Chudleigh, the most lovely of the royal mistresses. Sir Crisp Gascoyne was not so austere that he failed to steal a peak at her celebrated bosom; it had been famous ever since she'd appeared at a masquerade in a flesh-colored costume so daringly naked that the scandalized princess of Wales had thrown a shawl round her shoulders.

Lord Sandwich was close enough to overhear the lord mayor purring, "So gracious of you to say so. Both you and His Majesty do me too much honour."

A tall horsy woman hove into view, Lady Caroline Fitzroy on the arm of one of her Italian lovers, probably an obscure count, who had a pretty spit curl on his forehead.

"Your obedient servant," the lord mayor said with a bow.

"You have done yourself great honour," said Lady Caroline. "To think a man of your station would treat so compassionately with a low gypsy woman. It is wonderful."

"I'm obliged for your kind words."

God save me but the fellow takes to compliments like a starved cat laps up milk, thought Lord Sandwich. Then he put himself deliberately in the lord mayor's path. "Let me congratulate you on a diligent pursuit of justice."

Gascoyne bowed low. "Your lordship does me too much honour."

"What of the Canning girl now?" Sandwich hoped to sound casual. "Will more be done to her?"

"I should think so. Indeed, milord, it's likely. I should think her liable at least to a charge of perjury."

"Bah, no jury in the world would bring in guilty such an innocent young girl." Noting the surprise on Gascoyne's face, he added, "I mean, the riffraff wouldn't allow it."

"I own they're a difficulty," the Lord Mayor said coolly. Rather than deal with more such questions he turned to receive more praise. The beautiful Gunning sisters were moving their hooped skirts in his direction. They wished to make their own curtsies to the lionized lord mayor and gain more admiration from him than he gave to their Chudleigh rival.

Sandwich moved away from the circle of admirers. He couldn't abide such ladies with their beauty patches and clattering fans any more than he could endure such a coxcomb as Gascoyne. In the crowd he came upon George Selwyn holding a long-stemmed glass by its foot. Connoisseur, wit, man of great wealth, indifferent M.P., Selwyn enjoyed nothing more than attending an execution. Once he'd traveled to Paris for the sole purpose of watching a man torn apart by horses for attempting to assassinate Louis XV. Always in fashion, Selwyn wore a bag wig of a new as yet unnamed style: his hair was encased by stiffened taffeta drawn tight with a string and set off by a diamond-studded bow. A silver-hilted sword that would never under any circumstances be drawn was hanging at his side.

As his wont, Selwyn had the latest gossip. The duke of Newcastle would be at Ranelagh tonight for the purpose of commending the lord mayor.

Thus the delay of music, Sandwich thought bitterly. It would not begin until the duke arrived, although the tone-deaf hypochondriac couldn't tell the difference between an aria from Gluck and a country reel.

"Wilkes has set his sail for you," continued Selwyn. "He's about tonight, drumming up support for his go at Parliament."

"Support the man will never get from me." Sandwich had already received word of his antics. In frantic search of political advancement, the man had come in from the country to hobnob with his betters, smirking from one of the ugliest faces in creation, hoping for preferment any way he could get it. In him was more insolence and crudeness of nature than a drunken waterman. "If Wilkes is here, I'll take my leave willingly. The duke of Newcastle and John Wilkes. That's a combination to send me packing."

"Ah, my dear friend, what we're in need of is Medmenham." Selwyn laid a manicured hand on Sandwich's arm. "I declared it to Wilkes, who heartily agreed."

"I can't see why the fellow is ever invited."

"Well, he has a modicum of wit. He said Medmenham's the very thing for someone in need of religious solace."

"I agree with the fellow that Medmenham's needed, though I dare say it's the only thing we agree on. But I'm gone. I've no stomach for bumping into Newcastle."

But unluckily for him Lord Sandwich never made it out of Ranelagh without seeing the duke — without nearly bumping into the man at the entrance.

A kerchief at his nose, his long thin body wrapped in wool against the spring air, the First Minister of England intoned rapidly in a fussy voice, "Ah, milord Sandwich, this is indeed a pleasure. I was only telling the king in his closet this very day we have much need of seeing our good Sandwich again. Indeed, a pleasure." And he swept forward with a train of sycophants in his mincing wake.

Furious, Sandwich strode away, leaving Ranelagh without hearing a note of Handel. It would be ten more years before he had the most fascinating musical experience of a long life, right here in the Rotunda: an Austrian but eight years old named Mozart would play the harpsichord without looking at a score, his feet dangling high above the pedals.

In the night air Lord Sandwich called loudly for his carriage, giving the coachmaster a guinea for bringing it up without delay. Soon he was rumbling along streets that were lit fitfully by dishes of burning oil.

Flesh? Or faro?

Only this afternoon his man Scarrat had put him on to a new songbird in Covent Garden. His lordship knew the bawdy house and the mother who ran it, a vicious creature who'd have robbed him a dozen times had she not feared his station.

Flesh. Tonight it would be flesh. Flesh would take him away from his cares. What he craved at such times was a lousy and contemptible doxy on whom to vent his frustration. The common lot had no conception of what it meant to grow into manhood in full awareness that the future of England rested on your shoulders, though any scheming puppy could push you out of office by the vilest of stratagems. Damn the duke of Newcastle. Damn Bedford, Anson, the Canning slut, the lord mayor. Damn Wilkes. Damn Selwyn for the simpering fop he was. Damn Judith and her whist games and extravagance. Damn women.

Tapping the carriage roof with his cane, he gave Thomas the address. Lanes and squares flew by. Shadowy bulks leapt from the path of the mud-spattering hoofs. Then Thomas reined up with a hoarse cry in front of a three-story house near a market.

Milord Sandwich stepped clumsily from the carriage, assisted by two postilions, one holding a torch.

Had he not been thus accompanied to the brothel door by stout guards, his lordship might have suffered the fate of other Londoners this night — assault, robbery, and worse. He might have encountered a large growling animal and a former postilion of his household who'd have welcomed a chance for revenge. He might have met the Dog Cull.

Part Four

THE DOG CULL

[21]

SHORTLY AFTER Susannah Wells had been branded, Ned Carleton met the dog. It happened in a narrow lane off Cheapside, near a tripe shop. Sometimes mongrel dogs, when not chased away, fought over scraps of offal thrown out by butchers looking for entertainment. Ned had seen many such dogs roaming through London with lolling tongues, sway backs, hungry eyes. He'd paid scant attention, as they skittered underfoot, their tails drooping between withered shanks.

But Ned stopped in his tracks when he saw this dog. It reminded him of sheepdogs back home, a kind of brown and white collie, weighing — he judged with a practised eye — perhaps five stone. Obviously the animal was sick, for it hacked repeatedly and a purulent discharge exuded from its eyes. Its rough coat, which should have had a feathery sheen, was dull, patchy, lank against its ribs.

Yet the dog had survived a harsh winter without becoming a bag of bones, as many did. It must have fought hard; indeed, scars on the brown muzzle attested to that. Ned couldn't take his eyes off the animal, as it paced in front of the tripe shop, avoiding wheels and hoofs.

Kneeling some feet away, Ned whistled — a low cool sound like a bird call heard at twilight, which only shepherds made — but the dog responded with no more than a quick disdainful glance. It continued pacing, its muddy paws in restless motion. Again Ned whistled, and this time the dog ignored him. Good, Ned thought. The dog — he saw now it was female — had an independent spirit.

Someone must have brought her as a pup from the hills and probably lost her in London. He judged her to be about three years old, the same age Sandy had been when he sold her before leaving Warsop. Sandy had been a good dog — no, a very great dog. The memory of her still haunted him, coming at odd moments but especially often at lambing time. At that time she'd rarely slept, but remained in a state of nervous excitement, as each morning they went into the fields and found lambs born overnight. How gently she carried them by the neck and offered them to the ewes for suck! Again and again she'd haul a newborn lamb to its suspicious mother until at last the skittish dam accepted it as her own. Without help Sandy could handle a flock of thirty Lincolns, circling them like a schoolmistress, staring recalcitrant old rams into submission and scaring off wolves if need be. Each evening, without leaving a single stray behind, she'd funnel them through the winding hills to the meadow and keep watch till every sheep was settled down for the night.

Despite a mangy coat and sick eyes, this London dog reminded him of Sandy.

He walked past her into the tripe shop, where he purchased a beef heart. When he emerged with the meat on a piece of newsprint, the dog was still pacing, still waiting for something. Just beyond the shop door Ned knelt and held the meat at arm's length. At first the dog regarded him coldly, her black nose twitching. Then, warily, she approached in the low crouch of her breed. Halting inches away from the meat, she regarded Ned steadily from the suppurating eyes. Then with a single motion she snatched the meat up and with it clamped in long jaws trotted away at a gait so familiar to Ned that his heart hammered. He recalled something beautiful — the sight of Sandy bringing the flock to pen with effortless mastery.

Next day he returned to the tripe shop, crestfallen not to see the dog. But the following day she was there again, pacing restlessly. Again he whistled, again she ignored him, again he bought meat, again she took it warily and trotted away.

This ritual continued for a week. Ned looked forward to his daily visit to the tripe shop. His pace quickened as he neared Cheapside.

On the eighth day when he emerged from the shop with meat, Ned didn't kneel near the door but kept walking and stopped halfway down the block. There he turned to watch her watching him intently. This time when he whistled, she took a step forward, but only one, and when he whistled again, she turned away as if uninterested, so he didn't give her the meat, but strode off. She didn't follow.

On the ninth day when he whistled, she came forward until only a few feet lay between them. This time Ned knelt and presented the meat, which she took with the same wariness, then trotted off. This procedure was repeated the following afternoon.

And the next day, when only a few feet separated them, Ned didn't kneel and present the meat, but walked off a few paces, turned, and whistled. His pulse leapt when the dog followed. He went a few paces more, whistled, and she continued to follow.

By this painstaking method, Ned managed to lead her almost a mile before kneeling and offering the meat, which she took with her snatching motion and trotted off.

On the twelfth day, after leading her from the tripe shop into a belt of greenery beyond Smithfield, he allowed her to take the meat without his whistling. She continued trotting away, so Ned thought he'd failed, but halfway across the field, she halted and lay down facing him and bolted the meat. When she'd finished, he whistled. After a long hesitation, so long that he thought for sure he'd failed, she got up and approached, halting just beyond Ned's reach. He didn't try to touch her, but swung round and walked to the edge of the field. Turning there, Ned saw her only a few paces behind him. When he stopped, she stopped. When he started again, she followed. He felt tears in his eyes.

A week later he touched her. By then they were fast companions, save when he went out thieving. Then she remained in his room, curled up in a corner. When he was able to touch her, he cleaned her eyes and groomed her coat. Her tufted brows gave her a look of amused intelligence, much like Sandy. He named her Sandy.

A change took place then in his habits. Instead of lounging in grog shops, he took Sandy for long walks outside of London into the spring countryside. These strolls renewed his own sense of the past, when dogs and sheep had ordered his life. Looking fondly at this dog who trotted by his side, Ned decided one afternoon that he must train her. It would be sinful for her never to use the instincts bred through generations. She must be trained, for at heart she was a working dog. There were no sheep to herd in London, but he must train her anyway. It was an obligation, just as if his father had ambled down the lane on a visit home and declared severely, "What's here? A dog good for nothing but sitting by the fire? Train her or get rid of her!"

With this resolve in mind, Ned sought out a neighborhood boy, a little West Indian whose father had died a servant and whose mother eked out a kind of living as a washwoman. There were many of these St. Giles Blackbirds — boys left behind by fathers who wasted away in the cold and drafty houses of England. Ned had often seen the boy playing in a garbage heap next to the lodging house. He was a solemn lad with large round eyes and glossy black skin. Even in winter he wore only a burlap pullover and patched cotton breeches cut off at the knee.

Ned found him on a door stoop, dangling the drawstring of a used linen armour. "I need you to work her," Ned said, pointing to the dog. "I'll pay wages."

Studying Ned awhile from his large dark eyes, the boy finally rose from the stoop without a word and stood ready. The trio proceeded out of London, reaching the open fields in an hour. Ned explained to the boy that he must behave like a flock of sheep. He must run wildly in one direction, then in another, to imitate the jerky motion of nervous animals. The boy said nothing, didn't even nod, but stood there small, black, and ready.

So the work began.

It was soon apparent to Ned that he'd judged right: the bitch had natural talent for herding, though her flock was only a boy. With increasing delight Ned watched as dog and boy worked together. Sandy approached at a low rhythmic crouch, ears flat, then curved her neck so that the snout was slightly raised. She stared tensely at the boy, warning him she'd attack if he failed to halt. He kept moving at a trot. Then the dog rushed him, giving him a sidelong blow with her shoulder that sent him reeling. Twisting round and returning, she crashed into him again, this blow throwing him to the ground.

Ned yelled at him, "When she crouches and looks at you that way, stop running."

The boy did, coming to a halt. His eyes widened as she fixed him with her own and brought him under control.

In succeeding days Ned taught her to move on whistled signals: one short whistle to herd the flock leftward, two shorts rightward; one long to bring them to a halt. She had the herding dog's instinct for moving obliquely in small, ever narrowing semicircles. The blood of centuries told her how to command the sheep subtly, eliciting obedience without commotion.

In two weeks she was capable of guiding the boy in any direction by whistled signal. She never barked, never lost her concentration. She fixed him with unblinking eyes, warned him with ears flat against her russet skull. Upon signal she dipped, hovered, coaxed, or threatened him into going right or left. She circled as soundlessly as a falcon, her ears stiffening in triumph like wings half spread in flight, when the boy, led where she directed, stood panting and submissive.

To his last day on earth Ned Carleton would remember this dog working in the windswept field. And from the boy's grave intensity, Ned realized that he too was affected by her performance, though the lad never spoke, not once, never a single word during all the hours of training, not even when Ned paid him each evening. A special feeling developed between dog and boy. Ned was determinedly the master, but at times he felt a twinge of envy for the black boy's rapport with Sandy, who in turn had created through her small companion a whole flock of Lincolnshire sheep.

One evening Ned was lurking near the flash house where Doctor Bostock and Lemuel had abandoned him months ago. He waited for a drunken client to stagger from the house; in the shadows Ned might take whatever the whores had left in the man's pocket. A richly appointed carriage drew up. In the light of a flaming torch held by a postilion he saw gold buttons, a velvet coat, ruddy cheeks, all of which reminded him of Lord Sandwich. At odd times the memory of that nobleman left Ned breathless, as if the ermine robe and the flick of a ringed finger and the disdainful smile could smother the breath from his lungs.

He watched the coachman and postilion accompany the gentleman (taller and thinner than Lord Sandwich) to the flash house
door. Such fellows of wealth and power were never alone. They
couldn't be robbed and left with an aching head in a dark lane for
starving urchins to strip of velvet coats and buckled shoes. Such
men were never vulnerable in the way a labourer was. The worker
went homeward with wages clinking in his coat like the loud peal
of a foxhorn calling footpads to the hunt.

Ned took a few quick breaths, then thrusting the good hand into
his coat pocket, he trudged away. He longed for home where Sandy
would be waiting, tail curved upward, her clear eyes bright with
the pleasure of his return.

A strange idea occurred to Ned as he walked. London seemed to
encourage strange ideas, whereas at home in Warsop he'd never had
them. With sheep grazing round him, he'd seen the world clearly
and simply. Rain clouds brought rain; then the sun came out. Now
his ideas seemed to leap from the shadows, untrustworthy but
startling, like something dreamed up by Doctor Bostock.

This new idea was strangest of all. He leaned into the darkness
like someone hurrying toward a new and tempting destiny.

He began by enlisting more help for Sandy's training. They were
two white street urchins about the same age as the black boy; they
spent their time in upper windows of the neighborhood, fishing
with hooks on long wires for passing hats.

When Ned told the black boy of his intention, he met with strong
resistance. The boy shook his head with absolute finality and spoke
his first word. "No."

Ned offered to pay him more than the others because of his
experience with the dog. The boy refused. He said, "No."

"We can't complete her training without help," Ned explained
quietly.

"No."

"We can't."

The boy stood tight-lipped, fists made at his side.

"You are my man. They're only helpers."

Shifting from one foot to the other, the boy studied Ned awhile
before making his demand. "They must not touch her."

Ned agreed. In the black boy's presence, Ned made this stipulation to the recruits. They must never pat the dog's head or stroke her fur or fondle her ears. If they did, even once, they'd not get a farthing.

So the quintet left London for the fields where Sandy's training was completed. What she herded there was no longer a flock of sheep, but three grown men with gold in their pockets. Ned had begun training Sandy to no purpose but to honour her heritage. But a vision had revealed to him a different goal. If she was a working dog without sheep to work, why couldn't she work men?

Streets broadened into avenues in the fashionable West End and led to squares lined by brick town houses. This wealthy section of town was generally avoided by the thieves of St. Giles, who by their conspicuous shabbiness fell under the watchful eye of private guards and watchmen. Ned Carleton spent his last money on good clothes to rig himself out like a gentleman of the district. One summer evening, wearing a green fustian frock-coat and broadcloth breeches and a grey peruke under a beaver hat, he strolled into the glittering West End with Sandy loping a discreet half block behind him.

Three men ambled across a cobblestone square and proceeded down a street empty of people save for a few ladies and some merchants homeward bound in carriages. Ned was enheartened by the animated way the trio carried on their conversation — lively talk obscured danger.

So at a moment when the lane was clear, Ned whistled one long followed by one short, and within seconds Sandy bolted past him, her feathery shank-fur billowing. She swept in front of the three men, halted their progress, prevented them from taking a new direction. Bringing them around with feints and dashes, she parried their every step toward escape, until the astonished trio found themselves standing dead footed against a town house wall.

By this time Ned had reached them. His good hand was inside his frock-coat, on the walnut stock of the wide-bore flintlock blunderbuss he had recently purchased and which he understood thoroughly how to use, having been taught by a father who believed that no man deserved the name of man until he could handle firearms.

Ned quietly ordered the huddled threesome to give over their gold, while Sandy fronted them, ears flat, neck and head arched in snakelike concentration, a low growl coming from her parted mouth, as if she knew full well that herding men was far more dangerous than herding sheep. Stunned by this surprising method of being robbed, the men pulled out their money pouches and tossed them beyond the growling dog.

Without showing the pistol, Ned bent down and picked up the leather truffs, calmly informing the men that they must remain so, without sound or movement, or the dog would attack. Turning without a single backward glance — so confident was he of Sandy — Ned went down the street at an unhurried pace, doffing his hat to a lady coming along, her eyes squinting in the dim light of an oil lamp at three men and something like a dog crouching in front of them.

Only after rounding the corner did Ned whistle. Within seconds the dog was panting at his side, her arched brows giving her a human look of amusement as well as triumph.

In subsequent attempts Ned had like success with two, three, even four men. More often than not, they were herded together before knowing what was happening, and their amazement contributed to Ned's easy handling of them. He never had to show the pistol. The coves never challenged Sandy, whose cobralike muzzle, poised to strike, discouraged resistance.

A fortnight after the first West End robbery, a gazette ran a small news item about a strange cull who forced his victims into submission by using a dog. A month later there were more detailed accounts in which the dog was variously called a mastiff, a setter, a foxhound, a collie, and a terrier. The robber, nicknamed the Dog Cull, was consistently described as a well-appointed young gentleman whose polite manner belied his trade. The Dog Cull achieved widespread notoriety when a rich tobacco merchant, in the habit of walking his large otterhound near Grosvenor Square, was taken up at the insistence of fearful neighborhood women and handled quite roughly by the famous Bow Street Runners. The poor fellow was hauled before Justice Fielding on suspicion of being the notorious Dog Cull, whose activities had been listed in the Bow Street Register and described in the *Covent Garden Journal*. Of course, Fielding dismissed the charges within minutes of the tobacco merchant appearing at the bench, but he and his police force were for a few days the laughingstocks of London.

For the next month, before the excitement subsided, anyone with a dog heeling at his side was regarded suspiciously. It occurred to no one that the Dog Cull might have trained the dog to stay clear of him until the attack took place.

Though the hauls individually were modest enough, Ned was never in want again. His real satisfaction, however, came not from the booty but from his method of getting it. He felt the elation of having power over other men, and not just any men, but those special creatures who reminded him of his former master. Each time he demanded obedience from a group of fancy gentlemen, he saw among them the fourth earl of Sandwich. Each time he and his dog skulked through the twilight lanes of West London, he imagined Lord Sandwich being brought to pen like a befuddled ram. Each time he robbed a man of substance, Ned felt himself emptied of bitterness, although, like a bottle, he was soon filled up again.

He rented a small but cosy room in a good Holborn boarding house. When the summer nights grew suddenly brisk and chill, the landlady furnished a bedwarmer filled with coals and always kept a candle burning in the necessary behind the house. The lap of luxury, Ned told himself. He dressed every day in the fine lurries of a gentleman and bought a brass-headed cane better than the one wielded so majestically by Doctor Bostock. He was a successful cull, a fancy fellow, and might have moved into society had he also possessed a cultivated speech instead of his broad North Country accent.

But he must sacrifice for his new life. By making him famous the newspapers forced him into a change he hated. Ned had to give up Sandy's company. It was too dangerous for her to remain in his room, although the landlady took no special notice at first. Sooner or later she'd connect his pet with the accounts of crime from newspapers her crippled daughter read to her on Sundays. He had no choice but to put Sandy in the exclusive care of the black boy.

Each time that Ned took Sandy for an evening's work, the boy refused to let her go until he'd cradled her head in his black arms and whispered words only she could hear.

[22]

❡ Reader, bear with me, for though the succeeding lines may bore
you, they may also reveal something of me that you should know.

Though my youth was spent in a country setting, I have long
since considered myself a Londoner, for I have my home and living
in this place. In *Tom Jones* I made clear where my sentiments lie,
because life in the country is depicted as far better than life in
town. The farther Tom goes from home and the closer he gets to
London, the more he suffers from deception and hardship. Even
so, I have committed myself to London; as a citizen I must do what
I can to make life here better. And the focus of that effort, given
my magisterial role, must be to lessen crime.

This is difficult, Reader, when you consider the encouragement
given to it by the easy disposition of stolen goods, the general
reluctance of victims to prosecute their attackers, the legal escape
of felons because of our outmoded rules of evidence, and the
excessive clemency for the condemned through a frequent exercise
of the royal prerogative of pardon, to say nothing of judges who
substitute for the public good a misguided notion of fairness.

Of all aspects of this problem, however, what saddens me most
is the apathy of the general public, nay, not only that, but their
misconception of the rights of criminals. Many view the thief as a
kind of Robin Hood, a heroic upholder of freedom. They have a
thoughtless idea of liberty, judging thief takers contemptible for
arresting and prosecuting fellow Englishmen, albeit in recent
years the outlaws have made nightfall in London a time of siege.
To my endless surprise I find people adverse to halting crime even
as they suffer because of it. Only this week the complexity of this
problem was brought home to me by two events.

The first had to do with the arrest of a tobacconist who had been
in the habit of walking his otterhound near Grosvenor Square.
He was taken up roughly by two of my Bow Street Runners and
hauled here under suspicion of being the infamous Dog Cull. It
took little time for me to ascertain that a grave error had been

made, and I released the poor man forthwith, apologizing heartily, the which apology he did not accept but complained of my assault on English freedom and such and promised to bruit the mistake about town. He was true to his word, believe me, for my enemies got hold of the story and printed it everywhere, so that my plan for the suppression of crime suffered in the general merriment occasioned by the false arrest.

In fact, two recruits had made the error, but that meant little to the public, who eagerly grabbed at a chance to find in my plan an encroachment on their rights as Englishmen.

This afternoon, in spite of my wife's clear disapproval, I cracked a bottle of port with Saunders Welch. This was in preparation for discussing our response — I might say our vigorous response — to the criticism of Bow Street, for you must know by now, Reader, my enthusiasms tend to break their bonds when either good or bad fortune so much as winks at me. I told my colleague that we were bound to redouble our efforts in view of this setback. We must add on new runners, prepare to launch daily sallies into the lairs of known gangs, increase the reward to informers, campaign through public notices against felons — in short, declare war against crime. Saunders Welch agreed. A literate man, he then quoted the Bard: "Sweet are the uses of adversity."

Our conversation turned away then from our immediate concerns and ambled pleasantly along, fixing a while on the thief called the Dog Cull, who had contributed so peculiarly to our troubles. No accurate description of his dog was yet forthcoming — proof being the otterhound. He robbed but never did his victims bodily harm, at least not yet. He had a North Country accent, was young and in his prime. I conjectured that he used a dog because he must have deep knowledge of such animals. Saunders wondered if the cull was a shepherd and understood therefore how to train dogs. I hoped not, I said. What if all London was soon filled with shepherds on a stroll with their means of committing robbery? To which Saunders replied, But a good dog is rare. That truth was relief sufficient for us to raise our glasses in a toast. The bottle finished and with Saunders on his unsteady way, I considered the other event that weighed heavily on my mind.

The gypsy Mary Squires had been granted a free pardon. The officers of the Crown had then indicted Elizabeth Canning for wilful and corrupt perjury.

My part in the case was receiving its share of attention in a

disagreeable battle of pamphlets. I mention only one such
treatment written by the sensation-monger John Hill. I quote the
exact title of it, Reader, to give you some hint of its content: *The
Story of Elizabeth Canning considered. With Remarks on what has
been called A Clear State of her Case, by Mr. Fielding; and Answers
to several Arguments and Suppositions of that Writer.* He
admonished me for acting both as counselor and judge. To be
frank, his charge was not altogether without merit, for I had been
careless in accepting two roles in one case. I had allowed myself to
pursue the truth at the sacrifice of an appearance of caution. Yet I
had been consistent within my own nature, for I have always
believed that motive overrides action, and if I have erred on the
side of compassion for a badly used girl, then I am content with a
show of poor judgement in the bargain. But Doctor Hill reserved
the full force of his venom for my claim that the girl was
innocent — branding the girl's story as "absurd, incredible, and
most ridiculous . . . the reveries of an idiot."

In my own tract I stand by my original belief that the Canning
girl was innocent, this claim resting on a number of facts, not the
least of which is this: Although her tale seemed in the highest
degree improbable, yet in no particular was it impossible and no
proof against it had been conclusive. Of utmost importance was the
information given at Bow Street by Virtue Hall, who swore that
the gypsy had taken the girl's stays, then forcibly detained the
victim in the loft. The two girls could not have laid the story
together, for they did not see each other from the time of their
original evidence in front of Mister Tyschemaker until their
appearance before me. The following syllogistical conclusion will
make my point clear: Whenever two witnesses declare a fact, and
agree in all the circumstances of it, either the fact is true or they
have previously concerted the evidence between themselves.
But in this case it is impossible that these girls should have so
previously concerted the evidence. Therefore, the fact is true.

I might add that the failure of the defense to produce the Natus
couple in front of the lord mayor was also crucial to the trial. Had
either Judith or her husband Fortune or both of them given
testimony affirming their residence in the very loft where
Elizabeth Canning swore she had been held a whole month, then
there might have been reason for an acquittal of Squires. But such
testimony was not forthcoming. I suspect the Natus woman failed
to appear because of my admonition that, to protect herself, any
evidence she gave must be honest and true.

I am at this time as firmly persuaded as I am of any fact in this world, that Mary Squires is guilty; that the alibi defense is not only false, but a falsehood easy to be practised when there are gangs of people such as gypsies in the neighborhood and vulgar denizens of roadside ordinaries who are willing to swear to anything.

But my part in this peculiar case is not yet done. A fortnight ago I received from the Crown a request for affidavits held by me concerning the alibi of Mary Squires. I have no such affidavits, so I sent a law clerk to inquire of Counselor Salt if he had them. To my surprise I learned that Salt is no longer retained by the Canning supporters. The lawyer now is John Miles of Birchin Lane, who affirmed that such affidavits had been sworn before justices of the peace in outlying districts, principally in the neighborhood of Enfield. I asked through my law clerk to see them, but Miles put him off by claiming they were not in his possession either. Again I sent out the clerk to learn when they would be available. Miles replied they were being viewed elsewhere; he gave no assurance that their availability would be forthcoming. Plainly the Canning pepole were withholding evidence from me, albeit in my capacity as a justice for Middlesex I had a perfect right to acquaint myself with the documents. Their cause might be admirable, but their methods were lousy. So I reported to the Crown officers that the order for me to submit such affidavits had been given under a misapprehension, for I had none of them. To his grace the duke of Newcastle, secretary of state for the Northern Department, under whose name the request had been made, I wrote a reply and respectfully suggested that the Crown apply to John Miles, Esq.

And so yesterday I received yet a second request from the Crown for said documents! Out of all patience I have sent a server with subpoenas to the Canning crowd, demanding their appearance in my chambers to answer for their behaviour. I hope soon to be rid of the case, for though I believe in Elizabeth Canning, I have no faith in her supporters. Experience, let alone the philosophy of ethics, hath taught me the end cannot justify the means. I will lend the Canning girl my moral support, but I will not lend myself to the intrigues of pettifogging solicitors like Miles and rascals like that grey-faced fellow Scarrat who lurked in the shadows of her misfortune, seeking some kind of advantage of his own.

Leaving behind the law, I got up the stairway with the crutch and entered a far more pleasant world. Mary and the maid were in

the bathroom with little Sophia. To my joy I discovered that the
child was so well recovered that she could be bathed.

Sitting beside the tub, I observed her childish limbs glistening
from water, her squarish face not of great beauty but of a most
pleasant expression (like to her mother's), a countenance which
I venture to predict will bring ease and reasssurance to onlookers
in the future. Leaning forward, across the maid's washcloth, I
caressed Sophia's wet shoulder and arm, feeling a sense of wonder
at the touch of such tender skin, like to the sensation of touching a
lamb or a kitten, so fresh and new, untainted by the corruptions of
life, unweathered and as yet pristine pure, containing a gentleness
and warmth conveyed from the very heart of nature.

Then I was taken to see Louisa asleep in her crib. There did I
wait a long time to relieve my mind of worry and doubt, for I
especially dread sickness in so young a child, who cannot speak in
search of comfort or describe the pain of illness, who lies there
helpless and isolated by its own condition of infancy, much closer
to God than to us, yet capable of suffering and death as we
ourselves are.

I could never for an instant forget some five years ago that our
little Mary Amelia had been christened almost on the day I put
down my pen on the last written page of *Tom Jones,* hoping, as I
did so, that both children (for I considered the book a child of
mine) would lead happy lives, but alas, only one did, and that the
lesser of the two, because by the end of that year our Mary Amelia
was taken from us by a virulent fever.

Satisfied that Louisa rested easy in her sleep, I went from there
to the next room and found young William at his numbers, about
which I questioned him briskly. It pleased me to mark the success
of his application, which would stand him in good stead did I ever
provide sufficient funds for him to attend Eton, as I had done, but
where, it must be confessed, I spent more time than was fitting at
the Birchen Altar, a pair of steps on which we students knelt while
Doctor Black applied his famous switch in an effort to stimulate an
interest in good manners and Greek verbs.

From William I went into the next room and handed my wife
down the stairway to the dining room in spite of her protesting
that with one hand occupied by the crutch I needed the other to
grip the rail. Pshaw, I muttered, and gave her a good-natured
lecture on the delicacy of women in her condition and her need to
take special care; at which lecture even Mary could not fail to
laugh, because never was woman more fitted to the task of bearing

children nor carried in her face and form the appearance of more
vigorous health. Mary had but one burden in a physical way, the
which, since I am being frank with you, was her teeth, quite rotted
by her indulgence of sweetmeats, as the eating of them was her
single unbreakable sin. Quietly but firmly she had refused to have
the ruined teeth pulled, albeit a Frenchman in town could from all
accounts make perfectly good substitutes of ivory set in wooden
frames securely wired into place.

We ate a hearty meal, neither of us having a dainty appetite,
after which I retired to my bedroom for work on an essay. I
plumped the pillows and set paper on a drawing board in my lap,
with the ink stand on the bedside table, for an author is ever prey
to such little rituals. The task I had set myself was to write some
words on the topic of humour. I began with a short discussion of
Lucian and Cervantes and was proceeding to Swift when my
manservant, Joseph, burst into the room with one of his angry
schoolmasterly looks and informed me dryly that I had forgotten
to take my Drop for the day.

"Double Drop," I countered, hoping to get the better of
him. "Doctor Ward prescribed an amount double to that
yesterday."

"And here it is!" Joseph said triumphantly, pushing at me the
tray on which sat a large glass of the abominable liquid.

I took it down, but only after exacting from him the price of a
compensating glass of port. He left, not altogether victorious, as I
had not begged a second (having had my day's quota and then
some with Saunders Welch) and thereby denied old Joseph the
pleasure of refusing it.

Nor was I victorious either, as the act of taking the Drop made
me aware of renewed sweating; indeed, I somewhat marked it
while supping, but took it then for the effect of eating hot soup.
Along with the sweating was a racing of my pulse. Rising from
bed I shuffled over to the mirror (the wretched gout, you may be
sure, would not let me skip) and studied the familiar face, albeit
the puffiness about the eyes was not so familiar; on the contrary, it
was quite strange and a harbinger of nothing to my advantage, for
I was well enough acquainted with dropsy of the flesh to know
that oft-times it settles in the kidneys, the first indication being a
marked puffiness about the face and eyes. So what, Reader, do you
think I did? Why, I stuck out my tongue at the image, and, for
good measure, shook my fist, defying time and fate to do their
worse, because during most of the day I had forgotten my

infirmities and did not intend to dwell more on them, as there was still work to do.

I plumped the pillows, straightened the paper on the board, took quill in hand, when a sudden phrase came to mind, the wry words of Sophocles, namely, that no man loves life like him that's growing old.

I therefore took a deep purifying breath to rid myself of pity and went at humour with a will. To be sure, I had said my best on the subject in the preface to *Joseph Andrews,* but I wager few readers open the pages of that book anymore, now ancient at twelve years of age. In a brief time a number of thoughts on the matter of humour came to me, so that I forgot my puffiness and sweating and pulse. What was humour? It was a question perhaps ripe for someone who no longer practised it. Indeed, humour is nothing more than a violent bent or disposition of the mind to some particular point by which a man becomes ridiculously distinguished from other men. It occurred to me then that every extravagant passion may take on a tragic or comic aspect according to the mode of its presentation. I came at last to the conclusion that humour is produced by display in a ludicrous manner of extravagant peculiarities without regard to the rules of propriety. I sat back and considered the latter proposition, becoming more pleased with it as I studied its application to the masters and also not a little to those moments of humour which here and there seemed to have enlivened my own work.

Abruptly I felt drained of strength, so overwhelmed by fatigue that I could hardly put the writing materials aside and turn down the lamp. For a few affrighted moments I gasped for breath in the darkness, then a sense of vigour returned, allowing my mind to wander through memories of the countryside, when my own dog panted alongside me, and in the distance I saw the chimney, then the brick and fence of Charlotte's home, and my beloved running to the lane to meet me.

[23]

SCARRAT'S ALE HOUSE, The Sign of the Frigate, stood between sail-making shops near Temple Bar Gate with its broad arch where a half-dozen heads of traitorous Scots from the 'Forty-five Rebellion were still displayed on tall pikes. After eight weathering years the skulls looked like the broken shards of so many wine jugs, yet remained sufficiently intact to stare down on the multitudes below: the merry procession of London in sedan chair and wagon, on horseback and foot, blithefully carrying wicker baskets and buckets, twirling canes and parasols, all funneling through the arch toward Judgement Day under the empty glare of the rebellious dead.

When Scarrat entered his ordinary, watermen and stevedores looked up from their foaming mugs, greeted him boisterously, and called him to a pint. With feigned good humour, he waved back and continued past his ale drawer, Giles, who was turning the spigot on a stacked keg.

Scarrat went through the back door into his own room. Linens and breeches were drying on a clothes line stretched between walls. He did his own laundry, unwilling to let a washwoman in with a scrub board, her arms sudsy to the elbows, her filthy odour corrupting the air of his sanctuary. Aside from the clothes line, the small room was uncluttered, neat for that matter, the orderly stronghold of someone passionate about his goods.

On top of a mahogany chest was a row of clocks and in front of them pocket watches displayed in open cases. Each time Scarrat entered his room, he ran a kerchief over enamel, oak, and glass, removing the least speck of dust that might have accumulated since last he'd looked fondly at the steel parts clicking, rotating, ratcheting away. In one corner stood a grandfather clock with a face of brass engraved with cherub heads and banded with satinwood. It meant more to him than anything in the world. For two years he'd scrimped to buy it and was now collecting more gold (his money hid under a floor board) to purchase an ornamented canopy clock in gilt bronze, which had been cast and chased to perfection.

Scarrat could lose himself in watching the toothed wheels and pinions of a timepiece move. For long mystical stretches of time he'd study a mainspring as it transmitted energy by wheel train and escapement to the balance. Here was strength in predictable motion, here was comfort, here was security. Often he'd stop whatever he was doing and listen enraptured to the way a striking mechanism governed its blows against gong or bell.

His collection of timepieces was tangible proof of Robert Scarrat's climb to success in the world. Orphaned at five and thrown upon the parish, first laboring as a sweep, he served as a shoemaker's apprentice until the shoemaker's wife, taking on airs, hauled him from the garret workshop and installed him as a footman of sorts in her mean little household. At least he'd acquired sufficient manners to stand him in good stead when at eighteen he ran away to become a twang for whores. Then through a series of lies and some luck, he'd gained hire as a footman for Lord Sandwich, who had installed him finally in this tavern. He had come a long, long way. The metallic beauty which surrounded him belied the misery of his youth. When the clocks struck in concert, his lips broke into a proud smile of ownership.

Scarrat walked to the open window and regarded the back yard where, with his own hands, he had planted beds of flowers: lilies of the valley, sweet sultan, musty martagon, candy tuft, love-in-a-mist. Under a grey sky some of them were blooming, and their released perfume drifting into his castle keep added to Scarrat's sense of well-being.

He had struggled for everything here. He had eschewed good wine and fine clothes in favor of clocks and flowers. He had never let a woman get in the way of ambition. He had risen from the mire despite his grey ugliness, and nothing would ever dislodge him from his place in the world. Nothing. He had a name, a place, and fine goods. He was the proprietor of an establishment for the sale of spiritous liquors.

Yet he didn't hold the mortgage.

Each day that Robert Scarrat drew breath, the shakiness of his position rankled and embittered him. His independence was no more than an illusion without the continued patronage of a master too rich to be trustworthy, too high to be steady.

His lordship had never forgiven him for recruiting such an unreliable bitch as Betty Canning. And this recent charge of perjury against the girl had kept the error fresh in the nobleman's mind.

The indictment had come on the heels of a farcical business engineered by those blockheads, Wintlebury and Lyon. Incensed by the release of Mary Squires, they wanted revenge against those who had testified in her behalf. Smelling trouble, Salt had extricated himself from the affair after the gypsy's release from prison. The two bunglers had fallen into the hands of a pettifogging solicitor who easily persuaded them to indict the Dorsetshire men for perjury. Distrusting the lawyer, Scarrat had moved discreetly into the background while old Wintlebury and carpenter Lyon plunged into another trial.

It had ended disastrously for the Friends of Canning. The unscrupulous counselor never appeared in court, but sent a befuddled assistant who knew nothing about the case and produced not a single witness. Thus, the speedily dropped indictments against the Dorsetshire men served only to anger the court, rekindle public interest in the affair, and hasten a charge against Elizabeth Canning.

Her upcoming trial gave Scarrat yet another ticklish job: to prove the girl innocent of perjury. Quite understandably milord Sandwich demanded that every effort be made to settle the troubling matter for good and all. To this end Scarrat again moved to the forefront, leaving behind old Wintlebury, whose gout had flared up, and carpenter Lyon, whose legal zeal had recently been superseded by lust for a new maid. Armed with gold from his master, Scarrat hired a new lawyer, Mister John Miles, who had a reputation for winning cases by any means available. A short, thick-necked man with the puglike features and big loose mouth of a bulldog, Miles was ugly. Scarrat liked to deal with a man as ugly as himself. And Miles was a sharper who fell in easily with Scarrat's own brand of obtaining evidence and witnesses. They agreed that the best way to serve Bet Canning was to discredit the gypsy's alibi.

"We need affidavits proving the Squires woman was in Enfield all that month," Miles explained.

"I can get them."

"You have the means?"

"Never you mind. The Friends of Canning can raise whatever be necessary."

"I had no idea you people were so well fixed."

"I said never you mind."

"When told that, I listen," Miles replied sensibly, "and I stop minding."

This last fortnight Scarrat had busied himself further in the case, making sure of old witnesses and creating new ones. First he visited the neighborhood women who had attended Betty on her return and then the men who took part in the raid on Enfield, going over their recollection of events carefully, adding or erasing details as necessary. He urged them all to be safe in their testimony so as to protect the reputation of their district as well as a maiden's good name.

Scarrat was reasonably sure of the Canning women, for the mother needed gifts from the Friends to keep her in fripperies, and the daughter, who was escorted through swank coffee houses and given pouches of money at clubs, seemed to believe in her rigged tale with religious zeal. The two women spent long hours over their romances.

The mother declaimed from a calfbound volume: " 'He is gone; our more than father is dead! One universal lamentation filled the house.'

"What is tragical is so edifying," she observed grandly. But some of the passages so frightened the woman that she gasped for breath and laid the palm of her hand flat on her bodice. In *Charlotte Summers* three pillagers have waylaid the heroine, robbed, and tied her to a tree.

"I believe she is young; but young or old it is all the same in the Dark; do you stay here, and watch the Coast is clear. D — n me, but is a good thought; let us all have a Touch; but as she is my Booty, I will begin —"

More to the point of Bet's possible future, the widow read from *Matilda:*

"The Happiness of Lord Wilmot and his bride was now Complete, and the Tender and Virtuous Matilda forgot all her misfortunes in the blissful endearments of chaste connubial love."

So Widow Canning droned on into the night, while her daughter sat rigid, prim, absorbed, as if willing the pallor of her cheeks, her large eyes reflecting the memory of terrible adventures and wonderful marriages that had never happened.

Witness to their fancy, Scarrat counted on it along with their greed to keep them safe, yet he couldn't pry them loose from the infernal Methodists who trooped in daily with hosannas. He feared they might get sudden religion and in such a frivolous mood confess to the world what had occurred. That is, if the widow yet knew. His faith was in the girl's profound genius for dissimulation; it should protect Betty even from her mother.

Scarrat's chief effort was to collect secure witnesses from Enfield. He rode out there often, varying his approach according to the person interviewed. To make a witness safe, he used everything from bribery to threat and often rehearsed some empty-headed prater for hours to get the testimony straight. Even then he couldn't be wholly certain of the farmhands, servants, and tradespeople from Enfield and surrounding villages. Many of them couldn't tell one year from another and recalled Christmas of a season ago as something long buried in their childhood. Yet at this considerable task of establishing the whereabouts of the gypsy band in Enfield, he persisted with the passion of someone bent on saving his own life. Controlling his exasperation with utmost difficulty, he implored old women and dull-witted labourers to recall seeing the gypsy in their midst. Before they swore affidavits at the bench of local magistrates, they were schooled in precise details concerning their encounters with Mary Squires. She carried a blanket. She told a fortune. She drove two pack mules ahead of her along Turkey Street. She asked for a faggot to light her pipe. She lodged in a cowshed. She sat with a pork pie in the Wells kitchen.

Indeed, he created a complete fictional life for the old gypsy throughout the month of January 1753, and forced every particular down the throats of Enfield villagers, hoping they'd not only fix their marks to affidavits but also spew up the details from the witness box if it came to that. He gave a guinea to a gardener, to a serving girl, to a faggot carrier. He appealed to the pride of a glass blower and a tanner and a chandler, arguing that if they failed to so testify against the gang of gypsies, all London would think the people of Enfield encouraged bad company in their midst.

But Scarrat was not content even after the Friends of Canning had two dozen affidavits on file that put the gypsies in Enfield instead of Dorsetshire. He pressed forward, discovering people on the Hertford Road who would swear for a sum that they'd heard a girl scream for help on New Year night. He had good luck with the keeper of the Stanford Hill Turnpike, who needed money to clothe his children; for three guineas he would claim that on the New Year, between ten and eleven at night, he'd seen from the turnpike gate two fellows dragging a woman along. Then Scarrat got hold of a scurrilous rogue who maintained that during his stay in Bridewell Prison he'd overheard the Wells woman confess to keeping the girl locked up in a loft. A man of the same kidney would swear that Squires had made a like admission. Another Enfield couple in need of money was easily convinced that Judith Natus had confessed to them that she and Fortune had slept in the kitchen while the Canning girl was imprisoned in the loft. Scarrat sought out Virtue Hall and so frightened her with threats of facial disfigurement that she vanished forthwith and was never again seen in or about London. He also found the gypsy who, upon release from Newgate, had returned to the Dorset shore. He bribed her to emigrate with her family to Ireland, furnishing them with sturdy trunks, a bolt of bright silk, and a handful of newly minted guineas. As for Tabby Howard, who had actually imprisoned the girl, Scarrat merely repeated his warning: "One word of it from you will be your last."

All of these precautions notwithstanding, he feared the coming trial and, what was more important, so did his master. There was always something loose and difficult awaiting him: a drunken lout in the tavern to deal with, an aching tooth, a sudden fear of fire in the neighborhood. There was always a chance of losing this room, these clocks, the Frigate itself. There was always more to do, as if the solution to one problem created a host of others.

Today, for example, he and others had been forced to appear before Justice Fielding, who insisted on questioning the Friends of Canning.

Luckily, Counselor Miles had been a match for the truculent judge. They sparred back and forth: the hulking magistrate furious behind his gavel, and the pug-faced solicitor unfazed before the bench. Where are the affidavits? Fielding demanded a dozen times. To which Miles had a number of slippery explanations: they were being printed up or were being inspected by various justices outside of London or were being appraised by various solicitors for possible jurisdictional conflicts — until in exasperation Fielding gaveled him down.

The magistrate did no better with the Friends, some of them innocent of the recent legal intrigues and others fortified with sufficient gold to know absolutely nothing about informations given about anything. Scarrat laughed inwardly at Justice Fielding, as he often laughed at the high and mighty who felt they could control the vulgar when the vulgar were controlling them. But Scarrat had to admit that Fielding was not altogether a fool. There was wit in the man, enough to warn him there were those abroad who'd make a fool of him. Although his large frame was obviously wasted by illness and his keen blue eyes had gone watery and his pugnacious jaw and prominent cheeks were sunken in, Justice Fielding still had a spark left in him — a spark ignited into flame by his helpless fury, for helpless it was. Not a soul brought before him gave him satisfaction. He was indeed flailing in the wind.

And yet, called to the witness box himself, Scarrat felt a grudging admiration for the irascible and defeated man.

"Mister Scarrat, relate to me your opinion of the most recent activities of the Friends of Elizabeth Canning."

"Your worship, I believe the Friends do nothing more than solicit funds in our poor Betty's behalf." He took the full force of the judge's piercing eye.

"Mister Scarrat, I have spoken to an officer of the court who has gone out to Enfield. He says there appears to be considerable activity. By that I mean people are soliciting witnesses to sign affidavits. There is reason to believe you have been recently in Enfield."

"That is true, your worship. I have friends there."

"Apparently you have friends everywhere."

"That is true, your worship."

"Were you questioning, let us say, your friends in Enfield?"

"About what, your worship?"

"About the gypsy, Mister Scarrat. Answer plainly."

"I know nothing about the gypsy, your worship."

"You did not answer my question, Mister Scarrat."

Counselor Miles stood up. "Permit me, your worship, to rephrase the question for Mister Scarrat. Sir, did you ever solicit affidavits from people in or around Enfield?"

"No sir, I did not. I did ask contributions for the fund, however, on behalf of our poor Betty."

Fielding leaned far over the desk, his waxen face suddenly taking on color. "That's all you have to say? You'd have me believe your actions in this affair are above-board and selfless?"

"Yes, your worship."

Fielding seemed to be considering a course of action, and for an odd moment Scarrat half expected the ailing magistrate to come at him over the desk. Perhaps had Fielding been in his prime, he might very well have done so. Scarrat's admiration increased, especially because he had no need to fear the man. Miles had assured him that the judge from Middlesex had no power or jurisdiction over the matter of affidavits obtained in the neighborhood of Enfield. Fielding could only cajole and threaten, stir up a bit of momentary trouble. His powers extended only to the limit of righteous anger. His frustration, however, must be boundless, for he surmised correctly there were transgressions against the law. Fielding's day in court would accomplish nothing. So Miles promised.

And so it was. Scarrat and the others left that afternoon with a victory to celebrate.

For Scarrat a celebration was nothing more than a quiet evening in his room, away from his duties and the roaring laughter of watermen beyond the closed door. Yet he couldn't even celebrate his solitude because shortly after gazing at his flowers he was seized by a coughing fit. The furious coughing buckled him over. He hacked and hacked and hacked; while hacking, Scarrat fixed his eye on a wooden spoon that lay beside the clocks. He'd kept the spoon as a reminder of his youth, having won it in a donkey race for chimney sweeps held before a large crowd on Tyburn Road. The spectators howled with laughter as the sooty boys clutched their bucking mounts. He'd never forgotten the derisive laughter. Still coughing, he reached out and picked up the worthless spoon and turned it lovingly, as though it were an enameled watch from the atelier of Thomas Tompion.

No one was going to take away his name and position and fine things. No one.

He heard a commotion outside, announcing the arrival of another unruly crew of watermen. They were receiving taunts from rough fellows already in their cups. "Have a clank with us, old bumboats!"

"You still drinking? Your innards not rotted out?"

"Have a care —"

"Draw ale for these ladies!"

"Ladies? Don't go too far!"

"Sit down. I wouldn't fuck you for a shilling was I the worst slut alive. I never saw uglier. Sit down."

With a deep sigh Robert Scarrat reached under his pillow for the marlinspike he kept there. Tall but thin, he was no hulking brute, but encounters in his life had taught him defense, especially with a tapered weapon like a marlinspike or a wooden fid. More than one head had been split open by him in the Frigate, though usually he could solve matters with a few free grogs and some flavourful talk.

"Come athwart me, sonofabitch —" The scraping sound of a chair pushed back.

If only he might sit awhile in the garden, inhaling the aroma of flowers, while five clocks struck the hour simultaneously, but there was trouble afoot outside. Wiping his mouth of spittle, Scarrat hurried into the tavern.

[24]

JOHN HARRISON was at work on his fourth marine chronometer, a watch only five inches in diameter, but Captain Cook would take it on his second voyage around the world and it would enable him to navigate with startling accuracy. At Greenwich the astronomer James Bradley was observing eclipses of Jupiter's satellites in order to correct the existing tables for longitude, allowing him then to determine the exact locations of Lisbon and New York.

And Ned Carleton in the silence of his Holborn room was reading Robert Paltock's *The Life and Adventures of Peter Wilkins* — bent over the page in candlelight, his mouth forming each word as the adventure unfolded. The militant saviour of a winged people, Peter Wilkins listened to a recital of the land's history, which featured a Cain-like ancestor who with his wife was cast into a pit where they burned for seven thousand years, "till having with their teeth wrought a passage thro' the side of the mountain, they begat a new generation about the foot of the mountain." Peter Wilkins refashioned a primitive government into a constitutional monarchy, built a paper industry as well as a glider-like flying machine, translated the Latin Bible into Swangeantine, subdued palace plots, waged unremitting warfare against the enemy, and in the final pages was sending forth colonists to spread the Protestant ethic across the world. Ned thought it a rousing good tale.

Ever since Mister Scarrat had given Ned the charred remnants of *Joseph Andrews,* he'd wanted to read, and with his success as the Dog Cull there was leisure for it along with gold to buy books. He purchased a brand-new *Joseph Andrews* and got through it with the help of Nathaniel Bailey's *Universal Etymological English Dictionary,* though unknown to him a few streets away in a narrow house one lonely man was laboring hard on a far more monumental dictionary. In two years Samuel Johnson would publish his two-volume work, which would sell at an expensive four pounds ten shillings.

After *Joseph Andrews,* Ned had bought *The History of Tom Jones, the Foundling,* only to discover that this *Tom Jones* had not been writ by the same man nor was it nearly as good as the story about Joseph Andrews. It was much too fancy, with such as the following to pour over:

> Evil is an ill-natured Vice; it loves Mischief for Mischief's Sake, and takes Pleasure in Torment. It feeds on Stench, sucks Poison from Cordials, and Infection from Perfumes.

Unable to finish it, Ned turned to tales of adventure such as *Peter Wilkins* and *The Life and Adventures of Joe Thompson* and *The History of Jack Conner* and *The Travels and Adventures of William Bingfield, Esq.* and a book whose title was nearly as long as its contents: *A Narrative of the Life and Atonishing Adventures of John Daniel, a Smith at Royston in Herfortshire, For a Course of Seventy Years, Continuing the melancholy Occasion of his Travels. His shipwreck with one Companion on a desolate Island. Their Way of Life. His accidental discovery of a Woman for his Companion. Their peopling the Island. Also, a Description of a most surprizing Engine, invented by his Son Jacob, on which he flew to the Moon, with some Account of its Inhabitants. His return, and accidental Fall into the Habitation of a Sea-Monster, with whom he lived two years. His further Excursions in Search of England. His Residence in Lapland, and Travels to Norway, from whence he arrived at Aldborough, and further Transactions till his death, in 1711. Aged 97. Taken from his own Mouth, By Mr. Ralph Morris.*

Slipped into Ned's trunk was a copy of the real *Tom Jones,* which he meant to read when skill matched enthusiasm, and he could take easy pleasure from Mister Fielding's long sentences.

When not reading, he felt his loneliness, especially now that Sandy stayed with the black boy, and when he could no longer abide it, he went to bawdy houses to get there the impersonal relief that a few shillings could buy. Sometimes he talked to men in grog shops about the old days in the North Country. But most of these men had long ceased to remember their own childhoods. Life in the present was too demanding. They lacked the serenity to recall what had happened so much as a week ago.

And how, Ned wondered, might he explain to himself, much less to others, in what manner a stray dog had led him back to his own memories? During these days he often felt awash in sentiment. Bittersweet recollections brought him to the verge of tears. He recalled the old cottage, his mother working in the garden, a raw-boned woman with thickly veined hands and eyes steady enough to calm a nervous sheep. Certain images wandered into his mind: a loom by candlelight, a chestnut tree, a kettle hanging above the hearth, the dun-colored shops and bellied windows in the village of Warsop. Sometimes, when he lay immersed in such daydreams, he heard in memory the tolling from a church belfry, the lowing of cattle on their way to market, the amiable clang of metal in the wheelwright shop. He saw the palsied hand of an old chandler pouring wax into a mould.

Fidgety, beset by nostalgia, but unwilling to entertain the idea of returning to a place where Priscilla and her husband still lived, Ned sought reflief in the gaming stews of Smithfield. Often he played until daybreak. In this manner he began to lose most of what he took at footscampering, with the result that he and Sandy went on more forays, increasing the chances of being caught.

Late one afternoon, idly passing through the elegant district of Cornhill, he saw a tall young woman emerge from a millinery shop. It was closing time, and she stood in conversation with the owner, who then barred and padlocked the door. From the respectful curtsy the young woman gave the old man, she probably worked in the shop.

Her image went with Ned into the night. She reminded him of Pris, who had given him her heart, but not her hand. Pris languishing against a tree at sundown. Pris at the butter churn with cream to her elbows. Pris in his arms under the dappled willows. Carefree Pris, who had married well and practically. Tall, shapely, brown-haired, laughing Priscilla.

That evening at cards he thought of the girl at the millinery shop: tall, shapely, but dark-haired. She remained with him through heavy losses at hazard, so heavy that the next evening he went for Sandy and together at midnight they robbed two men in full sight of a coffee house. For the first time Ned had need of running from a group of shouting men until, in a maze of familiar lanes, he lost them.

Next day, haunted by the girl's image, he returned to the millinery shop for another look. Because the window was filled with ribbons and notions, he couldn't see inside. After a long hesitation, he entered the cramped little shop and saw the tall girl standing at a counter with boxes of goods piled behind her. He mumbled out a request to see laces, then studied her slyly as she set boxes on the counter for his inspection. Parted in the middle, her black hair was pulled taut from her brow and drawn under a muslin cap edged with lace. She wore a close-fitting bodice and a checked skirt which emphasized her figure. Around her neck was a lime-yellow ribbon. There was a fullness at her throat, as if gently swollen by song.

Ned purchased a piece of Irish lace for a shilling. He met her dark inquiring eyes with a timid smile. She did not smile back. Paying, he shuffled out of the store, feeling awkward, foolish, a perfect dolt — the selfsame dolt he'd felt himself to be that first time he spoke to Priscilla. At the corner he thrust the lace into the gnarled hand of a surprised beggar.

Next day he returned to Cornhill and hovered near the shop, feeling more foolish as time wore on. He might address her in language overheard during his service in the Sandwich household.

"And please you, madam, it would be benevolent of you to allow me to sup with you."

And if she protested, he'd coolly reply, "Indeed, you wrong me, madam. Upon my soul I mean no harm, I have no designs on your person."

And after more polite exchanges, she'd accept his arm and he'd say, "I'm infinitely obliged."

It was an elegant scene enacted in the shilling romances kept under the pillows of half the chambermaids in London, at least those who could read. It reminded him of the foolishness in a book he had never finished. Yet he continued to imagine such a brilliant meeting. Before he knew it, the sun had lowered below the rooftops, and the bent old shopkeeper emerged at closing time — with the girl.

Standing at the corner, Ned watched them talking in an earnest way. Finally the shopowner swung a tasseled cane, as if in irritation, and strode off. The girl remained in front of the shop, adjusting the bonnet ribbon under her chin and smoothing the fichu around her shoulders.

Taking a deep breath, Ned came forward to doff his tricorn awkwardly. "I was in your shop yesterday, miss."

She gave him a quick appraising glance from dark eyes. "I remember it." Readjusting the bonnet, she looked past him at the departing shopkeeper.

Ned was staring at the hummingbird fullness of her throat. "Can you," he began, "that is, would you come have a refreshment with me?"

Turning from the vanishing shopkeeper, she gave Ned her full attention.

"A dish of chocolate?" he asked hopefully.

The girl neither cried out, "Sir, you are overly zealous!" nor murmured with a demure blush, "Such a thing requires time to consider of." She merely said, "That would be pleasing."

They went to a pastry shop and drank their hot chocolate in near silence. Seeing her almost finished, Ned felt a touch of panic and blurted out another invitation. Would she sup in his company at a chop house? This she bluntly refused to do. However, at his shy but insistent entreaty, the girl agreed to stroll with him on Saturday afternoon in St. James's Park.

Having parted at the shop door, Ned called at her retreating figure, "Your name, miss?"

"Clare."

"Mine be Ned."

"Good evening, Ned."

He stood there thunderstruck by the beauty of Clare vanishing in the mist. Aside from being tall and shapely, the girl no longer reminded him of Pris. Her hair was darker. She was not so light-hearted, so gay, so quick to laugh. But she was somehow more than Pris could ever be.

They met as planned in St. James's Park. In the early summer air she wore a cherry-red cloak over a blue skirt and a white tucker; a slip of black hair curled under the bonnet down to her throat, her hummingbird throat. Ned was bewitched. Clare was nearly as tall as he — broad-shouldered too — yet his good hand might have encircled her waist halfway around would she give him leave to try.

With scores of other couples they strolled through the broad meadow, ambling under clumps of willows in a sea of frilled parasols. From there, exchanging but a few civil words, they walked to the Thames and gazed from the wharf at gilded barges, coastal packets, brigantines under sail, and countless bumboats rocking on the waves. Again she refused to sup with him, but after some hesitation agreed to see the fireworks at Marylebone Gardens with him the next day.

So the following afternoon they watched rockets bursting and pumped stars exploding above the heads of a spellbound crowd. Ned looked at the girl instead of at the fireworks and found, to his surprise and delight, his gaze openly, honestly returned. A rumour spread through the pleasure garden: four onlookers had caught fire from the display. But Ned and Clare scarcely heard. Their hands touched, drew quickly apart, came together again, as they strolled along the path, oblivious of the wagonload of injured spectators rolling past them.

They supped at a chop house near the Strand. They spoke little but regarded each other above a flagon of wine. When they left, she walked at his side, her hand clinging to his gloved bad hand — though at first, embarrassed by it, he had tried to pull the hand back from hers. Without hesitation, without argument, or even without agreement of any kind, she accompanied him back to his Holborn lodgings.

Looking around the small but comfortable room, Clare sat on the edge of the bed. "Do be gentle with me," she told him in a breathless whisper. Then getting to her feet, she began undressing.

He came to her awestruck, grateful, lusty. Taking her in his arms, he used the word he'd once used in the North Country, "Lass —"

"Not a word."

Their lovemaking began gently, but then she whispered in his ear, "Not *too* gentle, lad. I'm no virgin."

"Lass —"

"Not a word. Oh, just love me —"

*

In the morning, sitting cross-legged and naked on his bed, she methodically combed her tangled hair. Ned lay there in a helpless mood, watching her recede from him, watching her prepare to leave. He couldn't understand her abrupt coolness. Had he failed her last night? Dear God, that seemed unlikely, for she'd given him as much proof as a man would need of her own pleasure in their lovemaking.

While she was buttoning her bodice, he said, "When do we meet again?"

Clare shook her head. "Never again."

"Don't you like me?"

She turned her head and gave him a wan smile. "Yes, sweet lad, I like you very much."

"So see me again."

Until finished with her dressing, Clare said nothing. Then she agreed, with a frown and a sigh, to meet him the next Saturday.

"That's a long time off."

"Mark this, lad. Don't come to the shop." She was putting on the cherry-red cloak. "If you do, I'll see you no more," she warned severely.

Was this the passionate woman whom he'd held in his arms last night? At the door Ned put his gloved hand on her waist — he'd not removed the glove, not even to touch her flesh. "You mean much to me," he declared.

"Not a word of that." Gently but firmly she removed his hand. Her lips were trembling. "You mustn't tell me such things." She left then.

[25]

ALL WEEK HE TRIED to recapture those moments when, from the starchy petticoats, her body emerged like a butterfly from a cocoon. In his arms she'd been sufficiently bold and demanding to give him the confidence to seek fullest enjoyment. But he fretted over her strange behaviour of the next morning. She was a woman of her own mind, that was certain.

A week was a long wait, indeed. He felt woefully distracted, restless, in truth so petulant and unsteady that he never took Sandy on a hunt all week. But he did go to Black Boy Alley and bought linen condoms from the old woman there.

"Have you got yourself a good girl?" she asked, cackling.

Her jests in the past had never bothered him, but Ned was offended by such familiarity today. "These be for use with bawds," he lied.

The woman shook her head good-naturedly. "No, lad. See? Both your hands be trembling. Don't try and fool an old trollop like myself. You buy armour for a special miss. La, was I younger, I'd fight her for her place with you! Go to, you're bewitched." She laughed heartily. "I wish you joy of her," she declared with feeling.

Next Saturday they strolled again through the park, supped in a chop house, returned to his room. Again she was eager in his arms and the next morning, when sunlight awoke Ned, he turned to discover her studying his gloved hand. He had already told her about the fire, the sorry aftermath. But this morning she wanted to see for herself, and in spite of his mild protest removed the glove. Gently she pulled the calfskin from his fingers, held them in her own, and to his astonishment began kissing the scarred tissue. Then his heart went out to her, for he understood that by this action she was trying to share his pain and bitterness.

But later, while dressing, Clare turned cold again, even appearing reluctant to see him the next Saturday. At the door she kissed his gloved hand tenderly, but warned him again never to come to the shop.

Ned meant to heed the warning, but her insistence on it aroused the suspicions of a lover, and so he found himself, three days later, standing at twilight in the shadows of Cornhill. From a dark alley he watched as she left the shop with the owner, who swung the tasseled cane. Hailing a coach, the old fellow handed her inside, and together they rattled off into a mist.

Ned watched until the coach vanished, then hastened to a gaming house and lost in reckless play. The next night he almost pistol-whipped a cove, though the poor fellow had done nothing to warrant violence. The rest of the week Ned brooded, until by Saturday he was in a mood of suppressed rage.

But the girl's tall slim figure, dark hair, and hummingbird throat transformed his fury into an aching sense of loss. Taking her arm, he led her straight to his room. Clare smiled as they hurried there, as if this pell-mell rush was merely a delightful measure of his desire. Sitting down on the bed, she untied the bonnet ribbon. He sat on a chair, hands clasped, head bowed.

"Lass," he said finally, "I think you're the shopkeeper's wench."

When she said nothing to deny it, but took off the bonnet and laid it on the quilt, he added, "So it's true."

"Let it be, sweet lad." Removing the fichu from her neck, she started to unbutton the bodice.

"So it's true."

Her hands paused at the unbuttoning. "Do you want me to stay?"

"It's true!"

"You must have come to the shop. You saw me leave with him."

"You're his wench. It's true."

Clare began rebuttoning the bodice.

She was going to leave! Rushing from the chair, he gripped her shoulders, hovering above her as she sat on the bed. Clare held his wrists.

"Yes, it's true," she murmured, her dark eyes meeting his steadily.

Ned let go and returned to the chair, hiding his face in his hands. Time passed. Neither spoke.

At last Clare said calmly, "I shall go, lad. But hear me this last time. I came to London two years ago from Sussex."

She had come with a brass-nailed trunk and three guineas in a spring pouch. Her mother had just died, there was none in the world to help her, so she'd come to London seeking employment. At the staging inn a well-dressed middle-aged woman offered her lodgings and brushmaking work. Clare accepted the proposal eagerly and joined a half dozen other girls, all of whom worked and lodged in the brushmaking shop. Two days after assuming her duties, Clare was promptly raped by a watchmaker in a second-floor parlour where, at her employer's request, Clare had taken the customer a cup of tea. For the privilege of debauching the new girl, the watchmaker had paid Mrs. Adams handsomely. While Clare lay weeping on the couch, elegant Mrs. Adams came into the room and explained that a country lass could live vastly grand in London if only she would learn. So Clare had remained in the house, for want of elsewhere to go, and continued to receive the watchmaker, just as the other girls, she soon learned, received their own visitors. The watchmaker kept Clare six months before tiring of her, then sent along his friend, a silversmith, who in turn sent along a milliner, the man who presently employed Clare in his shop.

This, Ned knew, was a familiar enough history for a girl in London town. Had he not been so blinded by love, he also knew that he could have predicted it from the moment of first setting eyes on her. And surely he should have divined the truth when first he saw the pretty employee curtsy to the elderly milliner. What shop girl was ever safe, much less a country lass who came penniless to this town? It was a fact as inevitable as the sun rising, as the Thames flowing.

Having finished relating her history in a flat emotionless voice, Clare was tying the bonnet under her chin.

How could she leave? She had taken his heart.

"Lass, I'm glad you told me," he said gently, "but be assured of one thing. It's of no account to me because I love you."

She held the bows of the bonnet knot.

"But this shall be of account to *you*. I must speak plain and honestly. I'm no sheep seller. I work as a footpad. They call me the Dog Cull."

He waited for anger or horror or at least surprise, but the girl simply nodded, as if this revelation were as inevitable as the sun rising or the Thames flowing. In her quiet acceptance of this shocking fact there was a suggestion of terrible experience. Truly, Ned felt, she must have suffered and more than he could ever know. He wanted to comfort this wonderful woman, yet found himself accepting comfort from her — her hand stroking his hair, a motherly gesture, as he stood against her, hands lightly on her waist. He felt small, naked in the presence of her love.

"Come live with me," he whispered.

Pulling free, she walked to the door. "Such a thing's not possible."

"Because I'm a thief?"

"Yes. And because if you give it up, you'll have no money and if you have no money and I give up my shopkeeper I'll need to find another soon enough and you'll hate me for being a whore again and I'll hate you for not providing so I can be a decent woman and there we'll be, hating each other. Do you see? Nothing's possible for us." Leaning against the door, she began crying and in this vulnerability she allowed Ned to take her firmly against his chest in a comforting way.

"We shall marry," he declared, then repeated it in a surge of elation. "We shall marry!"

"Thank you, sweet lad, but we shall not marry. Didn't you hear me?"

"Do you care for me?"

"I love you, but marry you? Impossible." Avoiding his eyes, Clare pushed against his arms, separating herself from him. "I saw a woman at her man's hanging at Tyburn. She sat under the gibbet and bit her lips till the blood ran."

Ned sat on the edge of the bed, and Clare joined him at the other edge. They stared at the floor like children punished for the same misdemeanour. Finally Ned broke the silence.

"I'll give up scampering. In faith, I've never had stomach for it. I'll get a secure place. I've a strong back for work. I'll show you a man to count on." He hid his hand behind his back, though Clare wasn't even looking at it, didn't need to. It was on their minds like an absent enemy.

Suddenly Clare sighed and patted the bed. "This alone is what we have. We can't have more." Her voice was heavy with fatigue. "God help us."

Fiercely he drew her to him. "We'll have more! I vow it. Don't fear, lass. It won't go wrong with us!"

"You're a good sweet loving fellow."

Relaxing his hold, Ned held her gently, and even his love failed to protect him from the truth of London town: fate here was strict, implacable, unyielding.

*

Next day, when she was gone, Ned began to pace in his small room, prey to wild and numerous fancies. With his dog and pistol he'd become the richest cull in England. The world be damned; he'd give Clare everything she wanted. He'd dress her in utmost finery and escort her through Ranelagh so the foppish bloods might gape in wonder at her elegant beauty. Ned sat down, emptied of this hot fancy. He looked at the indentation left by her body on the quilt.

Clare was right. They were trapped, indeed. She'd not leave her shopkeeper for the uncertain, the terrifying, life of a footpad's woman. What if he got her with child and then one fine day was thrown into Newgate? An unprotected mother would surely land in the worst of stews. God in heaven, he'd seen them trudging from flash house to flash house with a child in tow, taking a customer into a room while the prattling toddler waited outside.

Nor could he, as he claimed, give up his footscampering. How could he? For what else? The ruined hand held him in an iron grip, securing him to the underworld.

There was, perhaps, a plain solution: he might return to shepherding. But where? Certainly not around Warsop, as he'd proved disloyal to the neighbourhood by leaving for a fancy life in London. And there was a strong chance he'd not be able to face such a simple life after the tumult of London. To become a shepherd after living as a footpad was like asking a grown man to behave as a boy. And the plain truth was he'd come to believe in gold, having seen what men would do to get it. He'd leave London only if his pockets were full. He'd not drag Clare penniless into yet more misfortune.

What they needed was a miracle, a miracle. His mother used to fling herself down and pray for salvation, so in desperation Ned sank to his own knees. But he couldn't pray. Instead, he roamed the West End that evening with his dog, taking from an old man two pounds six.

Brooding one afternoon on their unpromising future, Ned was walking in the Haymarket and saw through the crowd a long jaw, a grey face into which coal dust seemed to have been driven with the force of a hammer.

Ned had heard people say that London was like hell: you were sure to see old acquaintances in both places. Here was the familiar leathery face of Robert Scarrat. The sight of it had Ned tapping the charred book which he carried in his pocket everywhere, a kind of talisman against destiny.

Scarrat bobbed in the market rabble, like a fish swimming in a turbulent stream. Ned felt an irresistible urge to follow. On this dreamlike impulse he trailed the grey-faced man to an ordinary called the Sign of the Frigate. Watching Scarrat enter, Ned hesitated a few moments before entering too. In the doorway he looked around in vain, for the man had disappeared. All he saw in the gloom were watermen in briny slickers, their noses red, their faces fiercely bearded. A couple more swaggered in, jostling Ned as they did, and called out for mugs. Ned took his own place at a table, ordered an ale from a grimy-faced boy, and watched the men sit with companions, grumble among themselves, spoiling for trouble.

Just when two hot fellows rose to grip their oyster knives, a back door opened and Scarrat appeared, grinning but holding a wooden fid.

"Giles!" he called to the drawer. "Bumpers all around!"

The watermen smiled, sat down, and awaited their liquor, while Scarrat stood at their table and bantered freely with them in their jargon.

Turning to a waterman at the next table, Ned asked who that fellow was.

"That be the keeper of the Frigate."

Ned watched closely. Had he once seen his own salvation in such a funereal face? Had he believed such a man might do more than give him the gift of a burned book? He had in his innocence. But wise now to the streets, he saw something different in Scarrat. He saw the keen eyes of a ferret, cold and murderous. He saw the sardonic mouth of someone who could give a charred book to a young fool out of some misshapen sense of wit.

An apt companion for milord Sandwich.

He recalled the rumours about Scarrat and the nobleman, how they intrigued in some manner together. Here was proof of it, for the grey fellow had a tavern of his own. Surely his lordship had helped him to it. In recent months Ned had often glimpsed evil — a dull squint, a spiteful gain — but nowhere in the haunts of Smithfield had he encountered such taint in a face as in the one now hovering above the table of watermen.

Quaffing off his ale, Ned decided to leave. There was nothing for him here, no reason to stay. It had been the whim of a moment for him to follow Scarrat, just the memory of a face at a fire and then that same face inside a hated chariot on the day they branded Susannah Wells at the Old Bailey. He was remembering his rush at the chariot, his fist hitting the nobleman's crest on its embossed side, when suddenly his eyes met those of Mister Scarrat.

The grey man, having seen him, was now approaching, a smile on his thin lips.

"So it's you, lad! Welcome!" Scarrat chuckled, but his cold eyes were taking in Ned's frock-coat, linen neckcloth, parchment-colored breeches, neat bob wig. "What be you now, a prancer?"

"Why call me that?" Ned asked, startled and alarmed.

"To keep you in such fancy lurries, I wager you take purses on the road." Scarrat said it off-handedly with a smile, but his black eyes were still appraising.

"I work as a whoremaster," Ned said with a comparable smile.

"Have a dram," the tavernkeeper said, sitting down, and laying the wooden fid on the weathered table.

"I am beholden to you, sir."

"For a dram? Go to. I own the place."

"Beholden otherwise. On the day I burned this" — he raised the gloved hand — "you told me never to play a fool's game in London. So have I learned."

"Good. I thought you was a promising lad. By the look of these lurries, you've come on good times. A whoremaster? Is it true?"

Ignoring the question, Ned continued his own line of thought. "You told me the truth and asked me how I liked London. I like it fine now, only I hated it on the day of Susannah Wells' branding when I saw you climb into his coach."

"Whose coach?"

"Why, the coach of him who did me wrong."

Scarrat laughed uneasily. "Odd's fucking heart, man. What's your business?"

"I mortally hate him."

"Who? Your mind's no open book."

"Lord Sandwich. He wronged me."

"Be civil when you name your betters."

"The man did me wrong. I stole nothing. But the kitchen clerk

wanted me out because of a wench and it amused his lordship and
he let me go to keep peace. He treated me badly. The man wronged
me."

"I say, keep a civil tongue. It smacks of French impudence to call
a peer of England merely 'the man.' "

"I say he wronged me. The earl of Sandwich wronged me."

"So *you* say. But what's that to me?" Although his words were
contemptuous and belittling, a new look came into the grey man's
face at the mention of milord's name. Ned had seen this look when
Sandy ran a cove down. "I warrant you lost your place for good
cause," Scarrat added with a sneer.

"When next you see him —"

"See who? I can't follow your rambling."

"When next you ride in his chariot. I saw you do so on the day of
the gypsy trial. You went from Old Bailey to the chariot of his
lordship."

"Don't think to bite me," Scarrat whispered tensely, leaning
across the table. "I'm no coxcomb. I won't be laboured this way.
You'll get nothing from me."

Although the man declared boldly, Ned saw in his face a look as
if Sandy had herded him against a wall. "I came with no such
purpose. I ask nothing of you," Ned replied calmly. "But when next
you see him, tell him he wronged the postilion accused of robbing
the larder. Just tell him. Tell him I know him for unjust."

"You are mad. You're food for Bedlam."

"Tell him."

Scarrat got to his feet. "Do you think a great man cocks his ear to
the likes of you?"

"Tell him."

"Blockhead! You learned nothing since the fire. Get out of here!"
Scarrat howled, turning the shocked watermen from their mugs.
"Get out of here! Out!"

Without another word Ned left, hearing at his back the grey man
screaming, "Meddle in my affairs, you'll find yourself tucked up on
the hanging tree!"

Ned left without looking back, as he wondered what had happened in the Frigate just now. Touching upon the nobleman's name
had been like touching a rotten tooth. It was as if he'd stumbled on
the means of disconcerting and frightening the coldest man he'd

ever seen. But he'd also pitched on a way of vindicating his own honour. Go tell his lordship I never robbed the larder — that's what he'd demanded of a man whom he'd once regarded as far above himself. To be sure, Scarrat would never carry the message, but the honour of a Warsop lad had been saved. Let Scarrat threaten him and a nobleman laugh at him, for today he had stood up. Standing up mattered, his father used to tell him. Ned felt better for confronting the nobleman's creature. Perhaps in some mysterious way it boded well for the future. Indeed, it could harbinger the start of a new life. This at least was plain: his love for Clare had given him courage to stand up.

Part Five

———————————◆———————————

SURPRISES

[26]

WHEN NED REACHED the next street from the tavern, a tremendous wind began blowing through the city. Across the sky rumbled heavy ranks of thunderheads, promising a storm. Turning into a lane, he saw through swirls of paper and strands of wrapping hemp a crowd of people staring at a cobbling shop. Its thick wooden sign, wrenched free by the gusts, had carried with it into the street a ragged circle of brick, smashing the legs of a passerby who lay there chalk-faced, moaning, near death. Ned stood at the edge of the gathering crowd. Someone had thrown a rough blanket over the grievously injured man, whose fearful eyes reminded Ned of the woman in the burning house. The memory caused him to lift the gloved hand to his chest, while at the same moment he felt a sharp prod in his back.

"Be easy," someone whispered in his ear and again jabbed something hard against his spine. "Or have a brace of pistol balls through your guts."

Ned nodded in compliance, allowing the man to guide him from the crowd into a dark passage adjoining the lane. Two men came from the shadows with drawn flintlocks.

Ned pointed to the money pouch hanging from his belt. "Take my truff."

"Hold your fucking tongue, man," said the cull behind him. "See has he got weapons."

Searching warily, they didn't remove the money pouch. "No weapons," one said.

Their leader, a grizzled, heavy-set man, lowered his pistol. "Follow like a lamb. Hear me?"

"I do," Ned told him.

"That's a fine fellow, or count yourself cold mutton." He set out with his confederates flanking Ned. Leaning into the blustery wind, they tramped into a courtyard near Covent Garden. At the leader's command Ned rapped the knocker of a stately town house. A liveried footman opened the door and with a deep bow conducted Ned into a lobby, thence through a hall filled with people waiting on benches, through double doors into a large room lit by smoking clumps of candles.

Taking a tentative step forward, Ned stared at dark furniture, oppressive hangings. The parlour air was thick with the smell of incense. Through the hot cloudy atmosphere he saw a fat woman lounging on a settee in a corner. She held a Chinese fan and wore a crimson robe. On her massive head rose a columnar wig into which a number of jeweled pins had been stuck.

"Come here," she commanded sharply, while pushing away a plate of sweetmeats offered by a turbaned boy.

Approaching at her order, Ned could see through the smoke a wide mouth bright from carmine dye, cheeks eerily whitened by layers of paint. She had small darting eyes within folds of perspiring skin. She was grinning.

She was Jenny Rivers. Ned didn't need to be told that. She was known far and wide as the Queen of Foists, a female counterpart of the notorious Jonathan Wild. She commanded whole battalions of thieves and pickpockets. During her youth she'd become infamous for robbing people in church. Old now, she was wealthy beyond estimation and greatly feared. Ned recalled Doctor Bostock speaking of her in awe, equating her fame with that of Blue Sue and Dancing Doll and describing in detail her tragic love affair with Little Arthur Chambers, the Prince of Prigs, who babbled to the law. For this betrayal, so it was rumoured, he had been pinned down by Jenny's confederates on her order, then smothered to death by her sitting with her huge naked arse on his face. She ruled her motley kingdom with brutal efficiency, yet oft-times lent sums of money to footpads down on their luck or suffering from pox.

"So here's the Dog Cull." She licked sweat from her upper lip. The room had the feel of tropics — the haze and dark wood and thick drapery. "Where's your bouser?"

"I have no bouser, ma'am."

Jenny Rivers struck the fan hard against her palm; the sound was like a pistol crack. "Think you, lad, I don't know you? I'd need more than two hands to count the babblers who've come with tales of you," she drew breath, "and your bouser and the black boy that keeps it. Go to. The whole world's my eyes." She opened out her arms, the robe stretching across a vast expanse of bosom. "Sneakers and pinchers," she drew breath, "files and prancers," she drew breath, "all come to me with tales. From them," she drew breath, "I learned more than all your blockhead magistrates and your shitty bailiffs," she drew breath, "and such could learn from now till doomsday. This Fielding, I hear, thinks he's cunning enough to make a sainted church of London." She panted for breath. "A damn fool like him's born every minute. Boy," she said, "I'm no onion-breath whore slinking around your boozing kens." She was gasping for air. "I brought you here in admiration." She fanned herself, accepted a sweetmeat from the little turbaned servant, and then continued. "Boy," she said to Ned, "tell me plain how you work it."

Aware that the mansion must be crawling with experts at the knife and garrotte, Ned made no resistance but explained candidly and in detail how he used his dog to take coves down.

The fat woman snickered now and then, for she was vastly entertained by what she heard. When Ned finished his explanation, she tapped fan against palm in applause.

"A rogue clever and handsome. Don't fear I'd make bold to have my people copy you." She drew breath. "None trains a bouser that well less he's a shepherd." She drew breath. "And no bouser learns so well less it's of rare spirit. Will you take a glass of bub, boy?"

"No thank you, ma'am."

" 'No thank you, ma'am.' Hear that? The lad has manners. I've scamps here," she drew breath, "who form no words but shit, fuck, bitch, Stand and Deliver!" She leaned forward like a solicitous hostess to a guest. "On the table there you've got victuals of all kinds." She drew breath. "Whitstable oysters. Asparagus from Battersea. Watercress was brought in fresh this dawn to Covent Garden." She drew a few deep breaths. "And strawberries, boy. I have marzipan."

"No thank you, ma'am."

"You're not at ease."

"No, ma'am, I'm not."

"Is it you wonder why you was brought here?"

"Yes, ma'am."

Sitting back, she drew a crimson sleeve across her sweaty brow. Perspiration had streamed through the thick white paint, streaking her cheeks like tears. "To speak plain, I want twenty guineas delivered hence each fortnight. Without fail, mind. Or your bouser's food for worms." She drew breath. "You understand me, pretty lad?"

He did. It was common knowledge in Ned's world that Jenny Rivers extorted money from prosperous thieves. In effect she'd just threatened to kill Sandy unless paid a considerable sum of money every two weeks. Without fail. And there was nothing he could do about it. Having earned a reputation he didn't even want, Ned must now pay for it.

"Well, boy, answer me. Do you understand?"

"I do. I'll pay. But if there's a bad week —"

She interrupted him by smacking fan against palm. "Without fail. If there's no honour and discipline among thieves, where shall we find it? In return you have carte blanche to carry on your trade howsomever you wish." This was much to say between breaths and for a while she panted heavily. Then she moved the fan languorously through the hot, perfumed air. "Was I younger" — she pointed the fan at him — "I'd have you warming my bed, bless me I would!" She drew breath. "But as I'm in mellow years, I say to you, young fellow, God prosper such a fine young blood." She drew breath. "A fortnight from today, the first payment, mind. Give you or your messenger," she drew breath, "twenty guineas into the hand of my footman. He will sign for it as he can read and write. You can go now." Sitting back wearily, she motioned to the turbaned boy. "Bring a shawl. A draft has got in here."

Closing the double doors behind him, Ned started down the corridor, the marble floor of it making a resonant click at each step. He experienced the same sense of hopelessness felt on the day that

Lord Sandwich cast him from the household. The despair was caused not so much by the extortion itself — though the extra financial burden would keep him longer at grim work — as it was by loss of control over his own fate. A stupid thief was trapped by constables, a clever thief by other thieves. Did he take more purses, doubtless the extortion would increase as well. He was helpless to change the remorseless pattern. He'd never escape Jenny Rivers; or, if the fat old woman did manage to eat herself out of the last breath, then someone else would weave an invisible web across the rooftops of London and catch him in it.

So lost in his dismal thoughts was Ned Carleton that he didn't see, rising ahead of him from the hall bench, two persons who knew him — both open-mouthed, one plainly terrified, and the other with a black patch over one eye.

"Upon my honour and salvation," crowed Doctor Bostock, attempting to swallow his fear, "it's the lad himself! Jolly old cock, how do you?" But he held his brass-headed cane at chest level to ward off a blow.

"How do, Ned," said Lemuel with a broad grin.

Ned clapped him on the shoulder in a friendly way, then turned with a frown to the doctor. "Has she summoned you here?"

"We've been ill used, lad. We've come for solace, a bit of a loan to tide us over. God save us," Bostock wheezed, rolling his eyes toward heaven, then pointing at Lemuel, "this creature here lost a blinker and gained the claps almost the same day, the poor fool ninny. And both of us nearly kicked up for good." He studied Ned with open admiration. "Well, you're a dandy! Such lurries, Ned!" The doctor heaved a sigh. "You haven't fallen on evil times like your old chums." Reaching out, he shyly tapped Ned's coat. "Could you stand us a dram for old times' sake?"

Ned hesitated, but after a glance at pale Lemuel with the black patch and hopeful grin, he motioned for them to come along.

The doctor leapt to his side, unwinding a history of curious events. They'd met with a resurrection thief who dug up corpses and sold them to a peculiar fellow who fed the carnage to wild beasts he kept for pets near London. And in Moorfields they'd come across some bitter rogues who threatened to take them before a judge and charge them with attempts at unnatural acts did they not pay handsomely, which under the odd circumstances they most surely did, leaving them at the present moment temporarily embarrassed in a financial way.

Nearby was a tavern, which the doctor skipped to eagerly. After finding a table — he rejected two as unsuitable — Bostock waved imperiously at the waiter. "I do think," he turned to Ned, "a Welsh rabbit and some porter with freedom of spirit better than ortolans and claret with servility. I have eat beefsteaks with men less than you, lad. I set high value on the countenance you show me."

"Summers."

"What, lad?"

"Where be your old chum Summers?"

"Him? Pshaw!" Grimacing, the doctor turned to deal with the waiter. "The poor boy and me'll have a plate of tripe and a half of wine." Ned ordered nothing, though nodded approval when the doctor added, "Shall it be a full bottle?" Watching the waiter depart, Bostock licked his lips. "You asked of the man Summers. Would to Christ I had done for the bastard, as he was underhanded, irregular, a larcenous rogue without genius. What he lacked mostly was an overly scrupulous conscience. Betwixt you and me, there's no end to human perfidy. He was a stinkard, a coward, a *worse* than stinkard." Doctor Bostock pursed his lips judiciously. "Howsomever, I think he'll have his just reward — woman's his undoing."

"What did he do?" Ned asked with a smile. "As I remember, you was uncommonly fond of Summers."

"Aye, vent your spleen," the doctor murmured despondently. "Go to it, lad. I'll be the sport of you. I can't help it. Do your worst."

"You left me without a word. And without my share."

"To my eternal shame," Bostock admitted quickly. "It was him who tricked us, think what you will. Isn't it true, Lemuel? The vicious fucking rogue seduced us into a scheme that could not go wrong. And you shall know the true horror of it once our bellies are full, as your old chums haven't had so much as a biscuit these three days, as I am a Christian."

When food arrived, Bostock bolted his, sat back with a loud belch, picked his teeth with the table knife, and explained what he called the lumber drop.

It was a variation on the old confidence game designed to bilk country fellows with full pockets and empty heads. The lumber drop was the specialty of that scoundrel Summers. Three culls worked it.

The pickup, who'd been the good doctor, must charm a merchant into carelessness over a pot of wine. While sitting there, they watched two players at whist at the next table. One player — Lemuel, if you could believe that — won consistently, though of course the money was queer. Summers, the loser, loudly identified himself as a country squire with a landed estate and five thousand annual. The doctor then worked on the merchant's greed, whispering that this squire was obviously a fool anyone could beat at cards. So when Summers, glancing over to their table, asked them to join in the game, they willingly did. The merchant won until the stakes got high, then they sank him. Pretending to have a friend who'd loan money for another bout, the doctor took the merchant from the tavern. But naturally the lender was not to be found, so the doctor suggested that he continue the search while the merchant returned to the tavern where the players waited. So the gulled merchant found both men gone and his gold in the bargain.

"It happened thus five times," explained the doctor with a sigh. "Then we fell into trouble. I had our gull seated and bid the drawer bring ale. Our two came in and proceeded to play. Lemuel won, as usual, and Summers broached us to join the game. When I whispered 'Let's do it' to my flat — a brawny sort in boots and a great coat stinking of cattle — he readily agreed, but added to me, 'Think on this, sir: neither of us will nick the other. Bargain?' I told him, 'Bargain,' but didn't quite like the sound and substance of his words, as they smacked of a sly knowledge of the way things go. The game went as we would have it, but when I left the tavern with him to go seek my lending friend, he walked but ten paces, then stopped and faced me. 'Look you,' he said, 'is this a fetch of yours?' I tried to brave it out. I said, 'Insult me, sir, and I shall be obliged to go my ways.' I said, 'I'm sorry, sir, but you force me to be so ill bred, for I can't suffer an insult.' He wasn't listening, however, this big fellow. He was watching the tavern door, and, sure enough, a wink later out they waltzed, Lemuel and Summers. The merchant was on them before they had sight of him. They hadn't a chance on earth. It was then that Summers showed his true colors. The sneaking cur pushed our ninny here into the big fellow's path and himself

scurried off. The great oaf might have followed after Summers had
not poor Lemuel been fallen already at his boots. With a bestial cry
that brawling giant searched through Lemuel's pockets and found
not one farthing, for as author of the lumber drop, Summers had
the honour of being our bank. So in a fit of unnatural fury the huge
merchant drew his sword and nicked at the poor boy, popping his
eye out like a nut from its husk. Had I not felled him then with a
blow of vigour, he'd surely have done for Lemuel."

"*You* felled him?" Ned asked in surprise.

"As God is my witness."

"Did he?" Ned asked Lemuel.

"He did. With his cane from behind."

"Then you showed more courage," observed Ned tartly, "than
ever you did before."

"I couldn't let the monster do for my lad here, not I. He's more to
me than my own son, and I have fathered more than a few, I
warrant."

Ned regarded the doctor's grizzled cheeks, yellow teeth, fleshy
nose. A question would remain unanswered until Judgement Day.
Had Bostock acted to protect the boy or to prevent the merchant
from turning and running him through as well?

"I helped the lad to a surgeon," continued the doctor, "but nothing could be done, except with money we might have introduced a
wooden plug into the socket. His blinker gone one day, and then
the next this chucklehead came down with French claps."

"I did." Lemuel grinned sheepishly and scratched his shaggy red
head at the wonder of it.

"May my pistols misfire," said the doctor with a woeful frown,
"have I not told you true, sir. We lost our worldly goods in the
commotion. We are bilked. We are plucked chickens."

"I thought you was left without a farthing in Moorfields."

"Ah, that was another time."

Ned turned to Lemuel. "When did you lose the blinker, old
chum?"

Lemuel scratched his head again. "Some time back. I've changed
patches twice, I think."

"Go to," grumbled the doctor. "With him one month's the same
as the next."

"I think you've had time to restore your fortunes," Ned told the doctor with severity. "I'm not your keeper."

"Well, enough of this. Let's divert ourselves," Bostock suggested with a leer. "I know some wiggish tarts. For old times' sake, Ned?"

Ned threw down some coins for the reckoning and got to his feet. "Goodbye."

Staring at the money, Doctor Bostock sighed. "You've done well, lad. I own I take some pride in it, as I taught you everything. Recall how I fitted you with your first famstring?" He smiled meaningfully at the gloved left hand. "Remember? It was in Holborn I fitted you out like a gentleman. Those were good days. Those were good times when I still had my health. Come, sir, let's part in good humour. Would you favour us with ten pieces till the morrow? Give us your address, for we be duty-bound to repay."

Ned looked at the shabby man, at the one-eyed boy, then counted ten and four more shillings onto the table. He turned away, turned back. "Don't follow me," he warned.

"No, sir, not us. We —"

"Or I'll lend you something else to remember."

"Yes, yes, never fear." Bobbing his head, the doctor clutched the coins so tightly that his knuckles showed white. "What you command, young sir, is our duty honour-bound. But should you need us, we have a case next to the Hog's Head in Golden Lane. We're much obliged for the loan."

"Don't follow me." Leaving, Ned heard behind him the shrill cry, "Next to the Hog's Head in Golden Lane! If you need us!"

Just as Ned reached the street, the threatening storm broke in a fury over London. Cascades of rain swept obliquely across his face. Pulling his tricorn low, he hunched forward into the bluster of early evening. Pans of burning oil fastened to the street walls were extinguished by the downpour, leaving the way dark and gloomy. Within a few steps he was drenched, his boots sucking in the mire. A window casement, unable to withstand the onslaught of a high wind, blew free and careened wildly along the street, giving Ned a blow on the forearm that would have felled him had it struck squarely. He saw a horse rear in panic and overturn a vegetable cart.

Turning the corner of Holborn, Ned saw a figure huddled on the stoop of his lodging house. Approaching warily, he saw that it was Clare.

She arose, clutching a thin cloak to her breast, her long dark hair lank against her face.

He rushed to her.

"I need you, sweet lad," she said against his wet cheek. "I need you, dear, dear lad."

[27]

❡ Reader, I beg for your sympathy, for today I have been met with troublesome predicaments and continuous duties. While in my chambers, mulling over a case, I was greeted by Mary, who brought news of the butcher; he would give us no more meat, despite Cook having gone early in the morning and paid our reckoning which, to say true, was longer in arrears than I care to admit.

Then my tailor had called with bill in hand for a waistcoat delivered but not paid for two months ago, albeit in my defense I must say it was the last piece of clothing I had purchased (though loving finery, I had often been tempted) and that particular coat for reason of being honoured at a dinner as chairman of the Quarter Sessions of the Peace for the City and Liberty of Westminster, at which I delivered a new charge to the grand jury.

There had been yet another creditor at the door, a bookseller who didn't want to part with volumes on Roman Law or Cases in Chancery, Mézéray's *Histoire de France,* or even Francis Coventry's *Pompey the Little,* the third edition of which I am pleased to say was dedicated to me; no, would not part with any of them I had ordered from his stall until payment was forthcoming. Making a wonderful effort, Mary had sent him away, but kept the books, with the admonition that he must come again soon, for I would pay him in due time (I savour the vagueness of her diplomacy,

Reader), so he must not worry. Apparently the good woman had
sent him off as satisfied as if he had been paid.

I was delighted to hear that the children were well, so we could
proceed as planned for a stay in Bath, one scheduled for an entire
fortnight as a relief from London. Mary presented me with a list of
articles that must go with us in the stage, all of which I approved
to her satisfaction while adding, less to her liking, a full wicker of
Rhenish and a dozen bottles of porter, as it was not my intention to
enter the city of Bath bearing no more than a sack of tea.

No sooner had I returned to the case on my desk than Joseph
announced that *he* was at the door again. I could divine from
Joseph's testy tone that "he" was Samuel Bayse, an impoverished
scribbler and translator who applied to me whenever commissions
had temporarily run out or he happened to be in the
neighbourhood without funds for a touch of ale. I knew the poor
fellow's history well. Often he pawned his clothes and wrote his
pamphlets shivering in bed with his arms sticking through holes
in a blanket. He would modernize Chaucer for threepence a line;
four lines in a quarter hour got him a shilling; three hours, twelve
shillings, which was his maximum effort for a day. Had he done a
day through, Samuel Bayse might have suffered a bit of success,
but no such awful fate awaited him, since by writing a few lines
he worked up a thirst and must leave his room to pawn the
bookseller's text from which he was translating, and go for ale;
after which, the bookseller would redeem the book, allowing
Bayse the opportunity to translate a few lines more; and thus did
his literary career lurch along at these sorry fits and starts.

Much to Joseph's disgust, I desired Samuel Bayse to walk in.
He was a scrawny, long-necked creature with squinty eyes and
the smell emanating from him, Reader, you might whiff from
wherever you now sit. We spoke briefly of Molière, whom I had
translated in my youth, with less justice, however, than Samuel
Bayse would have done, he being superb in French, yet for more
money than my poor acquaintance could expect a bookseller ever
to place into his hands today. I gave him a crown and swore him to
secrecy did my wife collar him in the hall to inquire as to what had
transpired between us. Do not, Reader, I pray you, sneer at her
for a miser, as Mary is not so much parsimonious as hard pressed,
having to make ends meet in a household laid waste by a sick
aging fellow, who hath always insisted upon showing himself
amongst the society of London and Bath as if he could indeed not
only pay his butcher on a regular basis, but entertain royalty at his

table without their remarking any difference between the fare
served by him and the offerings they would have had in a palace.

Next I was informed that John Hill awaited my pleasure. I told
Joseph to inform Mister Hill that I was not available tonight or
tomorrow or ever to him. When Joseph opened his mouth to
protest this rudeness and hope for its modulation, I chid him for
disturbing me and waved him out.

I would not see a fellow like John Hill, no, not I, not even if my
life depended on it, for this person of considerable parts (I must
confess it, as he hath been actor, apothecary, botanist, doctor,
editor, librettist, and novelist) was also a vain, acrimonious,
hypocritical coxcomb, and an unblushing liar, who for a rival
journal once made a scurrilous attack upon my Mary's reputation
to which I referred earlier, and for whose vicious gossip mongering
I named him in an article *Mister Dung Hill,* "not only amongst the
meanest of those who ever drew a pen, but without exception the
vilest fellow that ever wore a head" — a hasty bit of vituperative
writing unmatched, I fervently hope, by any I ever writ elsewhere
and ever will write, as I do not know what is ultimately more
offensive to me, the reading of abuse or the writing of it. The
scoundrel had sent in a note by Joseph, asking for a few moments
of my time to spell out a project which might well prove of
financial consequence to us both. I tore up the note and requested
Joseph to place its pieces into the visitor's hand.

Such fellows as John Hill prove to me, if proof be needed, that
evil doth actually exist and can reside like a heavy stone in the
human breast. Only vigilance can save us from it. This John Hill
had the temerity to brook a money-making scheme with me after
so recently attacking my part in the Canning case, accusing me of
outright greed in giving my opinion to Counselor Salt and then
sitting in judgement of the particulars. I hold to my belief that
the child was abused, though all London is now torn by doubts
and charges and countercharges even before the poor girl hath
had a chance to defend herself in court. There is within myself
something which needs to protect injured innocence, and I find in
doing so a hope of more contentment than the applause of the
world can give. Many have already condemned the poor little girl,
but the fact remains she returned to her mother's home in a
deplorable condition after a month missing. Of course, I am well
aware of how easy it is to misjudge. To be placed above the reach
of deceit is to be placed above the rank of a human being. Sure I
am that I make no pretension to be of that rank. Indeed, I have

SURPRISES   223

often been deceived in my opinion of men, and have served and
recommended to others those persons whom I have afterward
discovered to be wholly worthless. But as to John Hill, I know my
opinion to be just. He hath taken the occasion of a poor girl's
misfortune to attack an old literary foe. Such a man remains below
my contempt. I will never see him.

This annoyance had considerably increased my fatigue, and I
found myself desiring to an intense degree some few calm
moments in which to compose my senses, but I heard a merry
commotion drawing near, and so I prepared to meet the breathless
onslaught of young William, who was racing toward the study
door and in moments would burst in upon me, panting, flushed
from his exertions, words tumbling one over another in his
eagerness to describe the giants and monsters who had roamed
with such spirit through his magical day.

Later, after a dinner much hurried by my obilgation to write
another article before retiring, I got no farther than my study door
when a bellow from below bespoke of my brother John's arrival, as
none other announced himself with such unbridled gusto.

Soon he and Saunders Welch were with me, desiring my time to
interview new applicants for the Bow Street Runners, as we had
additional funds now to recruit for the Newcastle Plan Against
Crime. So down I went with them to chambers where a half-dozen
men came singly before us to plead their cause for employment as
thief takers. Having selected two of the six for posts, we adjourned
for a glass of port. The embarrassing business of the Dog Cull was
still on Saunders Welch's mind. But by maintaining our register in
which information about crime was now daily entered, we were
able to form a better opinion of this miscreant. It was clear now
that his modus operandi depended upon utter control of the dog.
The difficulty in catching him lay in the fact that he never traveled
with the animal, leastwise never preceding an attack. Indeed, not
until the dog had cornered a victim did the cull himself appear,
and afterward, so accounts indicated, they went separate ways
again. The fellow had therefore to be apprehended during a period
not exceeding a minute or two. Saunders maintained there was no
chance of catching him unless through informing. I reluctantly
agreed. The grim truth is that there is small justice in justice, for
this fellow moves freely through our streets, taking what he pleases
with impunity, while the poor Canning girl must endure the cruel
accusations of opportunists like John Hill.

When my guests had gone, I sat awhile with quill in hand (and a

glass of excellent port at my side), attempting to go about the first
pages of an essay which would argue that the exercise of virtue in
human affairs can be looked upon in a practical way as enlightened
self-interest. But my attention waned and in its stead I thought
of my friend Ralph Allen in Bath. We would meet there soon and
I would ask him to do me the honour of serving as the executor of
my estate, such as it is.

With that in mind, I pulled from my desk an earlier Last Will
and Testament, which had named as executor my brother John,
who was as improvident now as myself for having sunk his
own funds into some of my ventures, like the newspaper and the
real estate company. With the old will as my model, I composed a
new one.

> In the name of God Amen. I Henry Fielding of the Parish of
> Ealing in the County of Middlesex do hereby give and bequeath
> unto Ralph Allen of Prior Park in the county of Somerset Esqr.
> and to his heirs executors administrators and assigns for ever to
> the use of said Ralph his heirs, etc., all my estate real and per-
> sonal and whatsoever and do appoint him sole executor of this
> my last Will Beseeching him that the whole (except my share in
> the Register Office) may be sold and forthwith converted into
> money and annuities purchased thereout for the lives of my dear
> wife Mary and my daughters Harriet and Sophia and Louisa
> and what proportions my said executor shall please to reserve to
> my son William shall be paid him severally as he shall attain the
> age of twenty and three. Then the shares in the Register Office
> divided between Mary and the Girls. Witness my Hand Henry
> Fielding signed and acknowledged as his last will and testament
> by the within named testator in the presence of ＿＿＿＿＿＿.

I left the names blank until I could provide witnesses; moreover,
I would insert the infant's name when it should be born.

Pushing aside the inkstand and throwing down the quill, I
breathed a sigh of deep melancholy, for upon my conscience was
the scant joy I had ever given my wife Mary and the niggardly
provision I had made for her future.

She had been Mary Daniel ten years ago when I hired her as a
nurse for my failing wife Charlotte, who could not get around
without help. I can't recall having thought one way or another
of the plain, sturdy, young woman who went about her duties in
a silent, almost grim, but very efficient manner. I think I first
noticed her a few weeks after the funeral, as she was still in the

household, going about the business of cleaning and washing and serving, more like a housekeeper than a nurse. I asked Mary why she was still here; to which she replied in a blunt manner that I would learn was characteristic of her nature, that no one had told her to leave. I asked her then to stay on, as I had released Charlotte's maid, having been unable to look at the woman with whom I so closely associated my departed girl.

For the next year and a half I went about with such a distracted air that some of my acquaintances considered me mad, and well they might, as I scarcely knew what I did, but carried out the daily labours of a barrister in a kind of dream, which did not encourage clients to beat a path to my chambers; and in the evenings I sat before a fire to drink the first glass of brandy, continuing until the bottle lay empty and there was some chance of my sleeping a few hours.

During that whole period I do not think I noticed the housekeeper a dozen times. She was simply there, a presence in black, flitting silently through the rooms, the tinkle of ringed keys faintly tracing her path. Then one evening, as I sat before the fire with my brandy, she flung into the room and spoke out boldly to the effect that I was not a good Christian father to little Harriet, who was seven years old then and rarely saw me, but spent her time sewing in a corner or talking to Cook or to herself.

I stared at the severe woman's steady eyes and her hair the color of chestnuts, half hidden beneath a low-crowned white cap. I thanked her for her words, which I declared to her face I must either heed or not count myself a man. Curtly she nodded and left briskly, as if she had merely completed another of her duties — say, dusting the furniture.

I admired immensely the way she had spoken up, without a trace of nonsense; and even more, I appreciated her concern for my daughter who, it was suddenly plain, had been suffering from a grief I had no right to impose upon her, as it was my own. From that moment on, I spent many hours with Harriet, much to our mutual satisfaction, and began to regard the housekeeper with a closer, more sympathetic eye. It had scarcely occurred to me hitherto where her quarters were in the house. Indeed, I would have been hard pressed to say whether or no she stayed here overnight. But I began to sip my brandy with less fierceness before the fire, as I listened to the floor boards creaking overhead, her footsteps crossing hither and yon at the bedtime hour. And I imagined the robust woman turning back the coverlet, her hair no

longer brushed severely back into a stiff knot but loosened for the
night, perhaps falling as far as to her waist.

In short, Reader, you must easily divine what happened next.
Fortified by brandy one night, I made my way slowly up the stairs,
a candle trembling in my hand. One soft knock upon the door,
and I heard her voice call firmly out, "Come in, Mister Fielding!"
With no other fuss, indeed, with a solacing candour, she opened
her arms and took me wordlessly into her bed.

So it began. Each night the ritual climb up the stairway, the
gentle knock, the brisk invitation, the silent forthright embrace.
She would not, however, suffer herself to move into my own room,
as I desired, because by that action methinks she would have
declared herself a whore, for let them say what they will, my Mary
is a woman of deep scruples, who surrendered to me her person
not for any gain she might have of it, but for the aid she might give
to a grief-stricken man.

That her charity did succeed in retrieving my spirits from the
darkest of melancholies was demonstrated most plainly by my
renewal of interest in literary composition. My hopes of legal
preferment had at that time faded, debt was upon me as usual, and
furthermore, it was rumoured that my rival in letters, Samuel
Richardson, was hard at work on a novel of great length, its first
installment soon to appear in print. That was a challenge to me, a
gauntlet, as it were, thrown down at my feet.

With a final push of encouragement, both financial and spiritual,
from Lyttelton and Allen, I began to sketch out a tale of a
foundling who, growing into a lusty young fellow of large heart
and little caution, after a series of tribulations wins the hand of
the lady he adores.

Two and a half years later I had finished *Tom Jones*. By then
Mary was sharing my bed in a legal manner, fortunately for our
William, who otherwise like Tom Jones would have come into the
world without a name.

[28]

Love changed nothing. Circumstances denied Ned and his Clare the natural hopes of young lovers, though on their strolls they might seem to passersby no more than a well-placed journeyman and his handsome wife. The notorious footpad and an old man's mistress never met without a sense of impermanence. Stripping their clothes off, they embraced always for the last time.

One evening as was his wont, Ned reached under the pillow for armour. Clare caught his hand to stop him — an astonishing thing, as she was ever careful. He'd never complained of using armour, though secretly he disliked the expert way in which she herself slipped the sheath on him and tied the drawstring with sure fingers, handling him as she must have handled the others, drawing armour onto the eager sex of watchmaker, silversmith, little old milliner. Now, however, she caught Ned's hand, pushed the sheath away, and whispered, "Only you."

With these words surely she had committed her life and love to him, yet the next morning, sitting naked on the bed to comb her tangled hair, she again refused to see him until Saturday. He knew why, of course. Sometime during the week — at the milliner's convenience — she must climb into a hackney coach and do what had to be done to assure herself of continued protection. Again she admonished Ned not to come to the shop, and he meant to obey. It would be too painful to slink around there and watch his beloved and the old man leave together. Nor did he beg for her address or try to follow her home. He'd rather abide by her desire for privacy than cause a rupture between them. Though by nature and upbringing a young man possessive of a woman he loved, Ned Carleton learned to restrain himself as though indifferent to what Clare did. He came to know a surprising truth of love — that it could demand forfeiture of a lover's most cherished demands.

And yet nothing had changed.

Taking the hand mirror from his small chest of drawers, Ned saw in its flawed glass the savage imprint of St. Giles, of Smithfield, of Barbican: the wary squint, the tense mouth, the set jaw — features both of hunted and hunter. He could never be a shepherd and sit on a hillside watching a flock of sheep graze. Nor could he find honourable work in trade, not with a bad hand and his only skill the training of a dog. Nor could he maintain himself indefinitely through crime. Jenny Rivers's extortion must surely increase like a rope tightening around his neck.

And there was another problem. Judge Fielding — he who wrote the book forever in Ned's pocket — had been urging citizens through journals and broadsides and advertisements not to carry much gold on their persons so as, in this manner, to discourage thieves. Only a night ago, Ned took but five shillings eight from a portly gentleman. Fearing the Dog Cull's anger for taking so little, the cove put blame on Judge Fielding. "It's not my fault, but his that I keep so little coin."

It had been nearly enough for Ned to throw away the charred remains of *Joseph Andrews,* for the author of it was contributing to his woes. Ned would have, save for a long-held superstition that the book, obtained in such a strange manner, had in some mysterious way a hold on his destiny.

Too restless for reading, Ned began to take long daily walks through London and during these walks he thought of home and imagined Clare and Sandy with him, the three of them on excursions through Nottinghamshire's Sherwood Forest. He found himself plunging deep into his mind as never before. Yet such reveries were broken these days by hawkers who cried the latest pamphlet about the coming trial of the Canning girl. From countless print shops he noticed her portrait staring out at him. Her mousy face trailed him through summer streets until he developed the odd conviction that somehow he knew the poor woman, and then, not only did he know her, but in some way his destiny was joined to hers. Indeed, it was true that their fates were both unsure.

Sitting in coffee houses, he began pouring over accounts of the Canning affair in gazettes and journals. His forefinger traced each word, as slowly he absorbed the mystery of the girl's life. Had she disappeared to get a cure for distemper or to rid herself of an unwanted child? Had she truly been kidnapped? Was she held for a

whole month in a room she couldn't describe? Indeed, was she ever
in the Wells house before the Enfield raid? If she lied, was it from
shame or fear? Had a callous rake seduced the girl, whisked her out
of London, and returned her home when sated?

The possibilities obsessed Ned, as if the answers to such questions would somehow provide answers to his own life, which
seemed equally uncertain. There were many people like himself and
Betty Canning in London. They were blown like so many scraps of
paper in the wind, blown and whipped around willy-nilly, until the
great maw of a justice not of their own making sucked them up and
then spewed them out.

Each time he thought of the upcoming trial, Ned harked back to
the Old Bailey where he'd watched in the rainy yard an old woman
be branded. From his reading he knew now that a chief witness
against her had been one Robert Scarrat, tavernkeeper, who —
unbeknownst to anyone save Ned — had gone straight from the
witness box to a nobleman's carriage. For months the image of that
grey face inside the coach had been as vivid as if only a minute ago
Ned had pounded on the dragon-crested door.

Then in the Sign of the Frigate that selfsame face had blanched at
the mention of milord Sandwich's name. Completing the circle of
his thoughts, Ned harked again to Old Bailey Yard and flesh sizzling against the snake-headed iron, so that the Canning affair
brought to mind the rear roost of a dragon-crested coach on which
he himself had ridden, arms crossed, eyes fixed ahead.

Had the girl lied from shame or fear? Had a rake whisked her off
somewhere, then discarded her when weary? Discarded her by
putting her in a loft from which, in truth, she escaped? Questions
took him back to the day when he'd struck a nobleman's coach.
Stones dropped into a pond, the circles of their motion crisscross-
ing — as were his thoughts.

There had been a time when he'd thrilled to ride on the rear roost
of a dragon-crested coach. He'd blushed if milord Sandwich glanced
his way while climbing in. He'd been in awe of the brilliant guests
who attended the musical soirées for which his lordship was famous.
But Ned knew now that the rich and the noble did more than buy
fine houses and listen to the strains of elegant music. From lousy
pimps he'd learned that noblemen loved to exercise their power in
special ways, as among them there was a rage for novelty. Whimsi-

cally they desired virgin milkmaids, crippled flower girls, the home-
less Clares of London. And they paid handsomely to gratify such
caprices. He knew that certain gentlemen of high rank had their
own personal twangs, who spent long hours procuring new dishes
for jaded palates.

And he harked back to that fateful day when a Canning witness
had left the Sessions House for a nobleman's coach. Had the girl
lied? And if so, from shame or fear? From fear? As the horses surged
into a gallop, the grey-faced man had stared from the coach like a
man hunted. And at the Frigate he'd worn the selfsame look at the
mention of a noble name.

Was it, could it be true? Scarrat a twang? Had he supplied a
mousy girl from Aldermanbury for a great nobleman?

Such questions followed Ned through the twilit lanes until sometimes he had difficulty concentrating on work. When he should be
choosing a proper cove, he let his mind cloud up with questions
that had less now to do with Elizabeth Canning than with himself.
To rid himself of the obsessive questions, he stopped reading the
gazettes. Even so, the questions remained, like ticks in a dog's coat.

One afternoon he went into a grog shop and quickly upended
two bumpers of brandy. Thus fortified, he prepared to rid himself
of the questions for good and all.

He set out for Aldermanbury Postern, an address now famous in
London. The summer air was sweet, and on every corner hawkers
offered gingerbread. He was munching a piece when ahead he saw
the narrow brick house wedged between bakeries on the crooked
street, just as described in a gazette. Approaching, he heard from
the second story a girl's voice pitched high in song. For a moment
he halted to listen. The gentle catch reminded him of Nottinghamshire, where the farm lasses sang on their way to kitchen gardens,
pig sties, hen roosts.

Knocking, he waited a long time until a middle-aged woman,
oddly dressed in a billowy velvet dinner gown, flung the door wide
and grinned at him. Over the bumpers, Ned had planned exactly
what to say — words of a madman, perhaps; surely words of a man
desperate from love and circumstance.

Removing his hat, he introduced himself to Widow Canning as
Mister Hill (a name taken from one of the Canning pamphlets), a
close companion of Mister Scarrat.

The woman's smile faded, but she recovered herself and with ostentatious courtesy begged him to enter. "Do sit down, Mister Hill, sir, pray do." She took a seat near the hearth, smoothing the rich purple cloth over her fat thighs, giving him sidelong thoughtful glances. "How does Mister Scarrat? A fine-spoken gentleman. I consider him the salt of the earth."

"Mister Scarrat sends his regards." Ned was staring at the muscled arms in all the finery.

"A fine-spoken gentleman." Parting her lips in a doubtful smile, Widow Canning held up a leather-bound volume. "A very pretty book, this. The heroine mistakes some friendly horsemen for attackers of her person and so flings herself into the river and cries out to her female retinue. Her words are very pretty." Opening the book, the widow found her place and read in a high thin singsong voice.

"What that beauteous Roman Lady Clelia performed to preserve herself from Violation by the Impious Sextus, let us imitate to avoid the Violence our intended Ravishers yonder come to offer us."

She lowered the book with a sigh. "I can't know who these Romans be, but the sentiment is very pretty, very fine spoken, and reminds me of your friend Mister Scarrat, sir. Has he sent you with some word?"

Thrilled by his own daring, which seemed to lead him down byways far stranger than St. Giles, Ned replied, "Mister Scarrat wishes to make sure of you."

"Sure of me?"

"At the trial."

"La, sir, say no farther!" The widow cackled merrily, but her eyes stayed anxious. "Sit your heart at rest, sir. We are safe indeed. Let them try to pump secrets from my girl, we are resolved. This very day I said, I told her, 'Girl, be a woman of spirit. Let them not shake you. Stay mum whatever.'"

"Let me see her."

At his blunt command, Widow Canning surged to her feet in the rustling velvet and with it flying about her white petticoats, rushed to the staircase and yelled shrilly, "Bet, come down!"

There was no response.

"Bet, come down."

When there was still no response, the woman turned with an apologetic sigh. "She's been in the sulks today. Sings up there alone." Putting broad hands on her waist and assuming a wide stance, the widow bellowed. "Girl! Come down! Come down, I say!"

No response.

"Leave off the whining! Look to business! We have got a gentleman here from Mister Scarrat!"

Almost immediately there was a step on the staircase boards. A short thin figure came down, then the pale face and enormous eyes that he'd seen in print shop windows. But in person there was something more to the girl. Her bland expression might be taken for the serenity of innocence, but Ned saw in it something different, as he had seen many a like expression in the stews of Shoreditch. It was a look full of stubborn control, of fixed and desperate confidence. Girls having it either clung to the main chance or went down to ruin. In this girl's determined face there was something of Clare.

Effusively the mother introduced her to "the gentleman from Mister Scarrat," then proceeded to busy herself with a tea kettle. In her finery she was a peculiar sight at the fireplace hung with pots and ladles.

"How be you?" Ned asked the girl, who had sat down and calmly folded her hands.

"Middling, Mister Hill."

"What of the trial?"

"Ready!" called out the mother, turning from the kettle. "My Bet's ready for it!"

"I am, I reckon," said the girl with a faint smile.

"You swear to it?" Ned asked boldly. "Mister Scarrat must be satisfied."

As if reciting lines from one of her mother's books, Betty said, "I was taken up near Moorfields by two bullies and mewed away in the Wells bawdy house where the gypsy Squires ripped off my stays and dragged me to the loft where I stayed till I got the board loose and came home."

"You see?" brayed Widow Canning. "None of your vain and silly girls here." She was beaming. "My Bet is safe, sir. I rejoice to hear her testify like that."

Ned could see that nothing would shake the girl free of her story. Nothing. Bullies in great coats, their hot breath pluming in the night air, their grip like iron, stays ripped from her waist, cold endless hours in a loft — Ned would have believed every bit of it save for the mother.

Turning to Widow Canning, who was pouring water into a teapot, he continued. "Mister Scarrat has asked me to make double sure."

The woman glanced fearfully at her daughter. "Tell him you be double safe, Bet! Tell him! Be quick!"

The girl said nothing.

Ned shrugged his shoulders and started for the door where he was intercepted by the widow, who still held the teapot. "Don't leave yet, pray! Are you, sir? Are you satisfied?"

"No, I am not."

Her hand flew to her throat. "Ah, believe me, she won't breathe a word. I swear it! She's playing obstinate now. All the attention has turned her head. But in the end my Bet is safe. God in heaven she is!" The woman threw a reproachful look at the seated girl with primly folded hands. "Albeit she played the fool once." Gripping Ned's arm with the strength of a labourer, the widow purred, "Pray tell Mister Scarrat we stay on a good footing with him. We know our station."

Ned's eyes met the girl's. Her face of stone gave off such inner conviction that he might have been watching his own mother at fervent and consuming prayer.

"Mister Scarrat," the girl said finally, "knows well and good I'm a good girl. I'm as safe and secure as any poor creature on God's earth."

If recent months hadn't sharpened his wits, Ned might have been satisfied even then that the girl was a simple innocent, that his queer suspicions were nonsense, but so many nights of danger had given him both a skeptical outlook and a flair for the unpredictable act. So he blurted out, "His lordship must be sure as well."

"His lordship!" exclaimed the widow. "Say no farther! His name was never spoke in this house till now. I swear! It is not true, Bet? Say no more, sir!"

Ned reached for the doorknob, but again the widow gripped his arm hard. "Satisfied, sir? Pray be! Tell Mister Scarrat we know our station. God never made a better man or I'm not of this world. Tell him. Tell him my Bet is safe!"

[29]

NEXT TO THE HOG'S HEAD in Golden Lane Ned found the lodging house where Doctor Bostock and Lemuel rented their tiny case.

Tiny it was, and with scarcely a stick of furniture. Sitting on a filthy mattress on the floor, the doctor held a bottle of gin. His cheek was swollen, he claimed, from a decayed tooth, and Lemuel had gone to fetch a poultice of juniper root, rock alum, and honey — to the doctor's specification.

"Oh, lad, I'm mightily glad to see you," the doctor told Ned with a drawn-out sigh. "Me and the lad have come on troublesome times. He's staunch enough, perhaps one day he'll be a brave spark, but he can't think. No. There's nothing up here at all," he declared, tapping his head and grimacing. But the low mood changed suddenly. "You should have been with us, old chum, two days ago! We set on this merchant from Sussex and took him." The doctor chuckled, but the motion gave him pain. "Damn tooth," he groaned. "Where's the ninny with my potion? What was I on to? Ah, yes, that clothing merchant from Sussex. Never did I fob a man with a better will, as the bastard felt himself much above me. We took two dozen of kerchiefs, some tie wigs of him too, a piece of broadcloth, a half dozen of linen shirts. But look at this." He threw up his hands in dismay. "We've no lock here. Have you a lock at home? Perhaps we might secure our goods in your lock?"

"I have no lock," Ned lied.

"All's one," the doctor sighed. "It wouldn't matter if you did. Last night a sneak broke in whilst we was out supping and nimmed it all, everything, the kerchiefs, the broadcloth, every last piece of goods. So now we've nothing, not a farthing for supper. Do you see our plight, dear Ned? Suppose" — he cleared his throat — "you was to provide us, old chum, with supper."

"Suppose I do more than that."

"Do you mean business?"

"I do."

"Then to business. If you've scarves and petticoats to deal, I'm your chap. If you've grander designs, so much the better."

At this moment Lemuel returned with a package.

"Here's our one-eyed dog of a cutpurse coming in," the doctor grumbled, and he watched cheerlessly while the two younger men embraced. "You fucking succubus," growled the doctor at Lemuel. "Where was you all this time? And my tooth near killing me! Give it here. Here, I say!" Soon the doctor had applied the poultice to his mouth. "These swagbellied surgeons with their five hundred per annum know nothing of toothache," he mumbled thickly. "Some people bathe the tooth in urine, but I can't abide the taste, albeit it's a goodly remedy. This poultice of mine is better than roasted turnip parings behind the ear, I warrant, but try telling surgeons that, especially those simpletons from the North Country — no offense to you, dear Ned. What can you do more than provide a supper?"

At an honest fee of six shillings a day and horse hire and food expenses which must be accounted for, Ned explained, they would follow someone and report back.

"Man or woman?"

"Man."

Doctor Bostock frowned as if disappointed that it wasn't a romantic intrigue.

"It concerns a business I have with him. I must know where he goes."

"And the nature of this business, sir?"

"That doesn't concern you," Ned declared. "What concerns you is his exact whereabouts each day."

The doctor slapped his knee. "Look, Lemuel, at our old chum! The lad has grown into a prig of circumstance, who has business at hand. I venture it's a bold undertaking, so we must have more."

They agreed on ten shillings, with Ned's admonition that they must work for it.

"On my conscience, we shall," declared the doctor.

The doctor's conscience was nothing to swear on, Ned knew, yet there was no one else to enlist in the enterprise, and spying on someone was the sort of thing that Doctor Bostock could manage, requiring little exertion of mind and body, but considerable curiosity of eye.

"We shall watch the man narrowly," Bostock vowed when given the name of Scarrat and the address of the Frigate. "We shall do our duty or the devil take me for a coward. We are in, lad. We are steel."

"I grasp little of it," admitted Lemuel.

"Of course you grasp little of it." The doctor yanked the poultice off angrily. "Washy damn rogue! Curse the day I made you my ward and took your welfare upon me." Turning to Ned, he smiled. "Have you the wherewithal, dear fellow, for our first pay and supper both?"

"I do."

Rising unsteadily, the doctor threw the wet poultice on the floor and patted his cheek gently. "Did I ever tell you of a patient of mine? I told him to eat properly, but he wouldn't listen, not he. His death was occasioned by the blowing up of his mammoth gut. I could give you a whole dissertation on the rarefaction in his stomach, but to be short, the heat and fermentation of what he took the previous night at supper was what destroyed him. What effluvia! I was not at his bedside, but they say he farted like a whale before kicking his heels up. You see, I was right, right again, in faith. Let's sup." He glared at Lemuel. "What does this booby gawk at from his one eye? Let's to victuals." He cinched up the rope that held his trousers around a shrunken paunch. "I wager," he said, winking at Ned, "we could bring all London to heel if we tried. It's good to have the three at work again, hey, lads? My gut's rumbling, so let's sup, and toast tomorrow when this Scarrat acquires a second skin."

The man whom they were hired to follow was at that moment accepting a commission of his own.

Medmenham, lively in the summer months, required a new bevy of beauteous nuns, and since John Montagu, fourth earl of Sandwich, had proved eminently successful at supplying them (through his agent Scarrat), the monks had honoured him with the task again.

And so Scarrat had been summoned to the household, where Lord Sandwich received him in the study. Briefly they discussed the Canning affair with Scarrat assuring his lordship that all would go well, for whatever happened to the girl at trial, she'd not be so foolish and pert as to jeopardize her good footing with her betters.

"By that," said Sandwich with a thin smile, "I think you mean you have frighted the bitch witless."

"That is so, milord."

Then the order was placed by his lordship for a dozen girls; for the next mass there would be visiting monastics also in need of spiritual solace. He waited to see a touch of smile on the narrow ashen face, but Scarrat remained impassive to the sort of word play that served as wit at Medmenham. A devil of a fellow, his lordship thought, when the tall lean figure in black, having vowed to have the women ordered before nightfall and having then bowed out backward, disappeared from the room as if an apparition.

Alone again, Lord Sandwich took from the desk drawer a pasteboard puppet that moved into grotesque positions when dangled on the finger. These *pantins* were all the rage. A few idle moments of play, and he tossed the puppet next to his snuffbox. Then he shuffled through papers in another drawer, emerging with a sheaf of poetry. A few pages came from a gazette called *The St. James Tatler,* but most of it from broadside collections found for his lordship by a bookseller on the Strand. All of this work was obscene. Some of it would be put to memory by his lordship, because, among the friars of Medmenham, he had a reputation for reciting the most lickerish of verses.

He meant to sustain his role, and for that purpose sat down with a seriousness to the perusal of some recent work. There was "Miss V——n enjoy'd in her Sleep," "The Microscope," wherein two sisters use such an instrument as a dildo, "The Death of Adonis," "Love's Subtilty," "On a Lady who shed her Water at seeing the Tragedy of Cato," and "An Epigram on Marriage," but none of them worthy of putting to memory. However, he rather liked this one:

The Court Rapture
Cry'd Strephon panting in Cosmelia's Arms,
I die, bright Nymph amidst your Charmss!
Chear up, dear Youth, reply'd the Maid,
Dissolved in Amorous Pain,

> All Men must die (brigh Boy you know)
> E'er they can Rise again.

He read "The Unfortunate Rake, or Love by Moon-Light, and The Fair-One Start Naked," which didn't live up to its provocative title. "A Moral and Philosophical Epistle by the Author of the Rape of Pomona" began promisingly enough.

> Can I forget the beauteous Emma's charms,
> The soft Elysium of her circling arms;
> The wanton jirk of those elastic hips,
> Which made the ermin'd sages lick their lips . . .

But it descended after that into the blandest of verse. There was a song based upon double entendre, though too long for easy memorization, which equated the male organ with a musical instrument.

> The Flute is good that's made of Wood,
> And is, I own, the neatest;
> Yet ne'ertheless I must confess
> The Silent Flute's the sweetest.

However, for his performance at the next meeting of the monks he chose the following:

> By the Mole on your Bubbies, so round and so white;
> By the Mole on your Neck, where my Arms would delight;
> By whatever Mole else you've got out of Sight,
> I prithee now hear me, dear Molly.

> By the Kiss just astarting from off your moist Lips;
> By the delicate up-and-down Jutt of your Hips;
> By the Tip of your Tongue, which all Tongues out-tips;
> I prithee now hear me, dear Molly.

> By the Down on your Bosom, on which my Soul dies;
> By the Thing of all Things which you love as your Eyes;
> By the Thoughts you lie down with, and those when you rise,
> I prithee now hear me, dear Molly.

By all the soft Pleasure a Virgin can share;
By the critical Minute no Virgin can bear;
By the Question I burn so to ask, but don't dare,
I prithee now hear me, dear Molly.

The next to the last line mystified him, but as the rest were quite tempting, it was worth his effort, and his reward for saying it with a roar and a wink would be the good-hearted approval of his brothers at Medmenham. Their last meeting had been enormously merry, so much so that they had scheduled a mass for each fortnight till November brought with it chill weather.

There was but one thing to rankle in milord's breast at the thought of Medmenham, and that was the continued presence of John Wilkes. The man was nothing more than a country squire, whom Francis Dashwood, superior of the order, had whimsically taken under his wing, perhaps because Wilkes, a distiller's son with a squint eye and a crooked jaw, had a singular talent for debauchery, but nothing more to recommend him than a rich wife ten years his senior. Surely there were things to condemn him. The last time out to Medmenham this ranting commoner had aired unpopular opinions. In the face of annoyance at supper he'd loudly praised William Pitt and boiled over with ill-informed theories of government. After supper, he'd managed to insult the earl of March by alluding to his bad judgement of horse flesh, though knowing full well that March prided himself on little save a capacity for drink and a knowledge of race horses. The aimless wit and irrepressible arrogance of this ugly fellow John Wilkes were enough to cloud the entire festivities.

Even so, Lord Sandwich looked forward to a few days hence when his carriage rolled out of London, its whip springs squeaking from the onslaught of potholes, and made for the road to Medmenham. If ever man deserved its special pleasures, surely he did: shamefully out of office, at loose ends, chained to a silly woman whose voice could put on edge the nerves of a lion.

Picking up the *pantin,* he dangled it from a finger. As it hopped crazily up and down, he turned to address his outstretched mastiff. "What think you of his grace the duke of Newcastle?" And with a vicious yank, he tore a leg from the puppet.

[30]

A FEW DAYS LATER, while three noblemen were traveling out of London, bound for a former Cistercian monastery within sight of the winding Thames on a stretch of meadow between Henley and Marlow, two shabbily dressed men, one with an eye patch, were solemnly watching the entrance of the Sign of the Frigate. Scarrat, having discharged his commission before they began watching him, gave them nothing to report. He went down to the wharfs and inspected kegs of spirits, bought sausages for watermen who liked to eat while they drank, oversaw the cleaning of his tavern, and once spent an inordinate amount of time at a watchmaker's shop. The good doctor sent Lemuel around the back of the ordinary in case the tavernkeeper was slipping out on peculiar business, but all the one-eyed spy saw through slats in a fence was the grey-faced man trimming weeds in his garden.

"I grasp little of this," confessed a dejected Lemuel.

To which his master replied angrily, "If you was hobbled and led to the rope at Tyburn, I'd not attend your finny, I'd not say a single prayer when they lowered you."

"But you would," Lemuel declared with a grin. "You'd not let me go without a last tear."

"Ah, you ninny," Bostock grumbled gently. "Just keep that blinker of yours open."

While this conversation was taking place, the trio of noblemen rode steadily in the chaise through the open countryside beyond Kensington. They had left London directly after attending a royal levee that morning.

The brutish temper of King George II had been somewhat mollified by a certain Doctor Ward, whose lucky first attempt had jerked back into place a dislocated royal thumb. Before the assembled court the First Minister, his grace the duke of Newcastle, had expressed confidence that Parliament would vote a message of grat-

itude for the doctor in public recognition of His Majesty's recovery
from the painful situation — and so forth and so forth, the sort of
droning obsequious speech for which the duke was famous and to
which even the vain king could not listen without fidgeting. All
present were aware of George's wish to be done with this tiresome
official levee, so he might return to a study of military history or to
a tally of his royal wealth, which he did frequently, like a common
pawnbroker. Rarely did His Majesty show enthusiasm for anything
save the whir of cannonballs or the fireworks display at Marylebone
Gardens. It was no state secret that this king was a graceless boor,
a bully, and a braggart who — his good taste in music aside —
enjoyed the coarse pleasures of a drill sergeant. Only yesterday a
performing Danish dwarf had been presented at court in the garb of
a medieval jester and had pleased His Majesty so heartily that his
heavy jowls swayed like the wattle on a turkey.

And yet Lord Sandwich, attending the dreadful levee, had been
pleased, because of news that the First Minister would accompany
the king on a trip to Hanover, to visit the ancestral German estates
there. It would be a relief to have the damned toady out of England.
In the month of his absence, decent men out of office might well
undermine Newcastle and force him from the ministry.

Rattling along in the chaise, Sandwich would have wished to
discuss this possibility with his companions. George Selwyn, however, in spite of the jostling ride, was snoring. In all his years in
Parliament Selwyn had never delivered a single worthwhile speech,
but confined himself to making quips in the lobby. To recommend
him, George Selwyn had a county seat in Gloucester, a manor in
Chistlehurst, a town house in Cleveland Court, and the distinction
of having been sent down from Oxford for immoral behavior.

Nor could Sandwich discuss politics in safety with the third
passenger, Bubb Dodington, who was astute enough behind his
sweaty porcine face, but thoroughly unreliable when it came to
allegiances. Only this morning he'd been criticizing Granville, actually the sole minister of true capacity in the privy council, a man
of enviable intellect who read Greek and Hebrew, though a sarcastic drunk when burgundy was at hand. Dodington had remarked
on Granville's arrogance, yet tomorrow he might well be walking
arm in arm with Granville at Ranelagh. Such nimbleness — fat
Bubb changed politics the way other men changed linen — had

kept him in government twenty years, weathering like a wine cork the floods of controversy which ebbed and flowed with each new administration. He was, moreover, a busy patron of the literary arts to whom that scribbling magistrate Henry Fielding had once dedicated a poem entitled "True Greatness." Of course, everyone knew that the impoverished Fielding, in need of wine money, had merely flattered Bubb, but Bubb proudly showed the work to visitors. And Bubb never tired of mentioning his friendship with another scribbler, that irascible and peevish and impossible Frenchman, Voltaire.

It was about Voltaire that Bubb chose to gossip while the chaise jolted onward. According to Bubb, naughty Voltaire had behaved disgracefully at the Prussian court, much to the dismay of everyone who knew him or had loaned him money. The incorrigible fellow had engaged in a bit of shady financial intrigue with a Dresden Jew; there was possible evidence of downright forgery, which had simply infuriated Emperor Frederick, and so Voltaire had skipped the court, and none but God Almighty could say where the wonderful rogue would alight next.

Bubb pointed a pudgy finger at the sleeping Selwyn. "Without a hanging to rouse him, he's a damnable bore. We've got into bad hands, John. Did we follow him, we'd sleep our time away in Medmenham."

"There'll be precious little sleep for us," Sandwich declared.

"I believe it. With you in charge of the handmaidens. You have uncommon talent, John, for pimping, do you not mind my saying so."

"Please do. Though you need correction. I have uncommon talent for discovering a pimp of talent. As for Selwyn, he won't disturb my pleasure at Medmenham. The one I fear is Wilkes for his infernal raving. His defense of Pitt is disgraceful."

"Well, well."

"You think not? Pitt's a warmonger who wants funds for the army and none for ships. He has no understanding of naval power. Such hauteur and arrogance. Haven't you heard him say time and again, 'I know I can save the country and I alone can'? Insufferable! He learned it all from his buccaneering grandfather, Diamond Pitt."

"I knew Diamond Pitt. A coarse and brutal man. I found him frightful," admitted Bubb. "I gather you still oppose Wilkes standing for Parliament."

"Oh, I don't care. He might bribe the constituents to the hilt, but they won't return him. He can't say a civil word."

"Don't be choleric, John." Reaching across the chaise, Bubb patted his knee. "Though I wouldn't want a mere moneyed man in Commons, I do think the rascal has qualities. Francis thinks him the most comical bitch in the world."

"Francis takes for merriment the least word of a parson."

"True, true," Bubb said with a chuckle. "But I say let Wilkes make one of us. He can do no harm, and he might afford some entertainment."

Sandwich grunted in reluctant agreement, for it was useless to pursue his dislike of Wilkes. Bubb would support the scamp in order to curry favor with Francis Dashwood. That was how a man remained in government twenty years. Bubb had never contributed anything, certainly not as he himself had done in the Admiralty, yet he was out and Bubb was in. Bubb was always in.

Francis Dashwood was surely a fool, as gullible as a chambermaid, buffeted here and there by strange religious obsessions, but in one aspect of his life he displayed a kind of genius: he had a keen eye for pleasure and the wherewithal to implement his pursuit of it. The man had taken a ruined old abbey, a low unobtrusive building of little grace, and transformed it into a charming hideaway where jolly friends might find relief from wives and the cares of state. Medmenham. No place like it. Next to his beloved Henchenbroke, it was the place milord Sandwich would most like to be.

A dry wind blew through the open window, giving him a fit of coughs. He pulled out a kerchief and held it to his nose. "A monstrous dusty road," he grumbled. Turning to Bubb for a response, he saw that the fat man had followed Selwyn into a doze.

Medmenham. Where a man could chuck everything for pleasure and lose himself in frolic and for a while forget the intrigues of London, the smirks, the sidelong glances, the casual hints that burgeoned so often into nasty rumour and brought grown men crying to their knees.

Their five-hour journey ended at the main entrance of Medmenham, above which was carved an inscription from Rabelais: FAY CE QUE VOUDRAS — an apt motto for a retreat devoted to one's whims.

They were met by a tall, lean, hawk-nosed man wearing a monk's habit. Secretary of the brotherhood, Paul Whitehead greeted them with a low bow of mock solemnity. To milord Sandwich he said, "Brother John, have you carried out your duty to the order?"

"In my office of subprior I have. The nuns arrive tomorrow afternoon."

"The superior will be pleased. He bids you join him in the library."

"What society's here?" asked Bubb.

"Half the brotherhood already."

The cowled Whitehead led the way down a dim hallway to a door above which was another inscription: AUDE HOSPES CONTEM-NERE OPES.

"O Guest, dare to set riches at no value," Bubb recited, as he always did — vain of his skill in Latin that enabled him to write obscene verses in the tongue.

"It's a pity," remarked Sandwich, "that Wilkes isn't with us now to translate too, as he believes he alone has gone to school to Latin."

"Wilkes is here," Whitehead informed them, opening the door to the library.

Dashwood, seated alone with a goblet by the fire, got up and rushed to the new arrivals. Muscular, boyish, exceedingly nervous, with a tic jumping at the corner of his mouth, Dashwood called out, "Tardy but welcome! Your superior welcomes you with all his heart!"

Sandwich, along with the other monks, was accustomed to Dashwood's outbursts, his habitual confusion, his silly impudence, and profound self-doubts that occasioned many long hours locked up in solitude. Dashwood alternated piety with the invention of insufferable pranks, a study of the classics with wild romps in the arms of bawds. Before a solemn mass, as was his wont, he drank excessively, as if the true aim of carousing was to deepen his belief in redemption — the sort of paradox that fascinated and mired him down.

Lord Sandwich never entered this library without feeling a sense of wonder. It was a large but lovely room, cluttered with treasures, where a recluse might stay for many hours in contemplation of beauty — and without a wife sending word of her silly needs. Many of Dashwood's most prized possessions had been brought from his estate at West Wycombe here to the abbey — objects secured for his collection by the art agents of Leghorn, the brothers Charron.

Candles flickered warmly on vases of majolica, on plump chairs, on rosewood tables, on a firescreen mounted in mahogany and inlaid with ivory, on a bust of Emperor Vespasian in basalt, on a bronze Caligula with silver eyes, on a richly enameled hunting horn fixed on the wall above a table of Sicilian jasper.

Among the objects which Dashwood especially valued and which Sandwich coveted were a manuscript copy of the Psalms in vellum, finely bound with gilt clasps, preserved in a satinwood case ornamented with lapis lazuli and agates; a bedwarming pan that had belonged to Charles II with its motto "Sarve God and live forever"; a cameo of an Egyptian duck; a jar of Roman faience; a missal attributed to Raphael; a young gladiator in bronze; Diana in serpentine stone; along with Persian shields and chinaware from Japan, Chantilly, and Staffordshire.

But as Sandwich glanced over this multitude of objects, he heard a fresh commotion at his back.

In came the little Welsh poet Robert Lloyd and elegant Thomas Stapleton and behind them John Wilkes, arm in arm with the earl of March, whom a fortnight ago the commoner had insulted in this very room by questioning his judgement of horse flesh. Clearly they'd all been drinking and roared out their welcome to the newcomers.

Taking a glass of claret from a servant, milord Sandwich stood aside and grimly listened to Wilkes declaim in thunderous tones about something or other. Somehow he turned to the subject of William Pitt and predicted that someday such an orator would fire up England to conquer the known world.

"If he doesn't end up first in the madhouse," Sandwich called out combatively.

Bubb Dodington guffawed. "Allow me an anecdote of another orator, Isaac Barre. It happened in Commons some time ago. He'd sat himself down after delivering one of his turbulent speeches and was munching a biscuit. 'Mercy,' someone exclaimed from a rear bench, 'does it eat biscuit? I thought it fed on raw flesh.' "

All laughed save Lord Sandwich, who boomed at the chuckling Wilkes, "Why, sir, do *you* laugh? How can you appreciate Parliament, whereof you have no knowledge? Have you ever stood for a seat, much less sat in one?"

For a moment the squint-eyed Wilkes colored. Then with a low bow, he said coolly, "My compliments, Brother John. A pretty *bon mot.*"

The tension was relieved by a butler appearing in the library entrance to announce dinner.

Wilkes took the occasion to stroke his crooked jaw and comment with a hearty laugh, "This interference at a moment of certain seriousness might have come straight from a play by Congreve!"

Dashwood stepped forward to demand of everyone in mock severity that they exchange their frock coats for monkish habits before going into the refectory. It was now necessary to take on the spiritual contemplation of friars preparing for a solemn mass.

They changed in a small room, then went into dinner. The long table there, aglow beneath the orange light of fire lusters, was set for ten. Thomas Potter, scheduled to arrive this evening, had not yet appeared. Next to Dashwood, in the place of honour, sat Bubb Dodington.

Their cowls pushed back, the drably gowned monks fell to the feast with a will. Servants in scarlet coats and white gloves brought in courses of pigeon pie, gulled turkey, truffled partridge, quarters of veal and ham, sweet creams, beignets. Burgundy and champagne went the rounds in abundance.

The talk turned quickly to politics, as the whole bent and view of the country was employed on the ensuing elections. But Selwyn, heartily bored by it, charmed the table by relating an anecdote about the beautiful but quite mad duchess of Queensbury. It seems that she'd been going along the Strand in her chariot when a cart blocked the way. Its carman had an unlit pipe in his mouth. Looking Lady Kitty full in her lovely face, he declared, "Little dear, my pipe's gone out. Pray lend me those eyes of yours to light it again."

March turned the conversation to horse racing. When this soon became dull, the monks broached the subject of the upcoming Canning trial, and a lively argument developed. Wilkes was loud and witty in his opinion that the girl had lived for a month with a hellrake lover, who'd then starved her into keeping their liaison quiet, but she got flauncy and escaped. Most of the table agreed.

Had milord Sandwich not been so dangerously involved in the affair, he'd have laughed outright at the irony of their view, for every one of them had seen the Canning girl right here at Medmen-

ham. Behind the black mask that hid her face had been the features
they'd all seen in print shop caricatures. But they had steadfastly
obeyed their own rules — not to take the girls' masks off publicly.

Fools.

And there sat the biggest fool of them all, that ugly Wilkes.
Milord Sandwich drank deep, savouring his secret knowledge. He
felt more at peace with himself than he had for months, and so when
Bubb, flushed from spirits, turned and said to him, "Brother John,
favor us with an effusion for which you still have fame at Cam-
bridge," he didn't hesitate. Rising unsteadily, Sandwich held out
his glass. Off-key, in a murky baritone, he bawled out a catch from
the free and easy days of his youth.

> "Prithee, fill me the glass
> Till it laugh in my face,
> With ale that is potent and mellow."

Draining off his brandy, he sang on.

> "He that whines for a lass
> Is an ignorant ass,
> For a bumper has not its fellow."

Prompted then to do more, he recited his latest obscene lyrics, for
which there was polite applause around the table. So pleased with
this reception was milord Sandwich that he even smiled at Wilkes.

[31]

THEY RETIRED to the library for a nightcap, although they
mustn't linger too long, Dashwood warned, because tomorrow was
a solemn mass.

As brandy went around, Thomas Potter arrived. Tall and
brawny, a notorious rake, Potter was the son of a former archbishop

of Canterbury. The tipsy earl of March wouldn't let him speak until he'd had a brandy. "Make one of us," March demanded blearily, "for there won't be a sober monk in the abbey tonight. Drink, fart bag."

Pouring one with good humour, Potter flung himself into a chair, complaining of potholes along the road. But soon he leapt up with a wild cry, waved a sheaf of papers at his companions, and promised the brotherhood a rare treat, for he'd brought with him a work of wonderful merit just off the printing press. It was authored by one of their own, Brother John Wilkes. "Implore him to read it!" Potter said.

At first Wilkes seemed reluctant. "I beg your leave to defer such a thing. I am tolerably shy."

Amidst shouts and laughter, Bubb Dodington bellowed drunkenly, "Read it and be damned!"

"So will you all be should I read it," Wilkes warned, but with a broad grin and a wink. Getting to his feet, he grabbed the pages from Potter and stood with his back to the firescreen. "But as you wish. I am your obedient servant. This verse by Pego Borewell is a companion piece to Mister Alexander Pope's *Essay on Man*."

"Can't abide Pope," muttered the earl of March.

"Have I the superior's permission to begin?" Wilkes asked.

Dashwood nodded with a guffaw.

"Silence!" cried Potter.

"Silence!" boomed Bubb Dodington.

"Good brothers," Wilkes began, "I shall read a passage from Mister Pope, then a passage from Pego Borewell, the which, I have faith, will be a considerable improvement on the original."

"No more palaver," said Bubb. "Give us the masterwork."

" 'Awake, my St. John!' " Wilkes declaimed with a grandiloquent gesture. "Thus does Pope begin. I must digress, brothers, for an observation which you scholars have no need of."

"Give it anyway," shouted Potter.

"If you insist. 'Awake, my St. John,' writes Pope. 'What St. John?' you may rightly ask. Why, that St. John more sinning than sinned against. That St. John who plotted treason but proved too faint-hearted to carry it out. That St. John Bolingbroke, papist conniver. That St. John —"

"No more speeches!" thundered Bubb. "We get sufficient of them in Commons."

Wilkes bowed. "I therefore beg your leave to start anew. With the Pope version." Taking an orator's stance, he recited with flourishes of his hand.

> "Awake, my St. John! leave all meaner things
> To low ambition, and the pride of Kings.
> Let us (since Life can little more supply
> Than just to look about us and to die)
> Expatiate free o'er all this scene of Man;
> A mighty Maze! but not without a plan;
> A Wild, where weeds and flow'rs promiscuous shoot,
> Or Garden, tempting with forbidden fruit."

Wilkes paused.

"Can't abide Pope," grumbled March.

"Mark now the heroic imitation entitled *Essay on Woman*," said Wilkes, rattling the papers.

> "Awake, my Sandwich!"

He paused, allowing the monks to grasp his audacious comparison: the traitorous St. John Bolingbroke and their own brother friar.

"You rogue," gasped Bubb. Everyone giggled, save Lord Sandwich.

"I beg your indulgence," said Wilkes to the stunned nobleman and gave him a low ostentatious bow. "This is not my doing, God forbid. In spite of what Brother Potter claims, the work in progress is not authored by me but by that noble poet, Pego Borewell. Believe me, it is solemn verse of exceptional merit. Permission to proceed?" he asked Dashwood, who gave it somewhat doubtfully.

> "Awake, my Sandwich! leave all meaner things;
> This morn shall prove what rapture swiving brings!
> Let us (since life can little more supply
> Than just a few good fucks, and then we die)

> Expatiate free o'er that loved scene of man,
> A mighty Maze, for mighty pricks to scan;
> A Wild, where Priapean thorns promiscuous shoot,
> Where flowers the monthly Rose, but yields no fruit."

All the monks were chuckling, save Lord Sandwich.

"A commentary by Reverend William Warburton accompanies the verse," Wilkes continued with a pedantic squint at the papers. "Line seven," he said. " 'Where Priapean thorns promiscuous shoot' has a note of explanation attached thereto." He looked solemnly at his audience. " 'The vegetation of Priapus — for it is a plant and nothing else — is most astonishing; it will shoot forth most amazingly, especially when placed in a hot moist bed, and as suddenly will shrink back. There is another plant called Clitoris, much of the same nature though seldom large. I mean in this country, for at Lesbos it is a formidable rival of Priapus.' So Warburton tells us."

Wilkes rattled the papers. "Now for more of the humbler verse of Mister Pope.

> Together let us beat this ample field,
> Try what the open, what the covert yield;
> The latent tracts, the giddy heights explore
> Of all who blindly creep, or sightless soar;
> Eye Nature's walks, shoot Folly as it flies,
> And catch the Manners living as they rise;
> Laugh where we must, be candid where we can;
> But vindicate the ways of God to Man."

Wilkes paused melodramatically. "Now mark the better version."
"Mark!" shouted Potter.

> "Together let us beat this ample field,
> Try what the open, what the covert yield;
> The latent tracts, the pleasing depths explore,
> And my prick clapp'd where thousands were before."

The monks guffawed, except Lord Sandwich. Raising his hand for silence, Wilkes frowned at them.

> "Observe how Nature works, and if it rise
> Too quick and rapid, check it ere it flies;

Spend when we must, but keep it while we can:
Thus godlike will be deem'd the ways of man."

The monks roared their approval, but again he checked them severely.

"There's a note to line twelve: 'And my prick clapp'd, et cetera.' With your indulgence, here is what the reverend says."

"Read!" brayed Potter.

" 'An earlier version has it, "And my prick crown'd." Note the change here: "crown'd" not "clapp'd." I take Pego Borewell's earlier version to be a better reading of the author's intent. It refers to the "corona veneris," the glory of the goddess Venus around the head of the beloved. Perhaps the passage is a parody of Lucretius:

> Insignemque meo capiti petere inde coronam,
> Unde prius nulli —

Et cetera. That is to say, "To seek there for my head that outstanding crown where before there was nothing." ' So says Warburton."

Save Lord Sandwich, the monks clapped wildly. Alternating between the first book of Pope's *Essay on Man* and his own *Essay on Woman,* Wilkes gave a bombastic recitation of ninety-four lines of each, along with commentary. He ended thus:

> "Who sees with equal Eye, as God of all,
> The Man just mounting and the Virgin's fall;
> Prick, cunt, and bollocks in convulsions hurl'd,
> And now a Hymen burst, and now a world.
> Hope humbly, then, clean girls; nor vainly soar;
> But fuck the cunt at hand, and God adore.
> What future fucks He gives not thee to know,
> But gives that Cunt to be thy blessing now."

"Warburton's final note." Wilkes shook the papers to command silence. " 'Line ninety-four: "But gives that Cunt." It can by no means signify a wife's cunt. Matrimony is a holy estate, signifying to us (as the Service says) the mystical union between Christ and His Church. Now, what has this to do with fucking?' "

Folding the papers, he bowed low to loud applause.

"Come, scholars, let's be merry!" Potter grabbed up a brandy.

Dashwood reminded the brotherhood that tomorrow evening was the solemn mass. It was time for bed. "We can't be fagged out for our spiritual duty."

"The superior has spoken," mumbled the earl of March, trying unsuccessfully to rise. "Stapleton, dear fellow," he said with a sheepish grin, "help me out of here."

Flushed, tight-lipped, milord Sandwich walked over to the seated Wilkes, who was finishing a bumper. "A remarkable effusion," the nobleman declared with suppressed fury.

"I'll inform Pego Borewell that his lordship has praised his work."

"You, sir, have a most elegant and distinguished character."

"Your obedient servant."

Sandwich moistened his lips. The room had become silent. "You, sir, will die either on the gallows or of the pox."

Squinting up with a cool grin, Wilkes replied without hesitation, "That must depend on whether I embrace your lordship's principles or your mistress."

Dashwood came between them. Taking milord Sandwich's arm, he said, "I beg all of you to retire. Tomorrow's the mass." He led the enraged Sandwich from the library.

Singly or in twos, the monks shuffled off to their cells. Each undressed and climbed into a man-size cradle carved from thick oak. The superior of the order had laid down a strict rule: on the eve of a solemn mass each friar must sleep in a cradle like the offspring of Satan, rocking in dreams of forbidden pleasure or nightmares of hell, though the superior was well aware that unlike himself none of them took it seriously, that none of them would do as he did on the eve of a mass — read William Law's *A Practical Treatise upon Christian Perfection* and contemplate the proposition that man arrives at good through evil.

The mass was over, and so was supper and the frolic afterward. With his chosen little nun Lord Sandwich retired to his cell. It had been a long day, and as usual the mass had both thrilled and terrified him, as doubtless it had done all the monks, all save Wilkes.

That devil Wilkes.

This morning Francis Dashwood had taken his lordship on a

stroll through the garden to see a new piece of sculpture from Italy. It was a naked Venus stooping to pull a thorn from her foot, and positioned so that her round marble buttocks faced the viewer. "Note the misapplied Virgil." Dashwood pointed to some lines of Latin chiseled into the stone. "I'm not, as Wilkes, a scholar of Latin, but this I know. 'Here is the place where the road branches off in two directions. On this side is our way to the Elysian Fields, but the other branch leads to evil Tartarus and exacts the penalties for wicked deeds.' I think it quite droll."

"I wish to speak of that insolent puppy Wilkes. Comparing me with a Jacobite scoundrel! I should have demanded satisfaction."

"No sword play here," Dashwood said in alarm. "Dueling would mean the end of Medmenham. You know Wilkes. It was merely a jest."

"Which I won't accept from him."

"Oh come, Wilkes afflicts me too at times, yet I've a certain affection for him."

"I wonder at your taste. He rails against his fellows, he has no knowledge of politics, and insists on defending that madman Pitt. He's unmannerly, without name, and his face is vulgar enough for a chimney sweep. I'm considering a demand for satisfaction."

"Careful," Dashwood said, placing his hand, as if in restraint, on Sandwich's arm. "It's known that Wilkes is a master of sword and pistol. He had a quarrel, as you can imagine, and the man demanded satisfaction. It seems that Wilkes tried to make amends, but the man would have none of it. So they met. Wilkes put a ball into him, and the man hasn't walked without assistance since."

"Ah."

"I'm convinced he meant no harm with you."

"To please you, Francis, I'll keep my indignation down."

"I rejoice to hear it."

"Though it chokes me. I can't like Wilkes."

But later at the noon meal, in the presence of everyone, John Wilkes rose to his feet and toasted his lordship, begging pardon for last night's little joke. "I confess, I haven't the stuff of a diplomat. For one thing my wig never fits, nor does my face." He went on a little more, attempting to charm his listeners, until the table murmured, "Here, here," and turned hopefully to Lord Sandwich, who could do nothing else but accept the apology. So it was over, although what he'd told Dashwood was true: he'd keep down his indignation without dissipating it, as he still found this man Wilkes presumptive and odious, a villain who wished to be the fashion of London.

In the cell now with his little nun, milord Sandwich poured a goblet of wine. Drained by the emotions of the mass, wearied of frolic, half drunk, he sat in a chair and studied the masked girl who sat opposite him, gripping her hands together. She was mousy enough, somewhat like the Canning chit, who, in this same room many months ago, had awaited his command.

"How long have you been on the town?" It was a question he always asked.

"I've not been on the town, your excellence." She was shapeless in a drab habit of the same coarse wool as that worn by his lordship.

"Your excellence," he repeated. He rather liked her quaint manners, yet felt a familiar urge to wound her, as he usually needed to do with a woman. "So you say you haven't been on the town? When a man pays for your favours, girl, you're on the town. It should be plain. You're a whore now."

Looking down at her nervously clasped hands, she murmured, "Yes, your excellence, I reckon."

"What? Don't mumble so. Speak up."

"Yes, your excellence!"

"Don't call me your excellence. Call me Brother John."

"Sir?"

"This is a religious order. I'm a friar of the order, just as you're a visiting nun. Didn't my man explain that to you?"

"He did," she confessed, staring at her hands. "But I understood little of it. I obeyed him like he said."

"What do you mean?"

"I spoke not one word to the other girls. We was all mum coming here. Like he said. I knew we was to wear popish clothes, that's all. I knew it was some kind of jest."

Sandwich sipped his wine and smiled, feeling better now that he'd insulted her. "I trust you understand music better than you do jest. I trust your voice is not the screech of a peacock."

"No, sir, I hope not. It's said I have a proper voice."

"I'll be aforehand with you. Please me and you shan't want a reward on your return to London."

"Thank you, your — brother."

"Strip off that habit." He motioned for her to throw it on the bed, which had replaced last night's cradle.

As she wordlessly undressed, milord Sandwich unbuttoned the breeches underneath his own habit and slid them off his plump legs. Looking up at the girl, who stood beside the bed, arms crossed over her breasts, he said, "The mask too."

"Sir, brother, I was told by your man never —"

"Remove it, I say. I'm your master here, not him."

She untied the mask, and a pale, almost haggard young face emerged.

Not unlike the troublesome Canning wench — probably cold mutton and a thin soprano. What was the world coming to, he asked himself bitterly, when pert little chits such as this could threaten the security of a peer?

"My man promised a songbird," he said irritably. "Can you sing a bawdy catch?"

"I know none."

"In the devil's name —"

"I'm recently from Gloucester," she muttered as if in explanation.

"I care not Gloucester or Russia. What then can you sing?"

"I can sing hymns. Hymns, brother."

"Hymns!" What in faith had the Canning girl sung? Not hymns, of course, but he couldn't recall anything she'd sung. One song ran into another, one little face into another, one woman's body into another. Heaven help him, but it was a mean world.

"Then do it," he said impatiently. "Sing me your hymns. But keep your hands at your sides and stand there naked as the day you were born." He slipped one hand inside his habit.

For a moment bewildered, then aware of what he was doing, the girl fixed her eyes determinedly at a spot above his head and in a sweet but trembling contralto began the first verse of "Hark! The herald angels sing."

"Ah, a good voice," he exclaimed, "hymns or no." While his hand moved within the monk's gown, he conjured once again the beloved image of a snow-breasted nanny who had taken him into her bed so many years ago. "Aye, good, keep it up," he panted. "Sing. Sing. Sing!"

The huge lawn across which his tall mother strolled toward

callers, ignoring him where he sat in a lacy costume on the grass. And his father bulling through the high-ceilinged room, with not so much as a glance at him muffled against the drafts.

And Nanny, warm and white, clasping his body to hers in the bed. She had sung O such lovely lovely songs, when he'd been a frightened lonely boy, and sickly, on the vast estate of Henchenbroke.

Part Six

———————————•———————————

REVELATIONS

[32]

In NEARLY A FORTNIGHT Doctor Bostock and Lemuel had nothing to report except that Mister Scarrat carried out the duties of a tavernkeeper, kept a garden, and visited watchmaking shops. Disappointed, doubtful that his suspicions had been anything but the fond daydream of a desperate man, he told them to end their spying, though to salve the good doctor's feelings (as he professed a deep melancholy for having failed), Ned gave them two extra days' wages.

As for himself, he was working hard to meet Jenny Rivers's demands for gold, and at least three times a week now he set out to rendezvous with Sandy. As always, he found her with the black boy, who wouldn't surrender her until his cheek rested against her muzzle and his lips formed secret words only she could hear.

Ned hiked into the West End with her loping far behind, her pink tongue lolling. It was twilight, a time just before oil lamps were lit, when homeward-bound gentlemen were less cautious, having had a few drams to relax after a long day of work. It was therefore the safest time to set upon a cove. Ned tramped a half hour without luck. It was getting quite dark when he observed, turning into a narrow lane, a man wearing the long frock-coat of a merchant. Ned followed, encouraged to see the passageway almost empty. There were five people aside from the man, then four, then two. When the fellow turned into yet a smaller thoroughfare, it was deserted.

Ned whistled. The sleek dog blew past him. It was all so familiar now: the worrisome arcs of her motion that grew smaller until abruptly she had the victim flat against a wall, her snakelike head pointed, her long body crouched.

Approaching, Ned said calmly to the man, "Your purse, sir."

Twilight had become night, so that all he could see was a bulky figure, a faint white circle of face, and one oblong of hand, the other kept within the frock-coat.

The dry click of a cocking lever had Ned yanking out his own flintlock. The stubby barrel of his own pistol wavered, steadied, wavered. He'd not be able to see the man's finger tighten on the trigger.

Sensing the danger, Sandy began to growl ominously.

It seemed to Ned that the three of them remained motionless long enough to make the tiny lane familiar, as if he'd traveled it for years. He heard from a window overhead a woman laugh drunkenly, a man curse. This was a bunter's lane, he realized suddenly. The man holding a pistol on him could well be a footpad like himself.

"It's even betwixt us," Ned finally declared. "But should mine misfire and you hit true, the dog'll have your throat out anyway. You can't win this."

There was another long wait. Ned could hear someone leaving a house nearby in the darkness, then go away. Sandy continued to growl, crouching just out of the line of fire. Ned felt his finger trembling on the trigger. He felt cold, though it was still warm summer.

Abruptly, with a sigh, the man let his pistol clatter to the ground. "You're right. You have me."

"The purse, sir," Ned demanded. "Throw it beyond the dog."

A long pause, then another object thudded on the stones near Ned's feet.

"Step back and clear of the pistol, sir."

The man did.

Bending to pick up the leather truff, Ned then moved cautiously forward and retrieved the man's pistol. Minutes later, with Sandy behind him in the darkness, Ned continued to walk rapidly. His heart was still knocking wildly. The heft of the pouch signaled a good take, though most of it would go to the Queen of Foists. In spite of his poor judgement, the affair had ended well for Ned. Ah, but such poor judgement. He should have realized that the narrow lane was most likely a hideaway for men like himself, fully capable of paying him back in kind. In fact, he'd even noticed the look of the lane, but without responding to its obvious danger. His mind was unclear. He shouldn't work when his mind was cluttered with schemes and questions and a longing for Clare, who persisted in seeing him but a single night in the week.

He returned Sandy to the black boy, who as usual was waiting on the door stoop. The boy must have been there the whole time, patiently waiting for her to come home to him. He would have waited all night and all the next day and God alone knew how long he would have huddled there, silent, grave, arms hugging his bony knees, until the dog rushed up to him, wagging her tail, licking his dark face. Ned said goodbye, saddened that neither seemed to notice his departure.

At home, flinging himself on the bed, he was unable to keep his leg muscles from twitching. He decided in this state of nerves to calm himself by at last beginning *Tom Jones*. Getting the book and slicing open its initial pages with his knife, Ned sat down to read. First he read the Dedication to the Honourable George Lyttelton, Esq.; One of the Lords Commissioners of the Treasury. Then he read an introductory chapter which talked of human nature and had lines from Mister Pope. This he found wearisome. But the first lines of the second chapter held his attention, and Ned found himself drawn into a world:

> In that part of the western division of this kingdom which is commonly called Somersetshire, there lately lived and perhaps lives still, a gentleman whose name was Allworthy, and who might be called the favourite of both Nature and Fortune; for both of these seem to have contended which should bless and enrich him most.

Four candles later, exhausted from the night's adventure and the work of parsing out Mister Fielding's difficult though wondrous sentences, Ned fell asleep.

He slept until the next day, when loud knocking at the door aroused him. Pistol in hand, he opened it and stared groggily into the beaming faces of Doctor Bostock and Lemuel.

"Heyday, lad!" cried the good doctor. "I come in triumph! You turned me off, but I told myself, I said, sir, do your duty to the boy even if he pays in nothing but good wishes. And so I've done." He looked uneasily at the pistol. "The devil. Lay by that nasty thing, man." He brushed past Ned with a scowl. "You was always a fiery sort, but now you're crabbed as a drunken tinker. It comes of being a footpad too long. Pray, draw no weapons near me. Be a chum and listen to the news."

But he wouldn't relate the news until Ned had put no less than a guinea into his paw. Then Ned had to give him and Lemuel a dram of gin.

At last he declared proudly that he'd never lost faith in the spying, though some did — with a scowl at Lemuel — as that grey-faced Scarrat had the look of a fellow with secrets in his mind. "The ninny and I kept as close to him as you had paid a king's ransom of the service."

"Go on," Ned said impatiently.

The upshot was that yesterday Scarrat had gone to a brushmaking shop in Bishopsgate. "This shop provides more than brushes. I heard from neighbour people the owner's a clever tart. She's stocked her shop with girls more skillful at lovemaking than brushmaking. Our man was in there long enough for congress with one of them."

That afternoon Ned Carleton entered the Bishopsgate brushmaking shop. A half-dozen pretty girls were bent over the brushes, inserting minute hairs into the tiny holes. The shopowner approached, smiling. She wore a white pinafore over a demure muslin gown and a lacy bonnet, but her friendly smile turned a sly appraisal when the customer explained that his good friend Mister Scarrat had recommended the store, did he wish to discover some uncommonly fine goods. "I'm especially interested," Ned added, "in goods favoured by Mister Scarrat, as he recommended them so highly."

"Molly," said the woman. A pretty brunette turned from her work and gave Ned an inviting smile. "Molly, sir, will show you the goods you desire. Go with the gentleman, girl."

Curtsying to him, the pretty brunette took Ned up a stairway and led the way down a corridor lined with doors. She opened one of them and invited him into a small but neat room. There was a washbowl, a pretty fan stuck in a mirror frame above a chest, a stool, a table with a vaseful of yellow flowers. Ned stared at the flowers, a touch of brave color.

The girl sat on the bed, fingers at her stays, and said with a coy smile, "I await your pleasure, sir."

Gripping his hat, Ned sat down on the stool and asked the girl when last she'd seen Robert Scarrat.

The name drew a frown, but she said nothing.

"He comes here, I know. I think you're the one he has acquaintance with."

"The name's not familiar." Kicking off a shoe and lifting her skirt, the girl with an efficient motion removed one black stocking, then the other.

"He has recently been here."

"I stay mum about my acquaintances, sir." Pulling her skirt higher, she let him see that she wore no underwear. "Let's say no more of another man. Let's do for you, nice gentleman."

"Give me information, you'll be rewarded."

In her eyes he saw a familiar look — it was the cove, the flat, the victim pressed against a wall.

"You'll get nothing of me," she said, and pulled her skirt rapidly over her exposed thighs. "Are you unnatural, sir? Do you pay to know what others have of me that you lack boldness to have for yourself?"

Her saucy reply came from fear, Ned realized. He'd get no answers from her.

Rising, he left the room and hurried downstairs.

Surprised, wondering perhaps how he could have satisfied himself so quickly, the girls stared at him over their brushwork.

Rushing up, the shopowner put a pink hand on his arm. "Not satisfied with the goods, sir? Tell me, as I keep a pleasing establishment."

"All is well. How much?"

Her hand shifted into the flat outstretched palm of a businesswoman. "Ten shillings. No less than that, even do you stay a short while."

As he gave her the money, Ned saw his own Clare coming into the shop. Their eyes met for an instant before she turned and hurried away.

The shopowner, her eyes studying Ned, asked again, "Be you sure all is well? Molly's a fine girl, but headstrong."

"I'm satisfied," Ned muttered as he turned and left the shop. He walked slowly until out of its sight, then sprinted in pursuit of the tall woman disappearing around a corner.

At midblock he caught up, spun her around.

"You followed me there," Clare said.

"I was there for other reasons."

"For brushes?" she asked with a sneer.

"Not for girls either. I want no whores!" He raised his good hand threateningly.

She stood ramrod straight, head high. "Go on. I can't blame you."

"You lodge in that shop?"

"I won't deny it."

"You have a second-floor room on that hallway?"

She said nothing, which he took for yes.

Pushing her against a wall, he slapped Clare hard across the face.

She didn't lift her hands in defense. "Go on, I can't blame you." The stinging blow brought tears to her eyes.

"Is this the shop you was first at?"

"It is."

"You told me you went from there."

"I lied."

"You told me when you was there they encouraged you to be a man's mistress. But nothing beyond that. Dear God, it's a bawdy house!"

She looked steadily at him through the tears; a red welt was appearing from ear to cheek.

"You have your milliner, but you lodge in a bawdy house. Why?"

She was rubbing the crimson streak spreading across her face. "For money."

"You work in the millinery, then go to another shop and take men there? You leave one shop for another and climb the stairs with anyone? Not only the milliner? With anyone?" He was pacing in front of her, as if Clare were a cove defenseless against a wall.

"I see my milliner once a week. Otherwise I take men at night in my room. I won't deny it."

"But why? Dear God!"

"I told you. For money."

"Gold? Here." Plunging his hand into his money pouch, he took out coins and flung them at her feet. "I can give you that as well as any man!"

Staring at the coins, she bent down and picked them up, one by one, slowly, then opened her own purse and dropped them in. "I'll hoard these too. It's not easy to save. I give Mrs. Adams half. That's to keep me safe, as it's a safe house, and for a physician do I need one."

"You whore yourself this way, but why, in God's name? You told me not to use armour. I thought you meant you was mine, lass."

"I did mean it. That night I knew it was your child I wanted and I thought no farther."

"And went back to your whoring." He kicked fiercely at the cobblestone. "Is gold worth hoarding up at any price?"

"Yes."

"Why? I ask why? I keep asking why, in God's name!"

"To get free."

"Of what?"

"Of London. Of dependence on others. Of fear and worry."

He kicked again, unable to meet her eyes, because he believed her instantly; indeed, with terrible ease he believed her. He could imagine her rising from a customer to enter in a thumbworn ledger the amount saved for a future of freedom. He saw it clearly, in a moment. Was he himself different?

Then he glanced up, looking in dismay at the ugly red mark on her face. God in heaven, he loved this woman. "The blow was wrong," he mumbled.

"I don't blame you. I kept back the truth. I lied."

"Forgive me the blow, lass. I'm sorry for it."

"It was forgiven when I felt it. Was I you I'd have done the same. Do you hate me now?"

He reached out and touched the inflamed cheek gently. "Would you come have a refreshment with me?" It was what he'd asked her long ago, in front of the millinery shop.

Smiling at the memory, Clare said, "Do you mean a dish of chocolate?"

"That was my thought."

"It would be pleasing."

He took her arm formally and like a couple newly met they went to a pastry shop. Chocolate would restore them, Ned thought. What happened in the brushmaking shop was of no account. Yet as he cooled the hot surface of his dish, an appalling image filled his mind: Clare naked, sprawling under a potbellied merchant. "Lass," he said in a tense whisper, "you must do it no more. You must leave the shop."

"Not till there's gold enough." Reaching across the table, she touched his ungloved hand, for the other he kept, as usual, hid in his frock-coat. "Not till we're free. I lacked faith to think we ever could be free, but I prayed to God every day for such faith, and I have it now. I do. I have faith we'll get free together. So I'll do what must be done till then. Say no more, love."

They were silent amidst voices raised over chocolate and pastry. Ned leaned over suddenly to whisper, "There's another way to get gold."

She looked startled, then fearful. "No schemes, lad."

"I know another way."

"I'd rather we use my body than risk your life. I can't abide the thought of you in the lanes at night. I can't bear it."

"There's yet another way."

"Take care," she said in alarm. "No wild schemes, lad."

"There's another way. And safe enough."

"Don't be rash! I beg you. I dream of you with a musketball in your chest. No schemes or we're done for."

"Hear me out." He revealed that a man named Scarrat might pay handsomely to keep certain information from public knowledge. "It's a safe way of getting gold quickly and enough at one swoop to free us from London."

"But how is that?"

"Gold would come from a rich source. It can hurt none, but help us. I swear."

"Can this be done, I'm for it," Clare said thoughtfully.

"Scarrat knows a girl in your house." He paused at what he'd just said, as if he were talking to a common whore. But he pushed on. The girl's name was Molly, he told her. Molly might know something important about the man.

"So you went to the house inquiring?" Clare smiled and shook her head. "Ah, you might ask the day long, she'd say nothing. No girl there would. Peach on a visitor, Mrs. Adams would have her revenge. I'd fear to cross the woman in such a way. Mrs. Adams would have Molly's throat cut."

"You mean that?"

"Molly wouldn't wish to learn for herself if the gossip was true. It's said a girl at Mrs. Adams's was once surly and did wrong and was found floating in the Thames with her throat cut."

"I'm done then," Ned admitted. "I can go no farther without information."

After a silence, Clare said, "On occasion I've befriended Molly. She might answer to me. But it'll take time, as you just asked today, and less I'm very cautious she'd be suspicious. You must stay clear."

"I swear to."

"Lad, do you love me true?"

"I love you true."

"I'd have your child. Willy-nilly. No matter if we get free or not, no matter what happens. It's wild and reckless but I want you never to wear armour. You see?" she said with a wan smile. "That makes you different."

"I could cut off my hand for hitting you."

"There's no blame. We lead a nasty life."

They had another chocolate, and he saw Clare looking anxiously at the door.

"Does Mrs. Adams expect you there this evening?" Ned asked in a flare of jealousy.

"I'm afraid, lad, she does."

He watched her rise and leave the pastry shop. This evening surely she'd lie naked beneath a panting tradesman, but it was of no account because she was his and he was hers forever. He'd not apply to her the notions of Warsop. What mattered was her courage and her love.

He mustn't fail her. He knew now what to do: pitch upon an act of incredible boldness, something at which Jenny Rivers herself would balk. It was an unheard-of deed that would have stayed beyond his wildest imagining a year ago. If fate lent him a hand, Ned Carleton was going to blackmail a peer of England.

[33]

⁊ This morning I arose with a will and took renewed satisfaction
in my surprising ability to stand unaided, without too much of
a vexing stab of pain in my left foot. There was a great bustle
through the house, as preparations were finally under way for our
journey to Bath.

At such fastidious work, requiring a clear sense of organization,
my wife was in strictest truth beyond compare, as nothing being
loaded into the coach and strapped on to the top escaped her eye:
portmanteau, food hopper, or chicken crate — she meant to have
our provisions with us, the which to escape the dear prices asked
in the pleasure spa of Bath. It was a far cry from the days when
I had my gilt coach and liveried crew and stopped along the way
to purchase anything of interest and at any price. Had I traveled
in Mary's style, need I tell you, Reader, I would not now be
having butchers refusing me service.

Saunders Welch came for a visit before our departure, and we
spoke of various things, among them this fellow the Dog Cull,
who seemed lately to have expanded his criminal enterprise
beyond the West End. From information filed at the Bow Street
Register, we were now convinced that the fellow had an injured
hand; either he kept it in his frock-coat or used it clumsily within a
glove. I thrilled to hear it, for I glimpsed in this piecing together of
facts a new way of tracking miscreants. It used to be by accident
that one was caught. A constable was in the right place or close by
or a crowd gathered round and in an angry mood prevented an
escape. The common arrest was hit and miss. But by gathering
our information in a central way and filing it for referral, we might
seek for a particular man on such information, without him being
witnessed in the criminal act. Saunders suggested, and I agreed,
that our runners be supplied with written details so as possibly to
recognize a criminal by the description of him and his means of
working his specialty, if, like the Dog Cull, he had one.

Shortly after Saunders had left, so did we, rattling away in the

coach, I holding the closely wrapped Louisa in my arms, with
Mary beside me; the other two youngsters and pretty Harriet
sitting on the seat opposite.

The summer sun beamed down on us and other travelers
proceeding south of London, while coming toward us was a great
colourful flood of wagons, horsemen, and herds, all funneling in
from country lanes and paths, streaming toward the city
thoroughfares, soon to empty into the squares and markets,
merging into the fetid atmosphere of the streets I love, for in faith I
do love them, their smell of burned charcoal, their Eastern spices,
their coffee and sewage and beer, their motion and colour all
drawing the life from outside into the insatiable maw of London,
for in truth this city is like a gigantic beast of prey.

We ourselves were then in the countryside, our spirits raised by
the sight of willows and poplars that marked the passage of little
streams, cows grazing in the distance, and overhead in a pure blue
sky a flock of sparrows dipping and curving in currents of air. It is
a scene beloved by English poets and made me wish for a voice like
theirs to speak in verse of such beauty, as Milton and Shakespeare
and Spenser have done in praising this blessed land.

At noon we stopped at an inn for refreshment, the which I must
say was hearty enough for any man, and delicious, as the cook
there had my favourite at hand, a hashed mutton with gravy, that
I washed down (avoiding Mary's disapproving eye) with three
tankards of strong ale.

But as we drew nearer to Bath, it fell out that a mood of
brooding melancholy descended on my spirits, and, as it were,
pinched them shut and left me unreceptive to the passing scene.
It was predictable, however, as it hath always happened in
recent years when I approach the town of so much earlier
happiness.

My love for Bath began with another love — my sudden
elopement with Charlotte Cradock after a protracted courtship.
Her mother, a widow, had never been sanguine, to say the least,
about her daughter marrying a man of the theatre, as such an
occupation was unstable at best and present good fortune could
overnight go sour (how prophetic the good woman was).
Wearying of delay, my beloved and I had hit finally upon the
scheme of running off to Bath.

I shall never lose the picture of Charlotte that morning when we
met on St. Ann's Street, just off Friary Lane where her mother and
sister lived. Critics of *Tom Jones* have complained that Sophia

Western is a heroine too good to be true, yet I swear she is nothing more than a faithful portrait of Charlotte Cradock:

> For, lo! adorned with all the charms in which nature can array her; bedecked with beauty, youth, sprightliness, innocency, modesty, and tenderness, breathing sweetness from her rosy lips, and darting brightness from her sparkling eyes, the lovely Sophia comes!

That was Charlotte on the morning of our elopement, no more or less. In that description, retained in my memory since the writing of it, I did not falsify one whit the girl's person, as she hurried toward me that autumn morning. I took her valise and helped her into the Salisbury coach then loading; we waited for what seemed an eternity, her warm hand trembling in mine, before the wheels turned and the stage set out for Bath.

It was a wonderful intrigue for a pair so fond as we. Obtaining a license under the fiction that we both lived in the parish of St. James, we were joined in holy wedlock on the twenty-eighth of November in the Year of Our Lord Seventeen Hundred and Thirty Four in the secluded parish of Charlcombe in St. Mary's, a stone church with an embattled tower overlooking a deep ravine, high on the slope of Lansdowne. The very thought of our hands clasped, our faces set toward the local inn where I had arranged for an accommodation, can still weaken me with tenderness and a pure joy: the room with a casement window, a tall vase of pink carnations, the twin flounced pillows.

Bath, the scene too of my triumphant retreats from London, when I had turned my pen most actively to political farces. What a merry time it was, as, buttressed by love, I feared nothing, not even Walpole himself, and in the service of the opposition against him and his corrupt government I wrote without stint, recklessly, happily. I took no warning from the First Minister's initial moves at suppressing the opposition, when a grand jury delivered into the Court of the King's Bench a presentment against several anonymous articles as false, infamous, scandalous, and treasonable libels against His Majesty's government. I continued to lampoon the hard-drinking unscrupulous Robert Walpole, half in admiration of his outrageous practicality in the use of bribes and threats, which had kept Parliament in line so many years. I was without apprehension that freedom of the theatre should be endangered, and so I went along prodigally.

Each time a new play of mine hit the boards, I purchased

complete new wardrobes for myself and my wife and pushed upon
dear Charlotte more expensive baubles than she in truth had desire
for. And as royalty we descended upon Bath where I often
received for such an outspoken stand against the First Minister a
rousing and widespread caressing from the fashionable public.

Therefore, it came as something of a shock to my pride, to say
nothing of my pocketbook, when the Licensing Act for the
Protection of Public Morals was pushed rapidly through both
houses of Parliament. The burden of it, as all London knew, was
aimed vengefully at me: under penalty of fifty pounds, no play
could appear unless sanctioned by letters patent from the Crown
or licensed by the lord chamberlain.

My loyal friend Lord Chesterfield argued against it as a breach
of liberty, but to no avail. So I left off writing for the stage when I
ought to have begun, being at the time but thirty years of age and
still in my apprenticeship. Had I worked with Garrick when he
came upon the scene a few years later, we might have given the
British stage a fame unequaled since the days of Shakespeare. So
say I, Reader. I beg you to be reconciled to my overweening boast,
as it lies like a poultice upon the wound I still carry from that
event. The censorship not only took away my principal means of
support, but to multiply the mischief, it closed down the theatre
of which I was manager, breaking the actors of my troupe, many
of whom were reduced to vagabondage and drifted into debtor's
prison, from which, given my own state of affairs, I could not
rescue them.

Thus, whenever the tile roofs and sash windows of familiar Bath
hove into view amongst the rolling hills, I see them, as always,
with mixed recollections of triumph and defeat, mixed feelings of
joy and sadness.

There was, when we entered, a great squeezing in the town, as
bathers had left the hot springs for the chop houses, the puppet
shows, the ballrooms. Our children were indeed weary from the
long jarring ride (though Louisa's cough seemed no worse for the
journey), and so in quick order we disembarked at a lodging
familiar to me for many years. Joseph, Cook, and my wife's maid,
following in the next coach, made promptly to get us comfortable
and by using the house kitchen to prepare, from our own supplies,
a bit of supper. After which, we all retired and looked forward
to the next day, which, as if by our order, dawned brilliantly,
providing us with a cloudless blue heaven and a scent of sweet
flowers, all balmy in a hint of breeze.

After breakfast, I took them to the hot wells, to that half acre starting close to Abbey Church, where everyone of quality in England sooner or later can be seen, for methinks I have seen them all, either at the King's Bath or Queen's Bath or the cooler Cross Bath, where gentlemen and ladies in gowns of stiff yellow canvas descend the short flight of stairs to the hot water, with powder and snuffboxes soon bobbing like corks before their heated noses.

The band had not yet tuned up, although a few enthusiasts were already at the pump, getting their cup of odoriferous sulphur water. I had never much cared for the stink of that place, which was hard put, however, to match the smell of the idle gossip drifting across the steamy surface of the baths and oft-times shouted through the band's blare so loudly that the gossiped-about were alerted to their supposed folly. No, I had no wish to display my dropsy of the flesh in that spicy pond or have myself wrapped in flannel and trundled homeward in one of those chairs that they line with red baise, not I, as if I were a fatted goose hanging from a pole and bound for market.

So after I had duly installed Mary and Harriet at a table near the Cross Bath, which they both preferred and which they would try whenever the few damp dressing rooms were freed, I took my leave ever so gladly. The truth was, I had important business in view, of a nature which I have already mentioned and which you will doubtlessly agree was best looked to without delay.

Not so foolhardy as to trust my quality of leg to a three-mile hike, I got a carriage and set out for a meeting scheduled more than a fortnight ago when this little expedition had first been planned. I meant to see Ralph Allen, friend and benefactor, who once had given me the use of his property at Twerton when I was composing *Tom Jones*. During that time I had dined almost daily at his Prior Park and, in truth, as some observers have suggested, I modeled good Squire Allworthy after Ralph Allen, who hath somewhat about him that doth certainly inhabit a few rare human breasts. The use of this talent is not so properly to distinguish right from wrong, as to prompt and incite others to the right and to restrain and withhold them from the wrong.

The estate of Prior Park sits upon a high hill overlooking Bath. To describe it adequately, Reader, would take the length of this volume in which I am now writing. The main house is splendorous indeed, with its creamy arcades and pavilions buttressed by noble Greek columns and its outflying wings leading the spellbound eye beyond the huge central mass to the flower gardens and horse stables and granaries and terraces and fountains and streams and bridges and grottoes. As far as vision can go, there is a cheery prospect presided over by a man of uncommon merit.

When my coach pulled up to the main entrance, Ralph Allen was soon at the steps to greet me, his ruddy face abeam, his sturdy figure a testament to a lifetime of hard work which Providence had chosen, and rightly so, to reward with abundance. We went into his study for tea and spoke awhile of other days when Mister Pope still lived and often resided for long stretches as a guest at Prior Park, a friend sorely missed by Ralph. He also spoke of William Warburton, both pastor and wit, who I must confess had never been a favourite of my own, as he had once appealed to me in my capacity as magistrate to retrieve for him a ton of lead which mysteriously had disappeared from his coach house. For nearly half a year he pestered me with urgent letters about it, as though I had nothing better to do in this life than tramp the lanes of London peering at trash heaps in search of his stolen ton of metal. Ralph and I spoke awhile of literature, for which he hath a genuine fondness, though he was never educated in it, a fact which he readily admits to but which no literary acquaintance of his ever found of consequence. We spoke then of a barrister mutually known to us who, after years of besmirching his honour through too much drink, had given the bottle up altogether and recouped his reputation.

Settling back deeply in his chair, my friend puffed on a pipe and observed that to retrieve the ill consequences of a foolish conduct and by struggling manfully with distress to subdue it, is surely one of the noblest efforts of wisdom and virtue. It must be considered strange indeed, Reader, how easily we can assign meanings to the words of others according to our present lights. In this instance I felt he might be touching on my own prodigality.

Having thus broached the subject which in fine I had actually come to introduce myself, I promptly requested him to do me the honour of serving as executor of my estate. His answer, as I would expect of him, was immediate and affirmative. Indeed, he seemed gratified and possibly quite relieved by my concern for the future. I showed him the proposed Last Will and Testament, which he read and approved. Upon my leaving, he pronounced himself overjoyed by my improved appearance of health since last we met. It was a pretty little speech. But I could see in his small blue eyes, which I daresay have rarely lost anything of what they looked upon, a troubled expression which confirmed the unspoken opinion of us both — that such a provision was taken none too soon. There was a further aspect of the matter left unspoken, but acknowledged by us both beyond question, and that was by making my friend — a most wealthy man — my executor, I could be certain of his future concern in every regard for my family, should I leave them slenderly provided for. I have long thought that men of highest standards must needs be rich, for the rest of us, though trying to scale the heights of ethical conduct, must slip now and then at the service of practicality.

Having thus settled this issue, I went to lodgings and arrived there just as Mary and Harriet returned from the hot wells. Feeling somewhat queasy, perhaps from the sulphurous fumes, Mary went to bed. Harriet took the children to a puppet show and the maid looked after ailing little Louisa, whose cough, alas, had come back on her. I was thinking of a chicken leg and a glass of porter, when Joseph came in with word that my sister was in the parlour.

I went down without delay, ever glad to see dear Sarah, the last of my four sisters who lived, the others having been lost in a terrible year of death that had also claimed poor little infant Mary Amelia.

The parlour of the lodging house was a dim, cramped affair with musty thick velvet hangings and a shabby genteel load of lace upon every chair and table. Sarah rose when I entered the room, and I must say her appearance appalled me, for though not much above forty, she seemed as wrinkled and careworn as a woman near twice her age (it is a woeful but true observation that we Fieldings do not age gracefully). But in her deep sunken eyes was the light of wisdom that I and many others had learned to trust. She was one of those persons of slender means who show themselves everywhere, not because they seek such exposure, but because others do, by discreetly easing the burden of expense, so as to have such calm and reassuring company on hand.

For that matter she had been befriended by Samuel Richardson himself, who, having hated me for making satiric fun of him in works like *Shamela* and *Joseph Andrews,* displayed a true regard and affection for my sister. It had once been reported to me that in his country house at North End, Hammersmith, with the usual covey of admiring females gathered round his plump little figure (for he loves a fawning audience, which is no more than a widely acknowledged fact, Reader), Richardson once remarked that my knowledge of the human heart was to Sarah's as the knowledge of the outside of a clock to the knowledge of its finer springs and the movement of the inside. I believe this report, as the comparison seems long and convoluted enough to have come from his brain. In truth, I believe him right about Sarah's depth of understanding, as in her novel *David Simple* there are touches that might have done honour to the pen of Shakespeare.

Sarah and I talked awhile about the present season in Bath. Our rich and powerful cousin, Lady Mary Wortley Montagu, was appearing every night at the Pump Room in fine fettle. Lately she had in her imperious manner asked Sarah of me. Lady Mary had especially inquired of my affairs, whether they were in some order. Doubtless there had been in her voice that tartness I have always found invigorating, no matter what the subject of her speech, when she told my sister, "Henry would still want money if his hereditary lands had been as extensive as his imagination."

To clarify that matter for you, my outspoken cousin was referring to the modest estate left me, which horses and hounds and casks of wine devoured in less than three years, a patrimony which, with good management, would have secured me and mine for a lifetime; the which was now but a memory.

The memory brings me again to Samuel Richardson. Soon after that financial crisis had made itself felt upon my all too buoyant spirit — meaning I had neither horse nor hound nor cask of wine left to sell in the service of my debts — I translated from the French a military history about the Swedish monarch Charles XII and proposed to make a few guineas, as well as amuse myself, by writing a somewhat racy burlesque of Richardson's *Pamela,* the current rage of literary London and admittedly a work of considerable power. What I found worth satirizing was the novel's hypocritical ethics, as the heroine guards her person from the seducer not for honour but for advantage; indeed, she must have taught every chambermaid in England that cunning, not virtue, is rewarded in affairs of the heart. Poor Richardson — how could this father of twelve children, half of whom lived, come up such a prude and declaim so against temptations of the flesh? But enough of that early *Pamela*. His *Clarissa* is a thing of beauty, a masterwork which shall outlast the lives of us all, and thus did I describe it in a letter to him, hoping thereby to patch up our quarrel and join hands, as two fellows should who labour in the solitude of words. He never replied to my letter, and now Sarah informed me that Richardson was here in Bath.

This in itself was reason enough to keep me from the crowded Pump Room that evening, for his star was high and mine fallen, and a watchful audience would remark gaily on the state of the literary heavens.

There were, however, other as pressing arguments against my appearance. It did not please me in my present situation to return to the scene of earlier days, when a head taller than most, I exchanged quips with the best of them. Nor would I longer be amused by the antics of Beau Nash, who in his plumed hat drew up to the Pump Room each evening in a post chariot drawn by six greys and with outriders and footmen trotting alongside and French horns heralding his arrival as master of ceremonies of Bath. The big, awkward, witty fellow! The ladies gushed over him as if he were the prince of Wales, a measure of the social graces of our time.

But the strongest reason for not attending tonight's gala had in truth to do with my wife, as Mary stubbornly refused to be seen abroad in polite society, whether with child or no, for the dear woman could never admit to herself that honesty of thought and plainness of speech and amiability of character and tenderness of soul could in their sum override the irregularity of our prenuptial relationship, let alone a lack of carefully nurtured manners. I once said to her, "Go to, Mary. The source of true breeding lies not within the confines of a drawing room but within the greater expanse of the human heart." To which pomposity the plain-spoken woman grimaced while telling me, "Go to, Mister Fielding, yourself!"

Our chat done, sister Sarah took her leave, but not before halting at the parlour entrance to touch my face lightly and study me from those limpid but sagacious eyes. Imagine my astonishment when she declared that I seemed younger today than I had been in a long time. I suspect this change in my countenance must have derived from my earlier meeting with Ralph Allen. I did indeed feel more sanguine about the future than I had in many a month.

Then, with an abruptly sorrowful expression on her aging face, Sarah murmured, "I pray no harm comes to you."

After she left, I mulled over her words that seemed not to refer to my physical condition but to something more profound, as if she divined a threat to the deepest core of my being.

[34]

BY DINT OF CUNNING and patience Clare was at last able to come to her lover with news of Scarrat.

They lay in bed, hands clasped, having sated the passions accumulated through another week's separation from each other, their bodies caught in the milky rays of late summer moonlight. Calm now, emerging from a shared realm of ecstasy, they talked in low voices while the outside world shook from the screech of wagon wheels and the clap of horses' hoofs and from voices raised in curses, in angry shouts, in gay laughter along the dark lanes of Holborn.

Clare had finally learned from the girl Molly that Scarrat did indeed visit her, but somewhat irregularly, perhaps twice each month. Such a man, Molly tearfully acknowledged once she began talking of him, she hoped never to deal with more, as his sharpest pleasure came from frightening her with the most terrible threats of violence if she failed to follow him in whatever he commanded. That meant in thought as well as deed, for he demanded absolute submission, and his favourite frolic was to have her come to him on all fours, like a dog, wagging her ass and barking. It was what she least liked, so he made her undergo the humiliation frequently, until it was all she could do to keep back a moan of despair whenever, while at work on the brushes, she raised her eyes and saw him slouch into the shop as grey as death. Like many taciturn men of restraint, in a rumpled bed Scarrat became a magpie, garrulous and boastful. He bragged often of his vast knowledge of women.

"Mark this," Clare said. "A knowledge that kept him in high favour with a nobleman."

"Meaning he got women for the nobleman?"

"Yes. And special ones. No matter how lousy or elegant, they must sing. Sing like a bird. Scarrat chooses only them that can. Otherwise they get no recommendation to his master. He combs London for them."

Sing like a bird, Ned repeated to himself. Near the Canning house he'd heard the girl warbling a pretty tune. Elizabeth Canning sang.

"He told Molly," Clare continued, "he got wenches however he could. Once he found a girl from the market nearby. A grocer girl."

"Can you find this girl?"

"I can try. And there's more to tell. Angry at Molly for sauciness one night, he threatened to lock her away in a wicked house."

"What wicked house?"

"Molly didn't say. But he warned the poor girl did she cross him, she'd get what another girl got from him — a month walled up and in the hands of a terrible old bitch. Molly fears him like the plague. Lad, what have you to do with such a mean creature as Scarrat?"

"No more than I must. Sweetheart, find the grocer girl."

"Is this scheme sure?" She turned to him, her eyes steady on his moonlit face. "I don't like it."

"You will when we get free."

"Ah, it's a pretty dream."

"But will come true."

"I want to believe it, love."

"I swear it!"

After Clare left the next morning, Ned lay a while longer in bed, thinking. Scarrat, close to a nobleman, threatens to mew a girl up in a wicked house. He tells her he supplies this nobleman with songbirds. Elizabeth Canning was a songbird who claimed to have been mewed up in such a place. What would the public think of such coincidences? There was true ground for blackmail of Lord Sandwich.

While dressing, he imagined the horror on the nobleman's face if Scarrat made clear the danger of discovery. It would fright his lordship more than Sandy driving him to the wall. It would loosen the great man's purse strings!

When Ned went to the case in Golden Lane, he found Doctor Bostock laid out on his mattress in a drunken stupor. Ned slapped his grizzled face and forced a dram of gin down the old rascal's throat, which revived him sufficiently to talk.

Yesterday afternoon he and Lemuel had followed Scarrat to a stable where he horsed and rode out of town. Good stalwart lad

Lemuel had horsed too and followed as best he could, until near the Hertford Road in a crowded thoroughfare Scarrat had vanished.

"The Hertford Road," Ned mused. "Does it lead to Enfield?"

"If not, I'm no honest man. You owe for Lemuel's rented mount, sir. I won't move an inch till the debt's honoured. I've a sure head for business, sir, though God gave me a gift for healing mankind. Would the world acknowledged it."

Having once broken Molly's reserve — the need to share fear greater than the fear itself — Clare easily learned from her the whereabouts of the grocer girl. But there a difficulty arose, for the grocer wouldn't let her talk during working hours and afterward spirited her away like a captive once the stall was closed down.

"It's possible," Ned suggested, "he has given the girl out to more than one man and fears someone might procure her away for a house and leave him without a helper or a source of other income. I'll to it."

So Ned went to the stall himself. The grocer's girl was dirty-faced and much too thin for beauty, but her voice rang out like a struck bell: "Fresh green peas, ninepence a peck peas! Gooseberries, green gooseberries, a penny a quart gooseberries!" She piped the produce, while her hunchbacked employer did the selling. "Sparrowgrass," she called prettily. "Buy my sparrowgrass! Fine Kentish cherries, a penny a pound cherries!"

Straightway Ned went up to the grocer and poured five coins into his hand.

"That, sir, buys a goodly deal of asparagus," the hunchback said.

"No asparagus. I'd rather your girl for a while."

Winking, the grocer called her over. "Go with this gentleman," he told her and returned to his work.

"Come along," Ned ordered the thin little songbird, who seemed bewildered when he took her into an ale house. Surely she'd expected to go with him elsewhere: perhaps to the dusty Mall, where, behind some bushes, she could bend over and pleasure him quickly with her skirts hoisted.

Ned ordered tankards and without more palaver demanded to know of her if a grey-faced man had ever taken her to a fine gentleman. When she said nothing, Ned shoved two crowns across the table at her. She merely blinked at them.

"Look, the fine gentleman debauched my sister. I mean to know where he and his servant took her."

"I be sorry, excellence, but I won't say nothing." She stared hard at the coins. "Please you, I'm frighted to death."

"Would you have me angry?"

"No, your excellence! But he'd have my gizzard did I say."

"And so will I, you miserable little bitch, unless you tell me."

The ale came. The girl gulped hers anxiously, then wiped her mouth with the back of a berry-smeared hand. She had soft, lovely, frightened eyes. "I was took out of London," she murmured finally.

"Where?"

"In truth I can't say. I never learned north from south."

Ned believed her. But he persisted until the girl remembered having seen fields from the carriage window and there were others like her, only no one dared speak, because the grey man threatened them not to, and they rode on and on in this fine chariot and in the afternoon they came to the popish cloister and there she and the other girls joined other girls all waiting in a damp cellar where they wore masks and dressed in gowns like infernal papists and then they were taken out of that cellar for song and gaiety somewhere with men in papist garb too and later a fine gentleman had her in a room that he insisted she call a cell and him call a brother.

"I sung for him," she concluded, a catch of fear at the memory. "God save me, I thought he was the devil."

"What made you think so?"

"He and his kind had fancy airs, but they swore oaths so terrible I thought I was in a fiery den of Catholics. God's mercy on me. God's mercy on me too for telling you. I'm frighted to death. Don't hurt me, sir. He said did I tell what I told now I'd not live to see next Christmas is what he said. But you have scared me witless too. God's mercy." Tears glistened in her eyes. She gripped the tankard with both hands.

"Tell me more of the fine gentleman."

"I can't, sir. I can't remember. They had me drink deep. I was fuddled. Leave me be, sir, I beg you." She was sobbing.

If he sat all day plying her with ale, he'd learn no more, Ned realized. The girl was terrified into a stupor. Rising, he touched her shoulder gently. "Here," he said, "you'll not come to harm. I thank you." Pressing two more coins into her hand, he left her in tears with the mug gripped so tightly in her hands that the knuckles showed white.

An hour later Ned had rented a horse and was riding toward the Hertford Road. Had he no other desire than to avenge the grocer girl, Ned Carleton would have horsed up and made for Enfield, as she had suffered in her soul for indignities to her person which only God and Lord Sandwich could know.

That evening a full moon rose high above the Hertford Road along which a tide of horsemen, coaches, wagons, and drovers with herds bound for morning markets was flowing toward city thoroughfares. Ned kept the horse at a rhythmic trot, breathing his last clean air before the fetid smell of street and lane and alley drew round him again the invisible net of London. Not having been ahorseback in months, he rode with zest, his sturdy thighs gripping the sweaty flanks of his mount.

His high spirits were added to by his success at Enfield.

He'd gone first to the house of Susannah Wells and there met the woman herself. That she was dull-witted was immediately apparent. She couldn't even remember Robert Scarrat or the name of the gypsy, but hunkered in front of an unlit fire, sipping a mugful of stale beer. She gave Ned a friendly but quizzical smile each time he asked a question. Perhaps the Canning affair had addled her further. She scratched her head in wonder at the dim memory of the trial: the gowned justices in curled wigs, the strutting counselors, the solemn jurors, the thunderous gallery, all came back to her in simple phrases.

"Odd's life, they was squeezed together in there like a pancake. They made proper speeches. There was bailiffs in gold buttons around." She never mentioned the branding, though when her hand left the beer mug, she exposed a thickly scarred palm. For one moment Ned almost lifted his own gloved hand and exclaimed in acknowledgement of their shared fate: here be one like it; and got as foolishly.

So he learned nothing there. But he fared better at the tavern across the road. The owner of the White Hart and Crown was Ezra Whiffen, who would later testify for the prosecution that the Natus couple had indeed occupied the Wells loft during the month at issue.

Ned didn't even consider a bribe, as Whiffen was eager to talk. He wanted to see justice done. He wanted to see Susannah Wells receive justice, though if she got it she'd not recognize it, for "she be the sorriest woman as ever God made. Her brain couldn't make up the measure of a spoon." He knew Scarrat. He had seen the fellow "as sooty as a chimney sweep" skulking through the village day in and day out, trying to find witnesses in support of Bet Canning. Publican Whiffen grimaced. "I wager he gets the girl off. Those London judges, they all be shitty mackerels. Take bribes like other men take supper."

"Where did Scarrat lodge when he came to the village?"

"At Tabby Howard's. Up the lane near Turkey Street, next corner."

"Scarrat is friends with this Tabby Howard?"

"That old turd Tabby have a friend?" Whiffen guffawed. "More like she'd put a blade in his back. She does some lodging when she can and waters horses and gives a stinking meal to travelers who don't want to spend the price of a good chop here."

"Why would he lodge with such a one? I think he's no skinflint."

"Who knows why any man could look that old sweatbox in the face? She must have been sorry enough sport even when a girl. I never saw a meaner visage in my life. I wonder if they have a scheme together."

"I wonder too," said Ned with a smile.

He found the Tabby Howard house and knocked a long time before the opening door revealed a tall, swarthy old woman who looked strikingly like print shop caricatures of the gypsy. Tabby Howard gruffly asked what he desired. Without replying, Ned shouldered past her into a room smelling pungently of gamy mutton.

"I come from Scarrat," he said.

"I know none by the name." She grabbed up a bottle from the table and held it threateningly. "Get out of here, you fucking sot! I know none by the name."

He could see now the full extent of her drunkenness. Studying the stairway to the second floor, he asked, "Is any up there now?"

"None now and won't be again neither," she grumbled, putting the bottle down as if unsure why she'd ever picked it up. "Grey bastard. Sends a rip here with infernal questions."

"Indeed, woman. Scarrat sent me. He wants to know do you keep an orderly house these days."

"What's it to him what I keep? Has he betrayed me?" That possibility lit up her face for a moment, like a candle in the dark. "Has he done me dirt? Tell him I'm quits with him. I'll deal with him no more. Sends a rip to check on me. Why? To turn me in, do me fucking dirt?" She picked up the bottle again, uncorked it, swallowed, her Adam's apple pumping rapidly in a withered throat.

"Want me to tell Scarrat you won't deal with him more?"

"Tell him! Yes! Tell him!" Tabby leaned against the table. "God's goddamn breath, what the devil can I do more? Which way turn when they everyone be fucking cowards and cheats?" She drank gloomily and retched. "Let him send every constable in the land here and be done with it. Tell him what you will, you cheat, you rip, you lousy asshole of a pimp. I'll none of his baggages here again!" she thundered. "I won't be knocked around more by the ugly rogue. I won't have lodgings for him or his sluts again. Tell him! Yes! Tell him!"

Ned moved toward the door.

At his back he heard her mutter thickly, "Sending rips here to haunt me." He closed the door behind him, hearing the crash of a bottle against it, a scream of drunken fury. Going around to the rear of the house, he found a shed beneath a second-story window. He studied the long drop to the ground. He was standing in the exact place where a frightened girl had stood eight months ago, after tumbling from the shed. This was the place she'd been held.

When he returned home to Holborn, he found a note under the door. From his beloved? Written in a large unsteady scrawl, the message on it urged him to the case next to the Hog's Head in Golden Lane.

There he found the good doctor and Lemuel at a bottle of burgundy, for they drank a finer spirit than gin on the proceeds of spying on Scarrat.

"Tardy!" cried the doctor, lifting his mug. "Tardy, sir! But we know *our* duty. I have uncommon news and you shall hear of it for two guineas, as it be worth every pence."

"You old scoundrel. One, no more. Or I swear to leave this place and you forever."

The doctor munched his lips thoughtfully before muttering, "Be a skinflint then, though it don't suit you, lad, a fine North Country gentleman like you."

Ned put the money on the mattress next to the doctor, who counted each shilling with the intensity of a child learning numbers. Then he gave a long rambling account, sprinkled with praise of his own cunning. Scarrat had done some marvelously strange things today. First, he'd gone to the White Swan near Clare Market, where Jews slaughtered oxen according to their heathenish custom — "a vile place for a Christian of my ilk to get into smelling distance of," he observed loftily, "but in the line of duty I was there."

"The White Swan, you say?" Ned was surprised. The White Swan was a house of call for buggers, where clients pretended to the names of women and dressed themselves in finery at cosmetic tables ladened with pomatums and carmines.

Scarrat went inside for a few minutes, then hailed a coach (we hired one too, noted the doctor, a debt you owe) and had it take him to the West End, where he disembarked at a modish house of accommodation. The house harboured more fine ladies of pleasure than any dwelling from Wapping to Chelsea, according to the doctor, who added, "For one of those fillies a man must give a small fortune, worthy of a prince of the realm, just for one night."

Leaving there soon enough as well, Scarrat flagged a chair (we did too, so another debt you owe) and was carried to the Magpie and Stump in Skinner Street, a boisterous stew where more than one murderous fight had taken place between men claiming the same trollop. Ned had passed it often. In candlelit windows the naked women postured obscenely, beckoning passersby to come in.

Scarrat didn't remain there long either, but continued on to a lodging house in Cheapside. "It wasn't a house of pleasure, mind you, though Lemuel kept an eye on the windows and saw more than one comely piece walk about."

"I did," Lemuel declared proudly.

"What was the place then, if not for bawds?" Ned asked.

"A lodging for decent young women. None of your nightbags there, none of your fire ships with the clap," said the doctor. "I'd have had one of my own daughters lodge there, did I know my daughters. Afterward Scarrat went straight to his taverns. He hadn't had time to sample a bit of goods anywhere all night."

"What do you make of it?"

Doctor Bostock pursed his lips judgementally. "As I am a scholar, I'm bemused by the man. Did I not know better, I'd say he was arranging to supply sweets for an army. What sort of man is it, seeking out so much pleasure without tasting it? Methinks this grey-faced fellow is a rip of exquisite merit. He knows the town stews and the lodgings, where to find corruptible innocence and dens of elegant pleasure and bugger houses and what have you — knows where to get what's needed like he knows the palm of his hand. He has talent enough to provide for an army. Damn, say what you will, the army's the only school for gentlemen. Do you think Marlborough beat the fucking French with Latin and Greek? Damn! A scholar when he comes into good manly company, what is he but an ass?"

"I thought you was a scholar," asked Lemuel with a puzzled frown.

"Only on occasion. At heart a military man." Doctor Bostock drank, belched in deep satisfaction, and regarded Ned with his shrewd, bloodshot eyes. "Isn't it time, lad, you confided in your best of friends?"

"There's nothing I need to confide."

"Ah, you're a prig of the new school. We old ones shared our woes and triumphs. We had jolly times and backed one another."

But Ned was too absorbed in his own thoughts to heed the good doctor. No man was infallible in his thinking, but Ned would have bet his life that Scarrat was collecting a batch of girls, a few of whom were not unlike Bet Canning. And as the grocer girl told it, they'd be taken out of London somewhere and served up to men of substance disguised as monks. Surely one of the girls hired by Scarrat could sing. The man was a procurer of exceeding merit, as the doctor maintained. Within a few days the girls must leave London, and Ned meant to follow where they led.

"What?" Ned turned to the doctor, who had just said something.

"Ah, lad, I'd not wish to have your thoughts. You're damn blown away by them. Methinks they're nothing good for anyone. Yet I'll willingly share them with you. I'll do my duty by you. I'm at your service."

Ned believed him. Smiling at the grizzled old man, Ned reached out and touched his patched elbow. "Thank you, my friend. I won't put you and Lemuel in harm's way more than I've already done. As of now this business is my own."

[35]

ＴODAY THERE WOULD BE an intellectual flurry in the Prussian court of Frederick the Great: the half-blind Leonhard Euler, Swiss mathematician under the emperor's patronage, had just brought forth a monumental study of parameters, another book in a lifetime's accumulation of sixty large quarto volumes. The irascible Voltaire, readying his *Essai sur les moeurs* for the press, had just broken for good with the equally irascible Frederick, and after a few ludicrous days of police detention in Frankfurt had rushed to Colmar in the fifty-ninth year of a wildly hectic life. The Swedish botanist Carl Linnaeus was editing the manuscript of *Species plantarum,* a binomial system of nomenclature that would endure.

Today Ned Carleton would weave one more strand into the thread of his destiny.

At dawn today John Wilkes, landholder settled with seven properties, husband of a rich but pious and aging woman who'd bored him from the moment of exchanging vows, Londoner at heart, snob, fellow of courage who wore a sword for more than decoration, wit, trencherman, successful rake despite his crooked jaw and squint eye, politically ambitious commoner — otherwise known as the Sheriff of Buckinghamshire, and later as the Patriot, the Martyr, the Exile, the Alderman, the Lord Mayor, the Friend of Liberty — arose, dressed, and went about his business long before the other monks of Medmenham had stirred in their cradles on this day of the mass.

Wilkes stole along the silent corridor to the chapel, and opened its door with the only key extant, save one carried by Francis Dashwood as superior of the order. Yesterday he'd wheedled from Dashwood the solemn honour of being the keeper of the chapel, an office giving him sole access to it. Sweet, gullible, cockeyed Francis.

Wilkes had been in a merry and triumphant mood ever since the last meeting of the friars, when that surly earl of Sandwich got what he deserved for trying to joust with his intellectual betters. His lordship's remark about not standing for Parliament, much less sitting there, had been ill considered. Did the fatuous nobleman really believe a merry wit would let him get away with such an insult? Wilkes had written *An Essay on Woman* over a period of weeks prior to the Medmenham meeting. The original first line of his imitation of Pope had been "Awake, my Fanny!" Half the brotherhood would have known it meant Fanny Murray, since half of them had had the pretty *fille de joie,* himself included, so her inclusion in a bawdy poem would be most proper and appreciated. What a frolicsome wanton she was! At present she enjoyed Stanhope's protection — so God help Stanhope. Stanhope was bringing the saucy redhead today, as she had a sacred office to perform in the service. He liked Stanhope, whose chief interest in life was building imitations of ruined castles. Wilkes liked anyone who went against the grain. He liked dash, courage, impertinence. He liked proud men save when they were proud of nothing more than titles. Not that a title was valueless, but without true manly worth it was a burden, as it must be for Sandwich, who could no more climb the rigging than could an ox and proved a swordsman only in the brothel. The poet Charles Churchill had once remarked of him, "The man looks half hanged, cut down by mistake." Typi cal Churchill — no, vintage Churchill. But none had ever brought Sandwich as low as he'd been at the reading of *Essay on Woman:* "Awake, Sandwich!" Since then many of the monks in private had congratulated Wilkes for bringing the shuffling coxcomb down.

Emboldened by the success of his bawdy poem, Wilkes had turned his mind to the working out of a wonderful prank. Making his way through the soft morning light to a wainscot chest in the corner of the abbey's chapel, he unfastened the clasp and emptied the contents: black vestments, missals printed at great cost privately because of their indecent prayers, a cracked chalice, a bell, a censer, a chamber pot. Having piled these ritual utensils on a table, Wilkes slipped out of the chapel and went to the stable yard, where his own coach waited. No one else was yet stirring.

He motioned for his coachman to climb down from the bench. Wilkes asked in a low conspiratorial voice, "Does it sleep?"

"Yes, sir, and will for hours on laudanum."

"Then to business."

Together they hauled a large object wrapped in burlap from the baggage rack and carried it into the abbey. There was a faint metallic sound from a distant passageway — cooks and helpers were busy with breakfast kettles. Wilkes and his coachman panted under the weight of their burden. Once inside the chapel, they removed the burlap and deposited the object inside the wainscot chest. Then the coachman attached one end of a thin wire to the metal clasp, while his master looked on, grinning. He ran the wire under a carpet along the floor and at the first row of pews turned to look quizzically at Wilkes.

"Go on, man," Wilkes told him impatiently. "Ram the wire through the carpet. Will do no harm."

So the coachman worked the wire through the carpet and tied the end of it to a bench leg indicated by his master.

"Sit in the pew," Wilkes told him, "and jerk the wire."

The coachman did. Yanking the wire caused the clasp of the chest to lift.

"Good. Put all in order," Wilkes commanded.

After the clasp was reset and the carpet smoothed, the wire was invisible in the chapel gloom.

"How long is the laudanum good for?" asked Wilkes.

"I wager till after sunset. I've tried it the last three days in such a dosage, and it proved to last about that long."

"Till after sunset," Wilkes mused. "That will do." He winked at the coachman. "Get you gone, saucy fellow. You'll have a faithful account of what transpires."

"I'd be curious of it, sir. Methinks, it's a wondrous prank —"

"Go, go," Wilkes muttered, whisking the coachman out of the chapel. Politics was the meat of life, but merriment was its drink. A month ago the brothers had a poem from him, and tonight they'd have a prank not easily forgotten. Especially not by Francis, poor sweet befuddled Francis. Until a rise into world view was possible, Wilkes reasoned that such little matters of frolic must suffice to satisfy him. He said out loud, "Wilkes, you're damnably clever." Then he tiptoed back to his cell, climbed into his cradle, and waited awhile before rising, so he could rise with the others.

*

By midafternoon (while Dashwood was meditating gloomily in his cell) many of the friars were taking the air in the expansive abbey grounds and garden. Stanhope was there, strolling with the earls of March and Sandwich, his shambling gait matched by that of Sandwich, while March lagged and coughed, suffering, as usual, from a hangover. Stanhope had brought with him Fanny Murphy, but the beautiful redhead was sequestered in an abbey chamber, as a rule forbade the daylight appearance of any woman.

Charles Churchill had arrived last night from London along with the Welsh journalist Robert Lloyd. They made an incongruous pair: Churchill, a great hulking figure; and Lloyd, frail, with tender eyes and a trembling mouth. For a stroll in the garden, however, Churchill sought out Wilkes, having wearied of the effeminate little Welshman.

Reaching the Thames, they contemplated a Venetian gondola brought here at great expense and moored permanently alongside a dock for twilight parties at times other than meetings of the Order of St. Francis. Then, with enthusiasm, the two strollers examined the obscene statuary placed strategically behind clumps of bushes or on secluded hillsides. They stopped to study the Venus bending to pull a thorn from her foot.

Churchill read the Latin on her marble buttocks. "Where the road branches off in two directions. The left branch leads to evil Tartarus." He winked at Wilkes. "I see no evil here. Both roads for me. Does Sandwich supply the nuns as usual?"

"He does. I submit that pimping's his best function in life."

"Well, there's merit in it. Even knaves have their virtues."

In a glory of early autumn light they trudged into the orchard, where under apple trees other monks had assembled in front of a prodigiously endowed marble Priapus. Churchill whistled in mock astonishment at the sight of cowled friars regarding such indecency with chuckles and guffaws, as it and the other sculptures had only recently been installed. "Small wonder Francis used no local labor in mounting these treasures," he said. "Did the common lot know of such wonders, they'd have every parson in England down on us."

"Well, it's best kept a secret," Wilkes observed.

"Best? My God, man, it *must* be kept a secret. Though poaching means nothing to Francis, he's hired gamekeepers. Their job is to keep out the curious."

"He can't hold the world out forever."

"I agree. But then you and I are commoners, not like most of our brothers here who think the world was created for their noble enjoyment."

"The earl of Sandwich."

"For one. I warrant our frolics here will end badly someday."

"But you don't care, Brother Charles."

"Nor do you, Brother John. Nor, I suppose, does Francis, though not because he's a rascal by nature as we are but because his mind's never fully where he is."

"If not where he is, where is it?"

"Wandering around eternity."

Wilkes laughed.

"Indeed," Churchill said. "In spite of his love of drink and trollops."

"And sacrilege."

"In spite of that as well." Churchill sighed. "In truth, if it were known, I wager no parson outdoes our Francis in pursuit of religion. If any among us be marked for heaven, it's our good abbot."

"I should think," Wilkes said, "he's marked for hell with the rest of us." Enigmatically he added, "There may be proof of that before long." Without awaiting a response from Churchill, he walked away, leaving the huge poet in front of the goat god who held in his marble hand a long phallic reed tipped with fire and at whose feet was carved the inscription PENI TENTO NON PENI TENTI — a reminder to the monks that they were not assembled here for penitence.

On horseback Ned followed the swaying chaise. The road west of Kensington had narrowed considerably from a broad avenue allowing three coaches to drive abreast. With clumps of woodland on either side of the dusty path, this was now highwayman country, so he kept a wary eye out for movement in foliage lining the way. He had no fear of losing sight of the rattling vehicle. It carried three girls who had stumbled this morning pale and bleary from the Magpie and Stump. Ned had decided to follow this contingent, although other coaches must be heading out of London, bound for the same place. An altogether different cargo would be leaving the

stylish West End house of accommodation: expensive young cour-
tesans in panniered skirts, no doubt twittering like gaudy birds.
And what of the White Swan? Would it supply an unnatural creature? And perhaps a naïve young woman or two from the decent
lodging house was also on the road, as Elizabeth Canning must
have been last year. Coaches were bound for a popish cloister where
men would have their various appetites served. Among such fellows
was the fourth earl of Sandwich.

Turning northwest, the road came upon broad patches of
meadow. For a moment Ned saw the lazy Thames sparkling in late
sunlight. Then the chaise turned suddenly into a beech-lined lane,
bumped alongside a tall stone fence, and passed through an iron
gate, when a big fellow, armed, opened it. Reining up, Ned had
glimpses of stone buildings in the distance and the coach with its
tartish crew heading toward them. He turned, trotted away, and
found a glen off the road where he could rest awhile, and think what
to do. Mounting again, he went down the road to a farmhouse
where he paid for watering and stabling of his horse. Then he
walked back a few miles to the iron gate, now closed. As he ambled
slowly by, he studied the long curving carriageway that led to a
hillock where buildings were clustered among trees.

The entire property was fenced in by stone, giving it the ominous
look of a prison wall. He suspected there must be gamekeepers
around, looking for poachers or for anyone else who proved curious
about the place.

Cautioned by such a possibility, he walked farther down the road
until coming to a portion of the fence hidden from view by a leafy
horse chestnut. He climbed over, jumped down, and at a crouch
moved through the undergrowth. Until leaving for London, he'd
spent many happy hours in the forests of Nottingham, and to feel
beneath his feet again the yielding earth, made softer by fallen leaves
and moss, was to reenter the world of his youth for a few blessed
moments.

The undergrowth began to thin, so he could see among a stand
of English oaks what was ahead of him. A shape flitted between
trunks — a man, a gamekeeper, with musket slung across his shoulder. That was sufficient for Ned to retrace his steps to a shady copse
of willows, beneath which he snuggled into a bushy recess and
waited for dark.

[36]

IT WAS DUSK. Wilkes and Churchill had been selected by the abbot to assist him in preparing the mass. The three monks entered the chapel carrying bowls of smoldering henbane and rue. Soon the chamber was filled with a thick demonic stench. Servants were not allowed in the chapel, so the trio themselves hung the walls in black drapery.

With grim care Dashwood laid the Ritual Book on a black satin pillow, and Wilkes filled the censer with coals brought from the abbey kitchen. Dashwood stared thoughtfully at the inverted cross hanging above the altar table. He glanced too at the ceiling, painted with obscene caricatures of the twelve apostles. Actually, he'd ordered this parody of the Sistine Chapel to commemorate a strange event. In his youth he had committed in that famous place an outrageous sacrilege. Entering the Vatican on Good Friday disguised as a Catholic penitent, he received the customary scourging whip at the chapel door. When the candles were formally blown out, leaving the room in darkness, the other pentitents disrobed and gently thrashed themselves in a symbolic act of flagellation. Enraged by their timidity and having come there for the express purpose of exercising his own justice, Dashwood pulled a long bull whip from his breeches and savagely laid it on right and left. Believing the Evil One was among them, the worshipers shrieked in terror through the chapel, and in the wild confusion Dashwood had made his escape. Now the ceiling of his own chapel bore witness to what, for him, had been both a reckless adventure and a pious act.

He ordered his two assistants to light the black candles in the black candlesticks. As celebrant of the mass, he put on a brown chasuble embroidered in front with the pine-cone symbols of the god Dionysus and on the back with Satan's inverted cross. It gave him a decided thrill to put on such a garment of spiritual danger.

Then he left the chapel and went down to the abbey cellars, where among casks of wine awaited the nuns brought in from London. Already garbed in black habits, sipping wine or gin, each sister wore a mask. None spoke, for so they had been instructed. One lusty girl straddled a hobby horse, carved with a rooster's head, and with its neck curved round so that the phallus-shaped beak touched her groin each time she rocked. It had been designed by Dashwood's former mistress, Lucy Cooper, whom a wit had once pronounced "lewder than all the whores of King Charles's reign put together."

Rather primly, causing a few girls to titter, the abbot told them that he'd come to instruct them in their duties. First he commanded them to raise their hands and swear upon their immortal souls never to reveal anything that happened this night. Breaking the oath would lead inevitably to "dire consequences beyond imagining." He said it with black conviction. Then his somber mood swung around.

"Visiting sisters, you're under no compulsion to take a vow of chastity while at our abbey."

Girls from the Magpie and Stump guffawed. The others smiled tentatively.

"For that matter, in the wall cabinet over there you'll find love potions to make yourselves piously liquorish."

A girl raised her hand. He went to her and she whispered in his ear, after which Dashwood told the group, "Our brotherhood will contribute to the spiritual enterprise of each nun's choosing on departure." The girl whispered again. Dashwood explained that he meant they'd be recompensed — paid, given their cole — when they left tomorrow.

Another girl raised her hand, and after going to her, Dashwood said, "Once alone in spiritual communion with a brother in his cell, you may remove your mask, but not until then. Now charmers," he said gaily, "be patient awhile. Tonight the cups will dance! Wait till the brothers call. I promise you a wonderful frolic."

Returning to the chapel, he knocked briskly on a side door until two masked women appeared: one in a nun's habit, the other nude.

Without a word the naked girl stretched out on the table, with her feet pointing toward the pews. Dashwood pressed her knees apart in fussy arrangement, slipped a pillow under her flaming red hair, and placed a black candleholder in each of her outstretched hands.

Tonight Fanny Murray would serve as the living altar.

At the chapel door, Celebrant Dashwood drew a sharp nervous breath, then banged the gong to call his brothers to mass, while Churchill and Wilkes stood beside the other sister, who impishly stuck her tongue out at both of them.

The stable area behind the abbey was crowded with horses and coaches. Some of the drivers, along with the stablekeeper, were at cards in the tack room. Thomas, coachman for milord Sandwich, had already made himself comfortable in the haymound, gripping a bottle of Madeira nimmed from the monastery kitchen. He drank alone, as no postilion accompanied the coach on such adventures. Before dawn Scarrat would rouse Thomas in order to hitch the team and whisk their master's girl-for-the-night back to London. His lordship disliked facing a songbird the next morning and always had Thomas and Scarrat return his "sister" separate from the others.

Scarrat didn't join in cards either, but climbed into the coach and curled up for a nap. He had no hope of sleeping soundly, as his master and the others would see to it, with their carousing, that none of the abbey slept well. Even so, Scarrat never begrudged the nobility their frolics. It was what they did. It was the way of the world and of Nature itself. It was like the sun coming up, like the land of England having a monarch. And if a fine gentleman were to stagger into the stable area in pursuit of a giggling toothsome girl — it had happened before — Scarrat would respectfully avert his eyes. Yes, respectfully. What he did and what a gentleman of merit did, though they did it side by side, occurred in different worlds. Let them piss elbow to elbow, the water fell in different places, for they'd never cross swords as old mates might do in jest.

He heard a gong boom through the abbey, calling his master and the other gentlemen to their peculiar games. So be it. He knew what those games were, and at certain times in the past had felt a sudden fright travel up his spine like mice feet. Then the sacrilege taking place nearby had overwhelmed him with visions of goatish devils romping through flames, while every one of the sinners, writhing below, possessed his own sooty face. These visions came from his earliest memories as a child in the St. Giles parish work-house, before he was apprenticed as a sweep. The foundlings slept eight to a bed and wore rags and learned enough reading to piece out prayers and listened dutifully to the ward nurse explain sin and the devil and the plain path to heaven, according to the teachings of John Wesley, who sometimes appeared at the workhouse to speak in thunderous tones of damnation. Wracked by fevers that ran through the ward like wildfire, Scarrat was told he'd brought them on himself by having immoral thoughts. He was whipped, made to stand naked and shivering in a corner, denied food. He remembered the warder's speeches, filled with rancour and disgust. "You should thank God we teach you to read so as you can know the Bible. As to other education, you should not receive it in such a manner as to put you on a level with the children of parents who have the humanity and virtue to preserve them and the industry to support them." He remembered every word, as if each were seared by a red-hot poker into his brain, for he'd heard these same words often, delivered in a high fierce voice of moral rectitude. He remembered the warder's instructional tales about good Christians. There was the merchant in St. Martin's Lane who tied together the legs of his roosters so they couldn't mount hens on the Sabbath. There were many such good people, but none in the workhouse, for everyone here was the devil's disciple, the proof being they were here — so said the ward nurses, the warder, the workshop officers who came gloomily on inspection, shaking their heads, holding scented ker-chiefs to their noses against the stench.

Such memories disturbed Scarrat greatly. In truth they terrified him with a presentiment of hellfire racing through his veins, bones cracking in the heat, eyes popping from their sockets in the flaming regions of everlasting punishment.

For having been so close to the blasphemy taking place in the abbey chapel tonight, he'd pray on his deathbed for God's mercy.

To escape such thoughts he lay back at this twilight hour against the Moroccan leather of the coach and tried to turn his mind around. He reviewed in memory each clock which such infernal work had enabled him to buy. He considered with deep satisfaction how snug he was. He had clocks and a tavern with a garden of his own that he could view on balmy summer nights.

Robert Scarrat would not have been so tranquil had he known

that fifty yards from the stable, beneath the chapel wall of the abbey, crouched the former postilion who had impudently called a peer of England a mere "man," and who, having prowled dumbfounded through the obscene abbey garden, listened to the gong boom out to assemble the monks to their duty.

In single file they ambled down the gloomy hall and entered the chapel, where Celebrant Dashwood and his deacon Churchill awaited next to the altar — beautiful Fanny Murray, her sex displayed — as they shuffled to their seats.

His task of helping to prepare for the mass now completed, Wilkes took his place at the far end of the first row of pews. Thomas Potter, an indifferent musician at best but the only one in the brotherhood, went dutifully to the chapel organ and proceeded to mangle a Kyrie by Byrd. As the wrong notes quavered through the stone chamber, Lord Sandwich audibly groaned. The assistant deacon, Robert Lloyd, took up his own assigned position near the altar. Grinning, he held the censer from which a stinking smoke poured.

Scanning the assembled monks for a brief moment, Celebrant Dashwood turned with a nervous giggle and placed between the altar's spread thighs the cracked chalice. On top of it he put a plate holding a single turnip and in front of it a perforated container for holy water, an aspergill shaped like a phallus.

Lifting his hand, he silenced the awful music. The assistant deacon brought the monks to order by ringing a bell. *Ting ting ting!* Lloyd smiled broadly like a proud new acolyte.

Again lifting his hand to silence the ringing, Dashwood turned and bowed low between the altar's outstretched legs.

"*In nomine Magni Dei Nostri Satanas,*" he intoned, flinging his arms wide. "Before the mighty Prince of Darkness, the dread demons of the pit, and this assembled company, I confess my past errors. Renouncing all other allegiances, I proclaim that His Satanic Majesty" — Dashwood's voice trembled on the name — "does indeed rule the earth! I renew my promise to honour Him in all things. I call upon you, my brothers, to bear witness and do likewise."

Unlike their diligent prior, Churchill and Lloyd had never memorized the text, so for their response they read an invocation in unison from the Ritual Book.

Dashwood lifted the turnip high in offering. "Come, O mighty Lord of Darkness, look favourably on this sacrifice which we have prepared in Thy name." Holding up the chalice next, he repeated the words. During the blessing of the altar and ritual articles, Dashwood became increasingly somber, so engrossed in his self-troubling parody of the observance that he failed to see his brethren exchanging winks at his expense.

Nor did he hear Bubb Dodington whisper to George Selwyn, "Thinking he's a true priest makes half the fun."

It was as if he alone were defying the divine, rejoicing in the fraternity of natural men who believe only in themselves, and re-deeming Eve, the quintessential female, from the inhibiting curse imposed upon her by the Church. He motioned for Lloyd to give him the censer. Incensing the chalice and turnip host with three counterclockwise strokes, he raised the censer three times to Ba-phomet, the inverted cross, and bowed low. Returning the censer to his subdeacon and pointing his palms downward, Dashwood shouted, *"Salve! Salve! Salve!"*

Lloyd struck the gong thrice, ever grinning.

"Dominus Satanas Deus Potentiae," Dashwood recited in a deep resonant voice, *"Pleni sunt terra et inferi gloria. Hosanna in excelsis."*

So did he finish the Sanctus and move into the Canon.

"O Mighty and Terrible Lord of Darkness," called out Dash-wood, the sweat of tension oozing from his brow, "we entreat Thee to accept this sacrifice, which we offer on behalf of the assembled company, upon whom Thou hath set Thy mark. We ask Thine unfailing assistance in our particular need." Dashwood paused and a sudden change came over his funereal face. Chortling, he winked at the brethren in their pews. "Which is that we may fuck the pretty nymphs until our cocks fall off and drink until our guts burst open!"

The monks cheered.

Their frivolity in response to his own had an adverse effect on the celebrant. Instantly sobered, Dashwood raised both hands for si-lence and nodded approvingly at John Wilkes, who, unlike the others, had remained pious in countenance.

"In the unity of unholy fellowship," Dashwood continued, "we praise and honour Thee, Lucifer, the Morning Star. Then Beelzebub, Lord of Regeneration. And Belial, Prince of the Earth and Angel of Destruction. Then Leviathan, Beast of Revelation. Then Abaddon, Angel of the Bottomless Pit. And then Asmodeus, Demon of Lust."

"Amen!" called out the earl of March, who'd drunk all day and was the least likely to satisfy his own lust tonight.

"Enlightened brother," the celebrant said to Churchill, "we ask you to prepare the blessing."

Smirking, the deacon picked up the chamber pot and handed it to the masked nun who stood nearby.

The brethren knew her as well as they did Fanny Murphy. This was Kitty Fischer, a fashionable courtesan notorious throughout England for her escapades. Kitty lifted her gown, revealing nakedness beneath; snickering, she began to urinate into the chamber pot.

Churchill read in sonorous mock solemnity from the Ritual Book:

> She maketh the font resound with the tears of her mortification. The waters of her shame become a shower of blessing in the tabernacle of Satan, for that which hath been withheld pourest forth, and with it, her piety. She is a living fountain of pious water.

Lloyd stepped forward and took the chamber pot from Kitty Fischer and offered it to Churchill, who dipped the phallus-shaped aspergill into the urine, then held it up dripping and pressed it against his own genitals. Turning in the four cardinal directions, Churchill shook the perforated container twice and at each point intoned, "In the name of Satan, we bless you with the rod of life!" He often claimed that this part of the observance was his finest moment on stage.

Dashwood moved to the Consecration.

Lifting the turnip from the plate, he declared, *"Hoc est corpus Jesu Christi,"* after which he placed the turnip host between the lovely breasts of the altar, then touched it to her vagina, causing Fanny Murphy to giggle and a few of the monks to cry out "Huzzah!" Carefully the priest returned the host to the plate. Dashwood felt light-headed, both horrified and delighted by his actions in the dusky chamber stinking of rue and henbane. This was the height of spiritual danger; he felt that he alone understood what was happening: that behind their levity and boyish naughtiness was something real and terrible, the shadow of eternal death. And they were tempting it to come forward, teasing and cajoling it into entering this chapel one day in its hideous actuality, bringing them all trembling to their knees, slaughtering them righteously in the name of Jesus Christ! Sweat poured from his forehead. Holding up the cracked chalice, he recited tremulously, *"Hic est calix voluptatis sanguis."* He waved the bowl of voluptuous liquid three times above his head and then replaced it between the outstretched thighs of the beautiful altar.

Lloyd, smirking, struck the gong.

"O Infernal Lord," the celebrant began, gazing up at the inverted cross, "to us, Thy faithful children who glory in iniquity and trust in Thy boundless power, grant that we may be numbered among Thy chosen."

He paused for the deacons to recite their parts, and when they failed, having forgotten, he frowned angrily.

Churchill nudged Lloyd, who raised the Ritual Book. There was giggling from the pews.

"Shemhamforash!" cried the deacons in unison.

Dashwood's voice rose in fervour. "Our Father who art in Hell, hallowed be Thy name! Thy kingdom come, Thy will be done, on earth as it is in Hell. Lead us into temptation —"

"Amen!" blurted out the earl of March.

Glaring at him, Dashwood continued. "— into temptation and deliver us from false piety, for Thine is the kingdom, the power, and the glory forever!"

Turning, he frowned at the deacons, who read in unison from the Ritual Book, "And let reason rule the earth!"

"Deliver us, O Mighty Satan, from all past error and delusion."

"Shemhamforash!"

To begin the Repudiation, he held up the turnip host and extended it toward the brethren. *"Ecce corpus Jesu Christi, Dominus Humilium et Rex Servorum.* He raised the vegetable toward the inverted cross. "You, Jesus," he said, feeling the heat in his cheeks, "in my capacity of priest I force you to descend into this host, whether you will or no."

He glanced over his shoulder at the brothers, none of whom was chuckling or even grinning. At this moment in the service, Dashwood knew to his satisfaction, even this crew felt the awful danger of their action, as they were now tempting divine retribution of the swiftest and deadliest kind.

"Since the day when you did issue from the complaisant bowels of a false virgin, you have failed in your engagements, belied your promises. Centuries have wept, awaiting you, fugitive god." Dashwood felt his whole body trembling. "You were to redeem Man and you did not. You were to appear in your glory and you slept. Go tell your lies to the wretch who appeals to you and prays and gives offerings. Tell him to be patient and suffer, because finally the angels will succour him. Imposter!" Dashwood screamed with such vehemence that the brothers stared in amazement, though accustomed to his odd behavior during such a celebration.

"Imposter!" he shouted again. "Disgusted by your inertness, the angels have abandoned you! O foulness of Bethlehem, we would have you confess your impudent cheats, your inexplicable crimes! We would drive deeper the nails into your hands, press down the crown of thorns upon your brow, and bring renewed blood gushing from the dry wound in your side!" Dashwood flung his arms wide as if to embrace the inverted cross.

Budd Dodington leaned toward George Selwyn and whispered, "The canting fellow's as wild as a goose today."

"O Infernal Majesty," Dashwood went on, his voice at the edge of hysteria, "condemn this Jesus to the pit, evermore to suffer in perpetual anguish! Call forth Thy legions that they may witness what we do in Thy name. Send the gates of heaven crashing down that the murderers of your children, our ancestors, may be avenged!"

Having bellowed out that last exhortation, Dashwood snatched up the turnip and rammed it deep into the altar, who shrieked in pain and tried to rise. Pushing her roughly down, he withdrew the host and held it up triumphantly.

Bubb muttered, "Either he's silly or the devil's in him. He goes too far. I say, Fanny won't come back after such a handling. Look at Stanhope. He's furious."

Indeed, William Stanhope (her immediate protector) was starting to rise, but Paul Whitehead on one side and Thomas Stapleton on the other restrained and reseated him.

Waving the turnip host over his head, Dashwood cried, "Vanish into nothingness, Jesus Christ, you fool of fools! You vile and abhorred pretender to the Majesty of Satan! Vanish into the void of your empty heaven, for YOU NEVER WAS, NOR EVER SHALL BE!" Throwing the turnip down, he squashed it viciously beneath his foot.

Lloyd struck the gong continuously until the booming sound reverberated against the dank walls.

Repudiation finished, it was now time for Communion. With intensity the celebrant picked up the chalice and faced the beautiful altar.

[37]

ACCEPT THIS BOWL of man's voluptuous liquid in the name of the Infernal God!" He drank, repeated the words of communion, and gave the cup to Deacon Churchill, who drank from it.

There was a muffled commotion from a far corner, but Dashwood was too overwhelmed by the ceremony to notice.

Taking the cup from Churchill, he gave it to Lloyd with the same declaration. There was a muted banging which caused some of the monks to peer through the smoky gloom at the far corner.

The rapturous celebrant was now passing the chalice to each monk in communion. When Selwyn drank, he handed the cup back with a wry smile. "It may be man's voluptuous liquid to you, sir, but to me it's a tolerable brandy."

Dashwood didn't hear. Whipped by ecstasy and terror, having blasphemed with rare courage and even rarer conviction, having joined the celebrants of past centuries who failed to accept the strictures of Christianity and by so doing having perhaps joined them in eternal damnation, Dashwood was buffeted by conflicting emotions as he handed John Wilkes the cup.

A few more monks craned their necks to see what was thumping in the corner, but heedless of all save the ceremony, Dashwood continued to administer the defiant communion. When all had sipped from the chalice, he replaced it between the altar's outstretched legs. Extending both hands, palms downward, he recited the concluding prayer: "O Prince of Darkness, accept my humble service." Bowing before the altar, he turned to the brotherhood and extended his left hand in the sign of the Horn, the Cornu, intoning *"Ego vos benedictio in nomine Magni Dei Nostri Satanas!"*

This was the signal for everyone to rise, which they did, although Friar Wilkes bent down and yanked hard on the wire which protruded from the carpet at his feet. The forceful pull on wire caused the attached clasp to slip off the wainscot chest, from which the thumping noise had been coming.

To end the mass, Celebrant Dashwood was calling out *"Ave, Satanas!"* just as the lid bounced back, as if something inside the chest were trying to lift it, and then heaved fully open. A child-sized figure, dressed in bright crimson with two curved horns jutting from a black shaggy head, scrambled out of the chest. With a few nimble steps, it leapt grunting upon the table, then upon the altar's bare stomach.

Fanny screamed. She kicked, she hollered, she thrashed and nearly fell off, although the creature, once landed and thus agitated, hurtled again through the air to grip the stupefied celebrant around the neck, and they fell in a heap.

There was pandemonium.

Shouting for more light, the monks rushed about, while Dashwood, his face covered with both furry arms of the thing clinging to him, writhed on the floor of the chapel. The naked altar scampered through the side door. Kitty Fischer huddled hysterically against Potter's shoulder. Stanhope, having seen Fanny Murray disappear from the room, fiddled with his robe to locate and draw his sword. The earl of March cowered under a pew. Others rushed toward the chapel door. Holding his ground in the second row of benches, Thomas Stapleton, cousin to Dashwood, peered curiously through the gloom and yelled out, "Why, look, it's a monkey! Great God, look! A monkey!"

Leaning against a wall, John Wilkes was convulsed by laughter.

"Odd's life," grumbled Churchill. "It's no more than a monkey." Then he started to smile.

A new peal of laughter from Wilkes.

In a red suit, wearing a horned helmet tied under its chin, a chimpanzee hunched forward on the table, blandly hooting, scratching its backside.

"Damn but a monkey," Sandwich muttered.

"Who loosed the thing?" Whitehead demanded furiously.

Curled up on the floor, his face covered, Sir Francis Dashwood, celebrant of the solemn black mass, was groaning.

Wilkes, bent over, was chortling.

"There's the rascal!" cried Churchill, smiling.

More laughter from Wilkes.

"A corrupt prank," Sandwich declared. "As might be expected from the source."

"Let's go to better business," Whitehead said bitterly, and in the company of Sandwich strode from the chapel with as much dignity as he could muster after this scene.

Others followed, glancing back in wonder and amusement at the monkey that squatted on the table where minutes ago the lovely altar had lain.

Someone said, "Did you see March? Cowering under the pew? That sight alone was worth the prank!"

Lloyd knelt by Dashwood, whose face was still covered, his legs drawn up fetally.

Wilkes shooed the little Welshman away. "I'll minister to our abbot. Just tell the brothers to save us wenches."

Left alone with the celebrant and the monkey, Wilkes tried to suppress his giggling, then knelt and touched the fallen man's shoulder.

Hearing a choked sob, Wilkes turned to see Kitty Fischer hunched against the wall. "Leave us!" he ordered her sharply.

Staring at him through cupped hands, Kitty said, "What a fright you gave me, John! Bless my soul, you're a bastard."

"Leave us, Kitty."

"Gladly. God in heaven, I think I should reform. I thought for a moment it was the devil." Straightening her wimple and nun's habit, she added with a sigh, "I thought we was all for hell."

"Leave us!"

Shrugging, Kitty trudged from the chapel, picking lint from her robe, bound for the refectory where the men would be.

Wilkes bent close to the fallen priest. "Upon my soul, Francis, I meant no harm. It was a capital jest, I thought, that's all. I thought the brothers would be amused." Wilkes leaned closer. "May I hope your pardon? Had I known you'd be so —" He let the words drift off, as Dashwood uncovered a face set in terror.

Wilkes murmured soothingly, "I bought the beast for you as a gift. And I thought of this naughty way of presenting it, is all." He knew Dashwood's odd predilection for morose brooding on heaven and hell, but had no idea the prank would so horribly unsettle him. "No cheap goods either," continued Wilkes, glancing at the monkey, who was still groggy from its laudanum sleep. "I had it of a ship's captain, Francis. It's a mild beast actually." Wilkes stood up, uncertain what to do. "I'll put it in the stable. Tomorrow my coachman'll bring its cage." He stared uneasily at Dashwood, who still hadn't moved from his foetal position. "Dear friend, am I forgiven?"

"Get away."

"Had I known . . ." Wilkes began lamely.

"Get away."

Shrugging, Wilkes went after the monkey, taking from under his vestment a long chain so as to snap its hook on the beast's collar. The horned helmet was now askew, the long teeth showing in a drugged grin, but when Wilkes approached, the creature danced away, avoided the man's grasp, and sculling forward rapidly on all fours rushed to the chapel door and leapt into the outside darkness, with Wilkes following in vain and cursing.

After a few minutes, Dashwood sat up, the satanic chasuble sagging around his thick body. Never in his life had he been so terrified. That inky face looming through the brimstone air had belonged to a devil incarnate. In those terrible moments when the creature clung to him, questions had flashed through Dashwood's mind. Who had sent this scourge? Not Satan to whom he'd dedicated the service and in whose name he'd blasphemed. Had the Christ sent a demon to pull him down to hell? Entangled in the thick fur, smelling the hot animal musk, he'd waited in those horrible moments for the rending blow of death.

Unsteadily, he got to his feet. He couldn't continue with this evening, as fear had quite unmanned him. He'd retire to his cell and read *A Practical Treatise upon Christian Perfection.* He'd send word that a sudden attack of gout had indisposed him, let them think what they would. None could imagine the depths of his emotions, so let the fools laugh. He alone realized that both the mass and the prank, be they ever so comical, were tests of his soul.

Let that impudent Wilkes enjoy his brutish sense of humour. Shame on John Wilkes for a nasty child.

A pulse beat wildly in his temple as Francis Dashwood shuffled out of the chapel. The day would come, if not tomorrow or next month or next year, when he'd repay John Wilkes for this unbearable insult.

Beneath the moody orange light of candelabra, the frolic was under way. Monkish hands groped under the habits of rouged and masked and already drunken nuns. Expressionless servants trolled to and fro with sweetmeat trays. Country fiddlers brought from afar and handsomely paid for music and future silence played hearty jigs to which two girls from the Magpie and Stump danced naked.

Thomas Potter, still excited by the mass, went around shouting, "I'll drink blood! I'm of fire and brimstone! We should have toads to bite and mangle as they did in France centuries ago! Bring me a pretty demon! I'd like her better than a human wench tonight. You, are you demon or human?" he asked a quiet girl seated stiffly on a chair.

Stunned by drink, she seemed confused by these goings-on and somewhat shy. "Human, sir."

"So who's your monkish friend for the night?"

"I have none yet."

"Then you'll be mine. We'll see in truth just how human you are."

"What have we here?" cried Dodington suddenly. He'd thrust his hand under a slim nun's robe as they sat on a couch. "My God, this sister has a cock on her as thick as my wrist!"

The rouged and pretty boy from the White Swan stuck out his tongue lasciviously and rolled it around, wetting his lips. Dodington rose and huffed angrily away. Robert Lloyd came across the room to hand the lad a glass of wine. The boy fluttered his eyes.

"Look at that," Stapleton said to Selwyn as they sat with two girls in their laps. "My cousin Francis insisted an unnatural creature be brought for Lloyd. I call that villainy."

"No villainy," Selwyn replied. "Your cousin's the generous host, is all. Look how merry the boy has made our Welsh poet. I call that no villainy at all."

Across the room a girl had slipped her arm around the beefy shoulder of Lord Sandwich, but he pushed her away. He was staring at a stringy lass sitting half hidden near the wall. That was the songbird Scarrat had brought for him this time.

John Wilkes entered the room to shouts of gaiety. "The devil got away!" he shouted, his crooked jaw set in a grin. "We'll capture him tomorrow, but tonight he's roaming the grounds out there." Spying a girl from the house of accommodation, a tall cool brunette with full lips beneath the mask, he sat down and patted his knee. "Come here, lass."

She did. "None of your coquettish airs with me!" He pulled her down and kissed her resoundingly. She pushed him away, but he clipped her again. "Charmer," he cooed, nuzzling her throat till she laughed and tossed her black hair.

Freed by enough wine to make a bold advance, Robert Lloyd kissed the boy from the White Swan on the mouth. Avid response. They were the first couple to leave the refectory.

In the company of William Stanhope, her protector, Fanny Murray appeared to general applause. She wore a virginal white gown. Wagging her finger at Wilkes, she cried, "La, sir, you're as mischievous as a monkey yourself. You and your creature and Francis and his turnip have given me a fright and a pain this day. Shame on you both!" she said with a laugh.

A servant arrived with news of the abbot's sudden attack of gout. There was snickering.

The earl of March sulked drunkenly in a corner. The brothers had seen him scoot under the pew like an abject coward, his fat arse in the cassock like a bundle of coal stuffed under the bench. Since leaving the chapel, no one had shown him good cheer. Indeed, they turned contemptuous glances his way. Wilkes had been the agent of his misfortune. He too had a score to settle with the impudent fellow. As a brother friar, John Wilkes had managed to alienate Sandwich, March, and Dashwood, something of an achievement for a mere sheriff and commoner.

The carousing continued into the night, until two by two the monks and their visiting sisters left the refectory, leaving it empty.

Was it possible? From the high window directly above Ned had come sounds incomprehensible and mysterious, a foreign tongue, bells ringing, bursts of laughter, the names of Satan and Jesus Christ invoked continually. He crouched in stupefied attention, trying in vain to imagine the ceremony taking place but a stone wall's breadth away.

In his youth he'd heard stories of horned demons and blood rites in dark glens, of men gone mad from consuming gouts of sacrificial flesh, of women so unleashed from human decency that his mother had ordered him to stop up his ears against such horror. And now here, from overhead, came the sound of hell and the smell of it too, for the pungent smoke drifting into the darkness made his nostrils tingle, his eyes smart. Could it be true that Englishmen of quality and fortune, no more than a stone wall's breadth away, were denying the Lord Saviour in the name of the devil? Could anything be more damning to the soul of man? It made the prigs and whores of London seem like innocent children. And then a terrible thing must have happened in there, a wild commotion and cries of terror — and of laughter — and something scooting right past him in the dark, hunched, furious, a hooting sound in its wake like that of a demon from hell.

His own childhood fears rushed back, as he sat under a window from which brimstone and profanation had poured as if from the hot mouth of Satan. His mother had been an enthusiast, a follower of John Wesley. He recalled the church bells tolling, his mother kneeling in prayer among the assembled, while the tall bony figure of John Wesley stood in the open field like a rock within fire, his voice bellowing above the heads of a thousand listeners, "My work is to free you from the clutches of the devil!" and all shouting "Amen!" in reply and Ned's mother dropping to her elbows and screaming "Cry ha! ha! amid the trumpets!" and people thrashing on the ground, their eyes rolling up like the dead, and the whole meadow quaking from the tumult as if Judgement Day had come.

And then from the abbey window there had been a fading away of footsteps. From another part of the cloister he soon heard the sounds of carousing. It was what he heard in the stews of Smithfield: glass clinking, fiddling, feet stomping, laughter. There was no difference between quality and the common lot when it came to carousing, he thought. But never had he heard a cutthroat revile the good Lord as these fine gentlemen had lately done.

Crouching beneath a window, he listened to sounds of debauchery until they subsided, and the abbey lay wrapped in silence as it must have done long ago when papist monks lived within its walls. Then, incredibly, in the chill of night he heard a girl's sweet voice raised in song. Following the sound, he scrambled under another window and heard her sing a ballad familiar from his childhood. The singing was abruptly overlaid with the spoken command of his former master — no mistaking the cold ring of that voice — hoarsely ordering the girl to sing! sing! sing! and then, after a time, he heard the stifled but unmistakable cry of sensual relief. And then silence for a while. And then the harsh command for more song, and her voice rising, cut off suddenly, followed by a grappling muffled sound, the mutual sounds of groaning at love, the catch of breath, his outcry once more, but not hers.

Ned gripped his pistol, struggling with the notion of rushing in there, as the thought of Lord Sandwich in such passion infuriated him. But the moment passed. Knees to chin, he sat against the stone wall, letting his fury ease into the darkness.

As the night moved toward morning, he was filled by a grim yet wonderful truth: knowledge, not the word of God or his own desire for revenge, would change his life. He knew what others did not, and in this truth was power.

While the abbey slept, Ned Carleton drifted a few moments into a dream of his choosing. He stood on the threshold of his own wayside inn at the edge of a forest in Nottinghamshire. Clare was fluffing the pillows in an upstairs chamber. The black boy peeled onions for their supper in the kitchen. And Sandy slept on crossed paws in the glow of a winter hearth.

Part Seven

———————————•———————————

BETRAYALS

[38]

HE SIGHTED THE COACH through a morning fog that slithered across the road out of wooded hollows. Seated in the rich interior were Scarrat and a grimly pallid girl who looked strikingly similar to how Elizabeth Canning must have appeared a year ago, when she too emerged from the popish cloister and rode with Scarrat down this same road.

Was Scarrat taking this lass to Enfield and the tender care of the murderous old bitch Tabby Howard?

Ned rode perhaps a furlong behind the coach, having glimpses of the broad gilt rear through swirling fog. The sun would appear soon through the vapour, turning the chill grey into a warm and sunny autumn morning. And indeed, within a half hour the ground fog burned off in sunlight, making him visible from the coach, so he rode far behind it.

To his surprise and relief the coach didn't turn toward Enfield but continued into London. So she wasn't being taken to Tabby Howard. So he wouldn't have to draw on Scarrat if the coach reined up for another incarceration of an innocent girl. Traffic began to clog the road, rendering Ned less conspicuous and enabling him to ride closer to the gilt coach, whose driver hunched forward, intent on maneuvering.

As they entered London, Ned thought with grim pleasure of Scarrat sitting back against the costly leather without the least suspicion of being followed, as naive as a country merchant strolling through St. Giles. Finally the coach halted in front of a Cheapside lodging house, and the pale girl stepped demurely out. No sooner had her feet touched ground than coachman Thomas whipped up the snorting horses and drew away.

From his vantage point ahorseback, Ned watched the girl stand there and wait until the carriage swayed around a corner. She seemed to be lost in thought or maybe grief or sorrow. Her shoulders sagged like those of an old woman, her averted eyes traced her steps into the lodging house where she'd go among girls her age, having learned more about taint in the human soul in a single night than many of them would discover in a lifetime. Was gold worth it? Gold was worth everything to someone who had little or none. Look what he — and Clare — did for gold.

Having had little rest in the last two days, Ned went home and fell asleep instantly, still booted and spurred. Abruptly he awakened in late afternoon, thinking of Clare. Would she still agree to their plan did she know that a group of noblemen blasphemed in the name of Satan and that one of these blasphemers was to supply the gold for their new life together? Though a whore in the world's eyes, she was a God-fearing woman who believed in divine power and grace. Would she accept gold from a follower of Satan?

As for himself, he felt it was the king's business when men of consequence renounced God. He knew little of religion, less of government, but for centuries men of his family had fought and died for England. He was first, last, and always a yeoman from Nottinghamshire. It was nothing he must consider. It was like the Thames flowing, the sun rising. Perhaps he should go to a magistrate with charges against the blasphemers and ruin them in the name of God and country. But there'd be no money from it for him and Clare. He wasn't sure what to do.

Rising, he washed and hurried to the milliner's shop, waiting in shadows while bleary rag-pickers shuffled home from work. When Clare emerged from the shop, his spirits lifted. Ned could tell that seeing him had a like effect on her, though he'd broken the rule about coming here. She came forward boldly, and that surprised him, especially because the milliner stood in the doorway.

She took Ned's ruined hand in hers, while he glanced past her at the little old man squinting quizzically at them. Clare tossed her head as if to say, I don't mind what he thinks.

With Ned's hand in hers, she led him to a nearby square. Carriage wheels thudded on cobblestone. Over the rooftops the last light was settling liquidly, like a pool of shallow water. Holding his hand, Clare studied his face gravely, while people eddied around them, homeward bound, leaving them like two stones in a brook.

"I've news you may not like," she began. "But it's my own doing. It was in my heart to bring this about. And so it's come about." Letting go of his hand, Clare said, "I'm with child." She added quickly, "It's yours. Believe me. I know what I've done."

A child? Through his mind flashed an image of the little milliner swinging a cane and climbing into a coach with her. Other faceless men huffed over her in bed in the brushmaking shop, second floor. Whose child?

She answered the unvoiced question. "Yours, lad. Yours. I was always careful. I know." There was an iron railing nearby, and she leaned against it, her twilit face severe, determined, without guile. For a moment she reminded Ned of the black boy refusing to let anyone touch Sandy. "Mine is the blame," she said, "but the child's yours."

"I believe it." He must never question it again. Nothing mattered but Clare's belief and his sharing of it. The child was their child. He felt a sudden elation: their child.

"Ah, it's a fine thing," he exclaimed without thinking.

"Be honest, lad."

But he was. That night when she'd stopped him from using armour, perhaps without knowing it they'd both wanted a child. Yes, a child. His parents had had seven, two of whom lived. His mother used to say, "A child gladdens the heart." A child? None better under heaven than Clare to give him a child. "It's a wonderful thing," he said with feeling.

"You mean that?"

"I never said truer." This time he took her hand — in his good one — and led her through the dusky square, unable to say more. Yes, a child. He and Clare had come to lambing time.

They walked about a mile before Clare halted and shyly announced that hereafter she'd deny her person to all but him.

"Leave the milliner."

"I will."

"And stay no more in the brushmaking shop. And come to me."

"I will, do you want me."

"With all my heart. Come tonight. Now."

"I will."

"And we'll post banns."

"I'd not ask such a thing of you."

"We'll post banns and marry. So it will be."

"Then, so be it."

"Dear girl, I'm glad of the child."

"I ask nothing. I swear it."

"I'm heartily glad. You'll mark it in me in time to come."

But as they walked, Ned turned cold in his mind. He knew he mustn't dream of their life together or he might dream it away, because in London he'd learned a bitter lesson: without a clear, steady mind you were fair game to misfortune. The Dog Cull in Ned Carleton knew this. He couldn't go soft or let his mind turn vague and therefore untrustworthy. Withdrawing his hand from her, Ned vowed to tell her nothing and involve her no further in his scheme. The notion of a child separated them now in the sense that he could risk, but she must not.

"I'm going now, lass," he said. "I've business."

Clare narrowed her eyes and regarded him. "Dear God, not with the man who sees Molly! Not with the one who scares her."

"Pack and come to me tonight."

"Lad, please, no business with him."

"Pack, hire a chaise for your goods, come tonight."

"Let it be."

"I won't. I can't."

"Don't fright me with this," she pleased. "I fear him, I've seen the look in Molly's eyes."

Kissing her cheek, Ned was gone in rapid strides. Her voice rose behind him in such alarm that people turned to stare. "Let it be, lad! *Let it be!*" He didn't look back, but kept going, bound for the Sign of the Frigate. His mind was clear, steady, cold.

The long dusty coach ride into London with a sniveling wench had left Scarrat tired and listless. If she didn't want to put up with a nobleman in bed, then why go at all to Medmenham? These girls without a penny, who'd lost their maidenhead but a few times or a dozen and thought the thing still worth value, why, they whim-

pered and cried when a nobleman fucked them or did whatever else
that he paid for and gave him pleasure in the privacy of a silly room
called a popish cell. The nobleman was a child, the girl a needful
toy for that child, and this was in faith the truth of it. What Scarrat
hated was the pious aftermath of the "innocent" nuns. That scrawny
songbird, for example, had known full well what was expected of
her when she left the Cheapside lodging house. She was to spread
her legs or however a man wished to be gratified, and there would
be payment for her service. That was all. She knew. She knew as
surely as the trollops from the Magpie and Stump knew. Yet this
one, like the Canning girl and others like them, had to sniffle and
sob and declare she hadn't really known, expected, considered,
imagined, or whatnot that such demands would be made on her,
especially by a fine gentleman, on an innocent excursion out of
London. In truth such paltry creatures knew a man's desires. Perhaps it even excited them that these desires came from men of
consequence. And there was always greed, ever and always greed,
for who escaped it? Say what you will, Scarrat often declared to
customers in the Frigate, we're everyone alike — tall, short, fat,
slim, we quake in the nighttime and regret our lives in the wakeful
silence of it.

Bemused by his thoughts over a dish of tea, he looked up from
the table and saw in the tavern's doorway a tall, husky fellow. Fixing
his gaze on the misshapen glove, Scarrat grinned in anticipation of
having more to do with this country blockhead. He'd have another
chance to give the fellow a glimpse of pure trouble. As the former
postilion approached, Scarrat's grin became a broad welcoming
smile.

Turning, he ordered Giles to fetch a tankard for "the young
gentleman."

"So here you be again!" Scarrat called to Ned and motioned him
to sit down.

Ned did, placing his hands on the table — one gloved hand
looking as though it contained lumps of coal instead of bones.

Starting out as if in midconversation, Ned leaned forward and
said rapidly, "You was bowled over when you learned she got loose
of Tabby Howard and went home."

Thunderstruck, Scarrat managed to keep smiling. "Who was
loose of what? Speak plain, boy."

"Betty loose of Tabby Howard. Then you frighted the girl witless, so when you named the Wells house as her prison, she took it up like a fish takes bait. You can't deny it."

"In faith, man, deny what?" Scarrat made his mouth sneer, but his cheeks were burning. "I grasp none of this."

"Betty Canning and his lordship."

Glancing around to see if watermen close by had overheard, Scarrat muttered tensely, "Cock sparrow, I won't have his name spoken here. Say your business and get out."

"I was at the popish cloister between Henley and Marlow."

Scarrat smiled, wondering if his cheeks looked hot.

"I was under the window. I heard his lordship debauching a girl. I watched you bring her back to lodgings in Cheapside."

"Keep your fucking voice low. So what's your pleasure?"

"Gold."

"True of every beggar."

"Gold for silence. Otherwise the tale goes to Grub Street and the gazettes and thence to a magistrate."

Scarrat guffawed. "Upon my salvation, you've a vivid fancy! And what would you desire of a magistrate?"

"Punishment of blasphemers."

"Keep your voice low."

"And to find his lordship guilty of kidnapping Bet — "

"That's sufficient! I get your meaning, man." And he did. He'd as lief go a bout at single stick with a brawny waterman as attempt to wheedle good humour, let alone reason, from this fierce lunatic. "I see you're a religious sort, worried for God's name. Until gold's in view. Is that it?"

"Think what you will."

"When do you desire this black tribute, young gentleman?"

"You think it a jest? Try me."

"Oh, I believe you mean your demands."

"I want it on the morrow."

"Heyday! That soon?"

"On the morrow."

"And how much is the young gentleman's pleasure?"

"Two hundred guineas. Not a farthing less."

Scarrat put on a resigned countenance. This was no time to rouse the lad, whose eyes fixed the air with the intensity of someone plainly addled. "To be sure, I won't counter a firm fellow like yourself. You say two hundred, it will be two hundred, and not a farthing less. Go your way. Return at leisure."

"On the morrow?"

"As you please. Noon or thereabouts, tomorrow."

"You'll have it then?"

"We've settled on it," Scarrat said with feigned compliance, though he had no idea what might happen. Addled, he thought, watching the strange lad rise and shuffle from the Frigate like a sleepwalker. Young bloods thought they could lollop at their ease and keep good fellows at hard duty. Well, this one would pay handsomely for the privilege. He had picked the wrong man to blackmail, and by that Scarrat meant himself, having forgotten Lord Sandwich in the outrage done to his own honour.

He went into his back room and listened to his clocks tick out their pure certainty. The autumn loveliness of his garden was now shrouded in evening darkness. Even so, he stood at the window and stared through it, trying to recover from the shock of this development. He used to feel similar after the sweepmaster had boxed his ears: benumbed, contemplative, almost sleepy. How could he explain to his lordship, much less to himself, that a country bumpkin had sniffed out the Canning affair, discovered Medmenham, and coolly listened to the strivings of a peer of England at pleasure? This North Country gull, this bubble, this comical dungcart, this infuriating puppy, this ignorant stinkpot and impertinent asshole, this sapless fucking twig had connected his lordship to the Canning affair as none other had. The boy's country pride had been pricked, and that pride had led him to hatred of milord Sandwich. And nothing but hatred had pushed the lad into a bit of cunning. Hatred was a close ally of cunning, Scarrat knew only too well.

Sitting on his bed, he stared gloomily at the row of ticking clocks. What the country lad had done was a sin against Order: God, king, peer, and commoner all had their places in the world, as did every living creature, right down to the lice crawling in the collars of watermen. Yet this feebleminded nit had offended against Nature and with impunity. It was a considerable thing to think on. It was enough to make a reasonable man wonder if the devil had indeed been conjured at Medmenham and was in fact abroad now, doing mischief in the guise of a country fool with but one good hand.

Scarrat got up and threw on his coat. His was a grim task now. He must explain to his master something that properly belonged in one of the romances read by Widow Canning.

[39]

ROBERT CLIVE had just come home to England for a well-earned rest before returning to his post in India, where Europeans and nawabs contested hotly for control of the subcontinent. Not yet thirty years old, Clive had already distinguished himself by outlasting a fifty-day siege against his dilapidated little fort at Arcot. Though initially no more than a bookkeeper, Clive had behaved like a brave and experienced general, taunting the attackers by boasting that their rabble forces, though far outnumbering his own troops, were nothing compared to Englishmen in arms. One day he'd give his country an empire and live to see gratitude tempered by the envy of lesser men, but at present he was lionized as a fine young soldier in the better clubs of London, just as in India the natives called him Sabut Jung, "the Daring in War."

Tonight he'd not be at the cocking house in Birdcage Walk near Dartmouth Street by Queen Anne's Gate. Nearby, the visiting Swedish philosopher and scientist Emanuel Swedenborg was writing his *Arcana coelestia,* an eight-volume explanation of Genesis and Exodus according to his principle of correspondence, which is that all created things are aspects of divine love and therefore correspond on the material plane to spiritual realities.

Inside the towerlike building a crowd of gamblers were betting on a Welsh Main: thirty-two gamecocks paired off in match play until but one survived. In the candlelit amphitheatre of the cocking house there was a raised stage with a mat floor and a circular railing on which spectators were leaning. Beyond them were tiered benches where men of fashion rubbed elbows with cutpurses, all having one aim in view: to make a blind bet successfully on one of two cocks hidden in sacks lying on the pit floor. Cries of "Done!"

filled the smoky air as wagers were pledged. The truly blind Lord Bertie Albemarle held up a fistful of guineas. A merchant sneezed above his snuffbox. A deaf gentleman raised an ear trumpet to hear the bet offered by his companion.

In the second tier, along with two friends, sat Lord Sandwich, who was yelling at a gentleman seated across the pit, "Cock to the north! Twenty guineas! You! In the spectacles! Cock to the north! Twenty! Done? Done!" Looking around to close a last lay before the cocks were set, he noticed his man Scarrat coming through the crowd. He motioned for Scarrat to wait at the pit barrier until the match in progress was finished.

Cockwalkers had removed the black sacks and were fitting the birds with long silver spurs. The gamecocks had already been matched by weight, their beaks filed, their wings clipped, their hackles cropped. They were both Cheshire Piles, a breed much fancied by his lordship, who'd bet on the cock lying to the north, a handsome fellow whose weapons were murderous two-inch spurs, curved like surgeon needles.

The handlers held the cocks beak to beak, rousing their fierce spirits. When the birds struggled wildly to get at each other, the handlers loosed them to buckle to.

For a few moments they stalked to and fro, while the spectators shouted, "Engage! Engage!"

Wings flared, the Cheshire Piles circled warily, until in a swift paroxysm of fury one leapt forward, bringing its spurs down in a flashing arc that left the other bird ripped through the crop. There was another flurry, a windmill motion of feathers, and then another buckle to, a few more moments of circling, and yet another furious headlong crash. Abdomens gaped open, blood poured from combs, and finally one of the combatants collapsed, its legs beneath its body as if nesting, its wings spread limply, its beak touching the mat.

The room filled with groans of dismay and shouts of victory.

The winning cock leapt high into the air and thudded down again and again, scoring ribbons of blood through the yellow feathers of its fallen adversary. Then it crowed triumphantly, and the bettors rose from their benches to settle wagers.

Sandwich signaled his man and came down to meet Scarrat at the barrier. There was a hangdog look about the man that Sandwich didn't like. Amid so much noise in the cocking house, his lordship could speak out boldly. Straightway he said, "Don't tell me the last one's proved greedy too!"

"Milord?"

"She had no spirit. You didn't do well by me. And her voice was no more than middling. Is your mind elsewhere when you hear them sing? I should send you to music lessons."

"It's not her, milord. I come to speak of other bloody business."

In the thundering room Lord Sandwich listened to something that put him far out of countenance.

Finished with his tale of a former postilion, Scarrat looked down humbly at passing shoes.

"Well, go on," Sandwich said impatiently. "From the look of you, there's more."

"Yes, milord."

"Speak up, man!"

"He wants gold to hold his tongue."

"Naturally such a villain wants gold. But dare he go public about the affairs of a peer of England?"

"Yes, milord. He claims he'll go to Grub Street and magistrates."

Lord Sandwich guffawed disdainfully. "I can well imagine what an English judge would say of such charges from such a creature."

At this moment a bespectacled man approached to pay the wager he'd lost to Lord Sandwich. A score of guineas changed hands, and the nobleman bowed slightly. Fate had been kind to him all day. It was rumoured that the duke of Newcastle might fall because of heightened tension with France. And if the duke fell, the Admiralty was again within grasp. Full honours on tall ships. Cabin lunches with seadogs who reminisced about great battles.

And last night he'd won three hundred at faro and just now twenty in the cocking house.

In the face of such good fortune this Scarrat had thus appeared like a messenger straight from hell, with outrageous news of a former postilion who threatened to pull him down and put the Admiralty and other preferments out of reach forever. It was as if destiny had whipped around like a snake and struck at him.

"How much gold does he want?"

"Two hundred guineas." Scarrat hesitated, as if ashamed of revealing the full impudence of the demand. "Not a farthing less."

Clearing his throat, Lord Sandwich struggled to control his fury and frustration. "Very well, then. Thomas will bring the gold. When is it due?"

"On the morrow."

"Indeed. Then, tomorrow." He cleared his throat again.

"And it please your lordship —"

"Well, say it." A gamecock crowed from a black sack slung over the shoulder of a cockwalker, who was shoving through the throng toward the pit, where another bout of the Main would soon begin. Looking at the pit, then at Scarrat, Lord Sandwich said angrily, "I tell you, get it out, man! Say what you must say!"

"Give the rogue gold, he'll come back for more. If I know his sort, he'll plague us. I think, milord —" His voice trailed off into hesitancy.

"Damn you, speak up!"

Scarrat winced as if words from the nobleman were blows. Then he had a brief fit of coughing, which made his cadaverous face even more offensive to his lordship. "I think," Scarrat finally said, "we must do for him."

"How dare you say such a thing to me!" Sandwich could have struck the fellow. It was insufferable to have a common servant regale him with low intrigues. "Do what you must, but say not *we*. It's *you!* You brought yourself this trouble. Tell me no more about it."

"I'll have him took off, so your lordship can be free of it for good."

"I said, say no more! I'm free of it this moment! And don't cough in my face, damn you." Furious at himself for losing control, even in a cocking house where tumult reigned, he added in a calmer voice, "There's the other affair too, or have you forgotten there's to be a trial?"

"No, milord."

"Handle both affairs or you'll be quits with me. But say no more, not a word." Behind him there was a commotion in the crowded smoke-filled room. Drawing out a scented kerchief, he dabbed his sweaty brow with it. "Mark me, I said quits. Thomas will bring the money." Damn the postilion, damn the Canning bitch, damn the duke, and damn Scarrat too. "I wash my hands of it!" His lordship swung away, having a final glimpse of Scarrat bobbing his sooty head like a bird drinking.

Pushing through the crowd, Lord Sandwich reached his friends in the second tier. One was saying lazily, "I think of the court as nothing more than a cheap diversion. It costs nothing to attend a levee and you see much of the best company there. It's the most gossipy coffee house in town. John, you've won again," he said to Lord Sandwich with a smile. "This is your lucky day."

Having failed to make good on a wager, a tradesman was being hoisted into a basket by two husky workmen, thence to be raised by rope and pulley to the roof, and for failing to pay his debt in good and current money, thence to be pelted by spectators at their pleasure, with anything at hand. Except it was below his station to do so, Lord Sandwich would have joined in the punishment to rid himself of this grim feeling that fate had played on him today a most nasty trick. God help that man Scarrat.

A knock on the door brought Ned to his feet, the pistol under his pillow to his hand.

When he opened it, Bostock and Lemuel were standing there. Brushing past Ned, the good doctor exclaimed, "What a chum! We come to pay respects and you draw a weapon on us. The devil."

Once inside, Bostock threw down his battered tricorn and sat in a chair, blowing his breath out, sticking one thumb under the worn belt over which his belly protruded like a tight little melon. "I say, do you have some diddle here? Even a bit of small beer?"

Ned took a bottle of gin from a cabinet and handed it to the doctor, who removed the cork and took a good pull. "Ah, it's a lovely place you have. In ours there's a noisome smell of onions." He waved the bottle at Lemuel, who sat gingerly on the edge of the bed. "The ninny's doing. He dotes on onions."

"I do," Lemuel declared proudly.

Bostock sighed deeply. "I wonder sometimes what my chief disorder be. Stuffing of the lungs, obstruction of the viscera, dropsy, jaundice, scurvy?"

"You've come for something," Ned said bluntly but with a smile.

The doctor frowned in response. "Don't be proud and choleric, lad. Don't be peery. Aren't we chums?"

"I think we are."

"Think? Know! Haven't we done our duty to you?"

"You have. And I've acknowledged it."

"Pshaw. You mean by the shitty pittance you gave us?"

"Pittance?"

Bostock stroked his grizzled chin thoughtfully. "I'll be frank, my boy. I was strangely puzzled for a while, but now I've sorted it out. I had Lemuel here stay close in recent days and he saw you follow a covy of tarts in their rattler out of town. And you seem cheek by jowl with the grey-faced man too. You're on to something. Put on your considering cap, Ned, and ask yourself would I be such a fool as to not wonder what you was up to?"

"So you've been spying on both me and Scarrat."

The doctor shrugged and took another pull. "Each must do his duty to his own body and soul. The sum of what I came to say is this: Be a good chum and let us make one with you."

"One with me in what?"

"You've become a proper twang. Indeed, you must be supplying tarts for half of London, you and Mister Scarrat."

Ned laughed.

"I tell you I've sorted it out. You have a brave plan. Of that I'm certain. The boy and I simply want in with our old chum we've been loyal to —"

"Loyal?" Again Ned laughed. "When?"

"Lately, lately," Bostock said with impatience. "I swear it. Well? Can we say done? Shall we seal it by being merry now? Shall we find your miss and have her celebrate along with us?"

Ned, who had been leaning in a relaxed way against the wall, stood ramrod straight when Bostock revealed a knowledge of Clare.

"Don't, don't, lad," exclaimed the doctor, throwing his hands up. "Don't be fiery! Yes, I do know you have a fine fresh lass. No low brimstone, no impudent strumpet, no adulteress or wanton. I wish you happiness of her. I've seen harlotry enough and don't like it. I hate drabs and their ways. Love and a bottle have always been my taste. I am, however, the most honourable of men in my amours. I never abandon a woman to distress, as too many men of fortune do when they've gratified their desires. I warrant you're supplying maidens and strumpets and all sorts to such men of consequence, Ned, and —" The doctor leaned forward, his massive florid face abruptly fierce, intent, without a touch of silliness. "I urge you strongly to bring us in. Scout the idea of partners, Ned boy. Don't make a clumsy hand of it."

"How might I do that?" Ned asked quietly, looking from the purposeful doctor to the confused boy.

"By denying us. Look. We need some crop, we're out, we're empty, yet you must be riding high. It's not fair when we've been chums so long."

"You ran out on me. I've never trusted you since, though in truth I like you and Lemuel."

Bostock clapped his hands. "Good! If you find a failing in me, let me study to correct it. None bewitch me, lad. I'm my own man. Not all the bottled spirits in London could make me babble against you. You'll look back fondly on your decision. I say get your pretty wench and together we'll all make merry."

"No."

"Come, give me a civil look, Ned."

Ned sat down on the bed next to Lemuel. Reaching out with his bad hand, he tapped the boy on the shoulder in a friendly way. "I've said what I must. You're both chums, but I can't trust you longer. And even if I did, it's time to part. From this moment hence, I won't abide you following me. I'll stop you if I must."

Putting the bottle down on the floor, Bostock looked steadily at Ned, his loose lips trembling. "We are not contemptible, we."

"No, you are not."

"Let me entreat —"

"Good doctor, it's time to part."

"I beseech you. On my conscience we're without crop."

Ned went to his bed, reached under it, and drew out a money pouch. He counted out ten guineas, though in two days he must pay Jenny Rivers. "Here, friend, this is the last I will give you."

Taking the money, Bostock said, "I thank you for it, but it's paltry to what you must be doing, you and Mister Scarrat. Faith, I hate a liar." Putting up both hands, eyes wide, he added, "Not that I say it of you! But so many around us lie and cheat and withhold our rightful funds, and so we're empty and beseech you to bring us in. We can all share, though in conscience I believe your share would be twice ours, yes, twice." Regarding Ned closely, he said, "More than twice." He turned to look at Lemuel, who seemed on the verge of tears. "Don't stare at me, booby!"

Ned walked to the door and opened it. "I must stand alone, whatever you think."

"You've no more feeling than a deal board," grumbled the doctor, getting slowly to his feet.

"I'm sorry, but there's no other way. I must stand alone."

"Yes, you and the dog must stand alone. And the black boy." When Ned looked surprised, the doctor smiled bitterly. "Indeed, we know about them too. And have we done you harm by the knowledge? Bring us in, lad."

"Goodbye, chums. And good luck."

"About ship, ninny," the doctor called out to Lemuel, who finally stood up and followed to the door. "We're gone."

Ned stood in the entranceway, watching the stoop-shouldered old man and the skinny redhead descend the stairs. Had he done right to slough them off? As if he had a choice. He must go it alone now. Only one thing was on his mind — to get the gold and take Clare out of London.

[40]

❡ I believe, Reader, I reported to you my sister Sarah's most peculiar words at our last parting: *I pray no harm comes to you.* And I conjectured that they referred to something other than my physical condition, as if the core of my very being was threatened. That evening, as I stood at the open window of my lodgings and looked down at the torch-lit paving of Bath, I observed the lumbering chariots and the lively throngs of people on holiday, bound for assemblies and routs and masquerades, perhaps going to a concert where old Handel, nearly blind and like myself crippled by gout, might conduct a new and wonderful work of his. On the air were youthful voices lifted in anticipation of the evening, never a note in them of foreboding or malice, merely the sweet pure sound of hope and good cheer.

Life may be properly called an art as any other; and the great incidents in it are no more to be considered mere accidents than the words of a noble poem, than the modeling of a fine statue. Nor are they to be thought of as lacking the spontaneity that distinguishes all great art. In all honesty I consider my life an extremely flawed work, but at least a work of some liveliness, not without its beauty, not without its lyrical moments.

And yet had my sister, mistress of a discerning eye, seen danger to the life I laboured to shape into a design of some honour and worth? Mistaken often in my judgement, I have tried to be a man both of feeling and rectitude. I have tried to err on the behalf of good will. I have always striven to believe in a benevolent Providence and have hoped that intention triumphs always over form.

Returning to London from our stay in Bath, I penned another essay for the *Covent Garden Journal,* which argued that form in itself is a travesty of authentic order, that a natural opposition exists between a free flow of individual soul and the imposed rule of a public united principally by its vanities through ignorance and false opinions and inadequate understanding of the heart's needs. You may well ask if such thoughts go with a man whose sworn duty is to uphold the institutions of society. Indeed, I have asked myself that selfsame question.

As I have mentioned the *Covent Garden Journal,* Joshua Brogden conveyed to me this morning mixed news about its possible sale. A coalition of publishers wish to buy it, though at a price not calculated to make us overjoyed. No indeed, they mean to take it off our hands more as a favour, stopping just short of requiring *us* to pay *them* for their generous effort on our behalf. With a sigh I instructed Joshua to go forward with the negotiations, being heartily sick of the journal which had so drained the energies of my brother John, myself, and our staff without filling our pockets. But I did insist on the stipulation that the reconstituted publication must devote adequate space to the criminal notices which form an essential part of my plan for suppressing crime.

As for these criminal notices and their importance, let me relate to you an incident just today which may result in a spectacular success for Bow Street.

I was stretched out on a chaise lounge in my study, unable to nap because of considerable pain from the gout in my left foot. Worse than the pain was an incapacitating fatigue, as I have found it to be the true enemy, the evil minister who daily reports another loss of Henry Fielding's powers.

A clerk came with news of a thief awaiting arraignment in the Public Office below. Struggling to an upright position, I waited impatiently for Joseph to come with my black robe and full-bottomed wig. When the old man arrived, I demanded a dram of brandy in such a voice of authority that he acquiesced with a disgusted grimace and gave it to me. I sipped it while dressing. Then Joseph and a strapping clerk carried me down the narrow stairway, because this week the gout had been too much to bear, even with a crutch.

Oft-times the Public Office, where arraignments took place, was packed with bystanders, but today proved almost empty. Seated with my bandaged foot on a stool, I looked at the begrimed young man, muscular but dull-eyed, who was roughly brought forward. I listened to the constables, the witnesses, the complainant who had the devious face of a street rogue. The prisoner had stolen the complainant's money pouch by simply reaching over and cutting it loose with a knife. Here, I felt, was a perfect illustration of my thesis that crime is most often caused by the desire for luxury. This young fellow could get what he wanted through honest work, yet impatience, I felt, must have driven him to violence.

"What is your occupation?" I asked. He answered that he was a drover of cattle.

"Do you drive your cattle into Smithfield with a knife?" But his confused expression told me such sarcasm was lost on him and effected nothing positive. I asked him how did it come about that he robbed the complainant.

He'd driven his animals into Smithfield for butchery, then overwhelmed by the sights of London had simply wandered away and lost his chance to return home with the other drovers. After a while he tried to get work, but found none, as they wanted sailmakers and bricklayers and malt distillers and nothing of cattle drivers. So he robbed for food and shelter.

It had been that simple for him. For a lark he'd strolled beyond the circle of his experience, skills, and inclinations. I have long observed that no good ever came of leaving one's sphere of life. In a fond and thoughtless search for greener pastures, he'd ended up at a magistrate's bench.

"Instead of robbery, why didn't you think of returning home and getting work again as a drover?"

"It's hard to go back."

"It's hard to go back, whereas it's easy to rob, do you mean?"

"No, your worship."

"What then do you mean?"

"After London, I'm not the man I was."

For a moment I was taken by the simple eloquence and wisdom and sadness of his remark, but fatigue held me in its grip and I had to bring this arraignment to a speedy end. It was plain that the lad had taken money belonging to someone else. Without more questioning, I ordered him to be detained on the charge of grand theft.

The world seemed to make less and less sense. I had believed in reason all my life, yet coming perhaps closer to the end of it, I now had to struggle with the increasing conviction that men were ruled almost exclusively by passion. Had I, for that matter, been ruled otherwise? I too had been deceived by dreams of luxury. I too had wanted fine baubles and good wine, though fortunately I had not, as this young man, used force to get them. But, in faith, what had I used? Why, my dear Charlotte's inheritance, which I squandered on conviviality within a year of our marriage. Perhaps a thin line separated thief and magistrate. How bitter it would be to face the end of my life without faith in human nature. Having this forlorn possibility in mind, I nearly called back the constables. I would have hoped to give the lad another chance, just as, in the goodness of his heart, Tom Jones had given one to the defeated Blifil. Indeed, I wrote better than I lived.

Yanking off the wig, I flung it on the desk and looked at the varnished wood. On such a flat surface I'd filled sheaves of paper with my scribbling. My writing life should not yet end. I knew the signs when a story needed shaping in my mind. There were the sudden preoccupations; the uncontrolled absences of thought from the real world; the irritability and restlessness felt, as if a tiny cinder were in my eye; the troublesome connections between disparate events; the need to construct people and events out of vagrant memories.

I was recalling faces that had appeared before me at this bench, when the door opened and in came Saunders Welch, wearing a grand plumed hat and a velvet waistcoat, as the man's vice was vanity. He instructed me that a citizen had come to the Register Office with an interesting tale.

It is this tale, Reader, that I thought would best illustrate my belief that public knowledge of crime both discourages it and leads to its suppression.

Two men followed one of our Bow Street Runners into the Public Office. The younger one, redheaded and excessively thin, wore a black eye patch as if mimicking the manner of a true buccaneer. But it was the older one who caught my attention. He

was short, with a massive head, florid cheeks, and a shifty air, and
he held a brass-knobbed cane against his round paunch. Both were
shabby and came in hangdog, as though guilty of something. But
I soon let go of such an idea, so bowled over was I by the older
man's speech. It was full of "your worship" and "your excellency"
and polite little phrases such as "Upon my word" and "Bless me,"
but once I calmed him into some semblance of verbal order, he
claimed to have read our advertisement in the *Covent Garden
Journal,* requesting information about criminals abroad in our
town. He hemmed and hawed, but finally got out that he knew of
such a person and as a loyal subject of the king wished to report it,
adding in the same breath that he understood the capture of a
notorious miscreant must lead to a reward.

"Notorious miscreant?" I repeated with a smile.

"I dare to say notorious, though I've learned it to my surprise
only yesterday. I had counted him a friend, though when I learned
the truth I could no longer hold it back from scruple."

I could scarcely hold back my own snickering, for it had been
considerable time since last I'd met with such a fellow, the last
being in my theatre days. Colley Cibber was the name of this rival
manager and playwright, a vain coxcomb with a voice too shrill
and cracked for acting, albeit he trod the boards no matter how
fierce the catcalls. Unlike the garrulous creature before my bench,
Colley was uncommonly lean, a clumsy oaf, a scurrilous wit whom,
in an article, I once summoned before the Court of Censorial
Enquiry set by Captain Hercules Vinegar on an indictment for
murdering the English language. Those had been the days of
energetic literary battle in which nothing was wounded but pride
and that not for long. Colley is now a very old man, far gone in
dotage, and yet I dare say he'd rouse himself to answer back a jest
and squeak at me in that voice of his that he'd had the better of it.
In this ramshackle old fellow in front of me I had a renewed taste
of Colley's frippery so that I could no more detest him than I could
my own father.

This Doctor Bostock was still defending his honour against
unspoken insults and imagined charges of misconduct when
something came from him that had me leaning forward. He was
complaining of this friend whom he'd trusted with his very soul
and whom he'd uncovered by accident to be a thief and a notorious
criminal. "This fellow I once called chum has shown himself to
be immensely corruptible. He has one hand as ugly as charcoal,
and a dog."

"A dog," I said. "Tell me about the dog."

"Why, a black boy keeps it for him, and when he comes to take it on a stroll, believe me, your worship, someone will lose a truff."

"Speak plainly, sir."

"What you command, your excellence, I perform. I mean he uses the dog to run down coves and have their purses. Methinks you know who I mean." He grinned slyly. "With bowser along, he can mill a flat on any street in London, and be gone in a wink."

Questioning him further, I glanced beyond his shoulder to Saunders Welch, who exchanged looks with me. The thief was gentlemanly enough, of polite speech and manner, but with the dog he was will-o'-the-wisp, quite beyond capture.

This must indeed be the Dog Cull we'd come upon.

"Do you know where he lives?" I asked.

"No, your worship."

I suspected this fellow had perfect knowledge of the Dog Cull's lodgings. He merely wished to make sure that he distinguished himself sufficiently to collect a reward. And as a preference, I'd rather take the Cull at work than in his bed, to leave no doubt of his identity or of evidence. So I instructed Saunders Welch to take the doctor outside and speak further. Left alone, I wished with all my heart that I might work more closely with my men. Taking this celebrated thief would enhance the prospects of Bow Street and send through London a new respect for our efforts.

I yelled out for Joseph and commanded another brandy, this one less for courage than for celebration. Though I must resort to a petty informer, I saw Providence at work in bringing the old ruffian to us. It was totally unexpected. I have always preferred the art of comedy to tragedy because it permits an escape from the past and allows for infinite possibilities in the future. Richardson writes of man being driven to doom by forces beyond his control: one mistake leads inevitably to another and another until hope of redemption vanishes. I like to think that my work hath always been out in sunlight, shining on a world that can be pieced back together, though for the moment it lays scattered in ruin.

The world of London lay in such ruin because of crime. Perhaps we'd put it back together again, by starting with the Dog Cull.

When Saunders Welch joined me again for a dram of brandy, his elegant hat ensconced in his lap like a pretty bawd, he smiled and shook his head in recalling this Doctor Bostock. "Hard to follow the man's mind, but he seems to think the Dog Cull is out for big fish. If you ask me, it's Bostock who's fishing. He seems to think the Cull has gone from robbery to great intrigue and means to haul in a lot of gold."

"That would be a time to get him."

"Agreed. But can we trust Bostock? Since we established the Register, all sorts of queer folk are turning up with wild stories. It seems to make them feel of consequence."

"You want to give up on Bostock?"

Saunders Welch pursed his lips judiciously. "The deal I made was this. If he lit upon unassailable evidence of the Dog Cull in an intrigue, meaning we might catch him in the act of crime, then he'd send his boy to get us and we'd come mounted on the instant."

"A good plan," I told Saunders Welch, "especially since Bostock seems on familiar footing with culls and lifts and rogues. If it takes a thief to catch one, we may have the right man."

[41]

FOOTGUARDS AT ST. JAMES'S and horse grenadiers at Hyde Park were drilling today, though a furious thunderstorm last night had left much of London a sea of stinking mud. Pavements of cobble were sinking, and the sky remained a heaving grey mass similar to coal-fire smoke.

Though the town was a dreary sight, milkmaids were spruced up in white pinafores and black taffeta bonnets as they carried shoulder yokes from which buckets of fresh milk dangled. Stuffy, cramped, dimly lit shops were doing brisk business in clocks, fans, silver, sweetmeats, India silk, tobacco, tallow candles, spiritous liquors, clay pipes, corsets, wigs, lace, hoops, and breeches. Street singers, match sellers, and beggars came from dank cellars into the thick of above-ground London, where they competed with performing ponies and jugglers. Porters were fetching bales for woolmen and heavy casks for wine merchants, lugging Purbeck marble and Burford stone to masons, and hauling Scandinavian timber to joiners for making cupboards, to carpenters for making shelves.

Cinder sifters, all women, were hard at work in Tottenham Court. Other scavengers prowled the dock and warehouse areas, where vast swaths of fog swept in from the Thames like rolling smoke after battle. Garrick at Drury Lane was rehearsing his coarsened version of *Macbeth,* John Beard a farce at Covent Garden. Not far away a publisher was printing up a new edition of the popular book by Richard Russell, *The Uses of Sea-Water in Diseases of the Glands.* The author had just settled in the dirty little village of Brighthelmstone, which his theories on sea bathing would soon transform into the fashionable resort of Brighton Beach.

And Ned was setting out for the Sign of the Frigate. Contrary to his usual practice, he'd gone in broad daylight for Sandy. Ever since Scarrat had agreed without a murmur to pay the gold, Ned had felt uneasy. He wanted Sandy nearby in case there was trouble.

Last night, with Clare in his arms, his ungloved hands stroking the skin of her as yet flat belly, Ned hadn't rid himself of a vision of Scarrat's dark face, as sly as death. At their last meeting Scarrat had smirked like a whist player who loses a game but not the match. So Ned had decided to bring Sandy to this final meeting. His spine felt chill, as if his body knew what his brain did not: that someone was following him. Yet when he swung around, he saw only tradesmen and shoppers and hawkers of newspapers and sweetmeats. Not a soul gave him a second glance. If someone did trail him, it was no clumsy anchorsmith or aging constable.

Whatever the danger, he must go on. Glancing over his shoulder, he could see, among the legs of passersby, the sleek dog loping along against a wall, avoiding good-natured pets or nasty kicks with the single-mindedness of a trained sheepdog.

Just ahead was the dark door of the ale house. Ned halted before reaching it and whistled for Sandy to halt. He watched her creep alongside a building and sit on her feathery haunches — watchful, ready, impossible to distract.

Taking a deep breath, Ned entered the Frigate and instantly laid eyes on Scarrat, who sat grinning near the back wall. Otherwise the dimly lit ordinary was almost empty. One look at the grey-faced man and Ned tapped the outside of his frock-coat to make sure of his flintlock. As Ned drew nearer, Scarrat's smile became broader, though the dark eyes remained metallically cold.

There was movement next to a stack of kegs and a small man vanished through a back door.

"Rest easy," Scarrat said, watching Ned's hand move to his frock-coat. "It's my drawer, Giles. He goes for a keg I want. Sit and have a tankard. I'll draw."

"No ale for me."

"Then a bumper of Hollands?" Scarrat chuckled gruffly. "Calm down. You're nervous as a cat. I've been sitting here thinking to myself, How's the lad going to spend such a haul? Have you got a doxy hid away? Hey? Beware of women. They pick you as clean as a goose and think nothing of it. Put your gold into trade. Take some advice from a fellow who's seen the world. Leave off women and go into trade. Buy a boozing house the likes of mine. Nothing better. Steady profit. Mark me, I've turned a shilling or two here. Business. Much better than wenches. You see, it's simple — there's no treachery in gold. And each morning when you open your eyes, you know where the gold is. Have a Hollands. Or is claret more to your liking? Sit awhile. Tell me how you mean to spend this booty."

The man was chattering, Ned realized, with a purpose. Glancing around, he asked bluntly for the gold.

"Aye, here it is." Casually the tavernkeeper lifted a money pouch from his lap and threw it on the table. "Every farthing, sir." He smirked broadly. "Count it. The weight's like a bagful of musket-balls."

Stepping forward, Ned took up the pouch, peered inside, hefted it in judgement, and tied the drawstring to his belt. Without a word he turned to leave.

"May I hope your pardon," Scarrat called after him, "for any delay."

Rain had begun again. It was a drizzle so far, but chill. Pulling his tricorn low, Ned stepped back to avoid being splashed by a coach. He whistled and to his satisfaction noticed that Sandy stood up instantly almost a block away, shook herself, and turned her snout in his direction. She went forward half the block, then halted and waited for him to set out so she could follow, as usual, at a distance.

He'd taken but a few steps before noticing a figure waving at him cheerily, as if by prearrangement. Doctor Bostock! Years in the streets had given the old devil a talent for sniffing out advantage. He had a nose for it like a rat for cheese. There was nothing to do, Ned thought, but to give the rascal some cole for old times' sake. So he slogged through the muddy street toward the sly, bewhiskered face. He'd reward the old devil for untrustworthy friendship, for a sorry but merry life.

In the next moment he heard a cry of "Thief! Thief!" Whirling around, he saw two men in coarse smocks rushing from a nearby alley, pistols drawn.

So Giles had gone for assassins.

Ned was drawing his own pistol, when one of the men fired, and the ball whistled past his ear. At this attack on her master, Sandy leapt forward despite Ned's warning whistle. The second man, who hadn't yet fired, turned to see what the speeding object was; he pulled the trigger only a split second before she hurtled into him, so it seemed as if the pistol report and her snarling impact occurred together. They went down in a heap, but only the man struggled up again. Ned stared in disbelief at the limp furred body, then saw that the first man, having reloaded, would fire again.

Ned fired first and the man went down. The second man was scrambling in the mud for the weapon Sandy had knocked out of his hand.

"Thief!" sounded from all directions. A hand grabbed at Ned's arm. He flung it off, seeing as he did so the good doctor scooting round a corner and beckoning as he ran. Following into the lane, Ned saw Lemuel, mouth gaping in fear, pressed against a wall, and athwart the path ahead three men ahorseback.

One wore a plumed hat, the other two black caps. Seeing Ned, they spurred their mounts into a gallop.

"Thief! Thief!"

Turning back from the horsemen, Ned saw to his dismay a half-dozen workmen, roused from their shops by the commotion, coming into the lane with staves and hammers. Ned waved his spent pistol at them, and as they hesitated, he bolted through their ranks into another lane. Not ten paces within it, he heard the thud of hoofbeats closing from behind. On the horsemen's caps a large red B — Bow Street Runners. The doctor had betrayed him to Bow Street!

Abruptly he veered into yet a smaller lane, hearing then the sound of horses neighing in frustration — the mounted pursuers were being slowed among wagons in the crowded passageway.

Ahead was a scrawny mule loaded with barrels and carrying two riders on its sway back. As he came alongside, Ned yanked the animal's halter, which caused the mule to buck and tumble both barrels and riders into the mire. He heard curses, neighing, while racing on, as instinctive as a homing pigeon, he made for Black Boy Alley.

The rain fell with greater force, while behind him, at some distance now, the repeated cry of "Thief!" caused people to turn and stare in the direction of the noise and then at him running. A few joined in the pursuit, and one even reached out tentatively, but Ned's waved pistol made the arm pull back. On he went through the lanes and the alleys filled with prancing hoofs, ponderous wheels, with a roiling mob of humanity beneath the sooty downpour.

For a few moments he stopped to catch his breath, hearing behind him the irritable whinnying, the frantic hoofbeats, the shouted oaths of pursuers caught like flies in the muddy web of the crowded thoroughfare. Turning he saw through the slanting rain two horses break out of the traffic jam and surge forward, one of them banging a haywain so hard with its flank that the conveyance tilted sideways and nearly overturned. Ned began running again.

Coming to an intersection, he nearly bumped into the vanguard of a funeral procession, but managed to scoot past. His pursuers were not so lucky. One of the riders collided broadside with a drawn hearse. This caused one of the dray horses to rear and ram a front leg heavily into a brewery cart, throwing casks of ale into the mud and overturning the hearse so that half of the corpse slid from its coffin into a puddle. Hands grabbed at the dray harnesses. The thrown Bow Street pursuer had his leg pinned under a cask that had rolled down on him. The brewery cart driver was screaming at the hearse driver, who was screaming at the fallen Runner.

The hullabaloo gave Ned needed time. Only a short distance separated him from the safety of a hundred old shanties in Black Boy Alley. But suddenly a huge butcher appeared in a doorway and swung a bloody ax at his head. Luckily Ned caught the blow on his pistol barrel, the weapon spinning out of his hand. He didn't stop for it, but rushed past a huddled knot of startled beggars.

Once around this corner — once around it!

Summoning a final burst of speed, he turned into the familiar labyrinth, a teetering forest of crumbling brick and old wood. Again he halted for breath, seeing whores and footpads leaning curiously from open windows. Some gave him a cheer, for though they didn't recognize him in the gloom, they knew a man fleeing when they saw one.

He trotted forward, coming at last to an old house, whose door was always unlocked. In the days before becoming the Dog Cull, when he'd come to the alley for women and drink, Ned had known this house well. It was kept unlocked for denizens of the alley who were pursued. As Ned turned the door knob, he was startled to see the black boy rising from behind a pile of barrels.

"I heard the noise a long way off," the boy said. "I heard the hue and cry and thought it might be you and you'd come here if followed, and so you have, but I don't see her trailing. Where is she?"

Instead of answering, Ned pushed the door open and entered the house. Passing some bunters at dice in a shabby parlor, he went into a kitchen reeking of fish soup. Going into the next room, an old pantry, Ned dropped to his knees and tugged at a trapdoor hidden beneath some faggots. Before he could lift it and climb down, however, the black boy was on him, yanking fiercely at his arm.

"She didn't come with you. Where is she?"

"Gone," Ned panted, struggling to fling the boy off.

"Where? Gone? Where is she?"

Ned stopped trying to free himself, but stared down at the boy's black hand that clutched his arm like a falcon's beak. After a hard look at the pleading face, he couldn't tell the truth. "She ran away."

"No, no, never! You owe Jenny Rivers. You need money to pay her and right now and you don't have it and you had to get it. Sandy never ran away! You sold her!" the boy screamed, letting go of Ned's arm in his anguish. "Did you? Tell me! You sold her!"

"Well, I — I did. It's true. I sold her." Lifting the trapdoor, Ned peered into a dank-smelling darkness.

"Sold her?" the boy repeated incredulously. The features of his black face clenched like a fist. He jumped up and down in his fury and frustration. "You ought not! You ought not! You ought not!" he shrieked. "She was mine! You sold her! You ought not!"

There was no time for explanations, let alone the truth. "To a good fellow. She's well taken care of," Ned muttered and climbed down the narrow stairway, closing the trapdoor over his head while from above came the muffled cry, "You ought not! She was mine!"

[42]

Picking his way through a dark cellar, Ned no longer heard the boy. In the silence he bumped into rotted trunks, old lumber, broken wheels, heaps of trash from an earlier age. Around him was the rustling scamper of rats, the fetid stench of sewage that seeped down from streets of the district. He crept forward, trying to recall the way as shown him by an old neighborhood beggar whom he'd once befriended and fed and who, in gratitude, had given him a tour of the escape routes through Black Boy Alley. These bolt-holes and chutes had been constructed more than a half century ago by outlaws like himself. Indeed, very like himself. Ned felt a sudden kinship with them, as if their hovering ghosts were at his side, helping him.

Surely he'd get no help from the living. He'd expected none from Scarrat, of course. The waylaying outside of the Frigate was no surprise; indeed, it was in character for Scarrat. To do the dirty work of his master, he'd hired two sons of Belial who would slit their mothers' throats for a guinea. One of the assassins had been paid for his trouble. Ned had seen the ball from his pistol blow out a side of the rogue's chest.

But for Doctor Bostock and Lemuel to peach on him, let alone set an ambush with the Bow Street thief takers, was against the nature of friendship, a sin against the nature of man.

Yet as he groped his slow way through the cellar, Ned felt glad of the betrayal. It meant that he and Clare were truly alone in the world. He was beholden to nobody, and from this moment on he'd show cunning but no mercy, give better than he got and no quarter. It was as if for the first time in his life he felt released from any constraint, even from the fear of God.

At the far end of this long cellar, if he remembered properly, there would be a ladder. Shuffling forward with hands outstretched, he touched the rungs at last. Cautiously he began the climb. Reaching the top rung, he stepped into a tiny space, a false room just large enough to hold him, along with the ladder when he hauled it up. Shooting the ladder upward into the darkness, securing it against a wall, he climbed again, and in this manner mounted four flights of the hidden shaft. Before coming to London, he'd been told that the people of this grand town lived vertically. And this had been proven to him when he saw many houses of four or five floors, with a stairway to one side, and two rooms to the floor. But he'd never experienced such a sense of tunneling upward as he did now, moving the ladder from floor to floor, going past what in the old days had been kitchen and pantry, drawing room and parlour, dining room and bedroom, other bedrooms and ladies' closets, an attic and servants' quarters — lively rooms every one, built long before King Charles lost his head.

Ned whiffed the pungent odors of urine, gin, burnt charcoal, and heard behind a thin wall some people cackling drunkenly. He'd reached the attic, and they were in the servants' quarters. The attic had a single window from which projected a waxed plank slanting down to a window in the opposite building. He got on the plank and edged over to the next house, then shoved the wooden chute free to dangle from a rope fastened to the roof.

In the room he then entered, a man lay stretched out on the floor snoring, an empty bottle near his curled fingers. Through the torn shirt a shrunken chest rose and fell in quick gusts, reminding Ned suddenly of something he'd long forgotten: the old woman in the gin shop with her lappy companion who couldn't breathe because of — was it mercury? Was this the man or no? Anything was possible in the alley. Stepping over the sprawled body, Ned crossed the room to the narrow hallway. He didn't hesitate there, but opened the opposite door and burst in, surprising a naked girl swilling gin with a half-dressed customer on a mattress. A single candle glowed in the room, which seemed to contain nothing but empty bottles and the dirty mattress.

"Hey, nipper," the girl called merrily, "have some bub with us?" She lifted up the bottle.

But her customer was groping for his sword, which lay nearby.

Ned crouched, wishing for his lost pistol.

The girl took hold of her customer's arm, keeping him from the sword. "Stay, sweetness! Stay! I believe I know this lad. Leave him be or he'll cool your courage, Jack."

The man hesitated, then allowed her to embrace him. There was movement from the corner, so that Ned turned to it, again in the crouch of defense. An older woman, wrapped partially in a worn shawl, crawled on her knees out of the corner, yawning and rubbing her eyes and squinting to get a better look at Ned.

"Whoa! Leave him be!" she brayed, shaking her frowsy head. "It's a prig hereabouts is under Jenny's protection."

"Who's Jenny?" the customer asked in a surly drink-thickened voice.

"Jenny Rivers, and kindly watch how you say her name in these parts. Queen of Foists they call her. A terrible old bitch who'd murder you as soon as look at you."

"Go to," murmured the customer who'd surreptitiously got hold of his sword and held it across his lap.

The older woman sat on the floor, crossing her legs so that her sex showed in the candlelight. "Jenny Rivers once had a pair of wooden hands made and she'd sit in a church pew with the hands in her lap like a good Christian madam while her own were busy elsewhere, nicking purses on either side."

"Go to. Here you," he said to Ned, "don't move." With the point of his sword, he was following Ned's steps backward to the door.

"I told you," declared the older woman. "Touch him, you're dead. He's under protection of the great bitch."

"Leave him be," urged the younger woman.

Ned turned, opened the door and went out and closed it in one swift motion. Then he went down a floor to another room. Empty. And a false panel in it. He remembered that. Feeling around the wainscot wall, he soon found its edge, lifted the panel out, and replaced it after climbing into another secret alcove. He listened for footsteps. Nothing. From the window of this ancient closet ran yet another plank to another house, and so he edged himself out on it and continued in this manner through two more ramshackle hovels, surprising card players and whores at their trade until he'd gone half the length of Black Boy Alley four flights above the ground.

In the last house he descended a rear staircase and found in the kitchen another trapdoor under some straw. The neighbourhood beggar, with more gratitude than ever noblemen show, had repaid kindness with a map for survival. Ned climbed into the cellar and felt his way to the far wall. At its base he located the entrance to a tunnel hidden by old burlap. Without hesitating, he squirmed into it, hearing the nearby trickle of sewage water and smelling the rank odour of corrupted earth. He had scarcely enough room through which to worm his broad shoulders. Well into the passage he felt a momentary panic of being stuck. Pausing, he breathed deeply in the cool thin air. This must be, he thought, what sweeps feel, wedged in the bend of a chimney, unable to go up or down. Tiny creatures ran nimbly across his nose and cheeks. There was a tickling of myriad legs across his eyelids. Taking more deep breaths, he tried to move forward. Again he paused, took breath, and again tried to wriggle through the narrow passage. This time he went slightly forward, then a little more, inching along endlessly, it seemed. Endless was how it felt to him, yet the tunnel must not have been farther than he'd walk at a brisk clip in a minute. Was it blocked at the far end? That was the question, as the beggar hadn't been sure. The tunnel hadn't been used for many years, though its existence was common knowledge in Black Boy Alley.

Ned continued to inch forward, with beetles and grubs dropping lightly into his hair. The air grew thinner, his lungs ached, he anticipated more panic if he got stuck again, but most of all he feared a blocked exit. Then he could neither turn round in the tunnel nor back all the way out. He was starting to feel queasy and faint, when a little rush of air brushed his face like a feather. Ahead he saw a tiny zero of light. Shortly he emerged from the tunnel, crawling out into yet another cellar.

Standing up and stretching his arms wide, he felt clammy and dizzy but savored the release from terrible confinement. God in heaven.

There was light in the cellar. Late sunshine after the rain was pouring in milky streams through a small window. He found a couple of empty kegs, piled one on another, and in this way reached the window and wriggled through.

A one-legged beggar, leaning on a misshapen crutch, looked at a man flopping in the mud like a fish — looked without interest or concern and hobbled on.

Scrambling up, Ned studied the tiny lane. He'd traversed three whole blocks underground. He was now free of the neighbourhood and with this little space of safety to live in for a moment, he thought of Clare. In a short while he'd see her again, stroke her cheek, place the money pouch in her hand, and say, "It's done, we're free."

Sighing with relief, he trudged to the corner. Bending there to brush the damp earth from his breeches, he had but an instant in which to see the cudgel arcing down on him from the left. He felt it thud heavily against his shoulder, felt his body whirl down through the air. He saw legs around him, arms raised. Hands struck, gripped, yanked him to his feet. Hands ripped the leather pouch from his belt. Hands frisked his body for pistols, knives. Hands pressed his hands to the small of his back and bound them.

A face loomed in front of his. It belonged to the horseman in the plumed hat. "You are took."

Blood, sweat, and muddy earth blurred his vision, but Ned had enough left to see, beyond the ring of captors, one of the Bow Street Runners methodically counting out coins into the outstretched palm of the black boy.

The small hand closed like a clam shell.

As they began pushing him forward, Ned called over his shoulder at the boy, "I never sold her!" Someone prodded him with a blunderbuss in the ribs. He stumbled, muttering, "She's dead. She's dead, boy!"

Before the mob of captors could accompany him around the corner (Scarrat trailing them discreetly and Lemuel coming along, though the good doctor must have been left far behind long ago), Ned saw the dumbfounded black boy plummet to the ground, the guilty hand open, and the coins dribble out.

An especially virulent attack of gout had laid up Magistrate Fielding, so when Saunders Welch and his men returned to Bow Street in triumph, they were instructed by a law clerk to take the prisoner to the legal chambers of the earl of Mansfield, lord chief justice, who had kindly agreed to conduct the arraignment.

And so Ned Carleton was hauled there and disposed of in short order by a judge impatient to get to a comic opera written by Thomas Arne, who'd composed "Rule, Britannica!" Justice Mansfield was going in defiance of Dr. Johnson's judgement that opera was "an exotic and irrational entertainment."

The felon was then taken from Mansfield's chambers to a constable's house, where he was shackled and placed in a dingy room for which the constable received "lock-up payment" from the local parish.

Fettered by hand and leg to wall rings, Ned sat on a dilapidated bunk and had scarcely had time to glance at the scabby little cell before its lock rattled, the door opened, and Scarrat walked in.

"See, lad, you don't lack for visitors, though you've been here but minutes." Scarrat waited until the constable discreetly closed the door. "Paid a pretty penny for this opportunity, I don't mind saying," he said pleasantly to Ned and rolled his eyes at the door. "That constable, the washy rogue, has a genius for getting coin out of a man, though I warrant I'm mighty glad they brought you here and not to Bow Street, as there you can't get a soul to do anything you ask, no matter what you offer."

"Say and be done with it," muttered Ned.

Scarrat had removed his tricorn and held it at his waist in both hands, as if preparing to make a speech. Ned's blunt words apparently changed his mind. Scarrat came right out with it.

"I'd planned to turn you off, simpleton, but your damn bowser got in the way of my men."

Ned smiled bitterly. "That's something I already know."

"Then know this too. I know about your wench. I know where she was and where she is now and where she'll be if you don't listen properly." Scarrat laughed at the shocked look of the mud-bespattered, bloody-headed prisoner. "Did you take me for one of your coxcombs or foot scamps with no more brain than a chicken? You was bold to try his lordship, but even bolder to try Robert Scarrat. I was foiled on taking you off, but they secured you anyway, thanks to that avaricious black boy you was stupid enough to befriend. You'll be tried and hanged at Tyburn, that's sure." Scarrat paused thoughtfully and stroked his long chin. "I see into your mind, lad. You're thinking, let them dangle me, but before they do I'll talk of someone in a high place to a magistrate. Is that so?"

"That's indeed so."

Scarrat nodded with a contented smile. "But, lad, you mustn't do it. Bless you for a fool, you *cannot* do it."

"I can do it."

"Do it and the doxy's forfeit." He raised his hand to hold back a response. "I said forfeit! I said the bitch dies! You'd as soon go against the archbishop of Canterbury as go against me. You're a leaf in the wind, boy, and so is she, and if you desire her dead along with yourself, why then open your silly mouth and see her life fly out of it." Scarrat's voice was trembling from emotion, as if a Christian prelate were attacking a blasphemous heretic. "There's no more to say. Not one word. I haven't one more word for you, damn your stupid fucking hide, except if you squeak, if you so much as let his lordship's name cross your lips, I swear by my own life I'll do for the cunt, I'll have her throat slit and her body tossed in the Thames and you shall know the truth of it when I bring a handful of her hair and throw it at your lousy feet when you're carted to the rope. I swear it!" Scarrat turned and pounded hard on the door. He didn't glance back at the prisoner, but when the constable let him out, Scarrat called over his shoulder, almost gaily, "Pray to heaven, boy, for a swift end! That's what does for mercy at Tyburn!"

Part Eight

———————————•———————————

TRIALS AND
TRIBULATIONS

[43]

HAVING BEEN ARRAIGNED on capital offenses, the prisoner Nathaniel Carleton was transferred the next day from the constable's lock-up to Newgate Prison, where he would await trial at the Old Bailey on the charges of grand theft, assault, and murder.

On the way there by wagon, the constable tied a money pouch to the bound prisoner's belt.

"What's this for?" Ned asked in amazement.

"The grey man left it for you." The constable grunted ruefully. "I was afraid to cross someone with a devil of a face like that, or I'd not be handing it over."

"Why did he do it?"

"You need cole in prison."

"Yes. But why did he help me?"

The constable, whose merry eyes suggested a sense of humour, patted Ned on the knee. "Maybe he wanted you to last long enough to get a full taste of Newgate."

Ned wasn't sure what the fellow meant, yet he was soon to find out.

Newgate.

The ugly immense prison had been built almost a century before Ned passed beneath its archway. At the Keeper's Office he paid a shilling's fee for the privilege of going to prison. Then he was conducted by guard to the Fetters Room, where a powerful man stood at a long table loaded with irons of different weights and construction.

The fellow's manner belied his rough appearance. First, he removed the constable's irons and gave them back to him with a little bow. Turning to Ned, he bowed again. "When a gentleman uses me with civility, I do the best I can to please him. We have fetters here of all prices. Please yourself."

Ned regarded the table heaped with irons, fixing his gaze on the infamous Shears — three-foot bars of iron weighing fifty pounds each. When fastened to ankles and groin, they limited movement to a few painful inches, caused suppurating sores, dislocated bones, sundered internal organs. A failure to cross the fetters officer's palm with gold would bring on a load of irons, maybe even the Shears.

Counting out six shillings from the pouch at his waist, Ned studied the courteous officer. "Is this enough for easement of irons?"

"Eight will give you the easement you desire."

Ned counted out another two shillings. With a pleasant smile the fetters officer hammered on a pair of lightweight wrist cuffs which allowed Ned considerable freedom. He was spared the ankle collars altogether.

But then a bailiff took away Ned's gloves.

This had a powerful effect on him, for those gloves had become part of Ned's body, and their loss — especially of the one fashioned for his misshapen hand — meant worse humiliation than the rough manner of his capture. Looking down at the ugly flesh, Ned became fully aware of his lamentable situation and wished with desperate urgency for a chance to see Clare so he might swear again that he wanted their child.

From the Fetters Room a guard took him up a winding staircase to a second-floor ward and gave him over to a grizzled turnkey, who stuck out a dirty hand and bellowed "Garnish!"

Ned well knew that the fee of garnish was a turnkey's sole wage, so unless he paid well he could expect little mercy. He handed over ten shillings, which brought a nod of approval from the turnkey, who then unlocked the ward door. When it swung back on iron hinges, Ned saw a crowd of people blinking like rats in the sudden brightness. They stood against clammy walls or sprawled on the stone floor. A wave of them surged forward, crying "Pay or strip!" for they meant to have Ned's clothes less he threw them some coins.

Satisfied with the garnish and hoping for more from such a prisoner, the turnkey raised his cudgel threateningly. "Leave off! Harm one hair of his, I'll break your guts! Get back, get back!"

Men, women, and children retreated, allowing Ned to enter the dark room without incident, and the door shut with a metallic ring. He was prepared for an attack, but none came, as they feared the turnkey would flail at them with his stave if the new prisoner were hurt.

Sitting on a bench alongside a wet wall, Ned took a deep breath to calm himself and was nearly overcome by a suffocating stench. Candles burned here and there, casting hollow faces in grim relief, glinting on chains, for an instant illuminating rats that scurried underfoot as freely as lapdogs.

Here be hell, he thought. Scarrat wanted me comfy to begin with, so I'd have time to know fully each new thing. Indeed, that was the nature of Scarrat.

A tall, skinny, middle-aged man approached, hesitated, thrust out the candle he carried to have a better look at Ned. Then rather cautiously he sat beside Ned on the bench. "What do they have you for, sir?"

"Too much."

The man laughed. He wore a filthy bobwig, torn lace ruffles at the cuffs of wrinkled velvet sleeves. Half the brass buttons of his waistcoat were off. Both silk stockings had holes in them, and the garter at his left knee was gone. He looked like someone who'd entered this ward in splendid attire, but hard usage had reduced his finery to rags. And so it proved, as he had come to Newgate months ago on a debtor's charge. Gambling had brought him, a master baker with his own shop, to this sorry circumstance. A venal attorney by making endless and — it turned out — meaningless petitions had taken the last of his savings. Hope of an Act for the Relief of Insolvent Debtors, encouraged in such hapless people as himself by a horde of such lawyers, proved nothing more than a foolish dream. Now he wished only for transport to the Americas, and a chance for a new start, though he'd heard death was common for those bold enough to ship there. "How was you took?"

"By thief takers from Bow Street."

"Ah, Bow Street. Was you arraigned before Justice Fielding?"

"He was sick. I went to Murray."

"Fielding's a most comical fellow. Least in his works he is. He arraigned me for debt and I saw no humour in his face then."

Struggling with his fettered hands to get the charred book from his coat pocket, Ned finally held up *Joseph Andrews*. "It's always with me."

"So you read," the debtor said thoughtfully. "They have taken someone of reason and, from the look of you, of good presentation and handled you as roughly as a scamp. My, they gave you a blow in the head. Are you in for something of import?"

Ned gave him a little nod.

"Are you in for . . . capital?"

"I am."

The debtor shook his head sadly. "I'd clean your wound, but I've no cloth left. So you read Mister Fielding. A word of warning, sir. Say nothing about him in the ward. His Bow Street Runners are hated here. The ward's full of rogues. The next ward is where most debtors be and though I pleaded with them to put me there, they kept me here, as my gold is much thinned out by lawyers." He sighed. "Seems your book has seen as bad times as yourself."

By the next morning Ned's own clothes were impregnated by air so filthy that it also polluted his watery soup of carrots. He felt already as if he'd been in this place forever. Vendors came around throughout the day, selling bowlfuls of cheap gin which they hawked as STRIP ME NAKED. Many buyers vomited after drinking it, yet each time a vendor appeared, they rushed to buy more. Underworld skills were practised unabated in the ward. Lifts exchanged the tricks of their art, regardless of chains hindering their movement. Forgers clipped coins with tools that the turnkey allowed them to keep for a price. Whores plied their wares in the common room and with amusement taught curious children how to hoist a pocket watch while a standing client was in the ecstatic fit, demonstrating the technique graphically to the delight of some prisoners, to the disgust of others, for every sort of person had been tumbled into the ward — young, old, debtor, petty thief, cutthroat. Weazened pawnbrokers and haughty solicitors slunk through the huge cell, looking for business. Prisoners whose money had run out and could no longer buy a candle or even a penny loaf of bread were briskly removed. Ned well knew where they were taken, having heard chums speak with a shudder of Newgate's stone hold, which lay beneath the main gate near the sewer. In the stone hold, without light or water, inmates shared loathsome straw with all sorts of vermin. It was merciful when they died quickly of gaol fever.

With nothing to do in the twilit grimness of the ward, people jabbered about anything: food, sickness, God's will, the treacherous French, the treacherous Germans, the corruption of Parliament, but mostly about the upcoming Canning trial, for though many of them awaited their own trials, hers still captured the imagination. They were about evenly divided between those who thought her an innocent and those who took her for a liar and a damnable cheat. A few came to blows, and the turnkey, summoned, beat the fighters into submission.

Ned listened in a kind of panicky frustration. He wanted to stand up and yell, "She lied but in fear of John Montagu, the right honourable fourth earl of Sandwich, who took her to a popish cloister where he and great men of substance laughed at God and worshiped the devil! And she was locked up thereafter in a loft for being troublesome and where's the justice in that? Does her lying hold a candle to such things as our betters do?"

That would be a pretty speech, he thought bitterly. And one that would never cross his lips.

Ned husbanded his money, not sure when he'd have more. Clare hadn't come to see him — thank God for that. Probably she didn't know he was in jail or at least in which among many jails. He hoped she wouldn't find out. She mustn't come to this place with a child in her belly. That was the resolve of his mind, yet in his heart he ached to have her come to his side and whisper "Dear lad," and lay her cool hand on his cheek.

He bought a candle, a threadbare blanket that emitted a noxious smell, and food only when he was very hungry.

But on the third day he gave money to ease the irons of an aging man jailed for stealing a half-dozen almond biscuits and three gooseberry tarts. The fellow sat panting in the Shears, his eyes dull from impending death, while next to him languished his pretty daughter, who'd been jailed for eating the food he'd stolen. Though Ned helped the father, he could do nothing for the daughter, who was taken repeatedly from the cell by a succession of guards and returned each time in tears. Ned thought of Medmenham, of the girl singing for milord Sandwich. Finally he could no longer watch when the iron door swung back and a grinning new turnkey, having got wind of the pretty girl in this ward, came for her. All night, all day.

Once when she returned, a woman in rags knelt beside her and smoothed her matted hair. "Good little miss, there, there," the woman murmured gently.

"God save me," the girl sobbed.

"Don't ask God to save you, miss. Ask your belly. Yes, sure, it can save you. Be you charged a felon?"

The girl nodded.

"Then get with child, dearie," the woman advised. "Get with child and you can plead your belly at court. They'll set you free and you can sell the issue to gypsies. Get with child, lass. I wish I was young enough for it and pretty enough to have the lot of them come at me. Think yourself fortunate."

Onlookers agreed, while the dying father, too weak for protest, lay on his side and groaned within a hundred pounds of constricting iron.

The next time a turnkey came for her, the pretty girl went with him without a murmur.

And the next time a turnkey came into the ward, he brought news of a recent prisoner — the one with the ugly hand was the Dog Cull! The ward grew silent, as the curious — those with candles — stepped cautiously forward and peered at the rumpled young man sitting on a bench in the corner. Awed by his reputation, fearful of what he might do, not a single one came closer, but kept their distance from him. When he spoke kindly to the debtor, the man winced as if receiving a blow and retreated into the shadows.

So the notoriety of his career separated Ned Carleton further from his companions in woe. He sat on the bench or lay under it, spending his time trying to conjure Clare in his imagination. Alas, given the fearsome condition of his mind, she soon became a pale blur, a featureless circle retreating to the far darkness of his memory.

Then a queer idea took hold of him.

He was not the prisoner of man but of God. The Almighty God was punishing him for not making the sacrilege at Medmenham known. Newgate was hell, the warders fallen angels.

In the midst of such feverish thoughts he became aware of a new smell in the air. A kettleful of burning brimstone had been brought into the ward to clean its air. The brimstone rid the cell of noxious fumes but added its own, and the smell reminded Ned of the pungent smoke drifting above him from the cloister window. Indeed, he'd offended against God by keeping the blasphemy secret. He began to feel giddy, nauseous, hot, as if the vengeful hand of God were squeezing his temples. And then a group of gentlemen appeared in the ward to gaze judiciously at the wretched inmates. Their short plump leader often stopped to scribble with a quill. In his unearthly mood Ned took the writer for a dark angel of judgement sent by God. Leaping up suddenly, Ned declared that for his own part he'd overheard but not countenanced the praises of Satan. When he plucked the heavenly angel's sleeve to beg mercy, a warder felled him from behind with a heavy stave.

All night he lay half conscious in a pool of blood, helplessly aware of fingers rifling through his clothes. Next morning he had no money, but he did have gaol fever and would never be aware that the man whom he'd deliriously mistaken for an angel had been in truth Stephen Hales, scientist and clergyman, who was designing modified organ bellows to act as prison ventilators. And Ned would not have cared, for he lay helpless on the stone floor, racked by a deep cough. When vainly he tried to rise, his bowels went off suddenly with a looseness that befouled his clothes. He could see an ugly rash on his arms and took it for a scourge from heaven. His head ached excruciatingly, his chest heaved to get breath, he moved in and out of consciousness, pursued by nightmares in which Medmenham merged with Newgate and the abused girls of Medmenham and Newgate became Clare.

Warders took him up and carried him to the stone hold, into veritable hell itself, his body burning burning burning just inches above the stinking sewers of London.

[44]

IT WAS A BRISK SEASON. The Scottish chemist Joseph Black discovered carbonic acid gas. At Fareham, Hampshire, the construction of the first iron rolling mill was nearing completion. In France the painter François Boucher was putting the finishing touches on his *Judgement of Paris* series for the Marquise de Pompadour. And in Königsberg, East Prussia, the young philosopher Immanuel Kant was hard at work on his doctoral dissertation, "The True Measure of Forces," no measure of what in future years he would accomplish. And three thousand unsuspecting people were still a year away from dying in the Lisbon earthquake.

And the perjury trial of Elizabeth Canning was under way. It would last twice as long as the trial of the two women against whom she'd brought her own action more than a year ago. It came before Thomas Rawlinson, new lord mayor of London, though Sir Crisp Gascoyne appeared as a counsel for the Crown, his scrappy nature as yet unsatisfied with the matter.

After selection of the jury, the clerk of the arraigns called out, "Crier, make proclamation."

The crier thundered, "Oyez, oyez, oyez! If any can inform my lords the king's justices, the king's serjeant, and the king's attorney, on this inquest to be taken, of any crimes or misdemeanours done or committed by the defendant at the bar, let them come forth, and they shall be heard. God save the king!"

The lengthy indictment was read, then counsel Gascoyne rose to enumerate the alleged perjured statements of Elizabeth Canning and concluded in ringing accents, "Therefore, that she was on the trial of the said Mary Squires guilty of wilful and corrupt perjury; all of which is said to be done to the great displeasure of Almighty God, in contempt of the laws of this land, and to the evil and pernicious example of all others in the like case offending, and against the peace of our lord the king, his crown and dignity — to this, gentlemen, the prisoner has pleaded Not Guilty. We shall call our witnesses, and if we prove her guilty, you will find her so."

Having delivered himself of those austere remarks, the former lord mayor took his seat, trusting to the sublime law of England to maintain the universal order.

Yet another Crown counsel, Mister Willes, attacked the defendant in familiar Old Bailey rhetoric: "Gentlemen, the prisoner stands indicted of one of the most heinous of crimes. An endeavor, by wilful and corrupt forswearing herself, to take away the life of a guiltless person. And without exaggeration, in the black catalogue of offenses, I know not one of a deeper dye!" Willes clapped both hands hard against his waist for emphasis. There was something fiercely leonine in the way he tossed his wigged head. "It is a perversion and mockery of the laws of her country to the worst of purposes. It is wresting the sword from the hand of justice to shed innocent blood!"

The original trial clerk was called to read the minutes of the trials of Susannah Wells and Mary Squires.

Then another counsel, Mister Davy, took charge of setting out the full case against Elizabeth Canning. He was a thick-set fellow with the pugnacious look and stance of a bulldog. Unlike Willes, however, he didn't bluster, but put his questions with a subtle precision that came to be admired as the trial proceeded.

His chief aim was to establish the whereabouts of the gypsy at the time she allegedly robbed and imprisoned the girl. To this end he produced thirty-eight witnesses, all from labouring towns in the South, who testified that they had seen the old gypsy woman far from Enfield around the New Year and thereafter in January, the period of the alleged assault and incarceration of the girl. The gypsy's son, George (Mary Squires was safely ensconced in Ireland on funds provided by Scarrat and therefore unable to testify), was first called to the stand.

Crown: "We will move directly to your residence at the Wells house. Was it early or late January?"

George Squires: "It was late, your worship."

Crown: "You were not at the Wells house in Enfield on the New Year and days thereafter?"

George Squires: "No, your worship. I keep the days better than my mother or others I know."

Snickering from the gallery.

Crown: "So you were at the Wells house — when did you say?"

George Squires: "Late January, your worship. Isn't that what I already said, your worship?"

Crown: "It was, indeed, Mister Squires. When you resided at the Wells house in late January, did you see Elizabeth Canning there? I mean by Elizabeth Canning the young woman at the bar."

George Squires: "No, I never did. Never saw her in my life before we was took up. If I was to be racked to death, I'd deny seeing this girl. I'll stand with a sword at my heart."

Crown: "I think that will not be necessary, Mister Squires."

Laughter in the gallery was gaveled down.

George Squires: "I'll burn in hellfire if ever I saw this girl till she came with officers in a chaise and they took us up."

Then followed a procession of witnesses: innkeepers, rustics, a plasterer, a blacksmith, two carpenters, a schoolmaster, a maltster, a carter, and a glue maker among others. They all attested to having seen the gypsy during early and middle January in Dorsetshire.

Many of them remarked on her unforgettable ugliness. As a turnip merchant declared, "I never saw a woman more particular in my life."

Mister Davy's relentless case for the Crown was marred only by a rustic who had to be admonished for his appearance and conduct. "How many pots of beer have you drunk today?" fumed Davy.

"I cannot count them beyond my fingers."

Laughter in the gallery.

"You are drunk," declared the Crown counsel angrily, "and ought to be ashamed of it in His Majesty's courtroom!"

Having laid out an imposing array of evidence against the gypsy's participation in the alleged crime, Davy turned next to the Canning testimony. He concentrated on her initial description of the loft and her subsequent versions, attempting to establish the fact that she had constructed her story piecemeal and in truth had never been in the Wells loft until the raiders took her there.

Then he called the Natus couple, who both claimed to have stayed in the Wells loft. The innkeeper Ezra Whiffen swore that he'd seen the Natus woman lying drunk on a mattress in that loft in early January. Three tree pruners testified that they'd exchanged pleasantries with Virtue Hall (who, thanks to Scarrat, never appeared in court and was not, to anyone's knowledge, still present on the face of the earth). They claimed that Virtue and another girl had been leaning from the Wells loft window one afternoon during the time in question.

At the end of three days, having called more witnesses and marshaled more evidence than for any previous trial in the history of English law, the Crown rested its case.

To the relief and satisfaction of the Friends of Canning, her defense attorneys were able to produce twenty-seven witnesses who swore that they'd seen the old gypsy woman around Enfield at the New Year and throughout January.

Then people who'd observed Betty on her return home all testified to her deplorable state of health, which, counsel pointed out, could reasonably account for errors in memory, especially in the recollection of places and events. Moreover, a turnpike keeper on the Hertford Road swore to having seen the girl stumbling along on New Year's night, though at the time he'd judged her drunk. Three witnesses identified Betty as the girl they'd seen a month later walking from Enfield to London, woefully pale and thinly dressed and seemingly dazed. Others came forward to discredit the important testimony of the Natus couple by declaring: "They have very indifferent characters and ought not to be believed upon oath."

Robert Scarrat was called to corroborate the girl's initial description of her place of captivity. Much was made of his being a former constable.

On cross examination the Crown counsel suggested that this particular witness had wilfully encouraged the girl to name Wells and Squires out of some private motive of his own.

This accusation caused a murmur in the gallery.

Mister Scarrat calmly denied it. He stated further that he gave no testimony save the truth before God and remained coolly adamant when Davy questioned him about his repeated visits to Enfield, which were common knowledge in the neighbourhood. Scarrat claimed to have many friends in Enfield and often journeyed out there to visit them. Thwarted by the fellow's unruffled poise, yet generally confident of his own case, Davy chose not to pursue the matter and consequently dismissed Scarrat.

After three days the defense rested.

At a hurried meeting with Lord Sandwich, held in the gilt coach near St. Sepulchre's Church, Scarrat assured his lordship that no matter what happened, Bet Canning would remain safe.

"Safe if acquitted. Trouble if guilty," said Sandwich. "The chit could panic if she ends up in Newgate."

"Not this one, milord. I swear it."

"Yes? You seem to swear often and without success. I say I want her off."

Scarrat agreed. "And so, milord, do I, but I wish to convey the full nature of this girl. She knows where her interest lies."

"Huh, no chit does," Lord Sandwich scoffed.

"This one does."

Scarrat's insistence was surprising. Going up against his lordship's judgement was not what he often did. It made Sandwich's eyebrows arch in disapproval.

"But we should not worry ourselves," concluded Scarrat. "I'm confident the court will bring her in innocent."

"Your confidence is not catching," grumbled Lord Sandwich and waved him out of the coach.

On the seventh day of the trial the court recorder summarized all testimony, nevertheless giving greater weight to the Crown's case.

This was duly noted in the gallery.

He concluded ruefully, "I believe there never happened a greater contrariety of evidence — not to give it a worse name — during the course of any trial in memory than there has been in this one." He emphasized the infamous role played during the Squires and Wells trial by a partisan mob that kept crucial witnesses from appearing who might have prevented the branding of Susannah Wells, let alone the terror known by Mary Squires who could have suffered execution. In spite of Elizabeth Canning's enfeebled condition, which might account for discrepancies in her initial account, the defendant later failed to provide consistent testimony. Two Enfield raiders, Aldridge and Nash, having first believed her story, disbelieved it on discovering how easily she could have escaped from her alleged imprisonment in the Wells house. They'd have so testified at the first trial had they not feared reprisals from the girl's zealous followers. Moreover, although twenty-seven people claimed to have seen the gypsy in or around Enfield at the time of the alleged assault, no two of them could swear to having seen her under the same set of circumstances. The testimony of those people claiming to have noticed the girl on the Hertford Road on New Year's was based on probability alone. On the other hand, witnesses had clearly substantiated the presence of the Natus couple, along with Virtue Hall and another girl, in the hayloft during various times in January.

Admitting freely to his own bias in favor of the Crown's case, the court recorder thus concluded his remarks to the jury: "In the first place, you will consider whether the evidence the defendant gave against Mary Squires can possibly be true. And in the next place, whether you think it probable."

The jury withdrew and returned two hours later with a verdict of Guilty, but not of Wilful and Corrupt Perjury. Upon which the court recorder explained to the jury that he couldn't receive a partial verdict — either they must find her guilty of the whole charge or acquit her.

Twenty minutes later the chastened jury brought in Guilty of Wilful and Corrupt Perjury, upon which the defendant was swiftly ushered across the street and committed to the custody of the keeper of Newgate. By nightfall, a battalion of curious inmates — still divided in their sentiments — surrounded and gawked at this celebrated new prisoner. Some brought her sweetmeats. Others yelled, "Serves you right!" Through the milling and murmuring, Bet Canning sat primly with hands folded in her lap, her glittering eyes fixed straight ahead, a faint smile on her lips.

She had been brought to a ward two floors above the stone hold where the Dog Cull, another renowned convict, lay close to death.

⟡ I believe it was in *Amelia* that I wrote to the effect that misfortune never comes single. From a severe attack of gout I proceeded to fail of dropsy, so that my stomach was tapped and relieved of fourteen quarts of water. For a few days afterwards I was too weak to get out of bed, but then I rallied, for it is true of us Fieldings that though we age rapidly, in compensation we recuperate just as rapidly.

During my recovery I read with great distress the verdict in the Canning trial. I have not changed my opinion of the poor girl, as given in my pamphlet *Clear State of the Case of Elizabeth Canning* that "she is a poor, honest, innocent, simple girl, and the most unhappy and most injured of human beings." I ask her detractors

(who are also mine for my part in the affair) where the girl had
been all that month? Was it ever proved she was not held at the
Wells house? Not at all. And surely she returned home in a
deplorable condition, in rags and emaciated. How had this come
about? She had not earned a bad character in her home of
Aldermanbury. The malicious suggestion that she'd rid herself
of an unwanted child during that time was contradicted by
the medical evidence. As for a lover whisking her away, was
any fellow named, let alone produced?

I inquired of three of the seventeen judges on the bench at her
trial, and they all agreed that the girl's counsel made a poor figure
'in court, whereas the recorder, charged with giving an objective
and neutral account of the defense and prosecution's arguments,
did noticeably err in presenting the Crown's case more vigorously.

The fact remains there was an extraordinary conflict of evidence.
It was not, to my satisfaction, ever proved where the gypsy had
spent the month, nor was a plausible alternative given to Elizabeth
Canning's account of the incarceration. I can only conclude that
the verdict of perjury against this poor girl constitutes a grave
judicial blunder.

I think my risen ire at this miscarriage of justice had a
benevolent effect on my health, for when I climbed from the sick-
bed, I called for pen and ink and began a long cherished project of
mine, namely to refute the philosophy of Henry St. John, Viscount
Bolingbroke, as collected in five quarto volumes. The gloomy,
sarcastic, bitter man had died three years prior, but his *Works* have
remained to promulgate the ideas of deists, who wish to destroy
the tenets of orthodox Christianity. I do agree with the fiery
William Warburton, who calls the *Works* "bulky volumes of red-
hot impiety."

Having made a careful study of Bolingbroke's essays, I feel the
best way to assail them is first to point out their inconsistencies
of reasoning, their ambiguities, and their misinterpretations of
Christian authorities. But as is my wont, I'll approach my treatise
in a satirical way. I intend to suggest that Bolingbroke never
meant to be taken seriously, but in truth put forward such ideas
merely to expose and ridicule them while pretending to defend
such sacrilegious tenets. In other words, his *Works* were a jest at
the expense of fashionable attacks on natural religion.

Though a tempering of the gout has let me go abroad again, I
find more of my time, when not in court, is spent on literary
endeavours as of old. Along with the commentary on

Bolingbroke's *Works,* I have decided to ready a new edition of *Jonathan Wild* for the press. Originally a satire on Robert Walpole, I would change it to reveal the follies of all great men. The vehicle of this satire was the infamous Wild, who earlier in this age had fashioned a veritable army from hundreds of thieves, commanding them like a general. In wanting to prepare a new edition of this work, which features London's underworld as analogous to politics, I also thought of the Dog Cull, whom Saunders Welch had successfully taken. It is a sorry comment on our day and age that we lionize felons of his ilk, while neglecting men of genius such as Bishop Berkeley, who not only hath given us a philosophy of considerable merit but also such a medical treatise as *Philosophical Reflections and Inquiries concerning the Virtues of Tar Water,* which I have lately read and of which I approve.

Along with Doctor Ward's Drop, I have, in accordance with the bishop's prescription, begun an extensive dosing of myself, morning and evening, with half a pint of tar water, a beverage in common use among the Indians of the Americas.

I believe these remedies, together with the beneficial aspect of anger at the Canning verdict, are responsible for my improved health. I wish to write again, not only briefs and opinions of law, but stories — perhaps a long work similar to *Tom Jones.* Why should it be out of the question as long as I draw breath? Surely a new breath of hope and anticipation blows through me these days. So did I tell my sister Sarah, who hath come to live with us in the final days of Mary's pregnancy, as she wishes to be of help at the time of confinement. I told Sarah she could rest easy about my future. I was brisk as a colt. And I was gratified when Sarah put her hand on my arm and exclaimed, "Indeed, I believe you are." That ominous look of hers in Bath hath been put from my mind.

[45]

PRAISE GOD, he was coming around at last.

She'd been at his side for more than a week now — the exact

number of days forgotten — fearful, most of the time, that he would die. Praise God.

Clare dipped a rag into a bucket of water, wrung it out, and placed the wet cloth on his brow. Ned's eyelids were fluttering, as he began at last to come around. She looked fondly at the haggard face which had been so ruggedly handsome when first he'd asked her to take refreshment as they stood outside the millinery shop. She'd never confessed to it, but her heart had gone out to him even in those first moments, no matter how hard she would later struggle against it. She'd been drawn irresistibly to him in spite of common sense, for he lacked the bearing of a London merchant — the sort of man other girls had set their caps at. And by the time she was sure of what she'd already suspected, that life with him would be uncertain at best, she was hopelessly lost.

It was in truth a strange working of fate, because from girlhood she'd vowed never to join her destiny with a man who couldn't provide in a steady way. Her father had worked on a Sussex farm, a tall merry man till he lost his place and from the shame of it vanished one fine day, leaving her mother with a child to feed and no money. Clare had seen the drudgery, the loneliness, the twin horrors of poverty and ill health. She'd learned from watching her poor mother how a woman could labour herself into an early grave. She'd vowed never to face a similar fate, and yet what was she facing now? Her man lay weakened almost to death by fever, with a capital trial to come, while his child stirred in her belly.

But at least he was alive. Praise God, he was coming around. It was hard to believe now that such a sweet man had even taken purses in dark lanes, had ever threatened a soul. In his gentle hands a flower was safe. His hands. That ruined hand was the cause of his trouble. Those five fingers had in truth turned both of their lives around.

Dear lad. She'd suffered horribly when he failed to return from his business that day. In her mind she saw him lying dead among barrel staves and garbage, done in by the grey-faced man whom Molly feared so much. She'd been frantic frantic frantic from the moment he'd left her, ignoring her pleas, letting nothing move him from his purpose. And of course she understood the nature of his resolve. He was thinking of the child, no other's child but his. She knew in her heart he was the father. She'd have known it even had she not taken precautions, insisting on armour for all the others. God would not let this particular prayer of hers go unheeded. With him she'd had the overwhelming desire for closeness — no scratchy impersonal linen sheath, but the man himself, the dear man, his warmth and meaning and the pulse of his life.

Sometimes he reminded her of the young farmers she'd once known who came shambling into the village with their hard muscles and downcast eyes. When first she lay with Ned, her feelings had been strange. No other man had roused her that way, although in spite of revulsion at selling her embraces, she'd been brought by some of those men to the ecstatic peak. But none of them had made her proud of feeling such ecstasy until this lad came along. He let her feel both wild and peaceful almost at the same moment. Praise God for the feeling.

During the first days of his disappearance, she'd gone out of her mind in a different, most terrible way. She'd sickened herself on gin and prayed aloud to God Almighty, until she was hoarse, for a word of comfort.

Then the word did come, though it came not from God but from the grinning mouth of a stooped old man rakishly twirling a cane. He'd stood in the doorway of Ned's lodging, ogling her, mouthing a most peculiar speech about his chum Ned and improvident circumstances which somehow had led to him revealing for a few guineas Ned's whereabouts to certain people, though not with the purpose of doing harm.

What people? she'd asked with such eagerness that the startled old man, in backing off, knocked against his companion, a redheaded one-eyed boy, who fell flush against the hallway wall.

Clare had learned then from the stammering, sniveling, hangdog old man that Ned had been taken by Bow Street Runners, that he'd been held overnight by a constable, and the next day had been transported to Newgate. Anything more than that must be discovered through considerable expense, and since they, meaning himself and his ninny here, were short on funds at the moment, they'd come in humble appeal to her sweet generous nature for help, as the dear lad must be saved from the capital charge of murder of a vile miscreant who had, as they were staunch witnesses of the scene and presentable in a court for consideration of their time and effort, meaning they required but a pittance of recompense for such sworn testimony . . .

For a moment the old man forgot the drift of his words and scratched his grizzly chin to recall it. Then he continued, swearing on his honour that the brutish scamp had drawn on poor Ned first and wrongly and criminally and had killed the lad's fine sheep dog just before, in self-defense, Ned took him off with a pistol ball.

The old fellow was still sniveling and stammering when Clare had raced past the pair of them and down the stairway and into the nightmare world of Newgate Prison.

Events had followed too swiftly for her to sort them out well in memory: bribing her way into the stone hold; finding the dear boy raving of hellfire and his body as hot as that; arranging through another bribe for his removal to a cleaner ward; watching him hover between life and death for days, each of them seeming to her as long as her own life.

But he was coming around now, praise God.

A woman, ambling along through the ward, bent down and whispered in her ear, "Good work, dearie. You won me a bet. I put two shillings you'd get him around."

Ned's eyes slowly opened. He was saying something.

Clare leaned forward and heard him murmur, "Leave."

"I stay," Clare told him.

He spoke again, again she leaned close, and again he commanded her to leave.

"I stay." Turning, she yelled for the warder. She'd give the man money to bring a bowl of hot porridge.

For the next three days she rarely left Ned's side except to get food and medicine. As a few other wives of fortunate prisoners did, Clare paid daily for the privilege of remaining in the ward. Ned understood that her funds were rapidly dwindling, for everything cost dear in Newgate. Still, he stopped protesting, as nothing he might say or threaten in his weakened condition would stop this woman. What a worthy mother she'd make!

At night she lay beside him on the hay-strewn floor, wrapping them in a single blanket. Holding his hand, she whispered about the coming trial. Hadn't he shot in self-defense? And if so, couldn't he be granted transport to the Americas? Couldn't she arrange passage on the same vessel? Or on one leaving at the same time for the same destination? Or a nearby destination, so when she arrived she might book passage to where he landed?

Ned gave her short replies of vague hope. Often they said little for hours, merely holding each other under the single blanket, walling themselves off from the noise of cards and carousing in the ward. Their thoughts moved into a hoped-for future together, so that sometimes the past and present fell away. It was strange, but they both confessed to having a deep sense of permanence, as if this prison was the dream and their dream of a better life the reality. Their modest embraces within the blanket seemed infinitely fulfilling, out of time.

Then on the fifth day, without help, Ned got to his feet, walked unsteadily across the ward, and leaned against a wall. "Because of you, lass, I'm strong again," he said, and added bluntly, "so now you must go."

Clare smiled wanly. "You thank me, then turn me out?"

"This is a terrible place to be. You're carrying a child."

"I'll go but come back tomorrow."

"Don't come back."

"Ah, you vex me, lad."

"Swear never to come back."

"I won't swear."

"Swear."

"I won't, I won't swear, and I'll come back."

"What of the child?"

She patted her belly, a gentle swell beginning there. "What of him? He's fine. Tomorrow I'll be back."

Before they could part, however, a warder came along and informed Ned of his trial in two days at the Old Bailey Sessions. "Do you want me sending counsel?" asked the warder.

"No. I've seen them sulking around like rats," Ned said. "I've seen them bleed people dry. It's not the law they follow, it's their greed. I'll stand by myself."

Shrugging, the warder said, "Can't blame you. It's a rare thing to see an honest lawyer here. But standing by yourself? I don't know."

"I'll stand by myself and ask mercy."

"Ah, mercy." The warder spat and went on.

"In two days." Clare grew pale. "I'll be at the Sessions. You won't deny me that."

"No, I dare not," he replied, touching her arm with his bad hand, "as you'd be there anyway."

The next day two bailiffs took Ned from the ward. In the fetters office his irons were knocked off and in a nearby room he was ordered to strip and wash himself in a tubful of vinegar. This had been common practice since the Black Sessions, when four of six judges and forty jurors died of a fever contracted from prisoners brought into Justice Hall. Ned sponged himself with the vinegar, happy to do it, as the tart pungent liquid cooled and tightened his skin. The physical cleaning even gave him a moment of hope. Verdicts of Guilty for capital offenses did not always lead to Tyburn, given extenuating circumstances, and often a sentence of hanging was commuted.

But his hope faded when they took him through the south gate into the Old Bailey, where footsteps echoed like doom in the lofty halls. Daylight slanting down from high windows seemed icy, remote. Doors swung wide. In the great Sessions Hall, above the tall chair of the court president, stood a dun-colored statue of a relentless Madam Justice, who gazed sternly down on the prisoner, on the court officers filing in, and on the presiding judge, who held a brine-soaked kerchief against his nose to make the stench of prison — it drifted in with anyone brought from Newgate — at least tolerable.

Standing in the dock, Ned stared curiously at the curved bench, the black curtained windows, the heavy pillars behind which a number of spectators sat in a gallery (though his gaze went rapidly over them, as he feared what the effect of seeing Clare among them might have on him). Law was the glory of England. His father had once sat him down on the hearth and said, "Lad, you listen now. If it ever comes to the law with you, know that this is England. Nowhere under heaven can a man have justice save in His Majesty's kingdom. Stand for yourself. Trust the law and God save the king."

The idea of justice had Ned spinning, as he watched the officials move solemnly toward their benches. If he explained to them that he could get no work in London, perhaps they'd understand what had brought him to this day. As the court procedure swung into motion, once again his hope soared.

Without delay the jury was chosen. Since none were challenged, they were sworn forthwith by the clerk of arraigns: "You shall well and truly try and true deliverance make, between our Sovereign Majesty the King and the prisoner at the bar whom you have in charge; and a true verdict give according to the evidence, so help you God!"

It sounded fine and fancy to Ned. The severe words gave him hope of receiving just punishment, whatever that might be. He'd have it and suffer what he must and then take Clare and their child into the North Country and there do what he did best, herd sheep and train dogs, and think back on this as a kind of nightmare fashioned by God to admonish him for seeking his fortune in a terrible town.

The indictment was being read. Then the king's counsel identified himself, after which witnesses for the prosecution were called.

A rough-looking waterman claimed that the prisoner had ripped his purse from his belt. It was a thick purse, holding his whole life's savings, as he was taking it to buy a Thames boat. Another rough fellow in coarse linen swore to having witnessed the cruel attack. So did another. Three others saw the prisoner aim and fire his pistol at a gentleman who was crying "Thief" by way of helping the robbed victim. Ned didn't need to search for Scarrat in the gallery to know that the man would not be there, though surely as the sun comes up he'd sent these watermen. For not much more than a few gins, they'd readily perjure themselves. Bostock didn't testify, perhaps because he'd made himself scarce. Nor was Scarrat or Giles called, nor did a single witness mention them, though a horse dealer came to the stand and maintained having seen the pouch on the defendant when he'd left a tavern.

Having refused counsel, Ned had no right to cross-examine witnesses or address the jury or give evidence in his own behalf. The presiding judge, who sat tall and imposing on the bench above him, would ask the questions for him. Ned must depend, as his father had taught him, on the pure reason and balanced fairness and human mercy of English law. Ned looked up with a hopeful smile at the handsome man in full-bottomed wig, unaware that John

Swinnerton was sitting as a presiding trial judge for the last time, having just been appointed to the high office of attorney general, and for this reason had his mind fixed more on his own future than on the fate of a footpad who stood mute, without legal aid.

A constable went to the bar and set the amount of stolen coin at two hundred pounds.

Swinnerton raised his eyebrows — a theft of forty shillings was worth death. This saucy lad had got away with enough gold to buy a deserving gentleman a nice parcel of land.

Then a Bow Street Runner described the pursuit into an infamous part of London, where the thief was finally apprehended. No mention was made of a street urchin, a black boy, whose knowledge of the labyrinthine passages and bolt-holes of the district had enabled the pursuers to waylay the prisoner. By vigilance and new methods of thief taking, maintained the Runner, he and his companions had ended the career of a notorious criminal.

Then the king's attorney suggested that the prisoner was in fact the footpad called the Dog Cull.

Judge Swinnerton looked directly at the prisoner for the first time. "Was there on him a written name or other way to so identify him?"

"No, your worship."

"Inadmissible," Swinnerton ruled tersely, but continued to study the young prisoner with interest.

Swiftly the prosecution rested its case.

Swinnerton leaned forward to address the prisoner. "The testimony of witnesses has you robbing the man seated there and then discharging your pistol at a gentleman coming to his aid. What say you?"

"I never robbed that man seated there. I killed the man with him in self-defense when they both drew on me."

"It is your claim you never robbed the man."

"Yes, your worship."

"One witness has you coming from a tavern with the money. What say you?"

"No, your worship."

"That you had the money on you?"

"I had money on me, but I did not come from a tavern."

"You had money on you, so you did not take it from the man claiming you did."

"That is true, your worship," Ned declared with satisfaction.

"Was this money yours by honest labour?"

"Honest?" Ned glanced around nervously. "It was due me." He struggled for more words. The gold might be looked upon as a reward for . . . or more properly as a punishment of a great nobleman who had blasphemed . . . debauched . . . who had committed sins against — He felt suddenly confused in such a public view. It seemed impossible to explain with all these eyes on him how he must escape from London with his dear pregnant girl. "It was mine by . . . right," he said, pausing again.

"Perhaps, sir, you go by the principle that might makes right." Having tired of this questioning, the judge left off further examination and charged the jury.

They had no need to withdraw, as so often happened in cases of patent guilt. Whispering among themselves, they arrived at Guilty of Grand Theft, Assault, and Murder as Charged.

Judge Swinnerton gaveled. "Nathaniel Carleton, rise. You are a young man who does not in appearance seem hardened to crime, yet you've taken a man's life savings from his hands, which is perfidious enough, and then you've taken a man's life, the life of someone bent upon defending a fellow citizen, which determines me not to recommend you to the king's mercy upon sentencing. Remove him from this court." He thumped the gavel hard.

Rough hands seized the prisoner who, at this juncture of events, searched the gallery and found her face — her mouth an O of dismay, her eyes wide, her hands to her ears as if to keep out the memory of a judge's resounding words.

Then he was hauled back to Newgate, there to await sentencing tomorrow, at the end of current Sessions.

When Clare left, head bowed, she nearly collided with a man waiting outside the Old Bailey.

Looking up, she saw who it was and why she'd nearly bumped into him. It was Mister Scarrat.

"He's been a jolly good boy," the grey-faced man said with a smile. "But tell him we brook no defiance."

"I will, sir."

"Repeat what I said to tell him."

"He's been a jolly good boy. But tell him you brook —"

"*We* brook. Repeat it."

"He's been a jolly good boy. But tell him we brook no defiance."

"There's a pretty lass. Molly makes a good report of you. 'A good, calm, quiet girl,' she says."

"I thank Molly."

"Maybe some day," Scarrat said with a grin, "you'll thank me."

"Yes, sir."

"Go now and tell him." He handed over a small money pouch. "This is for the guard so you can stay as long as you wish."

"Thank you, sir," she muttered shakily.

"My pleasure."

On May 30, 1754, the countess of Northumberland wrote in her diary, "Yesterday home from cards. Voided a large stone, which gave much pain. Tired to death of too much company. Went to Ball. Tired to death of it. A bad supper. Miss Townshend drunk."

That same day the Venetian ambassador in a fine gilded barge landed with fanfare at the Tower.

That day, to prepare for Samuel Foote's new play, a theatre in the Haymarket had the chandeliers brought down from over the stage and the three hundred tallow candles replaced.

And on that same day Elizabeth Canning was taken to the Old Bailey for sentencing.

Her counsel's request for a new trial was denied, much to the satisfaction of Sir Crisp Gascoyne, who'd laboured so doggedly to see justice done and who heard through the announcement of denial the entire universe click securely into place, as if the huge key of English law had turned in an eternal lock.

Elizabeth Canning then rose and in a voice calm if scarcely audible read a prepared plea for leniency. "I hope your lordships will be favourable. I had no intent of swearing away the gypsy's life. What has been done was only defending myself. I desire to be considered unfortunate."

Eight members of the court wished to give her a light sentence of six months' imprisonment, but Chief Justice Rawlinson, fearing the sentence would be a diversion rather than a punishment, observed coldly, "Collections have been made for her amounting to considerable sums of money. If her sentence is merely to remain in Newgate for six months, there will be more sums collected in her behalf for assemblies of gaiety each night of her confinement."

Nine members of the court, a majority, voted then for one month in Newgate to be followed by transportation to an American colony for a period of seven years.

At last satisfied, the chief justice peered down at the girl and added, "If within that time you return and are found at large in any of His Majesty's dominions of Great Britain and Ireland, you will suffer death as a felon without benefit of clergy."

Making no outcry, the slight young woman bowed her head humbly and in wrist irons returned to Newgate. In satins, her weeping mother followed.

Another prisoner was led into Justice Hall for sentencing, this time with Justice William Murray presiding.

"Nathaniel Carleton," said Murray, "you stand convicted of capital crimes without any degree of mitigating circumstances. This court does therefore adjudge that you be taken back to the place from whence you came and there await your fate. Between twenty-five and thirty June, depending, you will be taken to the common place of execution and hanged by the neck till you are dead dead dead."

The prison chaplain, standing beside Ned, pronounced "Amen."

Judge Murray brought his gavel down and said, "Constable, do your duty."

Stepping forward, a uniformed constable slipped a leather cord around Ned's right thumb, thereby illustrating the meaning of the magistrate's words. As the noose tightened around the thumb, so would the rope tighten around the condemned man's neck.

At this very moment Samuel Johnson, who lived nearby in Gough Street, threw down a quill and kneaded his cramped fingers. For his dictionary he'd just finished a definition for the word *whist:* "A game at cards, requiring close attention and silence." Tomorrow he'd begin with the word *whistle.*

And whistle was what the grey-faced man did as he left the Old Bailey. People looked curiously at him, for such a merry sound seemed peculiar coming as it did from such a saturnine face.

This time someone was waiting for him.

Sobbing, Clare gripped his sleeve, which startled Robert Scarrat, who was unaccustomed to people touching him familiarly.

"Sir, please, I beg you —" she began.

"I know your mind, miss, so I'll be frank," he said in a chilling voice. "The man's a rogue, a thief, a vicious footpad who used a dog to rob innocents and took a man's life savings and killed another. These be facts. I'll have nothing to do with him."

"But you said '*we* brook no defiance.' You and others have been in league with Ned and now you've deserted him."

"He told you so?"

Clare shook her head. "He'll say nothing. But I beg you to help him."

"I did have minor business with him, yes, but it's scarcely worth mentioning. I'd no idea he was such a scoundrel. I command his compliance. Should he ever reveal that me and my companions knew him, it'll go hard with his."

"With his?"

Scarrat looked at her coldly. "With anyone having to do with him."

She took a deep breath. "Sir, I'll be frank too. I think you find me pleasing." She paused, studying his grey impassive face. "You led me to think so yesterday."

"And?"

"If you help him, believe me, my person is wholly at your disposal."

"Oh, I don't doubt it. At Mrs. Adams' shop it was quite at the disposal of any who had the price of it. Don't forget my knowledge of you through Molly. And I do find you pleasing." He doffed his tricorn in mock courtesy. "But that's for another time, miss, not now. I'll say it once and never again. The lad's been a good lad, and for that reason you're safe. Maintain that safety, miss. Say no more, do no more. Let justice be served and go your ways. Be so kind, miss, as to allow me to take my leave." Without a glance her way, Scarrat turned and hastened into a crowd milling about the entrance of the Old Bailey, where yet another sentencing was in progress.

[46]

❡ Reader, I first laid eyes on the prisoner during one of my tours of Newgate Prison, as it was my self-imposed obligation, when healthy, to visit each session the wretched inmates there, many of whom I had condemned to the infernal place. It was a grim duty, but undertaken to serve warning on myself that neither illness nor fatigue ought to stay the exercise of good judgement when I put on the wig of a magistrate. Though I was still possessed of a gout, an asthma, a jaundice, and of late a visceral dropsy, I had rallied in recent days sufficiently to hobble that afternoon into the prison.

A turnkey always accompanied me on one of these somber inspections, the aim being to protect the architect of Bow Street justice but also in hope of proper reward at its conclusion. Coming to the iron door of a common ward, I instructed him to open it, which he did with a scornful look, as if to say no good would come of a sick old man nosing about here. When the door swung back, I stood in the entranceway and looked at the pathetic crowd whose wretched faces were thrown into deep relief by glowing dots of flame from candle ends. As Virgil says, Now is the time for courage. But my own faltered at the sight of so much misery.

I walked among them awhile, protected by the turnkey's warnings and cudgel. When we returned to the hall and the door behind us shut with a metallic ring, the guard gave me a mean smile, having seen from my face how the ward had affected my humour. He wished to know had I seen enough for the day, and without awaiting my reply (assured he had it), turned on his heel to leave. But today the inspection would not be complete till I braved the Condemned hole. I felt the instructional need of looking into the eyes of someone awaiting the final judgement of our law.

Grumbling at my decision to continue, the guard led the way down to the basement cells from which the condemned were finally taken and thence carted to their deaths. As we went down slowly, the turnkey complained of Methodists, who had put him into a pet since morning. Dressed in somber black and granted permission by the keeper, they'd come marching, hymnals in hand, down to the Condemned hole where they sang and swayed and begged God's mercy for the prisoners.

Though in my opinion such zealots delude themselves with canting sermons — indeed, there's more gunfire in them than in a brace of cannon — I could see no harm in their visit. When I suggested the purpose of their coming here had been to solace the condemned, the turnkey gave me such a glance of temper that I gripped the head of my cane more tightly.

"Damned if they left a grain of spirit within these walls. Damn my eyes." Moodily he drew a dirty sleeve across his brow, then fumbled with a heavy ring of keys. "If these rascals here take to religion, you can look forward to nothing but sniveling in the carts. They'll die like so many psalm-singing weavers." He unlocked the first cell. "Save this one. He'll make your worship take notice. When they nub him at Tyburn, he'll do us credit or I never set eyes on a proper cutthroat. This be the Dog Cull, a likely man, say what you will."

The Dog Cull! An episode of gout had prevented me from arraigning him when my runners took him. I'd heard of this trial and sentencing, but had put him out of my mind until now. I was instantly curious to see him, in part for his reputation and in part as he'd occasioned a good public response to Bow Street's method of thief taking.

The turnkey pushed the door open into a tiny windowless cell, dimly lit by a single candle in a broken dish. There was straw on the floor, a narrow bench, but the prisoner wasn't sitting on it. Indeed, against a wall slimy with moisture stood a tall young man in rumpled clothes that had once been fashionable. He was fastened with three bars of iron that were clamped to his ankles and his groin — the terrible shears.

The turnkey called the prisoner "Little Dearie" and asked him if the darbies suited him that the fetters officer had chosen for his lordship with such diligence, judging a heavier iron more to his taste during his stay in the palace. He made other sallies meant for sarcastic humour, though none of them brought a look of anger or dismay to the Dog Cull's countenance.

In the flickering candlelight I studied his features and found them to my liking, for along with the ageless virtue of youth, they had manly proportions and spoke of confidence, though a gauntness in the cheeks hinted of a recent illness (and who better

than myself to judge of it?). I was particularly struck by the
forceful chin, the unwavering look in his eyes. He was not your
hard-bitten footpad with a glance of ratlike rapacity. Even in those
oppressive shears he stood as tall as I — and I stand taller than
most fellows in a crowd. I fixed my attention then on his
left hand, the fingers of which were absolutely rigid, as though
encased in plaster, set in a half-clenched attitude. A ridged scar,
covering it, gave his skin the webbed look of a duck's foot. While
I was appraising the prisoner's robust chest and the massive
forearms of an ironmonger or a village smithy, the turnkey
continued with his abusive humour.

I told him that was enough of that talk and asked the prisoner
his name.

"Nathaniel Carleton, sir."

"I am Justice Fielding of Bow Street."

Raising his eyebrows in what seemed a hopeful manner,
Nathaniel Carleton opened his mouth as if to speak. This he
appeared ready to do for a moment longer, but then, with a
dignity I couldn't help but admire, he inclined his head in silent
acknowledgement of my office.

Shortly thereafter I was following the turnkey up the stairway,
taking care not to stumble on the uneven stones and cast myself
down, as it seemed hardly reasonable to add a broken leg to the
sum of my infirmities. As we neared the prison entrance, I ordered
the turnkey to have the fetters officer strike off those Shears and
give the prisoner some wrist cuffs, as it was disgraceful to torture
a man soon to lose his life.

The turnkey growled deeply in his throat, so furious did my
instruction render him, and I had the feeling that the Shears
had been employed at his own devilish instigation, for nothing
more than the sport of it. To soothe his disappointment that the
torment would now end, I thrust into his grimy hand a crown
for accompanying me on my rounds — and for doing my
bidding. I hobbled a few feet away, then turned and cautioned
him of my intention to confirm on the morrow that my wishes
had been carried out.

Outside the dark walls of Newgate, I hailed a coach and was
soon on my way to an appointment at Clifton's, a chop house of
distinction in Butchers Row near the Temple. The late afternoon
thoroughfares throbbed with the sound of commerce and church
bells and street criers. Oil drums boomed on their thunderous

descent into shop cellars, hammers thudded in scaffolding, and pulleys whined as they hoisted barrels into warehouses. The clamour was loudest in lanes choked with delivery wagons and carriages, as carmen and drovers hurled indifferently meant oaths at one another and horses snorted in collision. I'd not have traded the rough lanes of London for all the grand streets of Rome and Paris. I was a true-born Englishman, come what may, who gloried in the coarse but vibrant sights of this town. Perhaps London pulsed that day with an especial vigour because of my visit to Newgate. I could not remove from memory the sight of that broad-shouldered youth standing erect against the wall, entrapped by a thick webbing of iron and awaiting the gallows. That we live while others die is oft-times an unfortunate but powerful stimulant to enjoyment, and thus did the streets of London seem aglow in beauty to a sick man who'd recently left the Condemned hole of Newgate.

When I arrived at Clifton's, my dining companion was already seated at a corner table before a flagon of wine, in his hand a long clay pipe.

It is, I think, a victory of consequence if, in later years, we can still number among our companions those with whom we spent our youth. Such a victory was mine through a continued friendship with George Lyttelton, a schoolmate at Eton. He got to his feet, a tall lanky fellow of awkward carriage and meagre face, to give me a warm greeting. His voice was as thin as his body, but capable of eloquent debate in Parliament. He was a man who kept his troubles to himself, though it was common knowledge that he'd married a shrewish woman hard on the death of his first wife.

I asked him how he did. As usual he replied that he did wonderfully. I might have been hearing again the voice of my schoolmate who, after punishment and with tears in his eyes, would turn to tell us all that he did wonderfully.

That day I showed a cowardly lack of restraint in airing the causes of my continued discomfort. Each ailment came in for its rightful share of the blame. Poor Lyttelton looked so distressed that I revealed my little secret — in recent days I had been rallying wonderfully.

Then I turned to my Newgate visit, describing the turnkey who would hang people like laundry, but dwelling most particularly on the young prisoner. Of course, Lyttelton had heard of him. I spoke at length of the windowless cell, the terrible Shears, and the dignified way in which Nathaniel Carleton bore it all.

Though a benevolent man, Lyttelton withheld his own compassion, for the broadsides hawked on the street corner were filled with sensational accounts of the Dog Cull's rapes and murders and torturing of children.

At this I laughed, and in the perspective of my laughter, he saw his own gullibility and joined me in laughter. I observed that if nature hadn't taken a provident care to do me otherwise, I might have been a footpad myself, awaiting the gallows rather than supping with a baron of England.

Lyttelton agreed with the sense of that observation, yet added rather trenchantly that too much leniency of spirit was perhaps a hindrance in my profession.

Our oysters came, Whitstable, none better in my opinion. But not even food, which hath always done so much to lift my spirits, could dispel the effect of his gentle criticism, for it came from a most generous man, who had used his considerable influence to get me my post of justice of the peace for Westminster. Our relationship forced me to defend myself from the charge of being soft in dealing with felons, as, in fact, I had never been.

If he suggested, so I argued, that men must sometimes restrain the impetuosity of their benevolence, I heartily agreed. I did it myself almost every day that I took the bench. A man of good nature ought to behold all injuries done by one person to another with indignation. A villain should be an enemy to every lover of mankind, as Cicero hath told us. Tender-heartedness in the face of barbarity, I continued, is barbarity itself, and resembles the meek spirit of him who would not assist in blowing up his neighbor's house to save a whole city in flames.

I wondered in making this somewhat pompous speech if I might not be protesting too much. So apparently did Lyttelton wonder, as he nodded gravely and said, "So you won't help this contemptible fellow to some kind of pardon?"

"It surprises me that you consider I might do such a thing. In fact, it wounds me."

At this juncture Lyttelton begged my forgiveness. Our mutton came, and with it a change of conversation. But even as we talked, I was in no small measure bewildered that my dear friend and I had come nearly to a warm disagreement over a condemned prisoner. Beyond my knowing, I had conveyed more feeling of compassion for a notorious felon — I, a magistrate sworn to uphold the law — than a man of conscience such as George Lyttelton could tolerate.

But a hearty meal and good wine have ever left me young again, as strapping in mind as once I was in body, and with hopes as high, so when we left the chop house and parted, I clasped my companion's thin frame and gave him the most affectionate of embraces.

Through the evening streets, now dotted with the bobbing torches of linkboys, I returned by sedan chair to my home in Bow Street. There, with more liberality than a man sensible of his pocketbook might have done, I tipped the two chairmen who'd carried me.

There was a lull in sessions and my brother John, as a recently appointed new magistrate, was on duty at Bow Street, so I had rare leisure the next day to do what I pleased. Bidding my wife an affectionate farewell, I pulled on a great-coat, gripped the damnable cane, and left the house. I would have walked through the brisk morning of spring had the gout given me permission, but considering myself lucky just to be upright on both feet, I took a hackney coach to Newgate. Indeed, Newgate. For I meant to see the young felon again.

How had a lad of such worthy bearing come to such a pass? I couldn't help but regard him as a singular illustration of my long-held belief that most crime results from an improvident desire for luxury. Perhaps he'd turned to robbery as a means of obtaining enough gold to show himself at Ranelagh or lay wagers on the cocks or buy a velvet coat. Surely of all men, I myself could understand a passionate love of extravagance in someone young. At a similar age I'd yearned for baubles and comforts that were forthcoming, not through violence, but through another method without honour — I had squandered the estate of my dear wife Charlotte, who was caused much sorrow by my unlicensed conviviality long before the Creator chose to take her from my grasp to His bosom.

Perhaps I was drawn to the Dog Cull because of the harm done by my own prodigality. Perhaps I was confirming my belief in a thin line separating judge and thief. Montaigne, that incomparable observer of the human comedy, hath remarked to similar effect that there is no man so good who, did he submit his thoughts and actions to the law, would not deserve hanging at least ten times in his life.

Upon arriving at Newgate, I did not encounter the irascible turnkey of yesterday, but was accompanied by one equally irascible, who complained on the way to the Condemned hole that some bastard had ordered the Shears taken from the Dog Cull. Just as we reached the Condemned hole, from the Dog Cull's tiny cell emerged a young woman in a black cloak.

Indeed, so great was her haste, that she nearly collided with my cane, and gave me a wonderfully startled look, for doubtless the sight of such a fellow as me in the dim hall of a dungeon might well have affrighted anyone, to say nothing of a young creature whose form and countenance I had but the flash of a moment to study, yet managed in that short time to commit (I'd realize by nightfall) almost perfectly to memory: the complexion of her oval face was fair, if a little impaired by the sun; her black brows had a curve to them beyond the power of art to imitate; her lustrous dark eyes were widely spaced above high-boned cheeks, giving her a somewhat feline expression; she possessed a soft round throat, as if filled by unsung song; of special delight was a wisp of auburn hair which, escaping the domino's hood, had curled below her dimpled chin to a finely turned neck.

The fleeting apparition of her splendid figure (for so it seemed within the open confines of her cloak) bid me halt in my tracks, crane my head around, and mark her hurried progress down the hall till she was gone up the staircases. Perhaps contributing to the strong impression she'd made on me was the surprise of our meeting in such a wretched place, but I beg you to understand, Reader, that I've rarely been so taken by female beauty as at the moment. Indeed, I stood leaning on the cane for some moments after she'd disappeared.

I was surprised again, as a turnkey had also emerged from the cell and was curiously regarding me. Then he and the warder who'd brought me down exchanged grins. Embarrassed by being caught at such close scrutiny of a young woman, I told them I was going in alone. My escort was to remain outside.

Inside the cell, though no longer wearing the Shears, stood Nathaniel Carleton — did he ever sit? I was gratified to see him wearing lightweight wrist cuffs, but the air here was filled with the stench of human offal. It shamed the humanity of Newgate's keeper to leave buckets standing uncleansed in the Condemned hole. Surely the practice was meant for punishment and humiliation, but it was not part of a man's sentence. I blushed at the thought that the prisoner's young visitor had been forced to converse with him so near to a degradation so intimate.

Yelling for the turnkey, I ordered him to replace the bucket, to bring a lantern, and to fetch some sort of blanket, as the bench on which the prisoner slept was unprovided with a covering at all. The turnkey hurried away to carry out commands delivered to him in the most imperious manner I could summon.

When I turned to the prisoner, he spoke his first words of the day to me, which were of gratitude for my making him more comfortable. His voice was deep and resonant, his accent of the North Country, but his manner of speaking was sufficiently unlearned to belie the dignity of his bearing. It was probable that while his education must have been modest, his instincts possessed a kind of fittingness which, as we all know, is often refined by education into delicacy of expression. I was all the more taken by him because of his untutored excellence.

I sat on the cold bench, the cane across my lap. Without more prelude, I bid him tell me his story.

Pacing back and forth, he spoke in a halting way, beginning with his arrival in London at about the same time my doomed child *Amelia* appeared in the bookstalls.

[47]

¶ The story he told differed in many ways from those I'd heard from the bench. What especially interested me was his vain attempt to save the woman in the burning building, as he had lost his goods and the use of one hand because of it. Cervantes, whose own life was filled with such ironical events, taught us to expect the opposite of what we think will be. This prisoner had meant to help and so was rendered helpless. An act of bravery and concern for one person led to crime against many people. Irony resides at the heart of things, I told him. Thus, good and bad often become each other. Indeed, the same reasons will equally prove the existence of good and bad, love and hatred. And I might have added, though it would have meant nothing to Ned Carleton, that I thus refute Mandeville's doctrine of pure evil, as nothing is pure.

Having delivered this little homily, I was surprised by the prisoner's smile, as if my words had amused him. I had the strange feeling of being smiled at by someone whose intentions were beyond my power to comprehend, whose eyes saw differently and whose heart beat to another rhythm. The disturbing sensation passed quickly, but the memory of it remained long afterward.

Then abruptly he reached into his coat pocket and pulled out the charred remains of a book. "Look, your worship."

I took the thing and was amazed to find it a copy of *Joseph Andrews*. "You took this away from the fire?"

"I have carried it since then."

"As a kind of good-luck piece?"

He nodded.

"Can you read it?"

"I read what I could, then got a proper copy and read it. I began *Tom Jones*." He gave me a sheepish smile as if to say what's begun is not always finished.

"It's a long book," I acknowledged. "I'm flattered you've read my work." I gave him back the charred *Joseph Andrews,* which he put back carefully in his pocket, hoping to keep its brittle blackened leaves intact a while longer.

Then he thanked me abundantly for my good will and for listening to the history of his misfortunes in London and swore with considerable feeling that it meant more to him than I could know.

As you may suspect, his effusion somewhat embarrassed me. To cool any prospect of hope he might have, I said bluntly, "I had wanted to know your story and compare it to my own knowledge of crime. This I apologize for, as I see now your trouble began with an insensitive nobleman and continued through such a pattern of ill luck that I'd be hard put to consider alternatives to what has befallen you. Even so, Ned Carleton, you've robbed men and you've killed. I wish it were not so, for I like and pity you." With a curt nod I began shuffling toward the door, turning before getting there, however, on an impulse coming from whence I knew not.

"Today," I said, "I saw a young woman coming from your cell. Had I the pleasure of seeing your wife? If so, convey my compliments. She's a charming lady."

I can well imagine I have startled you, Reader, with such overdone civility, coming as it did from magistrate to felon, and in fact I startled myself. Yet to be sure, the prisoner and I were already on a most unusual footing.

He drew himself up as if to match my formal manner and

disclosed that the young lady, having attended his trial, believed the wrong done him was greater than the wrong he had done. She was therefore no more to him than a disinterested well-wisher.

I was taken aback by the arrogance of the woman's declaration that implied *he* was the victim. With warmth I replied that his deeds had hardly been those of a victim.

For a moment the prisoner blinked at me, as if considering the truth of what I had said, then with a short cry fell to his knees and blurted out a confession — namely, that he'd lied to me. The lady was his sweetheart. His falsehood had been designed to enlist my sympathy. Aside from his dear Clare, none gave a damn if he died. He begged my pardon for this attempt at pleading the extenuation of circumstances, if not innocence, in the matter of guilt for his crimes.

"My sympathy you already have," I told him.

He remained in that conciliatory and almost prayerful position, the ugly hand grasped by the other. And yet again he smiled that strange smile, which like the flaw in a mirror distorted the favourable impression I'd come to have of him. Yet the moment was again fleeting, and I believed it to have issued less from his peculiar smile than from what I knew of his crimes, the which could scarcely be discounted in my assessment of his character.

Nothing more was said between us. I left the cell and gave the turnkey "civility money" to provide the prisoner with a clean bucket daily, an oil lamp, and a double ration of the two halfpenny loaves of bread customarily given the condemned — an amount of food hardly capable of sustaining life long enough to end it. In my opinion this is a most heartless practice, since the penalty of death alone ought to do for any man, however dissolute, and the addition of brutality to that ultimate punishment would seem at best unreasonable and at worst vicious. Perhaps, Reader, you will do me the honour of agreeing that it should become mandatory for a turnkey to meditate a whole day in a dark cell upon the two essential facts of life — its brevity and its uncertainty — as a means of softening his heart toward creatures but slightly ahead of him on the journey into the eternal.

Thoroughly fatigued, I left the prison and hailed a hackney coach, easing my bulk onto the leather seat, and proceeded home. I had earlier sent word to friends and canceled supper with them so as to remain near the children, both Louisa and Sophia having a croup again.

In the homeward coach I couldn't rid my mind of the prisoner's history. It was methinks Epictetus who hath told us difficulties are the things that show what men are. It's a proposition with which I generally agree. And yet I wonder how must the world judge of a youth without advantages who hath been hurled into the maelstrom of a great city.

Surely the difficulties which I encountered in my own youthful arrival here, so many years ago, would in retrospect seem pure fancies compared to those which faced Nathaniel Carleton. I came armed; he came empty-handed. Perhaps in some measure as revenge against my father for having so soon remarried after my mother's death — and to a papist woman of uncertain attributes — my grandmother had ever shown me (not my father's favourite child) special favour, the which acquired material form in the spending money I took up to London. It enabled me to find, at the outset, comfortable if modest quarters where I wanted them, in the neighborhood of Covent Garden, close to the theatres and shops of fashion and innumerable coffeehouses, which I frequented in the hope of glimpsing Mister Pope hobbling along with sycophants in his wake, and Mister Gay, whose *Beggar's Opera* was all the rage that season. I attended the opera where Handel sat in the king's box, rocking to and fro to the sound of his own music. Or else I set sail for a masquerade, a rout, a great squeeze of young bloods like myself and fair charmers, until in my sleep I could hear the rattle of vellum fans, the wooden swish of layered silk. In fine, I became adept at exchanging pleasantries with rouged fops and dallying with ladies weighed down by valances of lace.

And at the same time I dared to put to paper a theatrical farce of my own invention. I must avow that *Love in Several Masques* got to the stage primarily through the good offices of my influential cousin Lady Mary Wortley Montagu, who perhaps spoke in its favour to rid herself of a young pest. With this slight piece of intrigue cast after Congreve's great plays, I was more or less launched.

Before notable success came my way, however, I turned from the theatre awhile and enjoyed the privilege of studying the classics with Peter Burmann at Leyden University in Holland. Upon my return to London I tried my hand at some poetic effusions fortunately now lost and a few immature plays which thankfully were rejected for performance, as had they reached the boards I might never have had another chance or been trusted again to write a proper scene.

At twenty-three, an early enough age in truth, I had my first considerable triumph. Soon afterward, a parody of heroic drama which I called *Tom Thumb* secured me a limelight I wouldn't relinquish for some years, not until forced to do so by Walpole's vengeful government. Were you to ask me, Reader, hath there been anything from my pen of which I can be justly proud, perhaps I'd reply it was the final scene of *Tom Thumb*. It hath been reported to me on good authority that Jonathan Swift once remarked of his having laughed twice in his life, once being at that particular scene.

Burlesques, comedies, ballad operas, and other farces quickly followed, bringing me more than three hundred a year, most of it promptly wasted on idle wagers at Boodle's and all-night whist at White's and fancy bag wigs in Holborn shops. Beneath the brassy light of fire lustres in the great pleasure halls, I received on occasion more than one inviting glance above the edge of a fan. To say the strict truth, the sparkling eye and swelling bosom of a young lady were sights never lost on my passionate youth. To say further, I didn't balk at using my little fame to bring such delicacies as close as need be for our mutual enjoyment. But I must insist on making perfectly clear, as this hath great importance to me in preservation of her memory, that such adventures ended when there seemed a chance for my suit with Miss Charlotte Cradock.

But to the point. Before I'd reached a twenty-eighth birthday, as by then my reputation in the theatre was secure, I'd not only put sixteen plays on the boards, many of them under my own management, but more importantly I'd been honoured by the critical attacks of scribblers in the daily journals and by the busy intrigues of rival playwrights and managers. Difficulties? Of course. But none to speak of compared to those of a prisoner of the same age languishing in prison, awaiting execution. At that age my difficulties had been hovering in the wings, awaiting their cue.

———

"He came here again," Ned told her as they sat together on the bench and held hands. The turnkey, who was supposed to remain within the cell during a visitation, had been given ten shillings by Clare to wait outside — a common enough practice at Newgate, where any privilege could be bought.

"He sat here and I told him my history. He listened carefully and said things about love and hate. But I never understood much of that. I showed him his book. I never thought to meet the writer of a book."

"Will he help you?" Clare asked eagerly.

"I thought for a while he would. I never saw man listen so closely."

"Then he must help. And he can, being magistrate."

"He can but won't. In faith I was too forward in praising and thanking him, for he backed away and scolded me for my crimes."

"Ah." She dropped Ned's hand and placed her own upon her eyes and leaned forward, trying not to cry.

"He asked of you."

Clare looked up. "What of me?"

"Was you my wife. I told him first you came as a friend."

"Why, lad?"

"To show I had sympathizers. But then it seemed the truth would do more in gaining his sympathy."

"You did right."

They sat in silence awhile. "He can help, lad," Clare finally said. "We mustn't lose him."

"Perhaps he won't come back."

Thoughtfully, Clare reached out and took Ned's hand again. "Yes, I think he will. Mister Fielding will come back."

———◆———

¶ Reader, you will not, I believe, be surprised to hear that the following day I returned to Newgate for another interview with the prisoner. This time I brought ink, a quill, and paper with the intention of writing down the details of his history in proper sequence.

Flattered, he smiled the odd smile again, so to cool his expectations, for clearly he wished my legal help, I stated flatly, coldly, "You may refuse my request, Ned Carleton. I've of late wished to write again. Your history seems to have elements both common and uncommon. They smoke out the dilemmas faced by many young men who come to London. This is a selfish project of mine and of no benefit to you. Shall I go?"

"Please, your worship, let's begin."

And so we did, retracing our way backward to the offer of employment in Lord Sandwich's household.

We were not far into the narrative when a turnkey could be

heard swearing outside of the cell and a female voice rising on a note of alarm.

I yelled for the turnkey to open the door at once, instructed the prisoner to remain as he was, and with the cane struggled to my feet. The door swung slowly open, revealing the turnkey's scowl, behind which, partially visible, was the charming face of the prisoner's lady.

I asked the turnkey for an explanation of the trouble. He gave it in a most surly manner. This woman had come again to visit the prisoner after having done so once already today. In his opinion Miss Saucy Chops shouldn't be given leave to see the fellow twice.

Reaching out, I handed the young lady into the cell (the warmth of her fingers in mine would follow me all the way home), at the same time commanding the turnkey to return only when I called.

With a display of that untutored dignity I have already remarked on, the prisoner introduced me to his Clare, who in turn gave me a brisk but deep curtsy, much as a servant girl doth, and in a voice more nasal than you might have expected to issue from such rosebud lips, she expressed her gratitude for all I had done to succour her dear friend so untimely brought to this condition. She hoped I would continue to look upon them both with favour as objects of compassion. Her words, I must confess, had a most studied ring and not altogether fitting pronunciation, the sum of which brought me to the conclusion that, like her young man, she too had been given but meager opportunities in life to learn the ways of gentility, but relied for the most part — and indeed the best part — on a natural flair for civil, proper, and honest behaviour. You may perhaps understand me when I maintain that the servile curtsy and harsh voice and unmanaged language contributed to her charm rather than detracted from it.

I beseeched her to be seated. Retrieving my hat, I gave a slight bow of farewell and prepared to leave, as the young couple, who could look forward only to a pathetically short future together, had without doubt much to communicate in private. I was surprised by the prisoner's eagerness to have me remain. Indeed, he fairly rushed to the door and, in a manner of speaking, barred my way out, as a stream of words poured from his lips. He begged me to think well of him, vowing to describe his full history as honestly as God gave him the power, even though his words might tell against him.

When this hurried speech ended, I glanced at Clare, wondering how his outburst had affected her. Her lips trembled, her face had

turned pale. I told him there was no need to beg of me my good
will, as he already had it. I went further, acknowledging my
admiration for his honest treatment of me. I went even further,
expressing the opinion that perhaps his greatest sin had been to
come to London in the first place, as it had put his fate into the
hands of people ill disposed to do it justice.

Behind me I heard a sound that stung me to the heart, I being
aware even before turning, that the lovely woman was crying. In
truth she was dabbing at her dark eyes with a kerchief, the cloak
thrown back to expose a finely turned neck, below which a slightly
disarrayed fichu let more of her breasts be seen by me than she
might otherwise, when in better control of herself, allow.

"Come, come," I said, glancing from Ned to his Clare, "do not
yield to misfortune." Having thus Englished *Tu ne cede malis,* the
immortal Malo's bravest words, I added an emphatic thump of my
cane against the stone floor. "You must not be shut of all hope.
Promise me!"

"We promise, your worship," said Ned Carleton.

I turned and left, instructing the turnkey in no uncertain terms
to allow the young lady access to the cell whensoever she pleased.

The turnkey shrugged. "You treat these cutthroats so sweetly,
they'll come in off the streets by droves and abide here in the
Condemned hole with their whores, as it's not too damp and it's
cheap."

However reluctantly, he swore to pass the word to his relief
about the woman's permission to come and go as she pleased.

That night I couldn't sleep for thinking of my dear departed
wife. I was carried back in reverie to the time I first laid eyes on
Charlotte Cradock coming through an avenue of lime trees on St.
Martin's Street in front of my grandmother's house in Salisbury,
where I was resting from London, having written five plays in half
a year.

Two girls, tall and well formed, were strolling along, but one
had a sprightliness in her countenance that haunted me long after
the pair climbed the steps into the church. Many years later in
Amelia I wrote, "Oh! there is no true tenderness but in a woman of
spirit," having in mind my dearest Charlotte during those days
when in the assembly rooms of Salisbury she outshone all her
rivals in the charms of her person, and with a teasing lively spirit
turned me away. She kept me at arm's length for a long time,
until the poems I wrote with my heart's blood finally gained me
entrance to her affections. She blushed easily when the words were

spoken rather than penned, and she was quick, moreover, to rally me over some indiscretion of speech as we strolled in her mother's garden.

I knew her from the first dawn of her beauty. Her black hair was then so luxuriant that it fell below her waist, albeit years later, when finally she consented to marry me, she had it cut for the fashion. It would curl then gracefully at her neck, much in the manner of Clare's, and in the last vague moments before sleep at last overtook my thoughts, I seemed to have mixed the women in my dimming brain. Now this and now that lovely visage hovered above me at my bedside, as I murmured, as often I've done to keep my courage high, these words from Shakespeare: "What's gone and what's past help should be past grief."

[48]

AS SHE WAS ENTERING Newgate, Clare saw a familiar face ahead of her — the grey saturnine visage of Mister Scarrat. Staying far enough behind him in the crowd, she watched him make his way down the stone halls, certain he'd be heading for the Condemned hole and more of "his minor business" with her lad.

So Clare was surprised when he took a stairway upward. He seemed well acquainted with Newgate, greeting warders and turnkeys and other officials with a merry wave which meant to her that the man dropped plenty of coins into the palms of those who worked here. On the second floor he entered a ward.

Clare waited some time before he came out again, forcing her to turn quickly away or be discovered. Then she followed him down the stairway and watched him finally disappear down the stone steps which led to the Condemned hole. So he was going to visit Ned as well. Retracing her steps to the second floor, she gave a turnkey thereabouts some coins so she could visit someone.

It was not a large ward or a rowdy one, but obviously contained those with money enough to buy a little peace and quiet. There must have been thirty people there, none in chains or cuffs, about half of them women. Clare's practised eye told her they were probably debtors, no rough trade from the flash houses. Who had Scarrat visited here? Emboldened by desperation and curiosity, Clare went up to a middle-aged woman who sat on a bench and said to her, "Ma'am," and gave her a curtsy.

The courtesy disposed the woman to smile.

"I was visiting my cousin in a ward down the hall," Clare said. "And I was with my uncle who said he knew someone in this ward, but I look round and don't see him at all. A grey-faced man, tall and thin."

The woman nodded. "I saw him here lately. He come to see Bet Canning. See her? I warrant you recognize her from the broadsheets."

Clare followed the woman's gaze to a small, neatly dressed young woman across the room, who sat with a group of older women, one of whom was reading to them from a book. Clare did indeed recognize Elizabeth Canning, as drawings of her were everywhere — the girl in prison, the girl praying, the girl talking to the devil, the girl prostrate before Madam Justice. The plain, round, solemn face was everywhere.

Going away, Clare went next to the Condemned hole, where all the turnkeys knew her and let her into Ned's cell without a murmur, so cowed were they by Justice Fielding.

"I saw him come down here," Clare began immediately. "I saw Scarrat."

Ned had been reading *Tom Jones* by lantern light. He looked up with brow either furrowed deeply by the effort of parsing the text or by her sudden entry and remark.

"Tell me, lad, what's happening? The fellow went in another ward too and saw Betty Canning."

Ned rose slowly to his feet. There was an air of threat about him, as if she was seeing him loom out of a dark lane. This must be what the coves saw when he came at them. With both fear and awe Clare saw him as the Dog Cull for the first time. He was telling her in a low voice never to mention Scarrat. What was between him and Scarrat was over and done with.

"You fear him that much?" Clare said boldly.

"He's the deepest scoundrel I ever knew."

"I believe that. And I wish Judge Fielding to know that."

"He must never know that. We'll count on Judge Fielding's sympathy and nothing more. Leave Scarrat to the devil."

His words calmed her. She was agreeably surprised to find her lad better at the use of people than she'd believed possible. But when life's at stake, perhaps a man finds in himself a talent for deceit. As for herself, she'd learned quickly in London how to dissemble. Every girl thrown upon the town knew how to cozen, to bamboozle, to beguile. It had taken little of her attention to see in the ailing judge's eye a sparkle of interest. From his courtly manner he took her for a proper lady, and so she'd behave. Where this might lead, she didn't know, but lead somewhere it must and quickly, as the poor lad's time was getting near.

First she meant to see the Canning girl, as she'd not given up on learning Scarrat's part in Ned's life. Any girl on the town had met such men, lawless and powerful, who could bribe or be bribed, who changed what others could not, whose chief weapon was fear and whose own fear could have them suddenly scrambling like a kicked dog. Girls talked with contempt and awe of this sort of man, who revealed himself in bed out of loneliness and a desire to be known for what he was. Such a man was Scarrat. If frightened, he might do many things — even get her lad's sentence commuted to transportation.

Back she went to the second-floor ward where the elderly woman was still reading to the group, of which Bet Canning was part. Unobtrusively, Clare joined them, sitting cross-legged on the straw-covered floor.

"The rosy-fingered Goddess had now opened the folding portals of the East; and now the feathered chorister trilled tremulously through the grove the most melodious and enchanting lays; the sturdy plough-boy had drove his jocund team a field; in short, the sun shone so bright in Grant and Lyndamira's bed-chamber, that they rose three hours earlier than their time."

"Widow Canning," said a woman when the reader paused, "this part is either dull or beyond my brain."

"There are beautiful words here," replied the widow loftily, "no matter what their meaning."

"Betty Canning," said Clare, reaching over to the girl on the bench and touching her arm. "It would be agreeable to have a word with you. Please?"

The girl studied Clare a moment, then rose, and the two went to a far shadowy corner. When they were together, Clare claimed that she had followed the two trials closely and ached in her heart for the misfortune and the miscarriage of justice. "I wish you well," Clare declared.

"I thank you, miss." Bet gave her a bright smile. "You're a pretty thing and I like you."

"May I come again? It would be my pleasure to speak with you again. It must be tiresome here."

"Very such. Please do come again," Bet said and touched Clare's hand. "You're pretty and sweet and we could pass time together." She sighed. "Some of these ladies bring me down, and Mother reads ever too much."

They parted, but each day thereafter, before going to the Condemned hole, Clare went to see Bet Canning, who sat apart with her and talked of clothes and Vauxhall and Ranelagh, which Bet had seen in the company of well-wishers before the trial. On her third visit Clare mentioned Scarrat.

Bet Canning's eyes widened.

"This Mister Scarrat is grey in the face," Clare said. "He's been here to see my Ned." Earlier she had explained to Bet that her sweetheart was held here, which is why she came each day to the prison.

Bet Canning smiled faintly.

"I've never seen a greyer man."

Bet Canning said nothing, her smile growing tighter.

"He comes like a shadow and visits Ned. He's a man of particular character."

"Indeed he is," Bet said crisply. "I too know Mister Scarrat, who in the worst of my tribulation came to my aid. Without Mister Scarrat and others like him, I swear I don't know what I'd have done. He's the salt of the earth, none better, and he's honoured me by coming to Newgate to give me courage and some gifts of money, as he's the most generous of men. Indeed, he's a man of particular character."

Clare regarded the girl closely. There was steel in those eyes, in the set of those lips. It was grimly clear that the girl would reveal nothing to anyone about Scarrat. She'd die first, that was plain. But instead of hating the girl for such secretiveness, Clare admired her caution, intelligence, determination. Though Clare gave up at once any hope of learning more from Bet Canning, she continued to drop by the ward and visit with her. They sat together, sometimes holding hands, talking in low voices, sometimes even giggling like girls, while on the opposite bench, in new finery, Widow Canning read from Volume Two of *Memoirs of a Scots Heiress*, after explaining to her rapt listeners the plot heretofore. Cyril wants to marry Miranda, a Dutch girl from Batavia, who unfortunately has black skin. Miranda is afraid that people will scorn Cyril for taking a black wife — albeit she is half white — so during the marriage ceremony, out of deference to him and love, she wills her own death and keels over. The service is suspended, while people wait anxiously for her to revive.

The widow intoned:

"We waited in vain; the hand of death had sealed those eyes; the power of medicine failed; and sweet Miranda waked no more; but fell a sacrifice to love and honour, to her own too strong sensation and too delicate frame."

⁂ Next day, Reader, the household was amazed to see me come downstairs with neither cane nor crutch, as I had not done in months. Indeed, I felt upon waking a new kindling of youthful vigour, the which I was determined to enjoy as long as I could. Through the labours of morning and afternoon, I was jovial, perhaps overly so, but my excessively fond humour faded when I returned to the prison and unaided descended the stairway to the Condemned hole.

I was recalling the falseness of my behaviour yesterday in the face of that doomed young couple, who must have taken my impulsive quotation of Virgil for some kind of promise, which mistake in a moment of inexplicable cowardice I had failed to rectify. The plain fact was that I possessed the legal power as a magistrate for the city of Westminster and the county of Middlesex to order a temporary stay of execution on some pretext or other. I could then argue before the king's bench a case of irregular arrest or extenuating circumstances and through one means or another (for many judges have done no less) quite possibly obtain

for him a lesser sentence, most probably transportation to one of
His Majesty's colonies.

Such an action, however, would go terribly against the grain of
my past performance on the bench, as I had striven to cast myself
in the mould of a fair and honest judge and a stern disciplinarian.

In this regard I had written a public pamphlet in which I argued
the government's duty under the Riot Act to hang a young man,
one Bosavern Penlez, who was caught with goods taken from a
brothel pillaged by a group of drunken soldiers. Though Penlez
had not joined in the destruction, in point of fact he'd taken away
goods not belonging to him, but made available through such
destruction of the house. As a deterrent to others who might do
likewise in similar circumstances, I defended the government's
execution of him, his life being forfeit in the public interest. Thus
had I argued against a man who for a single impulsive moment had
become a looter, never a thief by trade and surely no murderer.

Could I now in all conscience plead for the life of someone who
was both?

Plainly it was absurd to harbour any idea of rescuing Nathaniel
Carleton from his fate. Entering his cell, it was my intention to set
matters aright immediately by informing him that under no
circumstances could I tamper with his sentence. But he gave me
no chance to so state, but pitched upon me with an exclamation of
surprise and delight that I had left my cane behind.

Then in the next breath he begged of me a most important
favour, namely, to carry a message to Clare. "I can trust none other
with it," he said, thrusting a folded piece of paper into my hand.

I asked him had a turnkey given him pen and ink, for such
generosity would go counter to common practice in Newgate.

He lifted the blanket which lay in the corner, discovering some
materials for writing that Clare had sneaked in. This little
subterfuge, by which to increase their means of communication,
went to my heart, for when she was not with him here, he must
write to her, a lover's procedure with which I was only too well
acquainted. I had practised it years ago in Salisbury, when
upon arriving home from an afternoon with Charlotte, I rushed
upstairs to fill page after page with my longing for her presence
and with interminable descriptions of the misery I felt at our
long separation.

While I slipped the note into my pocket, tapping it with a
fondness arising from memory, the prisoner took up his narrative.
Soon enough he broke it off and sat next to me on the bench.

Leaning earnestly forward and with his manacled hands held before him, he swore that none had ever come to harm through his activities save for the loss of money. He never touched a piece of jewelry or a watch or any object which might have the value of sentiment. Not one of his victims had been hurt in the flesh or threatened with death or affrighted by his pistol, as he meant only to survive like any man and would have worked to the limit of his strength at honest labour had his fellow creatures allowed him. The bloody tales which alas had created his notorious reputation were nothing more than the stuff of Grub Street fancy, for as God was his witness, he'd done no more than rob the rich, and that never barbarously. Upon his solemn word he claimed that in his entire regrettable career as a footpad, he'd never committed a single act worthy of the name of violence, save for firing at a man who had fired at him on the day he'd been taken.

At the end of this declaration, the prisoner got up and paced again. Despite my liking of the prisoner, a liking which had strengthened through acquaintance, I felt his argument to be specious in the extreme when he spoke of doing little harm — for what is taking a man's gold if not harming him? The loss of money, to say nothing of the mental shock occasioned by such a robbery, would suffice as harmful to any man.

I told him so.

For a few moments he continued his pacing, as though too deep in thought to have heard my repudiation of his sophistry. Then turning, he eyed me in a most profound manner and admitted in a trembling voice that there was withal no possible excuse for what he had done. Robbery was against the laws of man and God, and so must he pay for his transgressions and would do so willingly, but not, dear God, with his life.

"A life for a life," I replied coolly. "As Judge Murray so decided."

He begged me to withhold final judgement on his conduct and his life.

So he moved in his history to the account of meeting Clare. She worked in a millinery shop, where he bought a piece of Irish lace just to look at her, and having left the store thrust his purchase into the hand of a surprised beggar.

I was amused and taken by his account, as there are few things more radiant or foolish to be encountered in life than a young man who hath just become sensible to a particular young woman's charms.

It should come as no surprise that love wrought another change in him. He wished to give up crime and make a new start with Clare outside of London. Certainly she bemoaned the fact that her lover was a footpad.

At this point I intervened to ask when he had revealed the truth to her.

With bowed head he replied that he'd kept it secret until they lived together. They had meant to marry then, but a knowledge of his true profession determined her not to marry him.

"Quite right," I commented.

His desire to turn his life around was balanced by his need for money to keep his sweetheart from misfortune. It is small wonder that he'd learned through his own adversity to put considerable faith in a full pocket. Urged by the benevolent feelings which love for another person hath a way of extending beyond its own borders, he desired more than ever to make his way through honest labour in the company of honest men, but the ruined hand held him in a grip of iron to the midnight streets. He saw no other way of providing for their escape from London (as that is how he saw it) except by a few final robberies. He had concluded that either he must get the money soon or bid farewell to Clare, a woman of unsullied character and decent upbringing.

While speaking thus, he had been pacing. Now he halted and with a faint smile asked me was the hour getting late, because, if it pleased me to remember, I had consented to give Clare his message.

His eagerness recalled for me my own anxiety when the sun was lowering below the Dorset fields, and I'd not yet sent my latest missive of love to Charlotte by way of a manservant whom I kept as lean as a whippet by rushing him at all possible speed to the Cradock house with tightly folded little pieces of paper gripped in his hand.

Rising, I told the prisoner that a call at his lodgings would be the first business I discharged upon leaving Newgate.

Pounding on the cell door for the guard, I turned to say farewell and observed with dismay such a look of anguish on the prisoner's face as would have excited pity in the most savage breast.

He touched my arm, so in turn I touched — indeed, gripped — his in a gesture of affection and commiseration. Plainly he yearned at this moment not only for prolonged life but for the freedom to go himself to his sweetheart.

At such a moment, unfortunately for us both, he murmured, "Save me, I beg of you."

They were words that might claim from me but one answer: I cannot. To make perfectly clear the stance I must take, I said, "I will not. You were tried and convicted by your peers for Grand Theft. There were no extenuating circumstances by law. I will not release you or anyone from the punishment demanded for such an act." My voice rang loudly with conviction through the tiny cell, albeit hidden in my heart was the desire for mercy.

Once again I touched his arm, but without speaking, as though to imply I had an affinity for his character but none for his argument. I could have quoted to him Pascal, who says it's not permitted to the most equitable of men to be a judge in his own cause.

[49]

❡ It was with agitated spirits that I stepped out of the sedan chair in front of the lodging house on Holborn Street.

I can imagine, Reader, that you are possibly at one with my feelings on this occasion, mixed as they were of embarrassment and anticipation; the former from my refusal to exercise power in behalf of the man loved by the young woman upstairs; the latter stemming from my keen desire to see her again.

I mounted the creaking staircase with resolution, hoping not to favour the gouty foot, which I must confess was giving pain again. It seemed important that I not arrive at her door limping like a doddering old man.

Having knocked timidly and received no answer, my feelings mixed of relief and regret, I turned to descend. Indeed, I had started down the stairway at a clumping gait, when at my back I heard a cry: "Your worship! Your worship!"

The door at the top of the stairs was ajar, a white hand and slim wrist appeared, beckoning me vigorously, and then her pale oval face, smiling, looked out at me.

In moments I was inside the room which she'd shared with the condemned prisoner. Swiftly I took in its features, as I dared not look at her (and you will shortly know why). There was a fire grate with a tea kettle sitting on it, two chairs of the common ladderback kind, a small but heavily constructed breakfront with a tray and some dishes inside, a vase, and oddments. Linen was drying on a clothesline stretched between walls, reminding me with a sudden ache of my early married months with Charlotte.

I said, Reader, after entering the room I dared not look at the young woman. The reason was, I desired to give her a chance to more fully clothe herself, as all she had upon her person was a thin cotton shift and a muslin mob-cap perched back on her head, allowing the rich dark hair to snake round her bare neck.

Having walked about the room for some moments, giving her time for arrangements behind the hung laundry, I was surprised, when she asked would I take a refreshment, to find her still in the same delightful disorder.

A refreshment. She asked it with a studied coquetry, as though we both were dressed for high tea in a drawing room. I owned a dish of tea would be pleasant, then watched her go prettily to the grate to see if water was hot in the kettle. Her calculated gentility, somewhat like Ned's odd smile, was a distortion of countenance, and at such moments I was separated from them in ways other than age and health, as if they lived lives beyond my knowing.

Clare stirred the coals beneath the kettle with a poker, bending to the job in such a decisive way that the front of her thin shift billowed out, displaying what you may or may not blush to know, Reader, were two swelling white breasts of such beauty, that leaning forward where I sat at the table, I moved my head this way and that to have yet a better advantage for viewing those exquisite twin charms. Moreover, as she bent to the grate, the skimpy cloth inched its way breathlessly up on her limbs until the glory of her firm young thighs was revealed to my incontinent gaze.

All this time she was excusing herself effusively for not being more presentable to a gentleman of my quality, but she'd been cleaning the room in the fond hope that if the poor lad was released from prison, he'd come home to a place of good cheer.

"Pshaw, I know of course it's nothing but fancy," Clare said with a sigh and turned to look at me.

"I'm distressed to say I believe that's what it is."

"Can there be a stay of execution?" she asked, seeming on the verge of tears.

I explained, rather lamely, that such a stay might have the

doleful effect of prolonging his agony until the next session, at which time he'd most surely suffer. His crime had been of the utmost seriousness, I added as if to justify sentencing him myself.

The girl made no reply, but busied herself with the kettle. I fidgeted at the table, drumming upon it steadily and stealing further glances at her young body moving with such liquid grace beneath the flimsy cloth. Did I hear the catching sound of a sob? I prepared to rise, just as she straightened up from the kettle, brushing a tear from her eye as she did so. From the cluttered breakfront, she took two cups and wiped them carefully with a rag before setting them on the table. Then came the sugar dish and a pitcher of milk.

Suddenly I blurted out (I hope, Reader, you recognize the feelings that led to my request) a desire for a spirit stronger than tea.

She hastened to get me gin, though with an extravagant apology for not having better liquor and for not having offered it hitherto.

I begged her not to think of it.

She beseeched me to forgive her.

I pleaded for her to be easy, as there was nothing to forgive.

And so we were soon sitting opposite each other at the table with a gin bottle between us, and two cups brimming. Clare murmured with a bewitching smile that she'd join me in a dram, for though she rarely took strong drink, she would on such an occasion.

We drank. I poured myself another and upended it without further prelude in an effort to dull my lustful memory of her bending at the fireplace.

Sipping her cup demurely, her eyes downcast, Clare then begged me not to think ill of her for so speaking out, but in truth she believed the poor lad innocent in the eyes of Our Maker, for he'd robbed only to survive and shot his pistol only to protect himself from a vicious attack.

I would not answer.

With her dark feline eyes swimming in tears, she asked me had I ever suffered a thing in my own life compared to what faced her in such a few days.

Be obliging in your forbearance, Reader, for I must confess I seemed then to have lost all restraint. Whether from fatigue or gin or the powerful effect of her youthful beauty upon my senses or simply from the chance opportunity to unburden myself of an anguish which hath ever pressed on me, I began to speak of the

worst that had befallen me in life; in the telling of which I almost
forgot it was said out loud to other than my own afflicted soul.

We had been married, Charlotte and I, nearly two years when
the dear woman blessed me with a little girl on the twenty-seventh
of April in the Year of Our Lord Seventeen Hundred and Thirty-
Six. I insisted on naming the child after her mother.

During that joyous time I also had a success with *Pasquin* at the
Haymarket Theatre, a political satire which ran sixty days, nearly a
record for London, and drew the fashionable mob from Pall Mall,
Grosvenor, Cavendish, and Hanover Squares, the *bon ton* and
great personages sitting humbly in side boxes and liking it. Ah, I
was arrogant enough then for a dozen men. Never could man be
happier in his fate than I was. I had the woman I loved and an
equally beloved daughter beside me, and a plenitude of success
both in fame and fortune to serve us all.

For six years thereafter my family flourished, during which time
I was called to the bar at the Middle Temple after a period of legal
studies.

Then, without warning, Providence entered our lives with a
biblical vengeance.

It was a fierce winter that year which suddenly found me laid up
with gout in one room, my dearest child Charlotte dying of a
consumptive fever in the next, and my wife in a bed beside her in a
condition little better. Dante never wrote truer than when he
observed, "No greater grief than to remember days of joy, when
misery is at hand."

She was just a sweet and pretty little child who now lies in the
chancel vault of St. Martin's in the Fields.

After the death of child Charlotte, wife Charlotte never truly
recovered either in mind or body. It was a measure of her
continuing sorrow that once she claimed we had a single
consolation — namely, that our daughter would ever be spared a
mother's grief at the death of a favoured child.

Following this tragedy was a time of mounting debt, as I no
longer could write for the stage, having been censored out of it by
government decree. And my dangerously buoyant spirits, coupled
with fanciful notions of greater fortune to come, saw to it that the
monies from *Joseph Andrews* were quickly wasted. My fees as an
attorney at law were both meager and poorly managed. In brief,
we faced the bleakest of futures, and each day I saw the lively
woman move deeper into a melancholy from which I could rarely
rouse her either by wit or embrace.

The tall, sprightly figure seemed to bend and shrink in upon itself. Her cough at night drummed in my ear like a thousand hammers, as neither of us slept but fitfully. She became thin, piteously haggard, those eyes which once could have bewitched all Christendom with their dazzling lights grew dim and listless and darkly circled. The cough increased in its ominous intensity, her strength failed altogether, until the fateful day came, less than two years since I had lost one Charlotte, that I lost the other.

Helplessly at her bedside, I watched each cough take away from me a little more Charlotte. My hand in hers attempted in vain to transmit some warmth, and at length she coughed no more and the fingers clasping mine grew cold.

As I have stated, Reader, I had nearly forgotten to whom I was speaking, the recollection seeming to take place within my soul, and so it was with considerable surprise that I felt a warm touch against my hand that retrieved me from the past. Clare had reached across the table to lay her soft white fingers on mine. She spoke not a word, nor was there need of one, for I understood with gratitude the eloquent sympathy this girl expressed in a simple gesture.

Her hand remained. Our eyes, both in tears, met. And from hers, abruptly, there seemed to emanate something I'd not seen there hitherto, a certain softness — well, to be plain, a hint of invitation — a look I'd learned to read in a woman's eyes long ago, before I was old enough or humble enough to appreciate this signal of a growing closeness, of an intimacy as precious in its way as the final surrender to which such a look is often prelude.

Our hands remained touching. Indeed, my own turned slyly until the palm lay against hers. Her sloe-black eyes met mine with a directness which in a lesser woman would have been called saucily bold and coming, but which in her was something akin to the low whispering of a secret. At this propitious moment a little clock in the breakfront began to strike. The metallic harshness of the sound returned us to our real situation, and she pulled her hand back. I cleared my throat and thanked her in a lame-sounding mumble for having heard me out, for I well knew and regretted that my story could give her little comfort in her own distress.

Clare seemed flustered, her eyes downcast and now upturned to meet mine and now downcast again, her breath coming in gusts which had a turbulent effect on the thin cotton shift, fixing my attention quite beyond control upon her obvious charms. Then, abruptly, her eyes met mine without faltering, and this time with a fire that might have consumed what little scruple I had left to me. So, rising without hesitation, I picked up my great-coat and strode briskly to the door (only later aware of having forgotten the gouty foot), turning there and for wont of other to say, again thanked her for listening to my tale — and for the gin.

Again she performed the disconcerting little curtsy of a maidservant, which fortunately under the circumstances had the effect of shattering the illusion we were on equal footing, a mere man and a mere woman. Her patent deference simply returned us to what in truth we were: an aging judge and a murderer's sweetheart.

It occurred to me then that I'd completely forgotten his note, the delivery of which had presumably brought me to here. I handed it over, bowed, and turned to leave, but she called for me to stay a moment longer until the matter of the note was made clear. Unfolding the paper, she read with difficulty, as I could see her lips forming each word like a boy at Latin in the first form.

With a grimace of dismay she handed it to me. What the prisoner had set down in the most ragged penmanship was a list of certain clothes which he meant to wear to the gallows. He wanted them spotlessly clean.

"I told you before," I said to the distressed girl, "you must hold up. I have not done with it."

"You have not done with it, your worship?"

Turning without reply, I opened the door and glanced back at her oval face, highboned cheeks, catlike eyes.

"You may command me, your worship," Clare said in a voice barely audible, "what you will."

Nodding, I left, aware there was more in her words than empty form. But I dared not consider their possible import beyond civility, because at that moment they might have seduced me beyond all sense. I might have shamed us both with an unpredictable action — namely, thrown myself at her feet and declaimed wild words.

Reader, this is true. I burned to have her.

Part Nine

———————•———————

BEGINNINGS
AND ENDINGS

[50]

IN BATH THIS EVENING, Richard "Beau" Nash, the dandified and self-proclaimed master of ceremonies for this pleasure capital of England, was wheeled sick into the Pump Room of St. John's Court. He wore his famous wide-brimmed white and plumed hat and with a toothless, cynical smile turned from side to side to inspect the ladies and gentlemen assembled for their ritual drinking of the sulphurous waters. Arbiter of taste, tyrant of public rooms, Beau had the power to give such disapproving glances that they could herald for their victims the end of invitations, the demise of social repute.

This evening the haughty old man was introduced by Thomas Potter, habitué of Bath and monk of Medmenham, to the red-haired young beauty Fanny Murray. She had been deflowered at sixteen by the insatiable Potter, who later, when tired of her, had introduced Fanny to the earl of Stanhope. She had served (unbeknownst to this assembly) as the living altar for a solemn black mass and shortly thereafter had left the bed and board of her protector Stanhope.

People said, Say what you will of Potter, he's forever loyal and friendly to anyone he ever fucked. And so tonight he had brought Fanny to Bath in the hope of finding her a new protector.

None of the crowd in the Pump Room would have then imagined that such a frivolous chit, to say nothing of such a notorious courtesan, would have attached herself instantly to aging Beau Nash, whose taste hitherto had been for titled ladies and whose affairs had usually been conducted behind fans and at tea rather than in bed.

Yet this very night Fanny Murray would go into his house, where she'd live with him like a recluse, where for many years henceforth she'd administer to his cranky demands, bathe his withered limbs, read to him, feed him, endure his insults, cater to his towering vanity, and nurse him without stint until one day, without explanation or fanfare, she would leave Bath as suddenly as she had arrived, simply vanish from society, trailing behind her a memory of loveliness and devotion in the minds of Bath habitués, like the sweet fragrance of evening roses remembered by a man dying.

This particular evening the Pump Room was abuzz with the spectacle of the redheaded tart flirting so effectively with the morose emperor of town slumped in his wheelchair. Lord Sandwich, however, paid no attention. He had come down for a few days of relief from domestic life, to escape a family not one member of which could get through supper without tears or recriminations. So John Montagu was in the rollicking good mood of someone unleashed into freedom. He was especially happy because George Handel himself, though blind, would be at the harpsichord today for his Concerto Grosso in G minor. Handel, the temperamental bear from Saxony, was one of the few men his lordship could stomach for long. They shared a shambling gait, a taste for mutton and wine. Handel's diligence at work matched his own. Handel had once told him that between September 29 and October 30, 1739, he had composed an entire set of twelve concertos. Two had been written in a day, one at a single sitting.

No one sneered at Handel's Italian operas in hearing distance of Lord Sandwich, who even defended the composer's un-English use of those vile fat creatures from Milan and Rome who'd been castrated as boys to retain their soprano voices. His lordship never missed a performance of a Handel opera featuring women singers such as Francesca Cuzzoni (though short, ugly, and ill-tempered) and Faustina Bordoni, attractive enough for him to have once tried and failed to win her as a lover. One of his favourite stories of Handel — it endeared the rough German to him — was when Cuzzoni refused to sing the aria "Falsa immagine" from *Ottone* as it was written. Losing control, Handel had grabbed her and threatened to toss her bodily out of a window, bellowing "You may be a she-devil, but I am the chief devil!" Lord Sandwich would have done anything for such a man and in fact had once tried to supply the composer with a particularly fine young woman, only to have the gruff old Saxon mumble, "*Ja, danke,* but I get mine own."

Sandwich was also happy this evening because William Pitt had just launched a parliamentary attack against the duke of Newcastle.

His good humour was clouded, however, and had been for some time now, by the conviction of Elizabeth Canning for perjury. That left the whole affair in doubt, although Scarrat assured him she'd stay mum until transported, after which she'd count for nothing.

And then Scarrat had done for that impudent boy, the former postilion, although Sandwich had cut short his man's boastful explanation of how this had been accomplished. He was disinclined to involve himself in the vulgar machinations required to dispose of such carrion. In a sense he was sorry that he'd not arranged for the boy's servitude in the fleet. One word to an admiral would have sufficed to have the insolent postilion learn by hard duty at sea how to behave toward superiors. That would have been a punishment more delectable than the gallows, where the fellow would be turned off in minutes instead of daily absorbing the appropriate treatment for spying on betters. It put him in vapours merely to contemplate such rascality. It would have given his father a crippling fit to know that a stout English lad could even think of such impertinence.

Impertinence? Hardly an adequate word. There was no adequate opprobrium for such behaviour. It smacked of rebellion. Indeed, no Scot or Irish dog or Frenchman would do worse. He shuddered to think of England's fate should a hundred such fellows get loose in the land to break down the doors of privacy and thumb their noses at the peerage which, in strict truth, was the ultimate bastion of law and order.

Better by far to take arms against all of Europe than let such ruin occur from within. Had the postilion blabbed to Grub Street or a magistrate, the Medmenham brotherhood might have suffered grievous harm, and he himself, descendant of earls and heir to the Montagu name, would be prey not only to common censure but to that of his peers, especially to that of his brother monks who still didn't know that the Canning girl had once been among them. If they knew, he'd fall into a deep disgrace from which he might never recover and so end his days with a sorry wife, a scrawny daughter who would be a trial to marry off, and a stupid, lazy, malevolent son — tucked away with such creatures in cold dark rooms over a backgammon board, hearing the familial shrieks of complaint and with little escape save grouse hunting when the weather allowed. Hell itself held no worse terrors. The outside chance that something might go wrong before the boy hanged and the girl sailed for the colonies had suddenly blown away milord's good humour like a summer storm.

He went glumly and frightened to his seat for the concert. Old Handel, blind and crippled by gout, his fat bow legs fairly creaking like masts in a high wind, was led in and helped to a chair where by memory he conducted the concerto for viola, cello, four violins, and his own harpsichord as thoroughbass.

Seated in the front row, Lord Sandwich hummed loudly and familiarly through the five movements, especially during the third, a melancholy musette which awakened in him a pastoral memory of his ramblings through the woodland of Henchenbroke. His high-pitched, off-key humming irritated his neighbours, but Sandwich was oblivious of them, being wholly absorbed in the inexhaustible flow of musical invention. The music spirited him back into boyhood, when he stood on the balcony of Henchenbroke and gazed across the rolling meadows, tightly holding his nanny's hand.

When the concerto grosso ended, a choral group filed into the room and Handel conducted them in sections from his *Ode for St. Cecilia's Day*.

A tall, nubile, pink-cheeked young woman stepped forward to sing the soprano aria "What Passion Cannot Music Raise," in which Jubel's lyre is represented by a cello. Lord Sandwich was entranced equally by the girl's voice and her figure. If only he might run his hands gently along her satiny thighs while she reached high C!

After the musicale, he sought out Beau Nash, who knew everyone in society, to inquire after the girl. Fanny Murray did not step discreetly away to allow the gentlemen a word in private but stood close and let go a merry laugh. Ordinarily such effrontery would have brought from the old man a withering glance of scorn, but in Fanny's cheery presence he merely parted his lips in a silly smile.

"You wish to know of Handel's young singer," Beau said to his lordship. "The soloist's no more than a merchant's daughter. She's a Rae girl, the father's in timber. Martha's her name."

"Sir, I would deeply appreciate an introduction."

After studying his lordship a moment, the old man sighed. "Very well. I'll present Miss Martha Rae forthwith."

"I will be beholden, sir."

"Only the future can decide that," Beau commented tartly and had his attendant wheel him away — with Fanny Murray's hand proprietorially on the back of the chair.

Anxiously Lord Sandwich watched as Beau Nash was navigated toward the girl, who sat demurely with a fan at her lips beside Handel, who puffed for breath with a glass of port in his fist. The old German was notoriously jealous of his young singers. Had someone other than Beau Nash applied for the girl's attention, the testy composer would have surely warned him off and kept the girl by his side. If anyone might draw her away from Handel, Beau was the man. And so he did.

Just then the duke of Newcastle entered the Pump Room.

So intent was Lord Sandwich on the success of his application to meet the girl, he failed to notice the commotion attendant on the duke's appearance at any function.

At the last moment, when it was too late for Sandwich to avoid an encounter, he saw the infernal ninny approaching him with a lofty smile.

Sandwich nodded curtly. "Your grace."

The duke waved a lace kerchief. "Milord Sandwich, what society we have here, hey?" He was wrapped in a wool frock-coat with a scarf wound around his scrawny neck. "But it's drafty, drafty, not so warm as we could wish. I shall speak to Nash of it, you may be sure. More heat's what's needed. How does milord?"

With a slight bow, Sandwich mumbled, "Your inquiry is pleasing. Well, your grace. You may command me any service."

The duke had a reputation for touching people familiarly, and so he did now. His long bony fingers touched Sandwich's sleeve — familiarly — then the duke proceeded on his way.

Sandwich viewed his own obsequious behaviour as necessary to a man out of a post. Even so, the incident might have ruined his entire evening had not the girl approached then, walking on one side of Nash's wheelchair (Fanny Murray on the other).

Martha Rae was wearing a flounced gown.

When Nash introduced her, she curtsied low, displaying a delectable expanse of snowy breast with a star-shaped black beauty mark in the cleavage.

At that instant the fourth earl of Sandwich pitched irrevocably on her for his own. Returning her curtsy with a bow, he said, "Madam, your most obedient . . ."

Grinning with openly cynical amusement, Beau Nash withdrew with his own beauty trailing him.

His lordship complimented Martha Rae on her performance.

"You do me honour, milord. I confess I'd not known it was you I would meet. Mister Nash told me another —"

"Because he's a sly rogue. He wishes to surprise people. I hope with all my heart you accept my compliments as those coming from a true lover of music and not from some idle flatterer."

"Milord."

"I've long been an admirer of Mister Handel. He's played often at my house."

"I have heard of your musical interests, milord."

Just for an instant he wondered in alarm if her words implied more than they outwardly meant. But looking into her large hazel eyes, he saw no guile or sarcasm, nothing but innocence. He was enheartened then by her words; the girl wished to compliment him. "Are you fatigued?" he asked. "Will you have a dish of tea?"

"Thank you, nothing, milord."

He was beside himself. The girl wore no paint to mar the natural beauty of her face. No quacks for her, no potions that ate away the skin! And she sang like an angel. A bead of sweat on her upper lip fixed his attention wonderfully. "Pray, what can I get you?"

"I'm content, milord."

Gesturing toward the dining room, he said, "Let me lead you in, madam. I beg your leave —"

"Thank you, no, milord. I'm not hungry."

"Then — the garden?" He wanted her out of the Pump Room. Old Handel was nodding over another of port, yet on a whim he might call the pretty singer back to his side. Perhaps then, crude and outspoken as he was, old Handel might tell his protégée of milord Sandwich's reputation with women.

Or does she already know my reputation? he wondered anxiously, even while saying, "I hope you'll favour me with your company in the garden." He added recklessly, "I would reckon myself happy in yours."

Tapping her cheek with a fan, Martha Rae laughed. "Don't use me ill, milord. I believe you jest."

"Depend upon my behaving with the utmost civility." He offered his arm and after a moment's hesitation she took it. The light pressure of her hand through the velvet of his coat had him trembling and flushed. At this moment he'd have forgone any past pleasure with women, if only he could put this girl at ease. He felt silly and dangerously young as they left the Pump Room.

As they moved into the garden, lit by torches, he had a sudden and unsettling memory of Henchenbroke: his bedroom door opening, the moonlight streaming across the naked breast of his nanny as she opened her nightgown and approached him, humming softly . . .

Struggling free of the memory, he asked Martha if she'd come down from London.

"A fortnight ago. I have only lived in London this year. I shall die of London."

"How so?"

"It dazzles me so much. The crowds, the balls. And the work with Mister Handel. I return tomorrow."

"Then so shall I," he declared instantly.

Turning and rattling the fan, Martha halted. "Milord?"

"John."

"Then, John. Why are you returning?"

Staring in helpless fascination at beads of sweat along her brow as well as lip, he said, "If you return, then so shall I. I must see you again. It must be soon."

She whisked the fan in front of her face nervously. "If not in jest, what can you mean by such words?"

"What you think I mean. I am a man of passion."

"So I have heard," she replied coolly.

So she knew his reputation, but it no longer mattered to John Montagu. "You must see in my eyes a sincerity of feeling."

"What I see in them frightens me."

"The sincerity is all the more profound for being frightening."

"Then it must be profound, as I am frightened."

Yet in the ballet of their flirtation John Montagu was encouraged by the absolute lack of fear in her voice and expression. Standing as tall as he, her eyes level and steadfast — indeed, she'd lowered the protective fan — Martha Rae seemed capable of encountering passion, dealing with surprise, and shrugging off convention. All the attributes of a daring lover seemed to be hers.

"Tomorrow," he said, "I'll return to London and tomorrow night I shall call on you."

Eyeing him steadily, Martha Rae replied, "If you so intend, then so be it."

"I so intend."

Thus began a romance that would last for sixteen years, a phenomenon as amazing to the society of London as Fanny Murray's long and inexplicable attachment to old Beau Nash.

[51]

¶ Reader, the prisoner claimed during my visit yesterday that the notorious Jenny Rivers had schemed to bring about his fall, as he'd refused to join her gang. When I asked why he'd kept mum on this issue, he affirmed the danger of pointing a finger at a person who could find ways of taking revenge even in the confines of Newgate. But given his circumstances, the risk of naming her was no match for the inevitability of his fate if he didn't.

The sense of that I acknowledged.

As Ned told it, a waterman had come along and offered him the money pouch as a gift in good faith from Jenny if he'd reconsider joining. When he took the gold, another man nearby cried "Thief!" and shot off a pistol, after which, in self-defense, Ned had shot his. It so happened that his old friend Doctor Bostock appeared on the scene. Not knowing of Bostock's plan to collect a reward, Ned had followed where the old cheat beckoned, nearly running into the Bow Street thief takers who finally apprehended him.

I took his report as convincing enough for me to mount an

investigation of it. If his account were true, the worst in London had set a trap for him. If one element of a case proves unsound, so might others.

I went to the legal chambers of Judge Swinnerton in front of whom the Carleton trial had been heard. A clerk gave me to read the official transcript prepared by a recorder, William Moreton, whose reliable work was known to me. The testimony of witnesses seemed forthright and proper and in general harmony with what I expected, save in one vital respect.

A horse dealer gave evidence that the prisoner had come out of a tavern, the Sign of the Frigate, with a prominent sack swinging at his belt.

His testimony contradicted that of all other witnesses.

I took a hackney back to Newgate. Whenever the thought of Ned or Clare entered my head, a rattling bump threw it out, until I wondered, as the coach rolled on with its whip springs squeaking from an onslaught of potholes, if yesterday the girl's hand in mine, the looks exchanged, her final searing words of invitation, had been more fancy than fact. But it had happened, and her lovely countenance loomed out of nowhere, the which mental portrait filling me with a warm and yielding sensation, only too familiar from the days when Charlotte Cradock had lived in Friary Lane in Salisbury.

The plain fact was my heart was irretrievably lost before I knew it was truly in danger.

I confronted Ned Carleton with the most peculiar discrepancy between his story and that of the horse dealer.

"Did you come from a tavern called the Sign of the Frigate and with the pouch already on you?"

For a long time he hesitated, and my hope soared, for I felt he was struggling with a truth thus far withheld.

But he shook his head.

"Ned Carleton," I said in the commanding tone of a magistrate, "the Crown's case rested on your robbery of a waterman on the street. Did you rob this man or not?

"He gave me the pouch from Jenny Rivers."

"Which you didn't say in court."

"I stood mute."

"Why?" But from experience I knew that a good many young felons, especially those from the country, often stood mute in front of law as they'd stand mute in front of the Almighty — out of fear, respect, inadequate speech, or a combination of them all. So I forgot the question and started again. "Did you come from the tavern?"

"No, I did not." He paused like a schoolboy determined not to peach on comrades. "I never went into the tavern. I don't know the Sign of the Frigate."

"I don't believe you."

When he merely stared at me for a response, I continued. "Because if you came from there and had the pouch with you, you didn't commit Grand Theft, at least not in the manner for which you were convicted. And if you fired a pistol in self-defense against someone sent to trap you, then the charge of murder is moreover suspect. There would then be doubts raised to get you transported instead of hung."

"I never went into the tavern. I have no knowledge of the Frigate."

In sum the matter fell out thus to me: the record of testimony, save for that of a bystander who may have been mistaken, stood squarely against the accused. The jury verdict, given the character of the evidence, seemed reasonable. The sentence, given the severity of the crime of which the prisoner stood convicted, seemed just indeed.

The competent conduct of the trial notwithstanding, an advocate for the defendant might still wonder about the bystander's testimony, as it opposed that of the watermen, those denizens of the Thames who've never borne on their broad shoulders the heavy burden of a faultless reputation. Were it possible to prove that the watermen had lied in the employ of a notorious criminal such as Jenny Rivers, that Ned Carleton had not nicked the pouch but in fact had brought it from a tavern on his person (in which case Jenny Rivers's "gift" had been handed over there), then the charge of Grand Theft might be overturned. The capital charge of murder, if further pursued, would also be in jeopardy. The murdered man may well have been an assassin sent to kill Ned Carleton while in the act of a robbery that he never committed. But this was mere fancy if he denied the one piece of testimony in his favour. I had to believe the court, yet wanted to believe in facts that would justify a stay of execution. Mister Pope came to mind: "A curse on all laws but those which love has made."

For that matter, love's laws were murky enough in this regard, as I now cared for the beloved of a man whose life I wished to save, but on principle could not, and whose account of a crime would have led me, were I sitting on the bench, to judge it spurious at worst, suspicious at best.

I must not stop here, however. To be yet considered was Doctor Bostock, who'd been bold enough to inform against his friend, yet cautious enough to escape giving testimony at the trial. He was one of those wicked old opportunists who know more than they should in the hope of advantage to themselves. I'd send Saunders Welch to smoke out Doctor Bostock.

Here I must pause and make a frank revelation to the question that might be on your mind, alert Reader. Why should I desire to save the life of a man whose sweetheart I coveted (for such I freely admit)? I reply that my interest in Clare rather forced on me a powerful reason for working in the prisoner's behalf. Added to my earlier compassion for him was now the need to expiate a newfound sense of guilt. I had no idea what the future held for Clare and myself or how my awakened passion could be managed, but surely I must make every effort to see that the man who'd become my rival for a woman's affections (at least in my fancy) did not suffer for it. I could not live in the knowledge I'd used his misfortune to clear the way for myself, assuming there was any true hope of my suit, as I was old enough in the ways of the world to ascertain how much of these assumptions and possibilities were pure fancies of mine, without support in fact. Moreover, I had no intention of pressing myself on the girl, no, none, but meant to remain shut of involvement. Assuming (here again the intrusion of a heated imagination) the enchanting Clare might have a romantic interest in a sick old fellow like myself, I couldn't skip merrily to her side in total disregard of my loyal wife and family, whose protection and welfare must always be my principal concern.

Often in essays I had portrayed with indignation the corrupting effects of gallantry upon our nation's morals. Seduction and adultery were the toys of fashion, which had overridden principle as the chief motive of action in our national life and must be ended or England would go the way of imperial Rome.

Fine words indeed. Yet here I was, half contemplating what I had branded contemptible. To say true, the word "adultery" was almost on my lips when the shapely form of the girl appeared in certain lustful ways to my imagination. Throughout my literary life I made merry of affectation, unmasked the hypocrite who is the opposite of what he hath set himself up to be. Was I now in a fair way of becoming a farcical character of my own devising?

The irony hath not escaped your scrutiny, I am sure. Indeed, I may have lost all favour with you, but as this journal hath taken on the nature of a confession, I must chance the sacrificing of your amiable disposition toward me in the service of strict truth.

When I arrived home that evening, I found to my joy that Mary had gone early into labour and was delivered of a fine boy, who would have the name Ralph after my wise friend and benevolent patron, Ralph Allen. Both mother and child were out of harm's way, though no thanks to me as I'd been absent both in body and spirit. But I said a silent prayer for having been spared retribution, if not for my actions, at least for my thoughts, which I vowed to keep hereafter close to home.

Ned had many visitors today. The one he least wished to see was Robert Scarrat, who came frequently and checked on the prisoner's resolve to stay mum.

"I know Justice Fielding comes to see you," Scarrat said tartly.

Ned could see the bulge in the pocket of Scarrat's great-coat — a pistol to protect him from any violence on the prisoner's part. Though hating him, Ned could not but admire the man's judgement, caution, sense of purpose.

"Justice Fielding comes here, yes," Ned admitted.

"What could such a man have to do with you?"

"He wants to write my history."

Scarrat guffawed, then his grey face pinched into grimacing anger. "Go to!"

"He comes to know my history. He writes it down."

"What's in your history to interest a judge like Fielding?"

"He's also a writer of books. One you gave me."

"What?"

"At the fire. It was *Joseph Andrews,* half burned."

"Well, go on, go on," Scarrat said impatiently.

"He writes down how I came to London and became a footpad."

Scarrat, who'd been sitting on the bench, rose to his feet and for an instant his hand went at his coat, as if to open it and reach for the pistol. "Do you know me for what I am? Do you trifle and jest with me, you fucking scoundrel?"

Ned raised both hands, palms out, to calm him. "Nothing of *you* is in my history."

"And his — the other person close to this?"

"Only that I worked as a postilion, that he threw me from his household. Nothing more."

"Nothing more? I swear I mean to keep my threat if there's more!"

"Nothing of you and him."

"I see hesitation in your eyes."

"Methinks you see something else. You see in them my attempt to live. You see fear of death."

"Yes, well, go on."

"To gain sympathy with him," Ned continued, "I told the judge my capture was planned by Jenny Rivers."

"Ho!" After a thoughtful pause, Scarrat began to smile. "Extenuating circumstances. I see. To get you from hanging to transport. Well, it matters not to me what you do in that regard. I fancy your wench sorted it out."

This was true, and Scarrat's divining of it amazed Ned. She'd come this morning early with the scheme, having thought it out last night, after Justice Fielding brought her the note.

"Don't look so surprised, lad," Scarrat said with a laugh. "I know the fair sex better than you do. I know their gulling ways. No man's a match for a swindling bitch. There was never a trollop born who couldn't dupe an archbishop or a magistrate or a nobleman of England." Scarrat was smiling. "I'm glad the bawd has got your heart. It makes it easier to hold you. So go on with your Jenny Rivers tale, play your game, and praise God if you succeed. Only keep me and mine out of it."

"I will. I swear."

Scarcely had the tavernkeeper left the cell, than a fresh commotion began outside. Lifting in high dudgeon was the familiar voice of Doctor Bostock.

For a moment Ned made a fist of his good hand, then just as quickly relaxed it. Long since he'd resolved the matter of Bostock's peaching as no more than an expression of his perpetual need for illgotten gain. You could no more change the man than tell the sun to take another course through the heavens.

Once the argument with a turnkey subsided, the cell door opened and Doctor Bostock stuck his inquisitive ruddy face inside, his bloodshot eyes wide in hope and fear, with skinny Lemuel staring blankly from above his right shoulder.

"Dear lad?"

"Yes, come in, come in," Ned called from where he stood against the far wall.

"We won't be needing the guard? I told him I have faith in you, boy, you wouldn't jump us."

"No, come in."

"All forgiven?"

"I said, come in. All forgiven."

The two crept sheepishly into the cell, then turned to look behind at the turnkey who'd been paid to wait and see if the prisoner would set upon his visitors. Satisfied they were safe — no doubt Bostock had relinquished but half of the bribe and promised the rest if they lived — the turnkey pulled the door to and locked it.

At which point Doctor Bostock yanked a flask from his belt and drew the cork out with his teeth. He waved it around gaily. "A libation brought for old times! Don't look at it so appealingly," he growled at Lemuel. "Ned's first!"

Approaching, Ned took the flask and upended it, feeling the raw gin burn his throat. Bostock took it next and drank and withheld it for a few long moments before, with a sigh, he gave it to Lemuel.

"I'm heartily glad, dear chum, you was man enough to forgive and forget —"

"Forgive, not forget."

Rubbing his chin, the good doctor smiled broadly. "Forgiving's the better. We'd not have done it save the ninny was having trouble again with the lost blinker and needed a surgeon. What I've not done since taking him in to keep him alive and well and cared for! Lad, though you don't deserve such a place, you don't look the worse for it either. I'd not see you turned off without we was good chums again. And to that point, which is my sworn mission in seeing you, I give you Jenny Rivers' promise to make you comfy on the scaffold."

Ned felt himself smiling more easily than he had since coming to Newgate. "I make nothing of what you say."

"By that I mean I bring word of her intent to help you."

"To get free?" Ned asked eagerly.

"Ah, I think not that. But she said, 'I won't forget the fine-looking lad on the day they turn him off.' Jenny sat on her sofa in her heated room, as you remember how hot it is in there, and she told me there'd be two husky fellows at the gibbet. They'd stand in the front row, having bribed the constables, do you see, so when the noose goes round your neck and the hangman whips the dray horse and the cart moves off from under you and you swing, why, they'll run out, these two bully boys, and pull on each of your legs and that way rob the rope of a long tussle. Do you see the meaning? You'll have your neck broke clean and quick and that's a Godsend, boy, as I've seen them twist and jerk a quarter hour in rope as thick as your wrist, no better squeezer than a skinny bawd." He took a breath and sighed happily. "No one ever accused Jenny Rivers of forgetting chums and clients." He took such a heavy swig from the flask that there couldn't be much left in it. "Ah," he gasped and waved Lemuel off angrily. "Wait your turn, rogue! Ned's next."

Ned refused and the good doctor finished off the last few drops. "In your shoes, lad, I'd say hurrah, for Jenny means it. She's known for keeping her word as well as any thief who ever drew breath."

And after they'd gone, Justice Fielding came back to ask about the Sign of the Frigate. At that moment Ned Carleton saw a chance to escape, saw a light in his mind just as he'd seen light at the end of the Black Boy Alley tunnel. But to take that happy tack, he'd have to name Scarrat, and that he couldn't do, and the light shut off in his mind as if he'd never reached the tunnel's end.

Once again, before this crowded day was done, Ned received a visit from his sweetheart. He told her that Justice Fielding was still inclined to help, but few directions were left for him to go in. He didn't tell her of Fielding's interest in the Sign of the Frigate. There was no good in elevating her own interest in Scarrat. Let that be, Ned thought. His own chief interest now was to keep her clear of the murderous man.

"Yet there might be a way." Ned let his voice trail off, hoping to keep her steady with a vague little hope.

But she'd not have that. "For a judge there's always a way," Clare asserted. She rested her head on Ned's shoulder, in part so their eyes wouldn't meet when she spoke. "I'll do anything, lad, to get you off. Do you know that?" When he didn't reply, she went on.

"I've whored in this town to live." She felt his body stiffen next, but kept her head against his shoulder. "I did it hoping for money, for a man to keep me a long time in finery and good quarters. I've no scruples left. Lad, don't move! I've no scruples left. I've done everything under heaven. Lad. Listen! I'll do anything to keep you alive, anything. That's far more to me than money, and I did everything asked of me for gold alone. I've no scruples. None hold me. Nothing can stop me from doing what must be done with this judge, who seems a good man if a silly one. I'll use him as I must, and I'll get you free."

When he still said nothing, Clare continued. "I hope your silence means understanding and courage. You must tell him when next he comes here I love you no more."

Drawing away, Ned regarded her closely.

She gripped his misshapen hand in both of hers. "Dearest lad, hear me out. Let him think we're finished together. Do you understand?"

"You want him to think there's a chance with you."

"That's what he must think. He must feel I'm too much lady for a felon. He wants me, Ned."

"But he's old . . . crippled. The judge is a sick man." And he added, "A good, decent man."

"Sick, old, crippled, and good or no, decent or no, he wants me as a man wants a woman."

"I can't like it."

"Of course you can't like it nor can I, but it's your life, boy, and mine and the child's, so you'll tell him, you'll swear we're quits, you'll go through with it, you'll trick and deceive him till the man has fond hopes of me and is ready to do anything that makes them come true."

Abruptly rising, she ended the visit without even kissing him, but pounded on the door. "I am done!" she shouted.

Ned remained on the bench where he was, morosely watching her brisk movement from the cell. Unlike Scarrat he would never understand women, nor want to in the way that Scarrat did. All of the understanding and knowledge he had of Clare, in truth, was nothing more than the feelings in himself she aroused. He'd cut off his good hand to keep her from harm and dishonour. That's all he knew. But such resolve notwithstanding, he couldn't protect her, even if she would allow him to try.

[52]

DURING THE CANNING TRIAL London had roused itself to a fever pitch, which continued unabated while Betty languished for a month in prison, before the second part of her sentence was carried out — transport to the colony.

New pamphlets appeared. Causing a sensation, one was entitled Elizabeth Canning's *Declaration to the World, With an Account of her Late Visitation from an Angel with a Promise of her Deliverance in a few Days from Newgate*. The rhymed poem began with said angel addressing the girl:

> All hail, all hail, thou lovely virtuous maid,
> An angel's come to stay. Be not afraid;
> Tho' wicked men thy body does confine,
> The torment's theirs, the glory shall be thine.

Of Sir Crisp Gascoyne, whose stubborn refusal to let the affair vanish from public view and whose legal skill contributed to poor Betty's downfall, the heavenly visitor noted:

> He that at first persuaded Virtue Hall
> Her former affidavit to recall;
> He is resolved to try this skeem with thee,
> But mind him not, do thou be ruled by me.
> A curse upon his cruel savage nature,
> Thus to fly in the face of his Creator.

Then the angel dealt with the court's refusal to accept Guilty of Perjury But Not Wilful and Corrupt. Forcing the exhausted jury to bring in an amended verdict of Wilful and Corrupt was a violation of English liberty:

> You must bring her in guilty or not, says My Lord.
> Guilty, says they, tho' not with one accord;
> We recommend her to the mercy of the court;
> With lives and liberties they thus do sport.

The poem ended with the fervent hope that King George would intervene or else submit the country to heavenly censure:

> Before I fly up to the realms of bliss,
> I must acquaint His Majesty of this;
> He must take it into consideration
> If he expects a blessing on this nation.

Foes of the girl, challenged by such effusions on her behalf, resurrected old charges of pregnancy and pox. They insisted that throughout the trial she'd been calmed by wine and tutored in composure by Methodists, who buoyed her spirits with ecstatic promises of heavenly intervention. This last charge drew a protest from an Anglican clergyman who went to Newgate and swore that the girl had fallen to her knees and joined him in her poor shabby cell "earnestly in the devotional offices."

Of all her loyal adherents who came with silks and baubles and fancy dishes to tempt her palate in the best gaol suite in Newgate, the most generous was the former constable Robert Scarrat. He came almost every day to pay his respects to Elizabeth and the widow. When he appeared, the two women rushed to greet him with full curtsies. Had he been the king, so claimed witnesses, the man could not have been more respectfully received. Widow Canning often pleaded with him to sit awhile and listen to a wondrous new romance, a task which sometimes he performed with dignity and patience.

So until the day of her transportation Elizabeth Canning would bask in fame and nourish martyrdom and for the mitigation of her suffering was given certain proofs of disinterested sympathy by an unnamed man of power and fashion, through his trusted agent.

*

When Clare left her lover's cell, having instructed him how to behave toward the judge, she went upward in Newgate with the intention of bidding her friend goodbye. In a few days Elizabeth Canning was scheduled to board the *Myrtilla* and sail for Philadelphia in the colony.

Clare had hopes of her lad doing right. He was no talker by nature, but adversity had lately loosened his tongue, and he'd always had a good head on his shoulders. She trusted him to do his task well for the three of them, as that's how she thought now, even though her belly had scarcely begun to swell.

She climbed to the second floor and entered what had come to be called the Canning ward.

There was Bet, wearing a new frock with lace at the sleeves, receiving the attention of well-wishers, all women, and her mother sobbing into a kerchief and being comforted by ladies.

Seeing her friend, Bet disengaged from the crowd and went with Clare to the other side of the ward.

Clare regarded the round-faced rather plain girl with deep feeling. She felt there was between them a sense of danger, a memory of insult and injury, a continuous fear, a secret knowledge of the world, perhaps even an exaltation in the face of ill fortune that only two young put-upon women of London might share.

"So it's very soon," Clare said with a sigh and took her friend's hands in hers. "I'll sorely miss you."

"And I you. How is he?"

"We don't talk of what's to come. About the time you board, it'll be happening."

They were silent awhile.

"And you, dear Bet, how do you see tomorrow?"

Bet smiled, it seemed, with genuine happiness. "I'll be frank. It gets me from home and mother and the old ways. Staying here would have me married to an old brewer, as that's what mother wishes. She brought him round the other day. Pshaw! Wide as a barrel with a breath full of onions. I'll be better off, I warrant, over there. They tell me Philadelphia's a fine town."

"But what of the murderous red Indian savages? Will they be there?"

Bet shrugged. "We must trust in God."

"Do you believe that, miss?"

Bet smiled.

"I wish for your courage."

"And I for your prettiness. You won't have long to suffer, Clare dear. Someone'll come along and see to you."

"It's only him I want."

Again there was a long silence. Drawing her hands away, Betty raised one to stroke Clare's cheek tenderly. "Dear, I'm fond of you as can be, and so I'm telling you what I've learned of life. Do nothing without it's for your own precious benefit. If you act on your own behalf with your whole heart you come to believe whatever is best." Her eyes were shining with conviction. "I've learned nothing can break the spirit be you willing to protect it. And protecting it is not hard if you've the will. You stand fast, come what may, and pay no mind to anything else. You have open eyes but they be truly closed to what's outside. They look within."

Clare felt she'd never seen anyone so strong. It was almost fearsome in such a slight girl.

"I confess," Clare said, "there was moments when I felt you wanted to tell me something to ease your heart. I felt you trusted me, knowing I'd forgive you whatever it was, as surely I'd have done. But now I see you've nothing to hold back." Clare opened her hands, palms out, in a gesture of finality and completeness. "You're Bet Canning, sweet Bet and strong Bet, and what I see before me is only you, all of you, and you're at peace."

Bet laughed with sudden coarseness at these words. "Did you think I had a secret? All London wonders too! Do you see only me, all of me? Do you truly think so?" The idea seemed to amuse her, giving Clare a few moments of puzzlement and consternation, but then Bet leaned forward and embraced her, kissing her with affection on the cheek and brow.

When they parted, both were crying.

———◆———

❡ When next I saw him, Reader, I spoke no more of my little investigation as it would give rise to false hopes. Perhaps I might prove that Jenny Rivers had hatched a plot against him, but until I could offer at least a bit of solid hope, I'd say no more. Meanwhile, as if hearing each second tick away, he seemed hardly to notice my presence, but paced at a regular rhythm, his good hand forever rubbing the scarred surface of the other. He spoke of his home in Nottinghamshire, of his seafaring father's death.

Halting to stare at the clammy stone wall, he added in a voice low from emotion that at least his mother had mourned his father's death, whereas none would mourn his own so soon to take place. A few days more, and he'd be gone without so much as a tear.

Here I interrupted to remind him of his sweetheart, who would shed tears enough for a prince to envy. I bid him brace up and think of that.

He then laughed so unpleasantly that for a moment I wondered if the strain was unhinging him from reason.

Without looking my way, he told me there was a confession to make. He couldn't expect the consolation of which I had spoken, because in plain truth Clare didn't love him, nor had she loved him before he was taken up. She'd never reconciled herself to his thievery and criminal ways, and as much as he tried to convince her of his intention of giving it all up, she'd never believed him capable of leading a humble life after a taste of London.

Had he not been captured, most likely she'd never have seen him again, as they'd been apart for a fortnight before then.

A fortnight apart.

I was thunderstruck by this revelation, the implications of which surely required no study. If Clare was free — But how was it possible, given what I knew of them?

There must be a divinity behind the working of fortune, for certain it is there are some incidents in life so very strange that it seems to require more than human skill and foresight in producing them.

To gain a semblance of clarity in this affair, I asked the prisoner why Clare had been so faithful during his incarceration if she no longer cared for him.

He regarded me with the saddest eye possible before replying. It was, he explained, in the nature of a last Christian act for her to give comfort to someone for whom, after all, she'd once felt a strong attachment.

I said nothing. I believed such a thing of Clare.

Once again he laughed in that piteous lost manner, before observing that the girl meant to plead for his life, not from love but from duty, as she was the most Christian person he'd ever known of her sex, the most charitable and obliging in her nature. Reader, I am translating his plainer words into my own to give you the effect of his subtle and profound feeling.

Finally he broke off, unable to extol longer the virtues of someone whom he could no more call his own. It was a terrible moment for me, acting as witness to his despair while basking in the hope of my own undeserved happiness. I could no longer stay in the cell for fear of revealing the ruffled state of my own feelings. I bid him a hasty farewell.

But I hadn't reached the door without his grabbing my arm with truly awesome strength and begging me to save him. He pleaded with me to see his former sweetheart, who might argue for his life more eloquently than he could himself.

I told him that the young woman needn't play advocate in his behalf, as I'd already intended to give this matter my continued attention. But I warned him I could not — or to be more blunt still — *would* not intervene unless there proved to be solid ground for it.

Pounding for the guard, I glanced over my shoulder at Ned Carleton, now leaning against the wall. His unshaven face turned toward me, his eyes regarding me with their old liveliness, he smiled that odd and unsettling smile again, concocted of knowledge denied me. It seemed almost as if he were a parent who observes a child plainly bound for folly.

But this presentiment I packed away and quickly forgot in my eagerness to reach Clare.

[53]

¶ I once wrote, "Enough is equal to a feast."

Indeed, as I rushed from Newgate and found myself a chaise and set out for the house on Holborn, my hopes soared beyond all reasonable degree. If she didn't love the prisoner, then perhaps I had a chance in her affections. Not even then, however, was I insensible of my age and infirmities, all of which must count against me (though I was going about without aid of a cane, and my cough in the springtime air had subsided). But in my favour was a merry wit, could I regain even less than half of what I once had; and a standing among the gentlemen of London that might

do any suitor of a girl's impressionable heart; and a disposition
inclined to the romantic, which is to love as water is to a plant.

Smile, Reader, at my reckless anticipation, but it would be more
to the point to frown at my heedless rush into a most unseemly
situation, indeed an impossible one, hardly suited to a man of my
responsibilities in life.

Yet I couldn't help myself. Each time the truth of my position
edged forward in my mind, the chaise hurried me forward into
destiny, and a devastating image of the charmer blasted all
obstacles and common sense away. I leaned forward with the
eagerness of a stripling in first love.

But mounting the stairway toward her door, I brought myself
up short and fairly smiled. It struck me like the blow of a cudgel
how silly I was. Up there was a young woman who'd burst out
laughing did she know what fancy was seething in my feverish old
brain. With a sigh of relief I continued to climb, having with one
fell swing of reason swept away the potential folly. I prepared for a
sober interview with the prisoner's advocate. I'd discuss nothing
but Ned Carleton's chances for a stay.

There was a long delay when I knocked at her door and called
my name out, then noises, and her voice rising in a tone of
excitement, "Ah, it's you! It's you!"

So my hopes rushed back — to strain a metaphor, a howling
mob of them — at the sound of "It's you!"

Nothing there of "your worship" or "your honour" or even "sir,"
but "It's you!" You — the caressing pronoun I'd heard so often
from behind the door on my return from somewhere to dearest
Charlotte.

Nor was I mistaken in my hope of more than a formal meeting
after such a welcoming exclamation. When the door swung back,
Clare stood before me in a night-dress, without a cap, her hair
fallen to bare shoulders. Fortunately, she gave me no curtsy, but
rather a bold and taking smile. She apologized for her appearance,
as she'd been in bed throughout the day, having felt faint from an
attempt to move the breakfront from where it stood, obscuring
the window.

I did not avert my eyes, but looked at her with meaning. Gently
I ordered her back to bed as she might take a chill.

"What," I asked, "might I provide for your comfort?"

She made no reply, but climbed into bed, without pulling the
coverlet all the way up.

"I shall see about the breakfront," I said, removing my coat and regarding that piece of furniture. Though plain in construction, it was heavily made, of solid blocks of English wood of which our artisans are so proud. No girl could move such an object. Sizing it up, I judged that few men could move it more than an inch. Small wonder the effort had given her a faint, though I admitted to myself that a strapping fellow like Ned Carleton could manage it with ease.

So might I have done in the vigour of my youth.

Behind me the girl murmured something, but I didn't hear, so intent was I on the piece of furniture. Without more ado, flexing my hands and bending my knees, I grasped the central portion of it in a bear hug, my cheek flat against the enameled wood, and with a tentative application of back and shoulders attempted to lift — alas, with no discernible result. So reapplying my grip, seeking a firmer purchase (I heard her voice rising in alarm, begging me to stop, the which only urged me on, for I'd not have her think such a petty adventure could better me), I jerked forward with all the power at my command, the strength coming from my gouty toes, it seemed, the effort spreading through every muscle I possessed, until I felt to my inexpressible delight (and surprise) the piece of furniture leave the floor, so that I had it in my power as Heracles did Antaeus.

For a few seconds I didn't know what to do with my triumph, but then, with tiny steps moved leftward, away from the window, and set it down with utmost care, for having succeeded thus far I didn't intend ending on a false note.

Then I backed off, without looking behind me at Clare, it being my aim to keep my countenance from her a moment, as it must surely reflect the pain and exhaustion of a man who'd pushed himself to the limit of his strength and beyond. I gasped for breath, feeling the sweat pour from my brow, my heart pound wildly.

In a most concerned voice she asked was I afflicted in any way and begging my pardon for putting me to such exertion.

I couldn't yet speak, but half turned to nod feebly, as if to indicate that the effort had been only a small one, of little consequence.

I then turned more to look at her lying on the narrow bed, propped on one elbow, her eyes round and liquid, as if on the verge of anxious tears. The darling girl was like a naiad freshly come from swimming in a brook and now took her ease on a lawn of grass, with time stopped, in a magical wood.

At last I found voice enough to ask if the breakfront was in a place more agreeable to her.

Clare didn't answer a question which, you'll agree, was both foolish and boastful. Instead, she beckoned me with an enchanting gesture of her slim white arm. I went toward her as in a dream, sitting myself on the edge of the bed, trembling as much from her near-naked closeness as from the exertion that still besieged my whole frame.

With the gravity of a pastor, she said that the breakfront had fatigued me overmuch.

I denied it, declaring that I could never be fatigued in her service.

She thanked me with a smile that made me wonder if I'd intended a double entendre. Her breath seemed to come in gusts, moving the swell of her bosom above the thin night-dress. I divined in that sweet flesh a softness of purest satin.

I said that she had obliged me by allowing me to serve her.

She thanked me again, adding that she had no doubt of my ability to serve her and that perhaps it was her turn to serve me.

We looked at each other a lengthy time, till there was nothing else to do but for me to murmur, "You've bewitched my heart," to which, sighing, she threw herself into my arms.

Reader, I draw a veil over what followed between us, not that I'm prudish, but that I'm convinced the nature of some events puts them quite beyond words, just as I'm further convinced such moments as I knew then are worth purchasing with whole worlds.

"Love comforteth like sunshine after rain."

There came a time when our disarray had to have an end. I in my breeches and shirt, she in her night-dress, we sat together on the bed with cups of tea. You'll be indulgent if I say in all sincerity there was never in my life a cup of tea so delicious.

To confess the degree of my infatuation, I couldn't keep free of her for a moment, but continued to touch her hair, her lips, her throat, her bosom, as if to reassure myself this had not been a dream. Her breath was as sweet as a nosegay. I have only known one other woman with skin so lovely and smooth and warm to the touch.

Returning by degrees to sanity, having finished our tea and after still more kisses, I disclosed the nature of my earlier conversation with the prisoner. In the process I closely regarded her reaction when repeating his claim that she was no longer his.

She nodded solemnly and gladdened my heart by swearing he

had, in fact, told the truth. Imperceptibly through the weeks and days of his criminal activity, she'd lost her affection for him.

I could readily believe it, having seen the women of felons in courtrooms. They lived in constant danger of their men being took. It wore terribly at a woman's soul, for anxiety is an abrasive that grinds until the person it rubs against must change, as wood changes from the action of a pumice.

At this point the dear girl sobbed, so that I cradled her as close as if she'd been my own daughter (to tell the truth she was hardly older than my Harriet). Then Clare pulled away. I asked why. She tearfully explained the horror she felt at the thought of our being happy whereas the poor lad awaited a fate for which she was largely responsible.

I told her it was true our happiness was clouded by his distress, but she could hardly blame herself for what faced him.

Clare shook her head in violent disagreement. In trying to rewin her by piling more gold at her feet, Ned had set aside all caution. He'd tried to please her with riches without first conquering her heart. A bewitching smile followed her comment.

I asked how I might conquer her heart. Though it needed no pointing out, I added, "Over twice your age and often sick."

You have already done so, she declared. By tenderness and strength and wisdom. And by compassion and generosity, she added. Without further warning, Clare begged me to save Ned Carleton for the sake of her own peace of mind, as she couldn't rid herself of guilt of having authored his folly. His death would be forever on her conscience.

I calmed her with caresses and the promise to see what further could be done.

So vowing, I got to my feet and finished dressing, resolved to continue the investigation without delay, for time was indeed short.

The winsome child pleaded with me to disclose my plan for rescuing the poor fellow — "rescuing" was her own pretty word, learned perhaps from shilling romances. Unwilling to raise her hopes, for all might fail, I kept her in suspense. I told her so. I'd not get her hopes up without good cause.

To which the little minx asked why a stay of execution could not be ordered before evidence in his behalf was accumulated. I chid her for an innocent. Nothing could be done by me without sufficient cause. It was duty. Indeed, it was my sworn covenant with God and country.

Leaning against me — the warmth of her body like that of a fallen bird you hold breathing in your hand — she murmured her trust of me in all things, her faith being boundless.

When I took my leave with tardiness and regret *and* caresses, you may be sure, Clare touched my cheek with tenderness and asked had her surrender to me injured her in my regard.

"You have my heart," I told her.

Outside on the twilit street I didn't immediately hail a coach, for I couldn't keep my mind or body still. Through the surging crowd I pushed my way, exalted by happiness yet tortured by events I had set in motion.

The fact is, Mary was more in my thoughts than Clare.

I could not discard someone of such a kindly nature, whose ministrations had brought me virtually from the darkness of despair, whose body had willingly blessed me with children, whose concern was ever for my health and good cheer. Yet of equal if quite different persuasion was the feeling in my heart, the sensible pulse of new life and joy, which I'd not experienced since the loss of Charlotte. What was I to do?

It was surely out of the question that I act in purest honour by resolving never to see Clare again. There are men plain in their appetites: the toss of a gown, a bit of groaning, and they go away satisfied, never to return. But not I. The girl did in truth have my heart. I could no more resist her than the shore a tidal wave. But questions of the future lay in the future, in a more distant time than that still allotted to Nathaniel Carleton.

It was my immediate design to seek out the rascally Doctor Bostock and apply to him, by bribe or threat or whatever, for some truth that might save the condemned man's life.

To pursue this aim I set sail for Bow Street, where I hoped Saunders Welch had a good report on the old cheat's whereabouts.

[54]

HIS LORDSHIP had not been at home on two other occasions when Robert Scarrat begged for an audience, but at last he was ushered into the large study, whose grate was covered now in the summer months and whose mastiff, another fixture of the room, had been sent to accompany Judith and the children on a junket to Henchenbroke for a few weeks.

In ruffled silk shirt and cotton breeches, his lordship sat behind the desk, taking snuff when Scarrat entered the study.

Having bowed, Scarrat said with all the courtesy he could muster, "I thank you, milord. It's most agreeable to see your lordship again."

"Indeed."

Scarrat tried to gather his wits in the ensuing silence. The coachman Thomas had told him of Lord Sandwich's intense infatuation with a tall, rosy-cheeked singer here in London. Perhaps that's why, Scarrat had reasoned before coming here, his lordship hadn't recently needed songbirds.

"Most agreeable indeed," Scarrat said. "If I may be permitted to say so, your lordship looks hale and hearty."

"Indeed. Yes."

"I was wondering, your lordship . . ." Scarrat paused.

"Yes, man, go on."

"Was you in need of songbirds."

"Why?"

"You haven't sent for me, milord, and I was wondering."

"It is yours to wonder?" his lordship asked sharply.

"No, milord, please you, I thought . . ." Again he paused.

"I say, let them find their own."

"Milord?"

Taking another pinch of snuff, sneezing, Sandwich fixed Scarrat with a disapproving scowl. "They always ask *me* to get their wenches, but I say no more. I've no need of those services anymore, Scarrat. No more coachloads of hussies and drabs for Medmenham. At least not at my working."

Swallowing hard, Scarrat turned his tricorn around and around in his hands. "I'm at your service whatever, milord." He tried to make a smile. "Milord, the Canning chit's off to the colonies when the tide's right."

"So I've heard." Lord Sandwich at last smiled, picked up his letter opener, and dawdled with it. "I'm cosily quit of that affair."

"You are indeed, milord. I'm happy to say so."

His lordship leaned forward. "You're happy? Why, pray tell? How *happy*? That you got me a sorry bitch like that in the first place and in the second you stowed her in a loft and let her get free and near brought me the embarrassment of my life? That made you happy?"

"Ah, no, milord. I meant —"

Sandwich waved the knife through the air — a schoolmaster waving his birch rod above the head of a thoughtless boy. "Don't tell me, man, what you meant. Let me tell you what *I* mean. Canning's gone, good riddance to a bad whore. Granted you managed that, but not without my money. You was never a judge of women, as I can look back at what you've brought me over the years and say a thing good about scarcely a one. Now I've had enough of the pranks at Medmenham, those spoiled wags and naughty boys at their frivolities. I want no more of it, and so I want no more of your whores. Wait," he commanded, raising a hand when Scarrat opened his mouth to say something. "As for the Frigate, I've given it deep thought and I warrant there's no need anymore for me to support such a place of information. It's clear Newcastle has weathered another storm and my chances at the Admiralty rank nil right now. So I'm saying I don't need your services at the Frigate either. I could care a tinker's damn for your advices on what those rascally watermen do. Do you hear what I'm saying, Scarrat?"

"Yes, milord, but —"

"You hear but don't understand. Indeed, I see it in your face. I'm saying I no longer need *any* of your services." Putting aside the letter opener, he drew on his round spectacles and adjusted the wire hooks around his ears. It seemed as if he'd wholly forgotten Scarrat's presence, as he searched around the desk for something.

Then abruptly he squinted up at Scarrat. "Don't look so bedraggled, man. It's not the end of the world. Screw your courage up and go on. Have no fear. I won't forget you. I'll send a pouch around within the week. I've always appreciated your vigilance in my behalf, thank you, sir. Now be so kind as to withdraw."

Readjusting his spectacles, Lord Sandwich took up a quill, dipped it in the ink well, and scratched his signature on a paper, after which, looking up, he said in a stern voice, "I said, be so kind as to withdraw."

Scarrat did.

Outside on the street, after putting the hat on, he stared at his hands. The knuckles were still white from the tension of his fingers as they'd slid the black rim of his tricorn around and around and around.

———————

⁋ So, Reader, I had the address from Saunders Welch, who grumbled considerably at my insistence on going myself to smoke out Doctor Bostock. He muttered it was a miracle I walked at all and would be a second miracle did I go on such investigation alone and hold up. As two miracles in the same day couldn't be expected, I must take him along.

Recalcitrant all my life, I told my good friend and colleague he'd just made a mistake by saying "must." I bid him farewell, hailed a hackney, and set merrily off. Daylight nearly gone, in its stead a hovering night mist engulfed the chariot's wheels like a great black surf at Skegness.

On the way to find the doctor, I recalled Ned's history with Bostock and Lemuel, chuckling at the memory of Ned's initial encounter with them. Someone with experience of London would have suspected an evil design, seeing that none in this bustling city would for reasons of disinterested good will take a stranger off the street and provide him a costly supper. It was a measure of Ned's innocence, not the old scoundrel's cunning. I had only a faint recall of Bostock coming before me to sniff out a reward for turning a friend in. But I recalled enough to smile, as I've always discovered in myself a sympathy or perhaps even a liking for such rogues. There seems in their bluster less vice than I've found in many public men of fame and fortune. From the bench, of course, I'd not hesitate to sentence one like Bostock severely for his crimes, yet would I smile at his antics, having always had a weakness for such creatures who prance about and thunderously proclaim their excellence, while the very words of their boasting reveal their improvident character.

Since what I write is in the nature of a confession, I must describe my first encounter with a fellow of this hapless turn. It happened at home in East Stour during my youth, whenever my father (a retired army officer on half pay who'd once fought bravely under Marlborough) flung into a room with yet another illusive scheme for squandering his estate.

I say that encountering my father was my introduction to a sort of a reckless spendthrift. Later I met another such person who, if less vocal in his assumption of immediate prosperity, was equally gifted at wasting the capital he had. Perhaps you've already divined, Reader, that this prodigal was myself.

Such were my thoughts when the hackney pulled up to the decrepit little lodging house. As I entered the stinking lobby, a door opened to the side and an old woman peered out in a threadworn jacket held to her throat. There was a stuporous combative look in her narrow eyes. I asked the whereabouts of Doctor Bostock, which made the woman cackle humourlessly and ask in return had I come to take the rogues up, as I looked a gentleman and a thief taker. They, God's curse, were scum and rips and smugglers in the bargain if the truth be known.

Fishing out a coin, I held it before her eyes.

Forthwith she suggested I try a gin shop nearby in Dartmouth Street, as the scoundrel and his boy spent their evenings there foisting pennies and then rushing to a cocking house where they promptly lost wagers, for at heart they was dunces and chuckleheads and simpletons to boot. Handing the coin over, I thanked the woman, which only made her cackle louder.

And so, to be brief, I found them.

He pretended not to know me, even after I introduced myself while sitting down at their bench in such way that they couldn't get past me. I called the gin girl over and ordered rounds for the three of us.

That pleased the doctor. When the boy thanked me, that loosened the doctor's tongue. "Hold your tongue," he ordered the boy, then turning to me with the sigh of a martyr complained of Lemuel being a thorn in his flesh, as these youngsters today lollop at their ease while their betters are kept at hard duty.

I hoped to waste no time here, so launched into my questions. Having brought the Runners along, how had he discovered Ned's whereabouts in the neighbourhood?

"As the lad's regular in his ways, I know his paths," the doctor claimed, as if prepared for such questioning.

"Where was he when you saw him?"

"On the street, your worship."

"Coming from somewhere?"

The doctor eyed me shrewdly before replying. "I saw him on the street," he repeated.

"Not coming from a tavern?"

"To my knowledge," the doctor said, pursing his lips judiciously, "no."

"Not coming," I persisted, "from the Sign of the Frigate?"

"I can't say, your excellence."

"Can't — or won't?"

"I can't say where he come from. The devil take me if I say false to a magistrate!" Like a placating concession, he added, "Though I know that tavern, the Frigate."

"Does Ned Carleton too?"

"That wouldn't be known to me."

"Tell me of the Frigate."

"Frequented by the worst-drinking, swag-bellied, washy damn watermen your excellence ever saw."

"The waterman who was robbed —"

"What one was robbed?"

"Why, that was the charge for Grand Theft."

"As to that, I wasn't called to witness. I had business out of London, when the trial was on."

"Tell me, did you see Ned rob him?"

"As God is my witness, no. I saw no robbing, no shooting."

I nearly stopped there, for plainly I'd get no more from him. Though a rogue and a fool, he did have the cunning of the streets in his veins, and though bilked surely by his peers, he could hold up against the likes of me. But I asked one more question.

"What sort of lad is Ned Carleton?"

The doctor drank and kissed his dirty fingertips. "Salt of the earth!"

"Salt of the earth!" put in Lemuel.

After admonishing the boy with a heavy scowl, the good doctor went on into ecstatic praise of his dear chum Ned. "He was a fine, healthy, good lad till she come along," Bostock maintained glumly.

"Who came along?"

"Why, his bawd. The one he got from the shop where she whored and brought her to his quarters."

I managed to control myself. "Tell me about her."

"I never saw a finer skin in my life," he said, smacking his wet lips. "Nor I wager a more cunning jade. Got more sides to her than a king's palace."

"You say he brought her from a shop?"

The bewhiskered old countenance was less shifty-looking than usual. He seemed to be on solid ground in his report. "Yes, I know the place, a brushmaking shop that sells more than brushes. The best of young strumpets there. He brought this one home."

"Then did she part with him?"

The doctor chortled. "Part! Never a pair of love birds like them two! When I went to tell her poor Ned was took, her colour changed to the pallor of the grave, I swear. She was atremble and set sail past Lem and I like the fleet at battle station. Part them two? Not them never. Till death do them part."

"I see."

"No offense, excellency, but you look bamboozled. Such a woman bamboozles us all, as it's her nature. You'd think her a lady didn't you know better. No stinkpot that. No blazing fireship with the pox. No mean talk but nearly a pure speech. Ah, I had one like that in my youth but she dropped me for a poultry merchant."

"So he brought her from a brushmaking shop to his room, and they lived together when he was caught."

The doctor laughed. "I declare, sir, you look stunned and hoodwinked." Leaning forward, he nearly tapped my hand familiarly, but thought better of it. Then he smiled slyly and to my dismay he said, "A beauty, hey? Your worship, I warrant if the bitch leveled her battery of charms even at you, she'd win the day!" He drew back quickly, as my expression must have warned him of the fury his remarks had awakened in me.

Upon my feet, I said in a great effort to keep my voice from trembling, "You were there when Ned was set upon. You knew if he came from the tavern. And if he did, if he had a money pouch on him. You saw him accosted. You saw how the shootings took place. I could have you brought up on charges! I'll have you hauled into Newgate!"

I stomped out, forgetting the pain in my gouty foot. I had misused my power terribly. I had thrown down a gauntlet of fierce words in the heat of a moment — for which I'll ever be ashamed and can justify only as an expression of my passionate involvement in this affair.

You can well imagine my resistance to accepting the idea that a woman to whom I'd given my heart had so coldly fooled me, not only about her continued alliance with the prisoner, but apparently with any member of the male sex having means to buy her favours. No, I wouldn't believe it. Could I, a man of experience, be thus gulled?

Methinks, Reader, the answer had been hovering in the back shadows of my mind since I began hoping for her.

To my credit, perhaps, I vowed not to succumb to despair. On the contrary, I meant to govern myself sufficiently to let reason have a rightful share in my behaviour — for a change. I could no more condemn Clare on the claim of such a rascal than I could chuck everything else in my life and rush to her, begging forgiveness for having so little faith.

[55]

❡ Not too long ago I had ridiculed in public court a poulterer who, in his blind age, had thought himself sufficiently attractive to entice a young woman; who, in her own turn, had thought him sufficiently feeble in mind to be gulled by her. I had held them up in the courtroom for the dupes they were, both prey to an inability to see the huge abyss stretching between desire and accomplishment.

It was with such a galling memory that I reached the house in Holborn and mounted to Clare's room, one painful step at a time, my cane (for I'd brought it from Bow Street) drilling hard against the creaking boards.

In a fetching white bodice and a brown hoopless skirt, she opened the door and with a cry of delight flung herself into my arms, exclaiming happily that I'd put her in a fright, not having seen her since — she paused modestly — I had made her mine. After this declaration, she pushed away from me and whirled round like a child and turned to appraise me with a little groan of dismay at the cane I carried again. Then she declared her intention to rid me of the gout forever by her artful caresses. She begged me to sit and would have started to remove the slipper from the gouty foot where I stood if I'd not gripped her shoulders firmly and said no.

She regarded me closely, while on my own part I studied her with equal desire for understanding.

Abruptly she began to chatter like a girl and walked about, busying herself with the tea kettle, now with the fire iron, now with spoons and some dishes, as she'd bought marmalade and almond biscuits in the hope I'd come today.

This commotion of hers allowed me an undesired chance to absorb once again the loveliness of her person. In my growing dismay I'd almost put aside the memory of her charms, but now, with her moving about in such a lively fashion, I acknowledged with a sinking heart the perfections of her face and form, the which recall to me, as I write these words, those sadly wise lines of Milton:

> Yet beauty, though injurious, hath strange power,
> After offense returning, to regain
> Love once possessed.

Indeed, within minutes of being again in her presence, I was more than half in love again, and blindly, and nourishing the hope that my suspicions were groundless. I was bewitched, yes, but with a reservation now, because the substance of her chatter began to put my reason on guard.

Not only herself, she declared, had missed my visits, but the prisoner (for so impersonally did she call him) had missed my presence as well. Only three days were left in which to win a stay, she pointed out with a charming pout. It behooved the three of us (as if I was with them in a coalition) to act with dispatch, after which two of us (she gave me a fetching smile) would be free to pursue without guilt the joys already tasted but once.

A pretty speech.

She came toward me, her smile promising an amorous dalliance which I'd not be capable of withstanding. To avoid it and give a current of cold reason its opportunity for expression between us, I asked pointedly for a dish of tea.

This request and doubtlessly the tone of it had her again appraising me with sly glances. But she nodded in apparent cheerfulness and went to the kettle, where she was standing when I threw a thunderbolt her way.

My investigation having proved fruitless, I could not enter a stay for the prisoner.

I watched her shoulders and back, but they never flinched, nor did her hand tremble in lifting the kettle from the fire. It was a display of such admirable composure under stress that for a heart-lifting moment I was convinced again of her innocence.

But when she turned her lovely face to me, it spoke volumes with a different meaning: the gleam in her dark eyes, the parted lips, the knit brow, all told me what I needed to know. In retrospect, I think of all that I've admired in Clare I admired most her behaviour at that moment.

"Something has changed," she said.

"I mean to be frank."

"Do."

I told her of Bostock's claim that she'd been an inmate of a pleasure house and that she'd never faltered in her affection for her sweetheart.

Clare sat down wearily at the table and looked steadily at me from her large dark eyes. "I was indeed a whore once."

I nodded. "That's distressing, but nothing more. The most distress is in thinking you had to live that way. It would be a poor lover who felt otherwise."

She said nothing, but looked down at her hands.

"And the other part," I said. "Did you lie to me? Was it your plan to scruple nothing? By any means prevail on me to get him stayed?"

Her silence was enough.

Getting to my feet, I was ready to step out on the cane when she fell to her knees and grabbed my legs in a powerful embrace of supplication, begging me through sobs not to let him die, no, not her lad, not to let them hang the pretty lad of her heart, not to let him, no, not him —

And I saw clearly at that moment what I'd been pushing back into my mind whenever it bid fair to confront me head on: all she'd done had been done for the man she loved.

It was so clear and simple. It should have been all along had I wanted to think rather than hope: the flimsy shift, the fainting spell, the disarray, the liquid looks were the stuff of shilling romances.

With considerable effort I drew Clare to her feet and put my arms about her shoulders, for in moments I'd been transformed from deceived lover to someone of disinterested sympathy or perhaps into the father Henry Fielding would have been had my own daughter Charlotte lived and come to me in such distress. I'd been a dupe, a gull, a bubble in their hands, yet I could not — how could I? — blame Nathaniel Carleton for wanting to live or his Clare for helping him to do so.

Perhaps, Reader, you'd have known what to say then, but I did not, except to murmur the lame phrase which the afflicted only too often hear when real help has been denied: "I am sorry."

When I released her, Clare's eyes were brimming, her defense shattered, her heart exposed, her cunning failed. Yet in a voice that stung me to the soul, she again asked would I stay the execution.

"I cannot," I said, hating the words as I spoke them, almost as much as I wished at that moment to be someone other than myself, who had been in this young woman's life both judge and lover.

I had lied to Clare.

I meant to try one more time to discover evidence, however slight, that could allow me to enter a petition at the king's bench for a stay of execution on the grounds of extenuating circumstances. It was no rare practice, as some judges had come by small fortunes by doing so, while courtiers had merely whispered a little phrase in the king's ear and won clemency for someone. I was well acquainted with the meandering path the law might take with just a little effort: a slight distortion here, a conjecture there, the chance of a misrepresentation, a failure of communication between thus and so, a hint of judicial error lost in records gathering dust on a shelf long forgotten, the imperfections of eye and ear, the odd twists of aye and nay. Indeed, as Rabelais observes, Necessity hath no law.

To be sure, I still loved the girl to distraction, for, after all, "There's a beggary in the love that can be reckoned." Her loyalty to her beloved quite overbalanced the deceit played on me. Despite a battering from fatigue my mind was now clear enough to know that. Often in my writing I'd set forth an idea which Clare had amply illustrated — namely, the outward act is less than the motive for it, as a bad deed for a good motive is better than a good deed for a bad motive. So I believed, and so had Clare made me confront not in the abstraction of philosophy but in the conduct of actual life. With the hope in mind I could yet save Ned Carleton, I went home by sedan chair and called Saunders Welch to me from the register office. I made out a general warrant of disclosure, gave it to him, and instructed him to find the tavernkeeper of the Sign of the Frigate and bring him posthaste to Bow Street.

Then going upstairs, I was informed by the nurse there that little Louisa's croup had worsened. In the nursery I found a surgeon in the process of examining her. Such a pale little thing she was and so racked by a heavy cough, with her eyes half opened in a stunned way, as though she couldn't believe life could be thus. Indeed, she'd had scant experience of it and that painful.

I put my arm around Mary, who was gaunt in her anxious fear and still weak from the birthing bed.

The surgeon then drew us into the hall, where he removed his spectacles with a judicious air and informed us that, in his opinion, the child was in no danger — that is, he added, of an immediate nature. He would prescribe a stronger plaster and a new drop. Given no unforeseen developments, which of course in some instances did occur, we might well look forward to Louisa's full recovery, though when that might be was still difficult to predict with certainty, as these matters were never straightforward, indeed, often surprising in their twists and turns.

He continued in this infernal vein for a while longer, then left us. I restrained myself from criticizing him in front of my wife, who fairly devoured his words, taking their vagueness for hope and their qualification for assurance.

We had a grim meal that evening, not even cheered by the girlish chatter of Harriet, who was exclaiming over a ball attended last night. After supping, Mary and I sat by baby Ralph's crib awhile. Then in we went to Louisa, who had mercifully fallen into a deep sleep, which we both knew was a good sign, and so with mutual smiles we headed for our separate rooms. I knew that Mary would do scarcely more than rock all night in a chair and take frequent trips to the sick room.

In my own room I sat disconsolately on the bed, reviewing the state of affairs. A curious thought occurred to me which I hope, Reader, you will treat with forbearance. If only life might copy art, I could sit down with pen and paper and furnish the destinies of a felon awaiting execution, his sweetheart, and my sick infant daughter, bringing all to a happy conclusion.

Then a call from the doorway brought me back to this world. It was Saunders Welch, grinning, doffing his plumed hat in an ornate bow. "We've got the tavernkeeper downstairs, Henry. As grey a man as I've ever seen. He awaits your pleasure."

———————

Hours ago Scarrat had been sitting in his quarters behind the tavern, when Coachman Thomas came with a pouch from Lord Sandwich. At Scarrat's invitation the coachman sat down to have a brandy.

"I'm damned sorry, Robert, he let you go. We had times together, didn't we, going round and getting him songbirds." Thomas sighed. "His lordship's mean-spirited. But that's gentry. Can't see the world beyond their own hand. Nothing matters to him right now but dicking Martha Rae. Not even the Admiralty. I wager he'll tire of the girl soon."

"And ask me to get him songbirds again?" Scarrat asked.

Thomas shook his head. "He's weary of pranks and quick tosses. At least she's taught him that. I know the bastard." Drumming on the table, Thomas added, "There's something you must know. He's looking to sell the Frigate, so you'll be out of here soon."

"Ah."

"Well, have a look." Thomas pointed with his cup at the pouch lying between them on the table. "Let's see if his lordship was generous."

Opening the pouch, Scarrat was dismayed to find but fifty guineas, an amount his lordship might have given to a maidservant leaving the household after a year.

"Why so paltry?" he asked Thomas.

"I've served him long. It's what I'd expect him to do. He wants you to know you mean nothing. You've been used up, cast out. He wants you to know you're nothing but a dog."

"Ah." Scarrat pushed the pouch away and lifted up his cup of brandy. He rarely drank, and when he did he sipped, but now he knocked back the entire dram, coughing violently thereafter.

"Here, here, man," said Thomas in alarm. "There's more to life than working for him. Get out of London. Go back where you belong."

"It's here I belong."

"A real citizen of London town, hey? They're rare enough. I come from Kesteven myself."

"Would he help me find a footman's post, you think?"

Thomas shook his head emphatically. "You'd get no recommendation. He wants you out of his life. I'm sorry, man."

Thomas finished his brandy, patted Scarrat almost affectionately on the shoulder, and left.

And so Scarrat had sat alone in his room, with fifty guineas as the fruit of years of loyal service. He looked into the future and saw nothing. Getting up, he walked to the window and stared at his garden. Soon he must leave it — and for where? And what of his clocks? He went on an inspection of them. A large chest of fine mahogany contained row upon row of clocks and pocket watches, their steel parts clicking and whirring and ratcheting. Near the window stood the grandfather clock of walnut, his pride and joy. It had a face of polished brass engraved with cherubs' heads and banded with the most elegant satinwood. Here was another sort of world, one of order and calm, where Scarrat could lose himself in the contemplation of toothed wheels and pinions moving in predictable motion, their metallic beauty belying the miserable uncertainty of life around him, of his own life.

On the lower shelf of the cabinet lay another kind of treasure, bought also from a watchmaker. It was an Italian miquelet-lock belt pistol, with an inlaid barrel and long slim lines, far more elegant than the kind made by Swedes and Germans. He'd never fired the piece, though he kept it loaded. Next to it lay a paper cartridge for priming. Picking up the pistol along with the cartridge, he studied the flint held in the cock and the battery opposite it. When the trigger was pulled, the cock, impelled by a spring, should leap forward and the flint it held as a dog holds a bone should strike the battery, producing a shower of sparks, some of which should drop into the priming powder of the pan. This flash, penetrating to the bore, should ignite the full charge and propel the ball forward through the muzzle. He thought about this process, step by step, as it should develop. It was not as beautiful as the working of a clock. Sometimes the sparks didn't penetrate to the bore and fire the pistol, causing a mere flash in the pan. For a few more moments he compared the erratic event of firing a pistol with the elegant motion of a timepiece.

Then with his teeth, he tore open the paper of the cartridge and filled the pan with powder. Doing this slowly and with utmost care seemed to calm him. He'd been breathing heavily.

So the pistol was ready, though he wouldn't do such a thing. Why should he? Indeed his cough had worsened, but he'd lived most of his life with it. He had years left. Perhaps he'd become an ale drawer in a tavern like the Frigate. Perhaps the new owner would let him stay. Perhaps he might even keep his clocks and garden.

Perhaps.

Cocking the pistol, he placed the barrel in his mouth, and held the thumb of his right hand on the trigger. One moment after seeing a jittery flash as the cock hit the flint against the battery, he'd see nothing, ever again.

Nothing? This was not for Robert Scarrat. He'd come up from a parish workhouse and from chimney sweeping. He had pride and a standing. His life was worth living as much as any man's, as much

as that of Lord Sandwich. It was a revelation and so shook him that
he yanked the gun from his mouth.

No sooner had Scarrat replaced the flintlock in its cabinet than a
loud voice came from behind the door, ordering him to open it in
the name of the law. He was wanted at Bow Street before Justice
Fielding.

So now he stood in the Bow Street courtroom, at night, without
spectators save the fancily dressed man in the plumed hat. He
watched Justice Fielding hobble in, looking as woebegone as last
time Scarrat had set eyes on him. It was a wonder the man could
still do a day's work, with his sunken cheeks and swollen paunch
and sickly pallor. But his eyes shone with a fierce understanding,
and the hooked nose spoke of inner power and those ample lips,
slightly curled, gave him the look of someone both skeptical and
amused. Scarrat had rarely felt admiration for anyone — noblemen
he gave respect for their station only — but here was a man, one to
believe in and fear.

The questioning began. When Scarrat gave his name, he saw the
judge's eyebrows raise in recognition.

"I know you," said Fielding. "You were in the Canning affair."

"Yes, your worship. It flatters me you remember."

"Well, you're a memorable man," the judge said with a cryptic
smile. "Do you know one Nathaniel Carleton?"

Scarrat was struck at that instant by the absolute knowledge of
standing at a crossroad. He had little time to think through which
way to go, but he felt that his answer would determine the course of
his entire life.

"I ask you, do you know Nathaniel Carleton?"

"Your worship — I do." There. It was done. He had chosen the
road, and it would take him awhile to see the consequences of his
choice. He felt too that Fielding was helping him take this path.
They were strong men, equals, going this way together. "I knew
Ned Carleton in Lord Sandwich's household. I was once a footman
there. Ned was a postilion."

"I see. You've a wide range of acquaintances. Betty Canning,
Ned Carleton, the right honourable Lord Sandwich."

"It is my fortune." He was gratified to see the judge smile at his
way of putting it. Scarrat's hopes lifted then. He knew why he'd
chosen this way. It was taking him out of his difficulties. It was

making him newly free. He could see himself racing along in a postchaise.

"So you knew Ned Carleton. Did you know he was taken up on charges of theft and murder?"

Scarrat hesitated. This answer was not altogether easy. He had to think keenly or fall in a ditch. "Recently I've been out of town much of the time."

"Come, man, you must have known of his capture not too far from your tavern."

"Yes, your worship."

"Are you indifferent?"

"I'm sorry he killed a man."

"That day, as you recall, had he been in your tavern with a money pouch?"

"Indeed, your worship, as I gave it him." He could see from the judge's eager expression that he was going the right way.

"How is that?"

"He wanted a loan."

"Tell me about this loan."

Scarrat felt himself racing along, he felt free and easy as if nothing could stop him now. "The lad needed a loan to leave London and raise sheep. As he's stout and honest, I provided it at interest."

"So leaving your tavern, he carried money loaned by you?"

"That's God's truth, your worship."

"But you never revealed this God's truth at the trial."

"I was not in London. And" — Scarrat could see the road widening in front of him, sunny, cloudless — "I feared giving testimony."

"What did you fear? The courtroom? As I remember, in the Canning affair you had a liking of courtrooms."

"I feared for the reputation of Lord Sandwich, your worship. For he's often provided me with money to loan out. The interest we split."

Fielding guffawed. "Lord Sandwich, a moneylender?"

Scarrat bowed his head in respectful acknowledgement of the fact.

"So you wanted to keep secret that a peer of England lent money to sheepherders?"

"I swear it." Scarrat hastened to add, "I beg Ned's forgiveness. I'm heartily sorry."

Fielding waved off the apologies. "It's such dismal folly I believe it. Would you swear by affidavit to having given Ned Carleton money in your tavern?"

"I would, your worship."

"Two hundred guineas' worth?"

"I would, your worship."

"Did you witness the shooting that took place not far from your tavern?"

Scarrat felt on solid ground, pounding along the thoroughfares of England. "I did not."

"Because if you saw him shoot in self-defense, all charges against him might ultimately be dropped."

"I saw nothing, your worship. I won't perjure myself."

"Admirable." Fielding wore a skeptical look, but then sighed as if this were quite enough. "I thank you, Mister Scarrat. Your affidavit may save his life." As an afterthought he said, "Are you indifferent to that?"

"No, your worship. I am all too pleased."

Later, having read and signed the affidavit, Scarrat took to the streets, tilting his tricorn at a rakish angle. It was a bit of bravado, as in the calming aftermath of his meeting with Justice Fielding, he was no longer sure of his decision to acknowledge Ned Carleton. Time would tell if he was indeed on the open road, free, with Lord Sandwich at his beck and call.

Part Ten

TYBURN

[56]

THERE WASN'T much time left. There were things to be done. Ned got out his paper, quill, and ink. He wrote awhile, then tore up the paper. It was not what he wanted to say. He wanted to tell his child — boy or girl? — of his love for the hills of Nottinghamshire. He wanted to express how it was to live where trees after a rainstorm were so heavy with wet leaves that their branches touched the ground. He wanted to describe the amiable but lonely ring of a blacksmith's hammer at sunrise in a village, the dry rhythmic scraping of wagon wheels turning on their axles, the distant calling of nightingales. He wanted to recapture in words the sweet pungency of apricot tarts smoking in a pan on feast days. And most of all he wanted to tell his child of the way Grandfather would rise one morning when the sea whispered again and pack his canvas bag without a word; and the way Grandmother would hold back tears until the sailor vanished at a rolling gait. Ned felt he could have written such things down with but a farthing of the artful skill of Grub Streeters, whose words had first roused his interest in Elizabeth Canning. But gripped in his fingers the quill creaked like a door on rusty hinges.

With a determined sigh, he began again.

Deare Childe
Forgive yr Father for leving yr Mother to the sory lot of a hempen Widow. I be truly Gilty of the Crime I cd not git work in this place.

Remembr of yr Father he went to his Deth for the con [he crossed out "con" thrice and began again] convinece of his Betters. I doth not Wishe to Dye ere you be Borne. I wld hold You in my Arms.

Respectfully

Yr Father

Nathaniel Carleton

Folding the paper carefully, he placed it in his coat pocket, waiting for Clare to come.

He didn't wait long. She was dressed in a linsey-woolsey skirt and bodice, with a hooded cloak round her shoulders. Without a word she handed him a bundle. He knew what was in it: a clean frock-coat, breeches, stockings, and shirt.

"I thank you, lass."

"I took the old book to the black boy as you wished. I asked for the one who'd kept the dog and found him."

"Sitting on a stoop."

"It was like you said. He took the book and smiled."

"He saw me with it many times. No matter he can't read. He knows we're chums again. He was good to Sandy and she loved him more than me." Ned took out the folded note. "Keep this for the child."

Folding it tighter, she shoved it into her bodice. "I'll carry it next to my heart till he reads it for himself."

At last Ned smiled. "Can you be sure it's a boy?"

"Your son will read."

"And you, dearest lass, what will you do?" They'd not allowed that shadow to fall between them until now.

"Each day I go to sewing shops that give me work sometimes. I won't follow the old path."

"I believe you." They were quiet awhile.

"No hope, lad?"

He shook his head, watching her lips tremble. "The judge did what he could. I hold no grudge."

"I'm glad you don't." She lowered her gaze first. "Then, this is the last time for us?"

"I believe so, lass."

"No chance of a stay." She said it as a statement.

"There be at least fifty guineas under the floorboard to the left of the grate. You lift the edge with a knife. I've been keeping that back," he said with a smile. "For a surprise."

Opening her purse, she withdrew a pair of white lambskin gloves, one larger than the other. "This be my surprise."

She gave them to him. "See do they fit."

Slowly he drew one glove over the good hand, then the larger over the bad. "Yes."

"Good."

"I thank you, lass. Tomorrow" — he paused — "don't go to Tyburn."

"I will."

"Please do not."

"I will."

"There's your belly to think of. I beg you."

Studying him hard, Clare relented. "Do you wish it that much, I won't go."

"Good girl."

"Can I stay till tomorrow?"

Ned shouted for the guard. At the door he said, "Two guineas for her to stay tonight."

Looking past Ned's shoulder, the turnkey grinned. "For a toss that good, it's four." Then he shrugged. "Where you're going, chum, you won't need gold, less Old Nick stands at the furnace and you pay to burn. Give me five." Pocketing the money, he said, "Get her out at daybreak. They have a big day awaiting you."

Having old straw to lie on and one threadbare blanket and no future to share, they were awkward and shy at first, held back from each other by fear, numbed by thoughts of tomorrow, but after awhile their caresses took dominion and they let go, and for this frenzied time they forgot everything, felt everything, became what they'd always been for each other, and it was no different tonight from any other time.

As if they'd made a pact to let love speak for them, neither said but endearments. Tomorrow was not mentioned afterward, and the weary pregnant girl soon fell asleep.

Ned listened to himself breathing. How could he ever stop breathing? He could not. Yet tomorrow he would. And the next thing, the sinking thing he thought of was facing his last day. But how could it be his last day? Other days would follow. There would be a Thursday, a Friday, a next week. It didn't seem that Thursday could begin without him. How could it? It was day after tomorrow, and Clare would be breathing then, just as he breathed now. She'd be breathing for herself and the child, but he wouldn't be breathing. To understand that tomorrow was his last day of breathing was to penetrate a mystery beyond his knowing.

Fatigue overwhelmed him too. He was starting to doze off when a sound startled him. It was a booming, groaning, melancholy sound. It was the bell of St. Sepulchre and it would toll from midnight till execution time in the afternoon. Beneath the prison wall a watchman stood ringing his bell. He called up verses recited on the eve of a Hanging Day.

> "Forswear your sin, trust in Christ's merit,
> That Heavenly Grace you may inherit;
> And when St. Sepulchre's bell tomorrow tolls,
> The Lord have mercy on your souls."

Lord have mercy, Ned said to himself.

"Lord have mercy on us," Clare murmured against his neck, as the tolling bell and the watchman's voice had awakened her.

They slept no more, but lay together, wrapped in each other's arms. "Lass," he said toward morning, "you've not told me what happened with Justice Fielding."

"I thought you knew."

"I wish you to tell me."

"When he came to see me, I seduced him easily. Did you think otherwise?"

"It's what I thought."

"You're sorely tried by it."

"I can't deny it, though I wanted you to do what you did. I thought it'd make him more determined to get me off. He'd be . . . beholden, I can't deny that either."

"But because it didn't work, you think it was wrong? Lad, let it go. There's only hours left. Let go of it."

"I encouraged you."

"You don't know women, lad. You know sheep and dogs and something of men, but nothing of women. I'd give myself to a hundred if I could win you a day more. What does it mean to me in balance with your life? Men have no sense of importance. You hoodwink yourselves. You're beguiled by words. I wish to God you and the judge could make it over. I do. He's a fine good man. He likes you mightily, Ned. What he did was no more than other men would do."

"I'd not think it of him. He'd have his conscience. He's writ great books."

"See what I mean? You see him through a man's eyes. You don't see him truly." Turning, she kissed Ned. Somehow this conversation had relaxed them and recalled their domestic time together, when they talked for hours in love's aftermath. They both fell asleep in the early morning hours. Ned dreamed of Sandy and the black boy working in the open field, running and circling and coming back.

Stirring first, Clare turned to him. "Be you awake, lad?"

"I am. I'd like a pot of small beer and a bowl of porridge before going to the sheep."

"Be you really awake? Methinks you're back in Nottingham."

"Nottingham. Yes, that's where I was."

When he reached out to touch her, Clare moved away and sat up. "I'm going now. Don't get up, don't move. It's easier this way. Easier for me. Can I go this way?"

"Yes. Easier for us both."

On her feet, she dressed quietly, quickly, as he watched.

Going to the door she rapped hard on it, then went to Ned, knelt beside him, and said against his cheek, "A gentle, fine man, Ned Carleton. I'll be a good mother to your child." She kissed him tenderly on the lips. "Now touch my hands farewell."

He touched her fingertips.

When the door creaked open, she rose and left briskly, without a backward glance.

The last he saw was a black curl edging to one side of the hood.

Because employees wouldn't report to work on a Hanging Day, almost everything closed save taverns and courts of law. Apprentices and shop girls treated the occasion like Christmas. By mid-morning they lined the way from Felons' Gate to Tyburn, jostling for the front line along the processional route, bolting hot gingerbread and pies sold by strolling vendors. Before the June sun had risen directly over the crenellated towers of Newgate, many of the gathered celebrants would be tipsy. Ladies and gentlemen would be munching sweetmeats and sipping champagne in rented chambers with windows that gave them unobstructed views of the route below. In boozing houses the talk was rougher, as ostlers and stevedores awaited the sound of muffled drums, the beat of hoofs on cobblestone, heralding the approach of costumed footguards and horse-drawn tumbrels loaded with the condemned.

From St. Sepulchre the bell continued its tolling, a solemn hollow sound that had boomed across the rooftops since midnight. It was the first sound heard that morning by gout-ridden George Handel, when he arose to prepare for a Vauxhall recital, unaware that five more years of music and blindness were yet left him.

And it was the first sound heard by milord Sandwich, as he turned in bed and snuggled against Martha's naked buttocks. The impudent postilion would hang today, he thought with satisfaction, which made even more delicious his first morning touch of her young breasts.

And it was the sound that drilled into Ned Carleton's brain until he felt it was the only sound he'd ever heard. He sat against his cell wall, counting each toll as if it were a sheep coming in from pasture. Then the cell door opened and two bailiffs called him roughly.

They took him into a common ward called the Viewing Room, barred but allowing visitors to say farewell or stare at the condemned. Awaiting Tyburn along with Ned was a young housebreaker, a smuggler, and a celebrated highwayman of gigantic stature, whose chums — coming in droves to stand at the bars — called him Pup Nose, for his had been broken countless times and was spread like a lump of melted wax across his face.

The curious paid a shilling for the privilege of looking at them. Pup Nose gripped the bars and yelled at a smirking visitor, "I've fucked that cast-off mutton you call your wife a dozen times! Snatch me out of the world, don't I snap your backbone!" Although a bailiff rapped his knuckles sharply, he kept rattling the bars till the frightened visitor hurried out.

Soon he bribed a guard to bring in gin.

Before mid-morning a young man was thrown bodily into the Viewing Room. Sneeringly a turnkey called him Madam Soft Lips, for he'd been convicted of unnatural acts offensive to God and king with an old chandler in the back room of a tavern. Blood was streaming down his face, as he lay on the stone floor. Both he and the chandler had been sentenced to hang, but since the crime was so vile they'd suffered additional punishment by undergoing the pillory in Charing Cross.

Upwards of fifty neighbourhood women had been permitted by constables to stand round the stocks and pelt the miscreants with mud, stones, dead dogs, rotten eggs, potatoes, and bucketfuls of offal lugged from slaughter houses, and with fish guts, blood, ex-crement — the buckets supplied and filled brimming by enter-prising hawkers who sold the ammunition at exorbitant prices to participants so frenzied that they'd use their last shilling for the purpose.

Hit by a large brick, the elderly chandler had expired in the stocks. A rock had blinded the younger man in the left eye, and no one had cleaned him up before dragging him here from Charing Cross. He lay moaning on the stone floor when the prisoners' last meal was brought in. At this point all the visitors were ushered out, for it was prison policy that men in their last hours should have privacy enough to eat in peace.

The prison ordinary, a weazened parson of indeterminate age, came in with the food buckets to taste the pork pudding.

It was his grim duty to ensure that no attempt had been made to rob the Crown of its rights by smuggling poison to the condemned. Some years ago a prisoner had so cheated the gibbet. Incensed by his trickery, a gang of citizens had dug up the fellow's corpse, broken every bone of it, dragged his viscera down a road, and picked out his eyes. To forestall another such gruesome event, the ordinary had the task of tasting food given to condemned prisoners on the eve of execution.

While they ate, the smuggler described the famous Hanging Day when the benches at Tyburn suddenly collapsed, killing more than a hundred spectators. For the privilege of paying a crown to watch a man lose his life, they'd lost their own. The doughty old smuggler cackled at the irony.

During the meal, Pup Nose was strangely quiet, so turning to him the smuggler cried, "Come, you immense old fart, give us some gaiety! Don't be stale as last week's bread. Give us a story. Talk up your exploits."

"Wait," said Pup Nose, producing a guinea and rolling it between his massive fingers. He yelled at the turnkey. "Go you, good sir, and bring me a bouncy one. This gaol must hold some tasty strumpets, hey?"

Grinning, the warder took the money and left. In a surprisingly short time he was back with a swaggering girl whose face was deeply pitted with smallpox scars.

"Here, wagtail!" yelled the highwayman, who dropped his breeches before she could even cross the room. When she reached him, giggling, he pushed her down into a pile of straw and copulated with her at once. Done, he stood up, moodily wiped his mouth, and tossed her a coin.

"Pretty jade," he panted, "you be my last on this earth. Go tell them you had Pup Nose last and it'll bring you trade."

"Methinks it will," the girl replied airily, pulling down her torn woolen skirt, for Pup Nose had mounted without removing it and in his haste had simply ripped it. "You could be proper and give me for a new skirt."

He tossed her another coin.

"There's a dear," she said over her shoulder and left.

Then the fetters officer came into the cell with hammer and spike. First he struck off the housebreaker's irons, then turned to Pup Nose. Striking the manacles from those thick hairy wrists, the fetters officer stood back with a sneer. "Damn you, man, you be half-seas-over on drink."

When Ned had his turn, he watched the weights slip off and clank to the floor. The fetters officer tied a leather cord lightly around his wrists.

"Damn me, will you," yelled Pup Nose, rushing in front of the fetters officer, a big man too, who instantly raised the hammer.

The highwayman backed off, muttering, "Was I not on the way to Tyburn, I'd brain you for cursing me. I've done worse for less. But I need my handsome looks for the ladies."

The fetters officer laughed. "You'll do bravely today, big fellow. If only I could see it."

"Why wouldn't you?" asked Pup Nose, offended.

"I've duty here. But I wish you sport of the day."

When Pup Nose offered him the bottle, he took it with a good-natured wink and drank deeply.

"What of his? Don't you strike them too?" Ned asked, pointing to Madam Soft Lips.

"Let him wear them to the gallows," said the fetters officer. "You be decent fellows here, not scum like him. He can die in irons and the devil take him."

Ned sat beside the boy and with his own kerchief wiped some caked blood from the swollen face. "You've a bad fever," Ned declared. Hauling the boy into a sitting position, he asked Pup Nose for the bottle.

The highwayman swore irritably, but handed it over.

When Ned put the bottle to the boy's mouth, it wouldn't open, and the liquid dribbled out.

"Don't waste it!" cried Pup Nose. "Don't know if there's drink in hell!"

Ned stared at the injured boy. Pain alone was keeping him conscious. He was ghastly white, shaking terrifically, his one round eye pleading, bewildered like that of a dying lamb. Ned had seen many such lambs, but never till today the same look in a human eye. Bending close to the boy's ear, he said, "Not much longer now."

Getting up, Ned dressed himself in the clean clothes which Clare had brought.

The smuggler shouted his approval. "What a fine young gentleman!" He got up from the bench and clapped Ned on the shoulder. "You'll turn off with courage."

Ned, who'd removed the lambskin gloves yesterday to keep them immaculate, now drew them on.

The smuggler said in a low voice, "One thing, lad. Never show fright. It goes harder when you do."

Pup Nose hummed loudly as he dressed in finery brought yesterday by an old chum: blue pantaloons, a white silk shirt, a swansdown waistcoat, white stockings, a pea green frock-coat, and shiny black slippers.

"Good Christ." The smuggler whistled lasciviously, when the enormous highwayman began strutting and preening. "Damn me for a whoremaster, did I ever see the like."

Pup Nose turned on him threateningly. "The like of what?"

"Why, sir, of a prince of state. No lace peddler had better goods than you have on your back."

Mollified, the highwayman stuck out his hand. "Give me a good grip till we meet again."

A group of bailiffs entered the Viewing Room. Two pulled Madam Soft Lips to his feet and had to support him out of the cell. Another warned the whimpering housebreaker that if he didn't get off his ass, he'd have a hard blow.

"Hey, bastards," yelled Pup Nose, "leave off the boy. Can't you see he's got to piss?"

"Let him piss his breeches," snarled a bailiff. "And hold your tongue." He prodded the highwayman in the back with a cudgel. When Pup Nose swung round with his tied hands raised like a hammer, another bailiff drew a pistol.

For a moment the huge man hesitated, as if wondering would it be better to have it done right here than at Tyburn. But here he'd miss the crowds, the gaiety, the show. Lowering his hands, he spit on the bailiff's boot and along with the others left the cell flanked by guards.

From cells along the way, other prisoners called out encouragement and farewell.

"When they nub you, give the crowd a smile!"

"When they scrag you, fart in the hangman's face!"

"What a spark you look, Pup Nose!"

"Be brave, Dog Cull!"

"Hey, the loose fish has got to be carried!"

The procession stopped first in the prison chapel, where the condemned were ordered to kneel and pray. Ned tried to recall snatches of prayer, whereas he could think only of a feast day some years ago. The fat of roasted pig sizzled in an open fire. Beyond the smoke and flame stood a plump girl licking jam from her lips. On his knees, trying to pray, Ned could think only of the plump girl licking jam from her lips and swallowing. He could see nothing but the tension of her throat in the act of swallowing, like the rippling motion of a snake.

There was a commotion when a huge Irishwoman was brought into the chapel, her strong arms pinioned by struggling bailiffs. The smuggler whispered, "I heard she might go with us this sessions. That great whale strangled her husband."

Throughout the ordinary's sermon on hellfire, she yelled oaths and taunted the guards.

Taken from the chapel, the prisoners then entered the press yard of the Old Bailey, which was circled by mounted guards and foot soldiers bearing long pikes. When the prisoners were halted in the center of the yard, the sheriff stepped forward to give the chief bailiff formal receipts for the bodies of the condemned. The knight of the halter was stepping forward to wind a thick hempen rope round the neck of each prisoner, when an undersheriff hurried up and whispered to the bailiff at Ned's side.

With a disgruntled frown the bailiff gripped Ned's arm and started to lead him back into Newgate.

"What's happening?" Ned asked.

"Who said you was to ask questions?"

[57]

SPIRITED AWAY from the yard, Ned had no time to consider what was happening, but found himself quickly inside Newgate again, led roughly a few paces down a corridor and into a small room. It took a moment for his eyes to adjust, after the sunny press yard, to such dim light. Then he saw Justice Fielding seated on a bench near a table.

"Guard, wait outside," the judge ordered.

Ned stood there and by candlelight — no window in the room — studied Fielding, who seemed more frail than usual, perhaps because he hunched forward and his sunken cheeks had a sickly pallour. That suited Ned. Last night his suspicion was confirmed; this man had betrayed him with Clare and he himself had schemed to bring the betrayal about. "Take this note to her," he'd pleaded, meaning "Take her and give me my life." They were all three in on it, and the intensity of his feeling was such that an outburst escaped him.

"You had my sweetheart!"

"I find no pleasure in the truth of that. I was a silly old fool. She was a brave woman intent on helping the man she loved. Now think of the future."

The confession, though strong and simple, angered Ned. He wished to swing his misshapen fist at the sickly face. Instead, he said with malice, "She's carrying my child. She's with child by me. You had nothing to do with it. I know the child's mine."

"I believe it. Please sit down."

"I'm her man. It's me she loves."

"I know that."

Ned sat down. "She submitted only to help me."

"As I said."

Ned felt calmer; he sat back and waited. From beyond the room came the sound of hoofs on cobblestone. The procession was starting to leave the yard.

"You are stayed," Fielding declared. "Mister Scarrat signed an affidavit claiming you had money of him, so what was found on you when they took you was yours by right. At the king's bench this morning I pleaded error in the Crown's case. They accepted. As for the charge of Murder, that remains, but in the light of these circumstances, it's in doubt. The calendar was full this morning, so we reached a swift resolution. You'll be transported on the *Myrtilla,* along with a few other prisoners, in a day's time."

Ned had been listening intently, yet somehow the words rushed over him like a crashing wave.

"I could have held for a new trial," Fielding went on. "But Scarrat claims to know nothing of the man you killed. So he'll help you to transport but not to clearance of charges. Nor will Doctor Bostock do more. You might be condemned at the next sessions for murder. After all, a man died, and with so much perjured testimony already, who's to say there wouldn't be more to come. It would take all my Bow Street fellows to sort it out. And then there's Jenny Rivers. You've had dealings with the meanest woman in all England. I say, no more trials for you, Ned Carleton. This way you're transported. But you're sure to live."

"In faith, I'm to live? Scarrat signed a paper to save me?"

"Furthermore, he named Lord Sandwich as the lender, though that didn't go into the affidavit." Fielding added with a faint smile,

"It would have complicated things damnably. I am not thinking as a magistrate now. I am thinking as your counselor at law."

Ned looked down at his hands, fisted on his knees. Scarrat and milord Sandwich had saved him? Had he been told the sun had failed to rise it would not seem stranger.

"You're disordered."

"I am, your worship."

"What lies beyond understanding most often stays that way. For my part I believe Scarrat had control of you, but for his own benefit has decided to relinquish it. So be it, lad. Let it go and think of the future."

"You went to Scarrat? You got the paper from him?"

"I felt justice had not been served."

Fielding braced both hands on the head of the cane. His blue eyes glowed with a vigour that belied his shrunken frame.

Ned could not look at him, sick though he was, without a stab of jealousy. "Did you get me stayed because of Clare?"

"Surely. And because of you. I've been in a fair way of loving you as a son."

They were silent awhile, hearing from beyond Newgate a shout go up, as the condemned were being escorted through Felons' Gate to the tumbrels where a huge crowd waited.

"There are coffins in the carts," Ned said musingly. "I thank you for my life, your worship."

"I'm heartily glad you have your life, Ned Carleton."

"What of her when I'm transported?"

"I'll see she gains passage. And on the same ship. I've already inquired through my assistant. There's space aboard."

"You've done that too?"

When Fielding acknowledged it by remaining silent, Ned cast around for something to do, to say, that would match such generosity. He'd tell his secret, lay it at the man's feet like a gift. "I have a story, sir, that was going with me to the grave."

Fielding smiled wanly. "Those are the best stories."

So Ned revealed the whole affair, retracing each step that led from Scarrat to Bet Canning to Tabby Howard to Lord Sandwich and a popish cloister near Marlow where rites of the devil took place. All had been done for gold, for a way of bringing Clare out of

London into a new life. He was heartily sorry for the way he'd lived. He wished there had been another way. His path might have led to heaven rather than the maw of eternal suffering, the pit of hell.

Fielding raised his hand. "Wait, lad. You're not in the pit yet! You talk like a man facing the rope. You've escaped it, and from what you've told me, I hold you in admiration for a better sifter of fact than my Bow Street fellows. But what's the gist of your story? Why, that Scarrat is a pimp and a scoundrel, which I readily believe. That Bet Canning is a liar, which I accept with sorrow and think of myself as a dunce in the bargain. That Lord Sandwich and his cronies have a place for frolic outside of London, which is not surprising, as wayward boys like to thumb their noses at the world. To make their silliness known is of no great consequence, save the furthering of their reputations as fools. The criminal act is Scarrat's and Tabby Howard's; they detained the girl unlawfully. But where's the proof beside your word? At least your story confirms my view of Scarrat. He reasons you're worth more to him living than dead. Who knows his deviousness? I fancy Lord Sandwich will suffer from it somehow." Fielding cleared his throat as if tasting something bad. "You've told me a story too strange to put down on paper. In faith, did I write it I'd be taken for a fancier of wonders."

"You make light of it, sir."

Fielding nodded. "I do. I know you, lad. You had a childhood secure in religion. Then one fine night, below a window, you hear fine gentlemen blaspheme and make sport of your beliefs. Yet in the public eye there's more bubble here than weight. Why have you held this in? Fear of Scarrat?"

"He threatened Clare's life."

Fielding nodded. "Easily believed. You'd not bring him into the trial, you'd not even have counsel who might question him and learn of his part in this dismal affair. You prepared to give your life rather than risk her losing hers. In truth, lad, I suspect Scarrat's too cowardly to carry out such a threat." Slowly Fielding rose to his feet. "She has chosen a strong, decent man. I say it not as a magistrate who'd have sentenced you myself to transport. I say it as another man of folly." Fielding leaned heavily on the cane and took a step forward.

"You're leaving?"

"With your permission, I'll go and tell her to pack, as she'll be sailing soon. With your permission." Fielding waited and then said with a smile, "You have nothing to fear. I'd be pleased to ease her mind with your turn of fortune."

"You've my permission, sir."

"I won't be seeing you again." Fielding hobbled forward to the door. "I wish you luck with all my heart."

"And I you, sir. Forgive me the wrong I've done you."

"God forgive us all."

The bell tolled ceaselessly, and a few miles away from the procession's route Joshua Reynolds put the final touches of paint on his portrait of Commodore Keppel — the ocean surging in the background, the officer gripping the sword guard and striding foward into the history of art.

As the bell did its tolling, the grim parade wormed its way down Snow Hill, over the Fleet by the narrow stone bridge to Holborn.

Throngs leaned from windows. Oranges thrown from rooftops pummeled the cart of Madam Soft Lips, who huddled alongside his coffin. A group of boys precariously gripped the parapet of St. Andrew's to peer giddily at the sea of hats below.

Stretched out on the bed in a cotton shift, her gaze fixed on the ceiling, Clare remembered other Hanging Days, when, as most Londoners did, she thought of them as occasions for festivity, the idea of execution merely enhancing the air of excitement. She'd seen ladies and gentlemen holding long-stemmed champagne glasses, leaning from their rented chambers for a look at the procession. Some threw down bouquets of flowers.

Once Clare and another girl from the brushmaking shop had taken a day's excursion into the countryside that stretched toward the drowsy village of Paddington. They had sudden glimpses of cattle browsing in meadowland and then the chaise broke free of the narrow streets into the broad field called Tyburn. The girl with her had merrily described a scene here on a Hanging Day. Stalls for selling drink and sweetmeats stood in the crowd like rocks in a stream. On their solitary ride, however, Tyburn was silent and empty. It was not a tree, as Clare supposed from hearing people speak of "being turned off at the tree." Tyburn was a permanent triangular scaffold, large enough to hold eight swinging bodies from each of its three broad beams. As their chaise passed the old wooden structure, Clare couldn't take her eyes from it.

But she would not look at it today. She'd promised him that. Nor would she look down at the procession. She heard a steady murmur like the distant roar of the sea. That would be the mob lining the way, commenting on the prisoners in the carts.

What would she do when the mounted guards and tumbrels reached this house in Holborn? Ned below her, swathed in thick rope, sitting on his coffin?

Then there was a loud knock on the door and Justice Fielding's distinctively deep voice calling out her name.

So he's come for me on the day of my lad's death! Clare was thunderstruck. He must think of her as the commonest of whores, a rotten palace of pleasure. For a moment she nearly screamed out at him, "Get to bed with one of your quality ladies!" He knocked again, called out again. She might say, "I'll have a frisk, but not till you settle up!" And then out of the blue she thought of Bet Canning.

Do whatever's of benefit to yourself. Think of your advantage and whatever you do will be the right thing.

Good God, her lad passing below the window soon.

But tonight the man outside the door would be living, and her lad would be dead.

Again Fielding knocked and called.

He'd turn and go if she didn't answer. There was no leisure for fancy thinking. Clare got off the bed, pulled down the left strap of her shift, so that much of her breast was exposed, ruffled her hair, wet her lips, and went to the door.

Taking a deep breath, forcing a smile, she opened it. "Ah, I'm heartily glad you came," she said with a coy brightness.

Fielding steadied himself with both hands on the cane. "He's stayed."

Soon thereafter, before she'd been able to absorb the news, Hanging Day shuffled below the window, the mob cheering through the ceaseless boom of St. Sepulchre. Sitting on the bed, arms locked across her chest, Clare looked wonderingly at the judge who stood looking down from the window at the scene beneath. He was mumbling something about punishment; it should be administered without public fanfare. It should be to deter others from crime by the terror engendered in their imaginations at a prospect of similar consequences for themselves. To provide the mob a vicious spectacle was to emulate Rome.

It was a sensible kind of babble, but pompous and not in his nature. He was avoiding her through words. He was afraid to look at her, Clare realized. Though he'd moved heaven and earth to free her lad, he still wanted her person. She watched him fight his demons, as he turned to the subject of her ship's passage and promised to book her on the *Myrtilla*. The man was giving her and her lad their lives back, while struggling with the fear of his own passion. The power of it must have surprised him; in spite of principle and commitment to honour, he burned to lay hands on her. He must have told Ned not to worry, he must have told himself the same thing, he must have come here in a righteous mood, secure in his goodness. But now he couldn't look at her. Men never knew themselves.

Finally, however, he did turn.

Clare was aghast at the look of fatigue in his haggard face. Only his eyes seemed alive. Had he really made love to her? What an effort of will it must have been!

"Elizabeth Canning will be on board," he said. "Give her my respects and tell her I once believed in her."

It was an odd message, but Clare would have agreed to anything in the first throes of a euphoria that surely would take her by the throat soon.

He moved painfully to the table and put down a money pouch. "I had Joshua get me funds, but this is all I could raise in a short time. Once in America you'll have to follow him wherever he's indentured."

"There'll be work. My mother sewed like an angel and she taught me."

"Good. Well, then." He paused, looking steadily at her. She felt the longing in his fierce blue eyes. "A fine poet named Horace once said, 'This is the end of the story and the journey.' Now it's a beginning for you and Ned. And for the child."

"He told you."

"I'm heartily glad of it. As I'd be if my own daughter Harriet was

carrying. Dear Clare," he said, "dear, dear Clare." Taking an unsteady step forward, he bussed her on the cheek. Turning, he went
to the door; when she offered to help him, Fielding scowled and
waved her off.

"We shall never forget you! Never! None of us!" she called at his
rounded back as he went down the stairs slowly, painfully.

Back in the room, hearing the distant roar of the crowd from the
opposite direction, from Tyburn where the sweetmeat stalls must
be doing business, Clare stared at the black leather pouch on the
table. She was frightened nearly witless of going to America,
though she'd said nothing to him of her fear. Thank God for Bet
Canning. By the time they reached Philadelphia, she'd most surely
learn from the strong, inscrutable girl how to deal with murderous
red Indians.

Then, getting up, Clare flung on her clothes. She was going to
the lad. Euphoria had indeed seized her by the throat.

[58]

ALL HIS LIFE Robert Scarrat had tried to order things, to
ward off the blow before it reached him, to think before he acted.
Then one afternoon he'd seen nothing ahead but chaos, and in this
mood had nearly blown his head off. But he hadn't. He'd recovered
at the last instant and had been blessed since then with the knowledge of being as good as other men, not just sweeps and watermen
and ostlers and footpads, for whom he'd never had regard, but as
good as noblemen, judges, the *bon ton* of the world. This revelation
had led him through the tortuous meeting with Justice Fielding.
He'd been proud of himself. He'd stood on equal footing with such
a man, whereas most of his life he'd been rendered short-sighted by
the need to serve. Now he was free of such duty. The road ahead lay
open. And today his newfound freedom from servitude had been
assured by news gotten from a Newgate guard.

For a few shillings he'd learned of the stay and the prisoner's transportation. Scarrat's own fortune lay in a country fool's good luck. But for their destinies being thus linked, he'd not have helped the former postilion. Fate had forced him to save them both.

Armed with the news, Scarrat went straightway to the Sandwich mansion where he presented to the underbutler a folded paper on which he'd written, "To the Right Honourable Earl of Sandwich, Your Lordship, there is a spiritual matter of concern to you that I plead an audience with you to discuss, as it is most urgent and of high significance to your affairs."

He thought it was prettily composed, the way a gentleman might do, and indeed, after only a short wait the butler came for him.

He was once again in Lord Sandwich's study, where in happier days Scarrat had received his instructions for Medmenham and other wayward dalliances.

His lordship waved the note impatiently. "What, man, is this *spiritual* matter?" he demanded, so loudly that the mastiff, back from the country and lying on the Turkish rug, lifted its huge head from its paws. "Are you a wit now?"

"By spiritual I meant abbeys and monks and nuns and whoever knows of them."

"Well, say what you came to say. But I'm vexed you came here again, when I thought it was plain between us you're no longer welcome in this house."

"Your lordship, the man Ned Carleton —"

Lord Sandwich allowed a faint smile to cross his face. "I warrant he was turned off in style. The tolling from St. Sepulchre has stopped."

"No, milord. He's been stayed."

Leaning forward, snuffbox clutched in both hands, Lord Sandwich grimaced. "Stayed? How stayed?"

"Magistrate Fielding managed it."

"Ah, that busybody, that meddler!"

"On my affidavit."

His lordship put the snuffbox down carefully, as if it were an egg. "You have the better of me, man. I can't make sense of a thing you say."

"I signed an affidavit that Ned Carleton had money of me in the Frigate on the day he was took. Meaning he'd robbed no one. The money was his by right." Now it was Scarrat's turn to allow himself

an expression. Rare in him, he smiled. Then loving each phrase of
his explanation, he told his lordship that Ned Carleton had gained
transportation to the colonies. Indeed, he would sail on the same
ship as Bet Canning, a barque named the *Myrtilla*. So together they
were taking a knowledge of Medmenham and Tabby Howard with
them overseas.

How simple it was, Scarrat felt, as he watched Lord Sandwich
colour visibly. What a man had to do was see the nobility as they
actually were. If all the vulgar of England did thus, they'd bring
them down, the earls and viscounts and dukes, like a house of cards.
Scarrat was about to do an astonishing thing. He was going to
blackmail a peer of the land. And how did he like it? He liked it
wonderfully.

"The gist is," Scarrat concluded, "they're a ship's voyage away
from bothering you. But who knows what they might do? Scheme
together, write their histories down, tell others? Work to come
home by confessing the truth? Or they might settle themselves there
and do nothing. As I see it, milord, and with your permission to
voice such an opinion, they must be kept track of, as they both live,
know each other, and could marshal an offense against your lordship of great merit."

Sandwich nodded glumly.

"I've been loyal. I've always looked to your interests, milord, and
will in the future. Do you see the need of it?"

"Speak plainly, man. Go on." Sandwich reached irritably for his
snuffbox.

"I've not been on the waterfront so many years for naught. I
know who to ask, how to inquire of sailing men. I'll know where
Canning and Carleton end up in the colonies. As convicts, they'll
be indentured once there. I'll learn of their whereabouts from sea-
men, from ship captains, from watermen chums of ship captains. A
seaport's the best gossip in the world, if you know to listen. I can
follow their path forever."

"Go on."

"For this I keep the Frigate."

Taking the snuff, his lordship sneezed mightily.

"I not only keep it," Scarrat said in slow, careful measures, "I
own it."

"Own what? The devil take you, man! You keep losing me."

"I'll own the Frigate by deed. You'll deed it over. I'll own it without entail. It'll be mine. That way you remain safe, milord."

There was a moment of silence. Then: "You impudent dog! Rapacious! Threaten *me* with extortion? How dare you!"

Scarrat had waited for this point in their encounter. If he withstood the fury of Lord Sandwich, the road ahead was clear. "If you'd be so kind," he began, ignoring the outburst, "as to draw up papers today, milord, I'll learn what's to be learned before the ship sails. I'd be hard put later to know where they was once landed and placed in someone's hand. I hear the moment a ship docks, the convicts be parceled out and taken off to serve their sentence in places across the whole colony. There's not much time, milord. Please you, the papers today. They must be signed today." He watched with immense satisfaction how Lord Sandwich absorbed the painful truth of his plight. This peer of the realm would do what he was told.

And so it was.

His voice almost inaudible from suppressed emotion, Lord Sandwich said, "Come before sunset. The papers'll be ready." Then recovering his hauteur, he added, "If I'm ever troubled again by them *or* by you, I'll forgo my forbearance. Do you hear? Do you understand? I'll do *whatever* necessary to rid myself of the trouble for good and all."

That threat would remain with Scarrat, troubling him at odd moments. Many nights he'd wake and sit bolt upright, shaking at the prospect of his lordship finding courage enough to have him taken off. But leaving the Sandwich household this fateful day, Scarrat had a sense of reaching open country, a horse lathering under his flanks, a free and sunny world ahead, with Medmenham lying behind him in the dust.

A friar of Medmenham, George Selwyn, who never missed a Hanging Day, had been disappointed with this one. He'd observed the weathered gallows from a tier of benches, where the fashionable sat in velvet and gold: ladies with fringed parasols, gentlemen with tasseled canes. The problem, according to Selwyn, was that the whole affair had gone too quickly.

Madam Soft Lips, weighed down by chains, jerked only once. The smuggler had his family there, wife and two children, who ran out from the crowd and gripped his legs and yanked hard, turning him off before constables could stop them. The Irishwoman, in no mood to please the crowd, lunged forward while the hangman was adjusting her slip knot, kicked him hard in the groin, and jumped over the rail. The leap broke her neck.

Only the celebrated highwayman went out with style and questionable courage. When Pup Nose's cart pulled up to the gibbet, the hangman laid down the reins, jumped off the bench, and climbed into the cart. It was the signal for the chanting parson to shut his book and get off. Unwinding the rope from Pup Nose's chest, the hangman threw one end over the thick beam projecting above the cart, then drew it down with expert swiftness, tied a slip knot around the man's huge neck, and cinched the rope up firmly. He flung down the highwayman's plumed hat, so all could see.

"Give me my kerchief," Pup Nose asked in a suddenly humble voice. "God's fucking blood, I don't want these blockheads seeing me grin."

The hangman removed a lace kerchief from Pup Nose's pea green frock-coat and tied it across the highwayman's brow, with one end tucked up. Jumping from the cart, the hangman stood beside the drayhorse. For a few seconds more Pup Nose stared thoughtfully into the bright air, then by roughly yanking the kerchief over his eyes and mouth he gave the signal. Unfortunately, he yanked so hard that the cloth came loose and floated down to settle beneath the wagon. Pup Nose watched stupefied as the hangman, fearful of losing such a costly bit of lace, scrambled under the wheels to retrieve it.

"Cast me, damn you!" screamed Pup Nose. "Cast me!" His courage left him. His eyes bulged with fear, his neck twisted frantically in the rope.

With the kerchief safely in hand, the hangman returned calmly to the horse, flailed with his whip, and the cart lurched away from beneath the beam. The crowd was silent, then a roar went up, a delirious blare of approval and horror.

George Selwyn observed with the judiciousness of a connoisseur, "I own I'm surprised by that hangman. To be generous, he's inept. I've never seen anyone turned off so clumsily." His pink unlined face broke into a smile. "But what a strong brute. Look at him jerking like a bull!"

Soon the crowd began returning to London, bound for taverns

and coffeehouses, a mood-changing stroll in a pleasure garden. A milkmaid, buckets empty on the crossbar around her neck, was crying as she walked away. Onlookers nudged one another and winked. This must be her first Hanging Day.

From the center of the scaffold a constable lifted a homing pigeon and let it go. White wings flashed in the late afternoon sunlight, carrying the bird back to Newgate and assuring officials that the sentences had been carried out. Soon the tolling from St. Sepulchre ceased.

Across the ocean at the moment it ceased, Lieutenant Colonel George Washington of the Virginia militia, in command of one hundred and sixty men, led a surprise attack on an advance detachment of thirty French soldiers near Fort Duquesne, killing the commander and nine troopers, thereby starting the French and Indian War.

Long after the tolling had ceased, a wagon carrying the Irishwoman entered an open field called Poor's Hole, where unclaimed bodies of the poor and corpses of executed felons were set in racks to remain there until all eight tiers held coffins. A few angry citizens, looking on, wished to take up her body and hang it in chains as a warning to other hot-blooded foreigners from filthy Ireland. A peddler bought the clothes after the hangman stripped her, as was his official right. The lid was nailed down, and everyone set sail for grog shops.

In Surgeon's Hall, where Madam Soft Lips was taken for dissection, the doctors were disappointed, having found no organs in the corpse different from those of normal men.

On the Strand little boys were hawking broadsheets, one describing the last dying speech of the Dog Cull. "Here be the confession, life and character of the vicious Dog Cull. A penny for his history! Read his last speech! Read of his infamy! A flash cull with ten buxom doxies! They emptied his pockets as soon as he filled them! Went to the tree without remorse! A penny a sheet!"

In a broadsheet of scarcely more validity, a poem reputedly written by Pup Nose on the eve of his execution was addressed to his beloved sister:

> My loving tender sister dear,
> From you I soon must part, I fear.

Think not on my wretched state,
Nor grieve for my unhappy fate,
But serve the Lord with all your heart,
And from you He'll never part.

The highwayman, poet or no, lay in state in a St. Giles tavern where bullies had brought him from Tyburn. He resided in a gin-splashed coffin surrounded by burning candles. A doxy of his acquaintance, lying naked on its top, had received a few of his old visitors, but got off and covered herself when Jenny Rivers showed up to pay last respects. Rarely did she leave her heated room, so it was a great event in the underworld. Loyal as ever to her clients, she had the lid lifted and bending down kissed the contorted lips of Pup Nose. "You great old wretch," she murmured and chortled at some memory of him.

That evening the weather turned round. Storm clouds rumbled across the city, bringing gusts that blew down dozens of signs, one of which fell in Charing Cross and killed a linkboy. The sign at the Lion's Head in Eastcheap swayed and creaked on its hinges, while inside the tavern the swarthy hangman who'd cast Pup Nose was selling lengths of the hanging rope for three pennies each.

Doctor Bostock was in this boozing house and overheard the hangman boast of his day's deeds. "I knew him well who you turned off," declared the good doctor, though he'd never seen Pup Nose in his life. "Love and a bottle was his taste. He provided happily for nineteen daughters."

"What do you say?" roared the astonished hangman, who hunched over the bench from too much drink. "Nineteen? As I remember, he seemed a natural man."

"He'd never have gone to crime but for disease. I being a surgeon have seen all the disorders. The gout, the scurvy, the stoppage of the lacteals and misentery, diminished menses, stuffings of the lung."

The hangman turned bleary eyes to Lemuel. "What be your friend saying? I'm fuddled."

"Hear me," said Doctor Bostock. "I have seen the bad habit of body as brings on a nervous atrophy so that nothing a man eats will nourish him."

"Damn but your friend's a wonder," the hangman said to Lemuel, who grinned.

"This fellow you hanged today," continued Bostock, "had a disorder I warrant you never heard of. A sort of convulsion or hiccup in the ear."

"Go to," said the hangman with a whistle.

"Had he seen me aforehand and not gone mad, he'd have escaped the rope you hung him with today. I toast him farewell," declared Bostock and raised his glass.

"So do I," said Lemuel with feeling.

Squinting at the hangman, Doctor Bostock said, "You, sir, have you got a disorder to speak of?"

"That I do." The hangman clapped his hands against his genitals and grimaced. "A fiery discharge I got from some wench."

"That be the thing today with men of spirit. It's modern," said the doctor with a wink. "I've got a powder to cure it, though."

"What powder?"

"What powder he asks!" Bostock laughed jovially. "He's ignorant of whom he speaks to, hey, Lemuel? Lemuel!"

"Aye."

"Look here, my good sir, I have got a powder on me I guarantee will cure obstructions of the viscera, glandular swelling, hypomelancholy, and what not."

"I know naught of that," said the hangman impatiently. "But will it cure claps?"

"In a day," Bostock replied. "Cure it in a day. Cure it before you make more water or I'm no surgeon."

Turning to Lemuel, the hangman said, "Is this true?"

"A chum of mine had French pox," continued the good doctor, taking an orator's stance. "Those pernicious threads of disease drew under his delicate skin and sowed his blood with the minute seeds of hell, till his nose fell off, his blinkers went out, and he tumbled a victim for the grave."

"God save me," breathed the hangman.

"To your health, sir."

Minutes later the doctor and Lemuel left the tavern with eight shillings more and a vial of talc less, as they'd taken from the hangman a good portion of his earnings from sale of the rope. As they strolled along, Doctor Bostock upbraided his companion for being a dunce whose lack of enthusiasm had nearly cost them movables.

Lemuel listened dutifully to the scolding. At the end of it, he muttered, "We be eating tonight on rope that turned a man off."

"That's the way of the world, lad," said the doctor airily, nudging the door of a chop house open with his cane. "Think of it this way. Had I not spoken up for our chum Ned, it might have been his rope we eat on tonight."

"I thought you found out it was Mister Scarrat saved him."

"Hush, ninny. Never mention the name of the devil. Anyway, I gave Ned a good character to Justice Fielding, though I'm done forever with magistrates. I swear they all belong in Bedlam, locked in chains for babblers. Remember, *I* saved Ned. Tonight we eat on the rope that turned off Pup Nose. Don't look so lost, boy. It's the way of the world."

❡ Reader, I was heading home at last. My final stop was at the *Myrtilla,* which lay dockside. I had great difficulty ascending the gangway with my crutch, but with a kindly seaman's help I reached the deck. The captain, a grizzled and practical man, assured me of Clare's comfort when she was entered on the manifest, even showed me her small but neat cabin when gold had passed between us. I asked of the prisoners. Betty Canning's followers had arranged for her to have the finest cabin on board. More gold passed hands, and I managed to ensure Ned a clean straw place in the forward paint locker, though his irons would not be removed during the voyage. That was the rule on the *Myrtilla.* Irons on male prisoners were not struck till the other side of the Atlantic.

At least he'd not be down in the bilge area, with the rats and the damp. So having done all that I could, I left the ship, glancing back at its low-bellied silhouette and its three masts festooned by shrouds, footropes, stays, halyards. Tomorrow they'd rig the sails and if the tides held, top off and head out to Gravesend. They'd be together, Clare and Ned. I had arranged with the captain for her to visit daily, though "no dalliance," he warned, as that was against the rule.

As I wearily flagged down a sedan chair and climbed in, bound

for home, a great wind brought swagfuls of cloud, harbingeing a
storm. Seeing a flower girl on a corner, holding up lilies of the
valley, whose stalks swayed in the gusts, I had the chairman halt.
Searching my pockets, I found a few pennies and so purchased a
nosegay for a little innocent at home, sick with the croup.

Tomorrow they'd board and set sail for the colonies. I
remembered in our early days together that Charlotte and I had
once considered a move to India. I'd join the East India Company
as a clerk and we'd leave everything behind but our love. That of
course had been merely talk in the aftermath of passion, but I
recalled it vividly now. Clare and Ned would be living our fiction.

And Betty Canning would be sailing with them. I had been
wrong about her, wrong about Clare too. Perhaps it was my
weakness to create innocence where there was none, but if it were
in my power to erase that weakness from my character, I doubt I
would do it. No, I'd hope to keep such faith in the human heart, no
matter how deep the folly of it.

As I reached home, a black rain began to fall, a thick sooty veil
descending on the rooftops of London. It must have been filling
the open trench of Poor's Hole, warping the coffins there. Ned's
was not among them, thank God.

Limping up to the knocker of my door, I rapped hard, eager for
the sound and feel of my home, seeing to my dismay the flowers
go soggy in the downpour. The door opened, and you can
appreciate the happiness I felt in going inside. But instantly I felt
consternation at the sight of old Joseph's anguished face, as he
fell into my arms for a moment, sobbing. It was a moment
longer before I learned from him that baby Louisa had died not
an hour ago.

The world collapsed in on me, tearing off a fragment of my
sensible nature, so that standing in the foyer I seemed to be
standing alone in a strange place, looking down at the dear face
of my dying wife Charlotte, her hand in mine growing colder,
her parted lips in a whisper that was never sounded. For those
moments I was with her again, as oft-times I've been with the
memory of her in the night, in the day, half waking, coming
from sleep or falling into it, in the middle of a trial, with my pen
moving, her dead face rising into my vision like a fallen blossom
on the surface of a pond.

Then beyond the shoulder of the old man, I saw two affrighted
bewildered faces in the salon doorway. Kneeling, I beckoned the
children forward. At first haltingly and then in a fearful rush they

came to me, both of whom I gathered close to my breast and kissed their pale brows. Their eyes were round and wondering as they studied mine for a sign of comfort.

God hath taken your dear sister to His bosom, I told them, aware that the words would mean little to Sophia, though my caresses did; and I handed her the wilted flowers.

Solemnly William asked if his little sister was therefore inside God, pointing to his own bosom. To which I answered, I thought not, but resting close to Him even as they were now resting themselves close to my own bosom. You'll see your sister again, I told them with a nod of conviction.

William eyed me again gravely. Would Louisa be older when he saw her next, just as he himself would be older? I told him I could not answer for certain, as that was for God alone to know.

Is she dead? Sophia asked; and I said she was. And what was death? Sophia wanted to know; and I said, a journey into another world. And would she herself take that journey too? Sophia asked; and I said, yes, some day. She would know when; but I told her I couldn't know. And she asked did God know? I assured her that if it was known at all, God knew it, but for now she must simply live.

Caressing them both, I rose to my feet and commanded them to go have Cook give them both a tart. William ran off with Sophia at his heels, the flowers hanging over her grip.

"And little Ralph?" I asked Joseph.

"Hale and hearty, your worship. A bouncy little thing."

Refusing his arm, I began the long stairway up. It seemed a long, long journey, step by step, but at length I reached the landing and drew a deep breath. Hobbling to the door on the right, I opened it and saw seated there my dear wife, her eyes filled with tears, her arms slowly reaching out to me as I went toward her. I went to her thinking, I am here. I said, "I am here."

EPILOGUE

One month after the Hanging Day, the ailing Henry Fielding was carried by stretcher aboard *The Queen of Portugal* for the purpose of restoring his health in a milder climate. Two months later he died in Lisbon, burned out at forty-seven years of age, with his wife at his bedside. He was buried in a spot bright with geraniums and flowering shrubs, shaded by cypresses and often swept gently by the song of nightingales. His grave was marked by a plain stone. Little Sophia died not long after her father, so that of Fielding's seven children only one of his five daughters, Harriet, lived to maturity. Often called the father of the English novel, he stands preeminent in the annals of criminal justice for his heroic attempt to bring reasonable order into the enforcement of law. Through the continued efforts of his brother John, the force at Bow Street became the progenitor of Scotland Yard.

Eight years after the Hanging Day, some of the Medmenham monks played dramatic roles in English history. In the process of defying young King George III and a corrupt ministry, John Wilkes overturned the universally hated writ of general warrant, which neither named nor precisely described a person to be arrested. He strolled home from the Tower with an escort of ten thousand wildly chanting "Wilkes and Liberty!"

A second attack on him was launched by brother monks Sandwich, March, and Dashwood, all having scores to settle with the insufferable commoner. Sandwich was then a secretary of state, having survived the machinations of the duke of Newcastle. He managed to secure through bribery the proofsheets of the "Essay on Woman" in order to discredit Wilkes for authoring a libelous and sacrilegious work that threatened the national morals. The earl of March, who couldn't abide Alexander Pope's poetry at Medmenham, expressed his outrage at Wilkes's desecration of such a noble author's name and work. Sandwich piously read the indecent poem before the assembled House of Lords, which unanimously condemned the work and its author. Wilkes escaped to France, was tried in absentia, and found guilty. But the public imagination was deeply stirred by Wilkes's struggle against oppression. Overnight he became a folk hero. Shops were crammed with mugs and snuffboxes decorated with his ugly face.

As for Lord Sandwich, the press denounced him for obtaining copies of the poem in a fraudulent manner. The public contemptuously nicknamed him "Jemmy Twitcher," after a vicious informer in *The Beggar's Opera*. A Medmenham brother, Charles Churchill, wrote spitefully of him in widely published lines:

> Too infamous to find a friend.
> Too bad for bad men to commend.

Fourteen years after the Hanging Day, John Wilkes returned to England and launched a successful campaign to regain his seat in Parliament. Later he served as lord mayor of London. Before slipping into cheerful but insolvent old age, he bequeathed to his country rich and enduring gifts: freedom from arbitrary arrest, freedom from seizure of private property, freedom from parliamentary interference in legal elections.

Of his Medmenham brothers there is still this to say: While visiting the exiled Wilkes in the company of a fifteen-year-old mistress, Churchill succumbed to typhoid; his last words were "What a fool I've been." A few months later his friend the Welsh poet Robert Lloyd died, some say of a broken heart. Dodington drank himself to death. George Selwyn lived a long life, the high points of which were attendance at more executions. Sir Francis Dashwood became the worst chancellor of the exchequer in English history, having all he could do to add up a tavern bill. Later in life, reformed beyond recognition, he coauthored an abridgment to the *Book of Common*

Prayer with someone of equally dubious morals, the American gadabout Ben Franklin. Shortly before dying, Paul Whitehead burned the business records of Medmenham and thus deprived posterity of an enlightened appraisal of cash spent on oaken cradles, indecent hobby horses, obscene statuary, hellfire missals, inverted crosses, and baboon food.

Disgraced though he was by peaching, Lord Sandwich managed to continue in government. He regained his beloved Admiralty through powerful friends, but made the mistake of assigning departments to naval officers blindly loyal to his policies, which led to dockyard corruption worse than had existed earlier. Yet in gratitude for his help in fitting out vessels for the world voyage of 1778, Captain Cook named a group of Pacific atolls after him: the Sandwich Islands. Martha Rae was senselessly murdered by a young clergyman whose romantic attentions she had laughingly rebuffed. As a measure of grief, Lord Sandwich withdrew from active life. On his deathbed he heartily damned all his old enemies. Raising his head from the pillow, he gasped "Damn the . . ." with his last breath and was thus denied the pleasure of once more cursing the duke of Newcastle, who had predeceased him by many years.

Nineteen years after the Hanging Day, Elizabeth Canning died suddenly in Wethersfield, Connecticut, inscrutable to the last, a wealthy woman who had married a respectable if scatterbrained Quaker with whom she had five children who lived. In 1761 she had returned legally but briefly to England for the purpose of commanding a legacy left by an old spinster, who had been a faithful Canningite. *The Gentleman's Magazine* ended its formal notice of her death with this baleful observation:

Notwithstanding the many strange circumstances of her story, none is so strange as that it should not be discovered in so many years where she had concealed herself, during the time she had invariably declared she was in the house of mother Wells.

The Canning trial has a place in legal history. It was the first of those elaborately conducted modern trials in which time and expense are not spared by either side. It posed the melancholy judicial question, Can faith be placed in human testimony? In retrospect the collection of evidence was the chief problem. It was limited to obtaining affidavits from volunteers, and the reliability of witnesses was probed only on the witness stand. Trained investigators did not exist and would not exist until the next century.

Twenty-nine years after the Hanging Day, the permanent scaffolding at Tyburn was pulled down. Executions took place thereafter in an atmosphere of restraint on temporary gibbets erected in the courtyard of rebuilt Newgate. Although Fielding would have been gratified by the end of such displays, Doctor Johnson said of this change in capital punishment, "The age is running mad after innovation; all the business of the world is to be done in a new way; Tyburn itself is not safe from the fury of innovation." He continued fretfully, "The old method was most satisfactory to all parties; the publick was gratified by a procession; the criminal was supported by it. Why is all this to be swept away?" Nevertheless, despite his protest and that of other citizens, the spectacle at Tyburn passed into history.

And what of Robert Scarrat and Doctor Bostock and Lemuel and the black boy and others mentioned? Their names and lives are not recorded in history. As have all but a few, they dropped silently, unseen and unnoticed, into the ages.

And what of Ned Carleton and his Clare? Let us hope they had their child and perhaps other children and made for themselves a good life in America. Let us hope that they emulated Tom Jones and his Sophia, of whom Fielding wrote, "They preserve the purest and tenderest affection for each other, an affection daily increased and confirmed by mutual endearments and mutual esteem."